The Thunderbird Covenant

The Thunderbird Covenant

JOHN L. FOX

Dageforde Publishing, Inc.

Copyright 2000 John L. Fox. All rights reserved. No part of this publication may be reproduced, stored in a retrieval system, or transmitted in any form or by any means, electronic, mechanical, photocopied, recorded, or otherwise, without the prior written permission of the publisher.

ISBN 1-886225-46-X

Cover design by Angie Johnson Art Productions and J.L. Fox
Photograph of author by Dixie Knight Photography

Note: This is a work of fiction. Characters, names, places, and incidents either are the product of the author's imagination or are used fictitiously. Except for the news article in the foreword, any resemblance of this theater to actual persons, living or dead, corporations, institutions, events, or locales is coincidental, or used as public background.

Library of Congress Cataloging-in-Publication Data

Fox, John L., 1934-
    The thunderbird covenant / John L. Fox
      p. cm.
    ISBN 1-886225-46-X (alk. paper)
    1. World War, 1939-1945--Atrocities--Fiction. 2. Birkenau (Concentration camp) Fiction. 3. World War, 1939-1945--Poland
Fiction. I. Title.
PS3556.O935T48   1999
813'.54--dc21   99-35467
                                                                                              CIP

Dageforde Publishing, Inc.
122 South 29th Street
Lincoln, Nebraska 68510
Ph: (402) 475-1123 FAX: (402) 475-1176
email: info@dageforde.com
Visit our website: www.dageforde.com

Printed in the United States of America
10 9 8 7 6 5 4 3 2 1

FOREWORD

The awesome power of genetic engineering, while used by most scientists for the benefit of humanity, still strikes fear into the hearts of men and women. Such reshaping of the very components of life begs the question—who will define and determine what truly benefits the human race?

During the Second World War, elements of the Nazi regime believed that humankind would reach its zenith only when a "master race" of German descent controlled vast reaches of Mother Earth. To this end, techniques of thought-control, as well as genetic selection by eradication of "the unfit and the unwell," became the forerunners of modern-day genetic engineering. Among most German nationals, this concept, an enforced survival of the fittest, played quite well—especially since Prussian Christians believed they were ridding the world of the "Antichrist." It became a holy crusade.

To carry out Hitler's mandate, the German government set up extermination centers in conquered territories. One of these camps incorporated the Polish village of Oswiecim, renamed Auschwitz by the Nazi military. The most feared sector of this infamous killing ground was called Birkenau.

We do not know what permanent somatic and genetic DNA changes occurred under prolonged torture and electroshock therapy. Yet, it is safe to say that, even if the body recovered, the brain remained unmistakably changed. A new person lived inside that skin.

The surgeons of the *Schutzstaffeln*, the *SS*, went a step further in constructing a super race when Nazi physicians applied medical experiments on helpless children. It is alleged that some of the survivors suffered a new type of rebirth, as if they had undergone parthogenesis, a reproduction by development of the egg or female gamete without fertilization. Such girls and boys provided genetic grist for another super-Aryan pathway — the creation of the *parthenogenone*.

The Nazi concentration camps delivered many of their children to an asylum in Vienna, a psychiatric institute called Spiegelgrund. On September 26, 1997, the following news article appeared in the *Arkansas Democratic Gazette*. It is reproduced, in part, with permission of the Scripps Howard News Service.

Brain of child Nazi victim, one of 417 found, is buried

Vienna, Austria, 1997— The small square coffin was pushed by the rabbi along a tree-lined avenue, followed by 25 mourners. After a five-minute procession, during which they sang haunting Yiddish chants, the group arrived at a small plot in a Jewish corner of Vienna's central cemetery.

...The wooden coffin, draped in a black cloth, held the brain of Wilhelm Kaposi, age 12, who died on September 10,

> 1942. His death came just 3 ½ months after the Jewish boy was admitted to Vienna's Spiegelgrund psychiatric hospital, where he was diagnosed as an idiot.
>
> He was one of 417 children whose brains have been stored in jars in a memorial room in the renamed Baumgartnerhohe hospital for 55 years.
>
> Wilhelm's was one of four brains of Austrian euthanasia victims from the Third Reich to have been buried in Vienna in the past few days…
>
> The burial of the remaining 413 brains has been delayed until next year, pending the results of parliamentary investigation into a doctor who worked at the hospital…

Methods of enslaving human minds took a more subtle turn with the easy availability of heroin on the streets of America. Enemies of democracy enlisted warriors practicing a type of chemical warfare. The targets were the opiate receptors and DNA reservoirs of American children. In 1971, the U.S. Bureau of Narcotics was known as the Bureau of Narcotics and Dangerous Drugs, or BNDD. This agency was the predecessor of the present DEA, the Drug Enforcement Administration. Although *Thunderbird*, the spirit of a huge bird in North American mythology, was a (fictitious) code-name used by BNDD in 1971, its seeds germinated in the year 1943.

A Place in Zürich

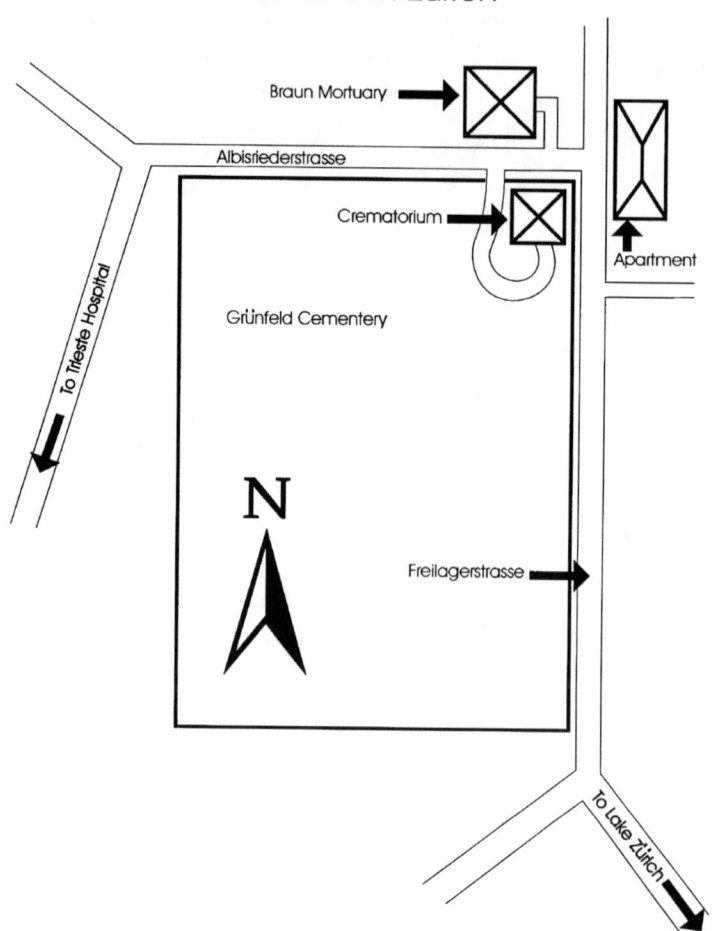

- Braun Mortuary
- Albisriederstrasse
- Crematorium
- Apartment
- To Trieste Hospital
- Grünfeld Cementery
- N
- Freilagerstrasse
- To Lake Zürich

PROLOGUE

Auschwitz, Summer 1943.

Halina, brushing away buzzing flies, squatted in the dusty yard. The child stared at a flower, sniffing its fragrance.

Blue and...the inner circle, yellow. Her eyes widened in awe.

"Ma...Mama! Mama. Look at the flower." The once beautiful girl, glancing about, stammered with delight in her native Polish language. She had forgotten her mother was away working in the fields.

Halina Vozniewski, clad in a man's tattered shirt, sighed and returned to her flower in full bloom. She remained oblivious to the din around her, the protective gap between fantasy and reality widening. She had this intimate friend, a silent companion.

Halina's eyes flared in brief excitement. With the left hand she could touch, actually caress, the blossom—without agony. Her right hand remained swollen. She could not raise her bruised arm well. Stabbing pains, the aftershocks of depravity, reminded her. She gazed upon the numbers tattooed in her right forearm and then looked back at the blue petals. She had never seen a real flower before. Or had she? Halina could not recall.

A wisp of wind from the free beyond touched her cheek. She sensed the sun's warmth building up on the back of her neck.

And then, a tiny, creeping shadow. Halina had company.

"Go...Go away, Mister Be...Beetle," Hali scolded the insect.

The determined black and brown predator stopped crawling up the green stem. Hali's left hand brushed him away.

She watched as the creature bounced off the hot dirt and scurried hither and yon. He ran in staccato-like fits and starts, first across the amber clay and then under moldy boards, finally slipping into a warm and wet resting place. A niche behind rows of white, corroding pillars of human teeth.

An hour later two prisoners jolted the insect's new home. The troubled beetle burrowed deeper under the dead human tongue. Outside, the alien creatures grunted and lifted his abode, a human corpse bouncing about while being dragged to the oven. One final shock resounded, the clang of an iron hatch slamming shut. Then the heat and the acrid smell of smoke rose up from burning flesh and bones. Spindly legs twisted into grotesque patterns, curling up against the smoldering torso as the bug's hard shell cracked. His miserable, checkered life ended. So simple. The sooted, red-bricked cremation chamber. The final solution for all undesirables. His remains, now dust, drifted through the air, settling into the lungs of Hitler's iron battalions. Settling and waiting.

The pungent odor of death.

Little Halina remained unaware, engrossed in her own reverie. With such total absorption in the rare beauty, her wise mind closed out the holocaust surrounding her. All she owned was her imagination, daydreams behind barbed wire fences, under the foreboding, skyward towers and sweeping searchlights.

"I'm go...going to call you Helga," the Polish waif stuttered, smiling at the flower. "I...I knew a Hel...Helga once. She was very pr...pretty. Bu...but they took her away."

Then Halina shaded her eyes from the sun and pointed to the distant, square, red-brick building, Block No. 25, the purgatory preceding the final release from earthly pain. The gray shadows of No. 25, belching black smoke, pitched against shadows of time, both lengthening as the silted sun rolled to the edge of a distant cloud deck, wavered, and then disappeared for a brief moment.

"Helga was mmmmy friend. She took care of me when Ma...Mama and Pa...Papa were sick. But now my Mmmama and Pa...Papa are alright."

A hundred yards away a soldier snapped his salute and moved out from a cluster of guards.

Unsuspecting, Halina hummed to herself. "Then Helga had to take her sh...shower. Mama said Helga went to another place and now she is very, very ha...happy." She paused. "Mm... Mama says maybe we won't go there 'cause we're not Jewish."

The man touched his holstered Luger, approaching the child. Her vision focused, Halina edged over, using her body to shield the lonely blossom from the fierce rays of the reappearing sun and the buzzing swarms of flies. The humidity was stifling. The mind of the four-year-old girl with stringy, blond hair judged only the omniscient present. The precarious future, like a foreign land, was too incomprehensible.

The Hessian boots drew closer.

For a moment, God-given synapses sheltered Hali from remembrance of the horror and smoke, gaunt faces, and sunken, vacuous eyes. Piercing screams and resigned sobs in the night. Continuous, putrid odors of discharged vomit and diarrhea, infected semen and urine, and blighted corruption and decay. This moment of reprieve from daily mayhem inflicted by giants in brown muslin uniforms and black leather boots secured her shriveled stomach a short respite.

The trooper stopped behind her. A tight grin.

Suddenly the insidious pain in her stomach returned, and Halina tilted away from the puzzled flower to wretch, spitting up traces of blood-tinged bile. She could not fathom whether the hunger or last night's boot to her tummy hurt worse. Hali turned back.

"Helga! Where are y...you?" she rasped. Her body shivered, nerve endings flooded with sudden panic.

Only a broken stem surrounded by a cloud of yellow dust remained where the blossom had grown. Next to the fractured stalk stood the child's daily reality. The boots. The heavy, black, leather jackboots.

Looking up very high with glazed, half-closed eyes, she pictured a distant head under a steel helmet, its edges reflecting streaks of sunlight. Vacant orbs long since devoid of feeling stared down at her, through her. She struggled to stand up, reaching for the flower in scarred hands. But the fingers of inhumanity closed into a fist, demolishing the blue petals.

Then, like a horse pawing the ground, the boots scraped the dry dirt, brushing her leg. Hali's throat constricted. Her heart, in a turmoil, thumped faster and faster against a fragile cage.

The awesome giant, uniformed in military brown, snapped her up and hurled sounds in a strange, guttural tongue. She could not understand his words. With huge strides the trooper transported the victim under his arm, drawing near a gray, shadowed monolith. She did not like that building. It smelled strange and metallic, dark and airless. The soldier delivered Halina into a damp basement chamber within the Birkenau sector. The walls were coated with crusts of lime exuding an earthy chill.

Her throat tightened, choking, "Mm...Mama. And Pa...Papa!"

Inside, her mother and father, dressed in their torn and soiled clothes of striped blue and white, except that the tops were absent, sat poised on iron seats. Their wrists were shackled behind their backs. They remained quiet, rigid, as if frozen, their hollow eyes projecting unspeakable terror.

"Ma...Mama, aren't you cold?" Halina's arid blues darted about, the icy ball of fear growing larger in her stomach.

"No, my darling, Hali." Tears choked back the last syllable of her name. "Our Lord is with me. Be brave, my precious."

Her mother's voice weakened, whispering prayers to the Almighty. "Dear God, I know our time has come. Please look after my child." Tears trailed through the dust on her cheeks. Not from fear of torture and death. She was already dead. But from the angst of her impending separation from Hali. A guillotine about to cleave away a part of her flesh on earth.

Halina knew they had been working in the fields, the burial pits, but it was too early for them to have returned. She shuddered, failing to understand. In bare feet she stood on the cement floor, her body trembling, unable to move, struggling to inhale the stifling air. Short, rapid breaths. Surrounding her were the harsh dripping of water, swinging incandescent light bulbs, and heels of jackboots cracking the silence, pavement underfoot ringing as they paced back and forth.

Halina did not like the new title the soldiers had given the Polish town of Oswiecim. She could not pronounce *Auschwitz*, a crazy collision of vowels and consonants.

Hali lived like a cockroach in this tabernacle of evil. She learned to swallow her cries when that booted giant touched her tense, puerile body in funny places. Then the leather did not strike her. If her hands played with that firm piece of flesh springing from between his legs, she received a piece of sweet candy. Every evening her bestial benefactor kept showing her how to do it. Again. And again. Using both of her hands she soon graduated, the seeds of male destruction irrevocably sown. Now the repulsive Nazi soldier would leave her mother alone.

Little Hali had discovered that when she stroked a soldier's penis, she also stroked his mind. Not sex. Nor love. But control.

Four souls shared bunks of rotting wood in Hali's world, her home roofed by green tarpaper. Halina, her mother, her father, and strange man called Sierpinski lived together. Jerzy Sierpinski, once a Polish engineer, had been a soldier until he was captured. He and Papa often talked about how things used to be, about something called communism as the only hope for everyone.

Hali did not like Sierpinski, the man with cold, gray-blue eyes, yet he often shared a morsel of food with her. From starvation and fungus infection all but the fringes of his hair had dropped away, making him appear like a vulture with stooped shoulders and swayed neck. When no one else would listen to his communistic preachings, he would select Halina as an assemblage of one, the girl with blond hair and deep cerulean eyes.

Mama, once a beautiful and blond Polish aristocrat, now dwelt in an empty shell bereft of her former self. Rotted teeth were falling out from the effects of the imposed famine. Atrophied muscles hung from string-like tendons attached to softened bones. Once vibrantly blue eyes were now lusterless, devoid of expression, seeing but not seeing. Halina had looked at a family photograph—her mother was so lovely back then.

Papa struggled with a severe limp, a tuberculous ulcer eroding into his right calf. In spite of the conditions of depravity surrounding him, the will to live was stronger than that of his wife. The left eye remained sightless following a bayonet injury by a Nazi thug—the day her father tried to keep the guard away from his Halina. The bloody wound puckered, the left eyelid shriveling above a white-scarred globe. These were mutilations that their four-year-old Halina also had to bear by watching, caustic engrams buried within an inaccessible memory bank, blood leaking away from the eye, dripping off the bayonet. Life trickling from a sadistic *SS* spear.

Halina's sunken eyes, now bottomless wells, in mute terror tracked every movement as her parents were strapped into the metal chairs. *Why?* she cringed.

The guard released Halina and tossed a ring of jangling keys into a cement wall inset.

"Papa, I'm so scared. What is going to happen?"

Bared copper bands snaked around their exposed torsos. On command, a soldier clicked his heels in salute and proceeded to paint a green X on the woman's bared chest, red for the man. Halina trembled again, eyes darting from red to green, then green to red. Then she saw someone new arrived, someone exuding evil.

"Ha! Herr Doktor Niemeier, there you are," exclaimed the big man with the decorations on his black tunic, silver *SS* lightening flashes of the *Schutzstaffeln* on the collar. As he spoke, Kommandant Heinz Baumann hung his black cap, also emblazoned with the silver eagle and flanking *SS* runes, on a wall peg and turned back.

"The subjects are in place," Baumann resumed. "Please announce your instructions to the attendants. I wish to see how this new toy of yours works."

"*Ja*, Herr Kommandant," replied the physician with a sunburned complexion, his magnified eyes peering through edge-thickened glasses. He saluted the acting Kommandant, polished jackboots snapping together on the cement floor, the malignant sound echoing in Hali's brain. "*Heil Hitler!*"

Suddenly Halina found herself lifted up and perched on a tall chair in front of an oak table. She was facing her mother and father. In front of her posed two foreboding buttons, each two inches in diameter. A green one on the left, red on the right.

"We know what will happen to the parents," crowed the obese Johann Niemeier, strutting about like a peacock in his earth-brown and well-pressed uniform, the doctor stalking a child's virgin brain. A brighter red suffused his jowls under a cap's insignia, a Nazi eagle with the silver Death's Head, the well-known pirate's attack emblem. He served Hitler's *Totenkopfverbände*, the feared Death's Head Squadron of the *SS*. "But it is the response of this...this wonderful little lady which utterly fascinates me. A unique study. An extraordinary cure for the diseased brain. An opportunity to make medical history!

"After stage one, Herr Kommandant Baumann, you and your wife must raise this foundling and provide her a secure German home, satisfying every want. At the Spiegelgrund Klinik in Vienna I shall keep copious notes on her mental and physical progress. A very detailed journal in my hospital files."

"Hali will not accept you as parents," cried her desperate mother. "She will always despise you!"

Halina looked at the two Nazis and froze, her stomach knotting up, fear sweeping her body, teeth chattering. At the same time, beyond awareness, a remote nucleus in her brain quietly filed their features away.

"We will erase all of today's memory with drugs...and my new techniques of Pavlovian electro-shock therapy. It's quite effective for the short term. I wish to discover if my methods still have their effect beyond childhood." The diabolical Niemeier, slamming his right fist into the left palm, spoke like a savage humanoid. He then hooked his cap on the wall peg next to the Kommandant's. Highlights reflected from the Niemeier's prematurely bald crown.

"You will rot in hell." Her father strained at his bonds, his searing, blue-glazed eye locked in a void toward his tormentors.

"Enough!" ordered Baumann, a brawny bull in uniform, his militant voice spitting out impatience. "My wife desires a child. And we shall provide her with one. However, Frau Baumann will never know the circumstances. Now, on with it." His left face twitched, the choreic movements quickening as the ultimate moment approached.

Then Niemeier turned to the helpless waif and squeezed a piece of sweet chocolate into her hand. He commanded her in Polish, an evil grin twisting thin lips, portals which Hali had watched writhe in their deadly locution.

"If you provide an outstanding performance, you shall receive more food, all the nourishment and clothes you want. Just like at Christmas time. Now, observe these two wonderful toys, Halina...that is her name?" The Kommandant nodded in affirmation. "The red button stops Papa from hurting." The doctor pointed at the wired, scarlet disc on the right.

"The green one takes the pain from your Mama. It's a game, my child. Press the correct knobs so that Mama and Papa will be free...free of all suffering. You are so smart. I am certain you can do it."

Hali, her head dipping a nervous nod, could not know that the emerald green disc not only stopped the torture to her mother but also activated increasing electrical current in her father. And *vice versa* with the ruby red button. The grotesque experiment would not end until little Hali's table-top toys had electrocuted both of her parents in a desperate attempt to save each. It would not cease until the chilling parthenogenesis of Halina was complete. Nor would it stop even then.

"Let it begin," commanded the perspiring Baumann, enlarging dark circles of moisture spreading from his armpits, the twitching in his left face advancing.

He pivoted to the left and clicked on his Victrola, a platter of music accelerating in its spin. With uncharacteristic reverence the Kommandant laid the needle in its groove and pushed the volume up until Hali felt the foundations of the chamber vibrating. "The Merry Widow Waltz." A beautiful symphony in stark contrast to an apocalyptic deed.

"*Los!*" snarled Niemeier as he snapped the switch, completing the circuit. The colorful buttons of crystal flashed.

"*Matka Boska!*" the Polish woman's voice erupted, her spastic body arching backwards. Mother of God! she wailed.

Little Halina, a lonely Polish atoll swept by an enormous Prussian tidal wave, hammered the flashing green light as her mother's succession of shrill screams fractured the air.

Frantic fingers pushed again, and the unwilling executioner left the woman weeping, catching her breath.

But then Halina shrieked as her father gasped, choking, his eyes bulging, the wound in the left lid splitting open. Her mind hurtled into a paralytic meltdown, crying, *The red. Hit the red!* The scarlet button blinked. *Nnno...no, Mama. Please sst...stop! Don't cry. Green.*

Gr...green! Her father convulsed, cauterized flesh filling the air. *Red! Green! Red! Gr...greee...*

Halina's fragile mind imploded, splintering into a thousand wounded pieces. Scattered shards within, the skull intact without, the arms locked in a rigor mortis of indecision as each compartment of Hali's brain closed down, synchronous with the final closure of sight in her mother and father, one after the other. At the end, even Kommandant Baumann and the guard had to turn away from the grisly theater.

While the child's heart continued beating, her head lay against the flickering red and green toy lights. Her parents had given her life. Now the ripping of their combined spirits from her little body was too savage, too powerful for her to defend.

The music stopped. Niemeier grabbed the discordant keys off the wall and clicked open the manacles. The dead couple's wrists dropped away, swinging.

An hour had passed before Jerzy Sierpinski, long bleached of all emotion, bore the unconscious four-year-old waif to a military ambulance. A small, dehumanized soul, a puppy-dog, hair now matted in sweat, began her journey from the Birkenau extermination sector of Auschwitz to the Spiegelgrund Psychiatric Hospital in Vienna—the brain of the changeling to receive new instructions as the ID numbers on her forearm were removed. Thence to Mainz, to the eye of the hurricane, the denizens of fascism knowing not what they had created.

Prisoner Sierpinski returned and stood at attention behind the officers. He listened.

"Well, what do you think, Herr Doktor?" Kommandant Heinz Baumann cocked his left eye. "The child comes from a good Catholic family. When might my lovely wife, Ingrid, be informed that she has a girl to adopt? She is ecstatic over the news and will smother her with affection."

"Very good. Never tell Frau Baumann what happened here. It will be the model psychological experiment, ultimately benefitting all of mankind. We shall deliver the subject to your home in Mainz within two weeks," reported the Niemeier as he wiped his spectacles. The two stopped and observed the limp swastika flag hanging from its pole. "Heinz, my friend. Himmler will recommend another silver medal for you when he returns from Berlin," prophesied Johann Niemeier.

"Herr Doktor, what was that our stuttering little animal was mumbling before you put her to sleep?"

"It sounded like the word *Helga*."

"Aha! Halina will be no more. From now on she is Helga. *Helga Baumann*," asserted the Kommandant.

"Excellent. She must never know who I am," proclaimed the surgeon. "In Spiegelgrund, I shall program a post-hypnotic directive into her brain. The talismatic words will be reinforced in Mainz. '*Die Sonne geht immer auf.*'" The sun always rises. "But first the cement must be cured, the steel tempered, the flesh annealed as it were, all memory frozen in the Führer's specialist clinic. Only *I* shall possess the key to the future reversal of a most exquisite metamorphosis.

"When this phrase from my voice passes her ears, our Helga will be triggered, nay...driven, to do as I command. With just a simple phone call to my new protagonist...anywhere in the world. You shall be amazed, Herr Kommandant."

"A unique method of purifying the human race, Herr Doktor...the noblest calling of the medical profession."

"*Ja*, it fits hand-in-glove with master plan of our beloved Hitler and even God himself. Imagine. Polish children rewoven into super-Aryans."

"All are candidates?" The Kommandant eyed the surgeon.

"None with a hint of Jewish blood, of course."

Baumann nodded. "Will you join me in another game of chess tonight?"

The ambulance and the first of the parthenogenones from Auschwitz roared through the gateway, a portal decorated by an overhead Nazi eagle clutching Mother Earth with its talons. As if heralding the birth of Helga Baumann, a siren warbled, then dissolved.

Jerzy Sierpinski watched the ambulance depart. He pulled a photograph from his back pocket, cast a cold gaze on a dated two-dimensional image of Halina and her parents in Krakow, and then ventured toward the Nazi officers.

PART I

1

Washington, D.C., Tuesday, May 4, 1971.

Waiting in the car, the blond assassin stared at the scene. She watched lightning bounce along swirling clouds and listened to sporadic gusts of howling wind interrupting sheets of rain. Like bowling balls, ear-shattering thunderclaps rolled back and forth across the heavens.

The night weather raked over the bullet-proofed Mercedes Benz lying in wait off Wisconsin Avenue. A damp chill crept in while the defroster and heater purred. The powerful motor idled quietly. Leather and faint perfume. The beautiful woman, a leopardess in human skin, twitched her nostrils, tracking the scent of her prey.

Alone, Helga gazed beyond the hazy amber street lamps while listening to Mozart's "Jupiter Symphony." Her blue-green eyes pierced into a different world, an unnatural existence learned from her Akido master in Kyoto. Mind and body armored, her driving determination for perfection did not abate in the two hours of waiting. Her eyes blinked, then shifted to the right.

A polyurethane box, insulated, pressed on the floor, passenger side. A cold and surreal mist hovered around the dark green casing, its insulated lid secured. The fog rolled to the floorboard.

The eyes of Helga Baumann narrowed — watching, waiting. Like a cat poised to strike, her head bobbed from side to side, hearing and eyesight honed to hair-trigger precision, the sensation of omnipotence unfolding within her. She stretched her arms over her head. Her black-gloved finger tips touched, yet not quite connecting. Stalking between the shadows of life and death, she could taste her victim, the energy boiling up within her.

"Edward Piccollo, you're so damn predictable," Helga sighed aloud. "I wonder what your wife would say if she knew you were fucking your administrative assistant again...Mr. Secretary of State."

Piccollo. He had gotten in the way. The Zürich connection had demanded that one of their own control State. This Swiss triumvirate ordered the termination of Edward Piccollo, and they handpicked Lance Masters to fill the void. This much Helga knew. Beyond that...

Helga released her arms from their cathedral posture and stretched a black beret over her long blond hair. And then, for a split second, the remote past slipped unbidden through her mind — the odor of burning flesh, a waltz in three-quarter time, her mother's hand. *From where? No! Please God. Not now.* The memory spiraled away as iron discipline reigned, her toe still slowly tapping to an internal beat. A beat that threatened to destroy her.

A townhouse door on the left side of the street inched open. A short block beyond Helga, music and light spilled against the marble steps and vanished into the mist. In front of the house on Dumbarton Street, a Cadillac DeVille waited. Drooping branches splashed its gray metal roof. The rasping leaves irritated the two agents inside, men from the State Department Office of Security assigned to protect the Secretary. They played gin rummy under the spill from the ceiling lamp. A tiny ember of cigarette fired out of the window, fizzed on the wet curb, died. The driver's window shot back up.

"Damn shitty weather. I promised the missus I'd take the kids bowling tonight. Now this piss-assed assignment," growled Joe Prolano in the Caddy. "Max, give me another Marlboro."

Helga glimpsed a brief flame inside the Secretary's car.

From the glove compartment in the Mercedes, Helga lifted a 9mm automatic pistol, Heckler & Koch, modified. "Someone else has to be promoted into your office, Edward," she whispered. "You're too chummy with Justice." Another gust of rain slashed the window, throwing down streamlets on glass, blurring the landscape.

As Helga screwed a silencer onto the burnished black weapon, her internal sphincters likewise tightened in programmed anticipation. A rush of air hissed into her nostrils. She withdrew a magazine of seven shells from the frigid chest to her right. The tips fumed from the special bullets constructed of dry ice, frozen carbon dioxide laced with curare. While the projectiles were not accurate at long range, the poison was lethal. Respiratory muscle paralysis. Termination from asphyxia. Only a fine tantalum powder, an invisible envelope forming the skin of the projectile, would remain in the tissues. Helga was certain that no one could trace the source to Switzerland. And Copenhagen was out of the loop.

The wind eased as the spring storm passed over. She slapped the magazine into her chilled H&K. It was time for the chameleon to change wardrobe, and within minutes the cat from Copenhagen wore a crone's disguise.

Helga stepped from the Mercedes and into the drizzle, the taut blonde now a stooped, shuffling bag lady splashing along in torn stockings and thick-heeled shoes.

The Thunderbird Covenant

A limp gave the appearance of an arthritic knee. Her black beret was covered by a clear plastic rain-shawl tied under her chin, dripping from the damp. A gray woolen dress hung in folds from slouched shoulders. Her left arm supported a half-filled food sack.

She could hear Max Chetler, the older of the security agents, chuckle. "Hey, Prolano. Wake up and get a look at that." He slapped his partner playfully on the back.

As the townhouse door slid open further, Helga listened to the laughing voices, a man and a woman gaily conversing, concluding another passionate tryst. For a moment, the roar of a jet ascending from Washington National Airport drowned out their merriment. Then Helga saw the three-piece, ornate vestibule lamp light up, illuminating the slick front walkway. She drifted closer, nearing the muffled words of the two lovers.

"Ed, darling, I hate it when you leave. Will I see you before next week?" Rose beamed a post-coital smile while combing her wavy, auburn hair. "Outside the office, I mean." She stroked his arm, her thoughts still lingering in the bedroom.

"You know I have to fly to New York, Rosy. I'll return in three days. Let's talk then." The handsome, rail-thin man pulled the raincoat about his waist and tied the belt.

"That infernal passport problem again?"

Helga approached the house. She stood on the walkway, her shaky legs weaving. Then she coughed and stopped to wipe her nose.

"It's more than that, Rose. Much more. Something terribly, terribly evil." Piccollo squinted, shading his eyes from the descending mist as he turned towards Dumbarton Street. "Uh…Madam, are you alright?"

"You got a few coins for an old lady down on her luck?" the voice rattled. Helga lurched, one hand grasping a low elm branch, its cold water cascading into her forearm.

"Hey, boys," Piccollo yelled to the men in his car, both agents laughing at the farcical sight. "Give the lady a couple bucks and send her on her way."

Helga tilted and then faltered again, the groceries dropping from her arms onto the brick walk. She let out a groan and staggered forward to pick them up. *Come to me babies. Yesss.*

"Max! Joe! Get over there and help her out. Get this drunken dame out of here." A sense of urgency seized the Secretary's voice. Fear, even.

Helga saw Piccollo's eyes, straining to focus, blurred with alcohol. As the two distracted guardians opened their car doors, the Secretary turned back toward Rosy. Rose glanced over Piccollo's shoulder, then suddenly on her tiptoes. She froze, her eyes expanding with shock. "Ed...Ed! Watch out! She's got a gun!"

The two Security Agents sprinted across the wet herringbone and towards the stranger sloughing her coat. Their fingers fumbled, unbuttoning, finally snapping .357 Browning Barracudas from shoulder holsters.

Helga raised her weapon, a blue flame hissing from its silencer.

The Secretary of State clutched his throat as hot blood boiled from the corner of his mouth, a small puncture painting widening circles of red blood on the back of his collar. Piccollo pivoted and spun to the steps.

Rosy, screaming in terror, reached for him, but then the second tracer tore through her chest, into her heart. Piccollo's lover tumbled down the front stoop, her torso slamming on top of him. A comb flew from her stiffened hand and catapulted into the hedge as she pleaded for help. The woman's ribs expanded twice more, then ceased as she drew her final gasp of breath.

Helga rolled over atop the slithery ground, both hands in finely insulated gloves and firmly on her gun. She fired the third missile. It struck the Max in the leg, his knees turning to jelly, the muscular body careening against a gnarled oak trunk. The transmuting feline sprang into a low crouch, weapon and woman propelled as one. She fired again, the shot ripping into his flank. Death followed as the thirsty veins of Max Chetler sucked in her poison.

The remaining agent, Joe Prolano, fired a fusillade at the cat-woman. Suddenly Helga screeched as she tripped over a tree root. She felt a white-hot burning in her shoulder, a bullet tearing through muscle. Her spine arched as the semi-automatic flew from her hand. Red stained her wet gray dress. She gasped, falling limp, barely breathing. Streams of bright scarlet flowed down over her chest.

"Who the hell are you?" Joe shrieked.

He rushed toward Helga and leaned over her, his own gun hand shaking. Her head coverings had fallen away, and the blond hair tumbled into wet leaves, eyes now like cobalt, appearing in a terminal gaze.

He holstered his Browning and ripped out his CB, punching numbers with the right thumb while searching for identification with his left hand.

"Don't die on me, you goddamn bitch. Who sent you? Who the fuck are you?"

I am your worst nightmare.

As he screamed into the two-way radio, Helga's frozen orbs spun alive. Akido-trained fingers shot to his throat, crushing the airway, cartilage cracking as he gasped for breath. He reeled sideways, trying to shove her against a tree trunk, to find a crack, a chink in her armor. But in this formidable death trap his oxygen seeped relentlessly away and his body fell limp.

A phone rang inside the townhouse.

Helga stood up, hands on her hips, tightly surveying the scene of destruction, her breathing now regular, controlled. Ignoring the pain in her arm, she retrieved her lethal weapon.

Lights from neighboring row houses lit up, one after another. A distant siren wailed.

With an ultraviolet flashlight, Helga quickly located and snatched up the fluorescent 9mm shell casings on the lawn. She stepped over the Security Agent's radio, still blinking under wet leaves, and hastened away, heading further up the street. She pulled a ten-speed bicycle from behind a hedgerow of dripping pink hydrangeas. Freed of her dress, Helga, now in black slacks disappeared into the fanged darkness and pedaled out of Georgetown, down into Rock Creek Park. Her hand fished out a flat box from a pack behind the bicycle seat, withdrew its antenna, and pressed the transponder button. A massive explosion rocked the neighborhood as her Mercedes gave way to ignited cordite.

It was time to report in. Overseas. To Jørgen Busche. Mozart continued twirling through her mind, masking a sinister, softer drumbeat from the past.

2

Tuesday, May 4, 1971.

Doctor Erik Landon was half listening to the strains of "The Marriage of Figaro" from his car radio. He had been operating at Washington Memorial Hospital most of the day. A diving accident. The teenager had leaped head-first into the shallow end of a neighbor's swimming pool. Erik had to realign and fuse the cervical spine.

His tired mind tried to relax as he transported himself back to Dartmouth and the thrills and challenges of college ice hockey. *College. Sex and Marlene. And chug-a-lugging beer with my frat brothers. If it weren't for Dad's genes, I never would have made the grades to get into med school. Good old Johns Hopkins.* Erik turned off the radio and began humming his old fraternity song, "Wings of a feather..."

Erik Landon had grown into a strikingly handsome man slightly over six feet in height. He had black hair and granite blue eyes. The hair and aggressiveness he inherited from his father, half English and half Polish. His eyes and patience, from his Swedish mother in Minnesota. The jaw, chiseled to command attention, projected slightly in a sharp, angular fashion. His only physical imperfection was an absent right toe, the result of an axe missing a log. He had been on a scout trip into the Canadian Boundary Waters and neatly cut off the appendage while demonstrating his axe proficiency to the younger scouts. He still winced when he thought of it.

Canoeing along the iron-rich waters of Minnesota and Canada during the summer months hewed Herculean muscle from young flesh. Like his older brother, Jeffry, he later stayed in shape by working out at the sports club, activities maintaining an upper torso and shoulders of broad proportions. He grinned as he recalled Marlene nuzzling his 'furry chest,' as she was wont to say.

A burst of thunder snapped Erik back to the present. He negotiated his T-Bird homeward, through the wet streets of Washington, wipers beating, thump, thumping against the windshield at midnight. He thought he might like to see the new movie, Kubrick's *A Clockwork Orange*.

His pager beeped. The Emergency Room at WMH."

Shit. Not another one," he cursed aloud.

Erik called from his car phone. Someone had been shot in the neck. The ER doc withheld details, but urged Erik's immediate return. A vague feeling of uneasiness swept over him as he pulled the T-Bird into a sharp U-turn, leaving a streak of rubber on the roadway.

Dashing into the modern emergency center at Washington Memorial, Erik saw doctors and nurses surrounding a stretcher. Police and plain-clothes suits stood aside, letting him pass, respecting his white coat. Beyond the double doors, news reporters were clamoring for answers.

"What's up, Harvey?" Erik grabbed the surgeon's arm and peered at the body on the gurney.

Harvey pointed his stethoscope. "Recognize him? Edward Piccollo. DOA. Others in his party also assassinated. They were taken to Georgetown and GW."

"Assassinated! The Secretary of State? Geez, how... what?"

"The ambulance brought him from a Dumbarton address. Shot once through the neck. Come...uh, excuse me officer...and take a look before the coroner takes over. Christ, Erik, the friggin' President and Congress already are howling for explanations. I figure we'd better get all of our ducks in a row. I'm certain the bullet went through the spinal cord, so we'd like your evaluation."

"I'm flattered, but he's dead."

"Aw, come on, Erik. The whole thing makes me nervous. Just examine the deceased and jot a few cogent notes on the chart. You know, from a neurosurgeon's viewpoint." The trauma surgeon pulled Erik over to Piccollo's side. "We'll get some x-rays and scans for documentation after you check him over."

Erik sighed, tired and irritated at the prospect of having to answer impossible questions from the press and the government. The corpse had already been stripped of all clothing. White linen covered the Secretary, two feet tenting up one end. Erik drew down the sheet, uncovering the upper torso. After completing his assessment, he wrote his findings in the chart. *Death confirmed. Entrance wound in the back of the neck, midline. Cervical spine probably transected. Exit wound in pharynx. But teeth not fractured. Where is the bullet?*

The detectives stated that no bullet fragments or shell casings were located at the scene. Agents from the State Department Office of Security, the Presidential Secret Service, and the District Police remained mum on further details. The FBI were just arriving, adding further clutter to the ER.

Erik was about to leave when State Security approached him. Another presence accompanied the agent and caught Erik's attention.

"Evening, Doctor," greeted the portly man in stiff pinstripe. "My name is Masters. Lance Masters. Undersecretary of State for European Affairs."

He appeared vaguely familiar to Erik and spoke with a deep, down-South accent. "Doctor Landon, perhaps you don't recall me? Ahh...well, it's been eleven or twelve years. You were the medical student at Hopkins." He pointed to a surgical scar in his neck. "I shall never forget all those rascally questions y'all bombarded me with."

"Oh, yessir. I think I recall now." The endarterectomy back in '59. Erik had been assigned to the case at Johns Hopkins. Did the pre-op H&P. Since then, Masters had become somewhat of a contentious diplomat in Washington, a rising star in the State Department.

Masters made a sketchy motion toward the body and said, "Well, my good doctor, I've talked with the officers here and have a fair grasp of what happened. We don't know how or why.

"Doctor Landon, Mrs. Piccollo is much too tired and distraught to travel to the hospital at this late hour. We would consider it an honor, and of course would compensate you well for your time and insight, if you would be so gracious as to join me in answering any medical questions she might put to us. Say, at ten tomorrow morning? At her house. Away from these annoying hospital smells." Masters crinkled his nose.

The idea bothered Erik, yet he had a widening curiosity — now that some strange fate seemed to embrace him. He had seen Dolores Piccollo on television, expounding on her many contributions to the arts. The deceased Secretary was well-liked in and out of government. But his wife was another matter. Erik's curiosity got the best of him. He agreed to go.

The next day, the butler, a dour Pickwickian, led Erik through Piccollo's Fairfax mansion and into a well-appointed guest parlor. Erik's nostrils twitched at the sweet-apple aroma in the lady's bubble of privacy. Masters stood up and pumped Erik's hand, then guiding him to a straight-back chair. Dolores Piccollo, studying a newspaper and seated next to a lounging Dalmation, seemed oblivious to Erik's presence. Erik had already read the releases.

"Dee, Doctor Landon is here. You wanted to hear from the neurosurgeon's own lips how Edward died."

She ignored the announcement, transfixed by the startling headlines of *The Washington Post*. The reporter detailed the killings, except that Rose was listed as Jane Doe, a young female.

**Secretary of State
Piccollo Murdered!**

...The President stated, 'The men responsible for these brutal murders will be found and brought to justice. On this you have my word.'

Only a deep gaping hole remains on Dumbarton Street near the scene of the crime. Authorities are certain that the scattered remnants of the car will lead to the identification of...

Erik observed her scanning further down the page and then tapping the newspaper with an arthritic finger. She turned to Masters, now sitting in the twin Philippine rattan chair next to her. "Well, darling, you're now the Acting Secretary of State. And that's just the beginning for you. Do you know the men who did this?"

Her tremulous hands, diamond rings reflecting, belied the otherwise placid exterior, a veneer of plasticized and powdered skin stretched over liposuctioned dough. Her painted black hair lay firmly pulled back and knotted. A cloyed picture of domesticity in wax.

"I'm sure the officials are working on that, Dee. I've heard nothing yet. Hmmm...what are you going to do with all that insurance money, my dear?"

Masters, almost forgetting that Erik was present, stared with arched eyebrows at the widow. A paternalistic hand reached over to pat her exposed knee, the leg dressed in stockings matching the blackness of her hair. Below a screaming-yellow chemise.

She shot a quick glance at Erik, returning to Masters. "Lance, honey, you are irritating at times. Charity begins at home," the lady bleated in a nasal, singsong voice. Her hair contrasted with the pallid face, a white death mask interrupted by thin lips scorched blood red. She hunched forward again over the newspaper, and Erik thought that her demeanor fluctuated between muffled hysteria and chilly hauteur.

Erik coughed, trying to attract her attention. But she appeared to be living on another planet.

"How strange." Her fasciculating eyelids shot upwards.

"What's that, my dear?" The southern accent flowed like molasses over rubbery lips, his mouth framed by a walrus mustache.

"The news article. Says the police coroner couldn't find any bullets in the bodies." Suddenly, she jerked her head around, facing Masters, her slate-gray eyes filled with darkness and venom.

"Lance, that mulatto bitch Ed was sleeping with... was...was she married?" There was a slurry edge to her voice, sliced with affronted dignity. Her features turned even more glacial as Erik heard her mumble something about purity of bloodlines.

"Say again, Dee?"

"Married. Goddammit, get a fucking hearing aid, Lance."

"Yeah. Married. No kids. Uh, Dee...the doctor. You asked to see him."

She paused, stretching her mouth into a broad line and admiring the gaudy diamonds, bejeweled fingers spread widely apart. Her eyes, pupils widely dilated, swiveled toward Erik.

"So you're the erudite physician. A brain surgeon, no less. Kind of cute, isn't he, Lance? Bet he's a trip in the sack."

It occurred to Erik that she had not asked him over to discuss the painful news of her husband's demise. The stories of her sexual conquests, even with her age and osteoporosis, were legendary. Erik wanted to leave, but the theater was like a magnet. Dolores Piccollo was unstable as hell and she had been drinking. She winked her false eyelashes at Erik while her upper torso teetered toward Masters.

"Lance?" she chipped in.

He coughed. "Yes, Dee?"

"Remember last night...in bed?" A thin smile again wrinkled the mask.

"Sure, Dee. You were great." His voice registered annoyance, his hand flying from her leg.

"Was I really?"

"Terrific." The Undersecretary attempted to make the scene appear inconsequential. But the more he tried, the more excited she got, aroused by reciting her pornographic tales in front of a trapped doctor.

"When I was sitting on you and, well, you know... I...well, I saw that tattoo on your left arm. What's it mean? Were you in the Navy?" She tried to restrain a giggle, wet gurgles spilling out. "It looked like some voodoo bird with its wings spread. Just the way I felt while I fucked you...and you with your hand on my tits. I was an eagle soaring in the wind!"

She pressed her hands against her crotch and briefly squeezed her eyes closed. Then, ratcheting the mood well beyond risqué, she shot a look toward Erik. "Maybe the doctor...Erik, isn't it, honey...would like to join our fine arts group some night?"

"Forget it, Dee. You best lay off the sauce." Masters stood up, preparing to leave, avoiding more questions. Erik started walking toward the door, struggling to withhold a chuckle.

She sniffed. "Forgive me, Doctor. I am so distressed by Ed's death." Then, as if governed by a schizophrenic mind, Dolores Piccollo trilled, "Lance, baby?"

"Yeah?" He stroked the brush on his upper lip.

"How soon before you can get me some more medicine?" Her nasal voice slipped into metallic pitch. "I control the money now, and I don't have to sneak around behind Ed's fucking back any more. I *need* something real soon. For my goddamn headaches."

For the first time Erik caught the needle marks on her forearms. The tremors in her hands were increasing, the Empire clock ticking, flashes from the muted television screen now exploding.

"Calm down, Dee. Drop by the church tonight and let Father Savalus listen to your confession. You'll feel better after that."

"Oh, Lance, honey. You are a rock in my hour of need. When will I see you again?"

"At the funeral, Dee. Doctor Landon and I shall find our own way to the door."

She cast hungry eyes at Erik, her hand with splayed fingers at the base of her throat. "Please, doctor. *Do* come back any time. It's such a comfort to know Ed was in your good hands at the end."

Thursday, May 6.

Narcotic Agent Harald Johnson telephoned Erik at his office the next day. Harald and Erik had been friends since Edina Junior High School in Minneapolis and continued to remain in touch, sometimes taking off on ski trips or canoe outings together. Harald knew that Erik had been one of the doctors examining Piccollo that fateful night. Harald's boys were three of the suits at the ER. Erik lifted the receiver.

"Doctor Landon speaking."

"Erik! It's Harald. Long time no see."

"Hi, buddy. Planning next winter's ski vacation already?"

"Don't I wish. Actually, my chief, Timothy Stafford, would like a word with you. He and Ed Piccollo were close. Golfed together. Would you mind stopping by the Justice Department and briefing us on what you saw at Washington Memorial? We still have the file from your laser research at Redstone...top secret clearance and all that. State is stonewalling our requests for more detailed intelligence. And the coroner seems brain-dead himself...if you get my drift. Shit. No bullets. And State is rushing into early burial services."

Erik hesitated, entering perilous waters without a map. "Okay, Harald. I'll rearrange afternoon clinic. Tell me where and when."

Erik gazed at a photo on his credenza—three teenagers holding hockey sticks and standing by Minnehaha Creek. Harald, Erik, and Jeffry. They called themselves the three musketeers back then.

3

Edina, Minnesota, December 1946.

At the age of thirteen, Erik's brother, Jeffry, loved the outdoors. Hazel eyes, tan freckles, and high cheek-bones graced his face. A ski cap often covered the mop of light brown hair. He was always laughing, fun to be with. And sought after by the young girls.

The third teenage musketeer was Harald, his name a Scandinavian word for "harbinger of things to come." Harald Johnson's right thigh muscles had atrophied from the effects of poliomyelitis. His frame was skinny, the limbs agile and otherwise muscular. The lad shot a mean hockey puck.

Crisp and snappy air breezed through that day of mid-December. Americans had seen the end of the terrible War, and the risk of sailing off to far-away conflicts was fading. After school, the three boys headed for ice skating on Minnehaha Creek, a strong stone's throw westward from the red-brick Edina Junior High School. A small dam under the West Fiftieth Street bridge had forced the stream to widen northward, giving a broad expanse of ice lined by congregations of trees and shrubbery.

At the frozen hockey field, a curious gentleman — Jake was his name — tended to a wooden warming shack near the west end of the dam. Inside the hut, a potbelly stove ensured warmth for the skaters as fire cracked and hissed within its iron paunch.

Old Jake, shortly past his seventieth birthday, was a tough codger dressed out with worn overalls, a red and black lumberjack's shirt, leather boots, and a coon-skin cap. He always had a pipe, generally unlit, squeezed between his teeth. Jake loved to chew on sunflower seeds.

On that fateful day, Jeffry and Erik skated toward their goal, both carrying hockey sticks that had seen better days. Warm breath condensed in the brisk, cold air as the ocher-orange sun spun into a grayish haze of fading luminescence, throwing tall tree shadows over the creek.

"Hey, you guys want to quit? I can't see that damn puck any more," Harald complained.

"Okay. Race you to the shack," Jeffry yelled.

Harald turned to streak away.

"Harald! Look out for the...," screamed Erik.

The warning was too late, and Harald tripped over a log serving as one side of the goal. His hand grabbed Jeffry's blue knit sweater, dragging Jeffry down with him. In a desperate attempt to regain equilibrium, Jeffry dropped the stick and lurched sideways, throwing his legs further off balance, his head pitching toward the black ice. Harald's skate blade became a rapier, slashing a deep wound into Jeffry's left forehead and eyelid. The blood poured in freezing droplets, congealing in an eerie, mosaic pattern of fractured rubies against white crystals of snow. Rubies and diamonds taking on a life of their own, a two-dimensional painting becoming a four-dimensional memory.

Erik, horrified at seeing Jeffry's white skull bone, took off his shirt and pressed it against his brother's hemorrhaging wound.

Jeffry stammered, "God, Erik. I can't see...I can't see!"

Erik cried, "It's just the blood, Jeff. You'll be okay." *I hope*, he thought. Erik put more pressure on the laceration while the brother he dearly loved lay trembling on the ice, the wounded head on Erik's lap.

"I'll get Jake. He'll know what to do," Harald hollered. Erik watched him dash away for help, a slight limp noticeable from the aftereffects of polio.

A week after the accident, Erik was skidding across the ice, toting his skates and a hockey stick slung over his shoulder.

"Hey, Erik. How's your brother?" Jake shouted.

"Oh, he's okay. Stitches are out."

Erik mounted the step into the warming-shack and dropped down on a wooden bench. With two thuds, his boots hit the floor. Firewood was stacked on one side of the cheery room. White smoke hissed up the stovepipe chimney as the snap and flare of incandescent gas escaped under pressure from blazing kindling. Erik loved the odor of burning pine logs. This was the first time he had returned since his brother's injury. He bent over to pull his skates on over a pair of woolen socks.

Jake fired a sunflower seed off his tongue and onto the hot stovepipe. "Hey, laddie, that was a neat job of doctorin' you did on your older brother last week. Professional I'd even say."

"Uh, thanks."

"Handsome guy like you, Erik. Intelligent, clever with the hands. Makings of a doctor, I'd say."

Another burning timber snapped.

"You know, Erik, that cut went clear down to the bone. Saw the white skull…clear as day. Where'd you learn to stop the bleedin' like that?"

Erik looked up. "We had some First Aid courses in Boy Scouts. Anyway, all I did was wrap up my shirt and hold it tight 'gainst his head." He fastened his leather laces.

Jake laughed in admiration and slapped his knee. "Well, it's lucky he was in the city. We had some nasty saw 'n axe cuts while loggin' in the north woods. No docs around then. Sweeney 'n me, we'd sew 'em up ourselves and pray a little. 'Course whiskey helped take the edge off. We'd just drink a toast or two. '*Skoal!*' we'd say." The right arm of Old Jake threw a dramatic gesture, a toast toward Erik.

Erik finished cinching up and scooted toward the door. "What's that mean?"

"What?"

"*Skoal.*"

"Oh, an expression from the old country. Means 'to your health.'"

That evening Erik tossed and turned in bed, sleep refusing to join him. His mind churned through strange waters, drifting in and out of a restless slumber. Searching for something. Like a tape waiting for a record. Agitated, his eyes cracked open.

"*Skoal?* What a funny word." He cast off the coverlet, leaped out of bed, and fanned through the pages of the dictionary lying ajar on his desk blotter. Next to the watchful eyes of Franklin Delano Roosevelt in newsprint.

Aloud he read to himself. "*Skoal*, cup or bowl. From Danish *skaal*." A few lines down another definition hooked his eye. "Skull—from *skulle*, of Scandinavian origin." The Norseman-of-old filled their cup, a real but inverted skull, with drink to toast their brethren. With a vague formless fear, Erik wrapped his arms about himself. Soon his tension ebbed into fantasies of Viking conquests, dreams of sailing ships carrying him back in time, memories of the white bone above his brother's eye. *Skoal. Skull.*

Upon awaking the next morning, he found the dictionary lying open atop the desk. A roll-top. His father used it when he was a high school student in Salina, Kansas. Jeffry didn't want the antique, but Erik thought it had class.

Now a Viking warrior, Erik swaggered in his pajamas to the bathroom down the hall. He pushed the gateway to the castle open, sword at the ready, and whispered, "Charge!"

Suddenly he stopped, the image in the mirror on a counter-attack. Erik studied the head of the enemy. Pretended it was Jeffry. "Take that! And that!" Swish. The left eye in the glass started bleeding. Erik froze and then blinked, a skull bone staring back at him. He thought he heard the thunder of war. And death. And troops in lockstep. The mirror blurred as it drew Doctor Landon back from the past, to the year 1971.

4

Washington, Thursday, May 6, 1971.

A glass-protected conference table reflected the faces of four men. They had gathered at the Bureau of Narcotics and Dangerous Drugs within the Justice Department. Erik's eyes snapped from the mirrored images as Director Timothy Stafford slammed the *Post* down, the edges of the rolled paper fraying. This large, imposing man eyed Erik and then the two agents.

"Shit. I thought this only happened in Colombia. It's got to be another drug hit from one of the cartels." Stafford glared at the ceiling as he drove his fingers through a thick brush of black hair, his suntanned forehead creased with anger. The deep voice rumbled, "Where did they find her, Harald? I know. In the goddamn Potomac. But exactly where?"

"Dolores washed up on Haines Point, chief," reported Harald Johnson, drumming his fingertips on the octagon oak table. "Shot up with smack before she drowned."

"First Ed, and now his wife. Damn. And Ed Piccollo was onto something big at State. Right?"

Harald nodded. "Some irregularities with passports and illegal immigration by hoodlums in the drug trade. State's playing it close to the vest. Lance Masters says it's all taken care of and no more problems."

Erik saw Director Stafford squint his way. "Sorry, Doctor Landon. This business with Piccollo's wife just came up. We do appreciate your input about the bullet wound inflicted on the Secretary. There is something you haven't heard, and it is not to leave this room for the present. Ed's body contained lethal quantities of curare. Same with the...uh...other targets. What's your take on that?"

Erik's mouth dropped open. "Curare! Good God. I'm sure the bullet cut the spinal cord, interrupting respiratory pathways. Curare takes several minutes, but it also would paralyze muscles, including those needed for breathing."

"Whoever wanted him dead wasn't taking any chances. And we still can't find the goddamn bullets."

"I dunno, boss. Seems like we're only seeing the tip of an iceberg." Terry Caldwell, a field agent with a tight crew-cut and sharp cowboy boots, tapped a pencil on his knuckles. "And no metallic frags seen on the x-ray films."

Erik looked at Terry and then at his friend Harald, not sure whether he would only muddy the waters. "Masters brought me to visit the grieving wife at her home yesterday." Erik reported the jist of the conversation in Fairfax, leaving out the erotic overtones. "I was there from ten until just before noon. She seemed a bit agitated. I thought she had been drinking, maybe on something stronger."

"Dolores was an embarrassment to Ed, in many ways... Well, I guess this investigation stays with our FBI brothers. For now." The square features of Stafford shifted, aiming back at Harald. "Keep me posted if anyone smells something. Harald, your ears hear more than most."

"You bet." Harald was thinking of Ezra Thomas, a black snake he had sworn to annihilate. At the time, Harald did not know that Ezra Thomas and Lance Masters sprouted from opposite ends of the same flower garden. Poppies.

Erik turned to look out the window. The President's motorcade, en route to a state funeral, was snarling traffic.

5

Washington, D.C.

Connecticut Avenue—home to princes and paupers, boutiques and bars, hippies and harlots. Helga, now a Gypsy girl garbed in an explosion of colors, leaned against a column of the grand Mayflower Hotel, south of Dupont Circle. Her gay bandana secured a coal-black wig. She tapped her toes to the strum of her Gibson guitar, New Orleans blues mixing with pedestrian chatter, baubles rattling amongst bangles and beads.

"Come on, Lance, baby. You know the drill. Call from a public phone," Helga murmured. "My bladder won't wait forever."

Inside the hotel, Lance Masters, the pro-tem power at State, stood at the podium of the East Room, a large chamber addressing the long promenade running north from the main lobby. The Acting Secretary was the guest speaker at the National Association of Airline Pilots. Relief flooded over him as the ten-thirty coffee-break arrived. He excused himself and hurried to a private restroom. And then toward a bank of public phones on the far side of the promenade. Two Security Agents accompanied him. They were his men, or rather their allegiance was to his money. Masters had selected his lieutenants with care.

The Acting Secretary wheezed as he steered his large torso across the grand hall of the Mayflower Hotel. Distant metropolitan hums and muffled roars swept through the high-ceilinged rooms. He stopped to catch his breath while leaning against a potted plant. An index finger pulled at the starched collar rimming a half-Windsor knot. Faustian eyes flicked right and left, and then he picked his way toward one of the phone booths. Masters' agents attended at a discreet distance.

The usually complacent features with creased, hooded eyelids had given way to a sense of urgency, consternation at not comprehending the whole picture. The laundered monies ferried into his clandestine account in the Bahamas would have to suffice. Any understanding of the mercurial boundaries of this underground Society would be incompatible with a long life.

The Undersecretary looked around, slid into the glass-and-bronze booth, and slapped the door shut. He squeezed half-glasses down on his slippery nose, hauled out a fistful of quarters, and dialed zero.

The New Orleans blues faded. Masters scarcely noticed a Gypsy lady stray toward the adjacent booth. After a Security man barred her way, she bumped against the kiosk and departed, tossing Hungarian obscenities over her shoulder.

As her screeching faded, Masters began, "May I have the overseas operator, please?" Perspiration beaded up on his forehead. Seconds played out into an eternity, straining his southern drawl.

Nearby, the blues guitar resumed, passersby tossing coins into a felt hat.

"Overseas operator speaking. May I assist you please?"

The faint sounds of guitar strumming distracted him. "Yes. Uh…yes, Miss. Copenhagen, please…if you would be so kind." He reeled off the number.

"How do you wish to pay for this, sir?"

"With quarters. I'll put in ten dollars worth now. Let me know…Oh, Jesus!…when I exceed my time." Loose change spilled on the floor, shattering a strained composure.

"Certainly, sir. Have a pleasant day."

Following the thuds and clings of the deposit into the Bell phone, Masters heard the series of couplet rings, interrupted by an electronic connection and a handset being lifted, the voice silent at the other end. Only quiet respirations.

"This is John Tempest," breathed Masters evenly, not wanting to sound stressed.

"Yes?"

"Jørgen Busche, please." The southern drawl stretched his words, one syllable becoming two. Two, three.

"Speaking." English with an Italian accent.

"Why…why the wife, for Christ sake? That was not part of our agreement." He already was missing his Dolores. Dee Piccollo had been his ally, spending lavishly and introducing Masters to sex-hungry wives along the underground political circuit. The fine arts club. He was an insatiable womanizer.

"We understand your position, Mr. Tempest. The decision came from higher up. Much higher up."

"The insurance money. She would have paid over huge sums."

"We are aware of that, but she was too unstable, a risk the Herr Doktor wished to avoid. Now listen very, very carefully, my friend." The voice paused. "Our dominion exceeds all rational comprehension. Indeed, the Society's retribution is well beyond any human endurance. A lesson even I had to learn. You now have a covenant with us. Do not...I say again...do not trouble yourself with the reasons and consequences of the tribunal's actions."

Stillness as the pregnant warning sank in. Busche added, "Now, my good man, are there any impediments to confirmation of your appointment?"

"Hell, no," drawled Masters in a rasping whisper, swallowing hard. "Perhaps...in a month."

Then the concluding click, the portal to a forgiving past permanently slammed shut. His hand replaced the dead pay phone receiver. Masters stared at the coils of its cord. His nerves on edge, he popped a Valium into his mouth. He pocketed his change and taxied back toward the East Room. His shoe snagged a carpet and one of the agents grabbed his elbow for support.

The guitar blues on Connecticut suddenly stopped. Helga skipped from the crowded street and darted down the promenade to the phone booth. She snapped a small magnetized box off the metal frame of the kiosk, dropped it into her handbag, and spirited the packet away. On Connecticut Avenue, a Mercedes Benz' rear door swung open and swallowed the Gypsy.

Friday, May 7.

A black limousine with smoked windows whisked up to the curb at Dullas Airport in Northern Virginia. The driver remained inside the Lincoln while a State Security Agent hurried out and pulled open the rear door. Masters exited, turned to the blond woman inside, and offered his hand. Helga, a compelling presence, grasped it and stepped to the sidewalk.

"Lance, dearest, I do love your tie selection." She fingered his cravat, her own lips in a tight smile.

"Helga, darling, my people are more than pleased with your brilliant success. Again. And, as always, I am supremely grateful. May I escort you to the Air France counter?"

"I'll find my own way, love. Please have your boys see to my luggage. Until we meet again…" She brushed his cheek with her lips and rushed off.

"When shall…" But he was left with his eyes trailing her backside. He couldn't get her out of his mind. The faceless syndicate in Europe had employed her as bait to snare him, and she had done so on her couch at the Connecticut Hilton. He knew he had been used. By Jørgen Busche of Copenhagen, a mastermind he despised. By Helga. But the memories of her heated body next to his even now raised a gratifying tension against the zipper securing his fly.

Masters shook his head. Helga. A drop-dead beauty of devastating proportions. He knew he had not seen the last of her, this mysterious temptress from beyond the Atlantic. She had assassinated Piccollo, the remaining obstacle to the rise of Lance Masters to fame and power. *Maybe even the Presidency*, he mused. She could have killed Masters with equal skill and aplomb, and he knew that. But Masters had chosen to serve. And serve he would.

She left the Undersecretary sinking with a certainty of his appointment to the lofty position of Secretary of State. She also left him with an unholy desire for her body, and he stood blinded to that risk. He could not know that when he copulated with Helga, he was also fucking an inner child, Halina, the Herr Doktor's corrupted prisoner. The risk? That one day Halina would remember. The year

1943. The terrifying medical experiments on little children at Auschwitz, at Birkenau, at Spiegelgrund.

Masters watched the silver Concorde hurtle eastward, disappearing at supersonic speed through thin air. Faint white streaks, metabolites of kerosine, trailing powerful engines.

Helga, tastefully dressed in muted blue silk and tight satin, rested in her seat. Earphones clutched her head as she listened intently with eyes closed, fingers twisting her pearl necklace. The tape of the overseas conversation between Masters and Busche intrigued Helga.

Lance, darling, Helga mused. *You're as bad at espionage as you are in bed. So now they call you John Tempest?* She opened her eyes, now ultramarine. *Still, a little insurance never hurts.* She pulled the earphones off her head, electrified hair clinging to the headset, and stowed them back inside her snakeskin purse.

Jørgen has another assignment for me. In Switzerland. Helga stretched, smiled, and shut her eyes once again. She was enthralled by the power wielded by this Jørgen Busche of Denmark. But there was more to the attraction, though she couldn't put her finger on it. Something evil. Another presence.

She knew that the Zürich connection employed their Copenhagen contact as a conduit for deliveries, orders, and payments. Yet Busche seemed to move within enigmatic circles of his own calling, deep inside lengthening shades of a different underworld, even beyond Zürich.

Helga felt a down draft, a perceptible draw on the Concorde as it winged its way toward Paris. She laid her head on a pillow, slumber overtaking the returning passenger as a changing Europe waited to embrace her. She dreamed of a love split asunder, unable to fathom the deeper meaning. Holyoke. In 1959. A part of her still ached for her Jeffry as she murmured, "Oh, Jeffry, darling. I still miss you so. Even after all these years."

She felt her eyelashes glisten with tears, Helga desperately wanting to understand as her thoughts rolled back to her college days in Massachusetts.

6

Holyoke, Massachusetts, September 1959.

A new musical, *The Sound of Music*, poured from a radio, "Do-Re-Me" drifting through the background.

"I love that song," said Emily as she hummed the tune and collected her school books. "It just came out."

"Hmm, so do I. It reminds me of holidays in Austria. Emily, are you going to study for the history test?" Helga, in jeans and a bra, was brushing her hair. She sat before a dresser mirror in the dormitory room which the two college girls shared.

"I'm hopping over to the library. Less distraction. Hope you like it here, Helga. Let me know if you need any help with the system. By the way, are you going to the dance Saturday? It's very informal and you'll meet some neat college guys from the Ivy League schools." Emily grabbed her book bag and pushed open the door.

"Hmm...maybe. Uh...who's the new instructor in English? He's kind of cute." She laughed and tossed the brush on her bed.

"Oh, you mean Mr. Landon. The guy with the ponytail. Jeffry Landon. I have him for English 101. He's terrific."

"Ponytail?"

"I don't know what you call it in German...the way he has his long hair braided in back. Must run. 'Bye." Helga's roommate dashed out the door.

"'Bye, Emily." Helga grabbed her textbook and pondered, *Pferdeschwanz*. Ponytail.

Two hours later, Helga Baumann, now an exchange student at Holyoke College, found herself drifting into a slumber, leaving writing pads and books askew on her bed. A sudden breeze from the east whistled through the open window and rustled loose papers. Helga had been studying a chapter in modern history. The Second World War. She became feverish, awoke briefly and took an aspirin, and then curled into a fetal trance. Globes moved rapidly under closed lids, tense fingers clutching the coverlet. She felt a tiny rupture from the guarded past. Little slivers of a broken mirror.

Pa...Papa, watch out! The b...b...bayonet! It's... Your left eye! Pa...! Muffled screams and the "Merry Widow Waltz" rifled through her head, eyelids squeezed together. *Matka Boska! Matka Boska!* Her Polish mother's voice leaked through from the forbidden sound-track, Helga's very soul bleeding from within. A brief scent of burning flesh. The lingering taste of Nazi storm troopers. Soon her rigid fingers relaxed as the painful cries receded back into an ancient, unconscious spiral, behind the mirror. Stretches of islands in forgotten time.

Then her dream state climbed through a higher plane of awareness. A caravan of images. Lavish parties in Mainz. On horseback, jumping hurdles. A telephone call she could not remember. Helga never felt the hot, wayward droplets streaming down her cheeks. The tears dried as the imago's dream, stirring through an ancient alchemical soup, evaporated from memory, leaving her with a heart beating so hard it hurt.

7

Washington, April 1962.

In the year 1962, President Kennedy ordered the blockade of Cuba, and Bob Dylan released his song, "Blowin' in the Wind." The genetic DNA code for a protein amino acid was just discovered. And Adolf Eichmann was hanged for his crimes against the Jews and humanity.

Erik had graduated from medical school and now was continuing his training, working as an intern at the DC General Hospital.

"Doctor Landon, please call the operator," an overhead page announced, calling the surgical intern on duty.

Erik picked up the wall phone and dialed zero.

"Doctor Landon speaking."

"You have an outside call, sir. Please hold while I connect."

"Erik, it's Harald. Remember that doll you met with me? You and your nurse friend went with us to see *The Sound of Music*."

"Sure do, Harald. Are you guys getting serious?"

"Sort of. The reason I'm calling is that she was badly hurt in an auto accident. On the beltway. I just got word the emergency squad shipped her to DC General. I'm really worried. You know how frail she is anyway. Would you see what's going on. I'm on my way over."

"Sure thing, Harald. I'll head on down to the ER now."

Waiting for an elevator, Erik thought about Harald's lifeline since their time together in Edina. After attending art school, Harald Johnson had emerged as a talented sketch artist and photographer for the Baltimore Police Department. Soon, the U.S. Treasury Department advertised for an artist skilled in the science and art of graphic portrayal of the most-wanted. Harald took the post and joined Treasury and the war on drugs.

Harald, carrying on the tradition of G-men, continued to accelerate through the ranks in Washington, sometimes at far-flung postings. One could still detect a slight limp when he walked. Chiseled features complemented a solid face, handsome and Romanesque in profile. Heavy eyebrows hovered over alert, iron-gray eyes. A rugged, unfinished look, the girls would say. He had yet to marry, though he and a young lady in her mid-twenties had something going. Her name was Lauri Tucker.

When Erik got to Emergency, he found that the chief resident in surgery had just performed a successful tracheostomy on Lauri. A fractured larynx. She stabilized and was admitted to the Intensive Care Unit.

Within a few weeks Lauri mastered a whispering speech by plugging her trach tube with a finger, allowing air to escape into the voice box. Lauri, a pretty ash blonde, and Erik looked forward to their daily visits during the mending. Harald joined them when he was in town.

One afternoon after checking patient charts with his medical student in the Surgical Stepdown Unit, Erik departed for a quick lunch. Upon his return, a distressed nurse ran down the hall toward him.

"Doctor Landon, come immediately! Lauri is hemorrhaging from her neck!"

Erik dashed to Lauri's room. Another nurse was suctioning the tracheostomy, but a blizzard of blood still shot out of the aperture in her neck. The hemorrhage was out of control. Red stained the walls and even the ceiling where forceful coughing had splattered Lauri's lifeblood. Terror gripped her face, the petrified green eyes, pleading with Erik, glassed over as coma took hold, blood and secretions strangling her oxygen supply.

"Start an IV *stat*. Nurse, keep suctioning." Erik was desperate to save the drowning patient.

After tearing off his coat, he inserted his right index finger into Lauri's neck between the month-old wound edges and the plastic trach tube. Soft tissues stripped away as his finger thrust deeper between the surrounding tissues and the tracheal cartilage, downward into Lauri's upper chest, her thorax heaving and gasping. Erik pulled his finger against a pulsating mass, the carotid artery. The deadly hemorrhage suddenly stopped.

"Suction all the blood out," he ordered. "Give her a hundred milligrams of hydrocortisone and one gram of Ampicillin, I.V."

The nurse ran to page the chest surgeon and alert the OR. Erik had handled the crisis, baptizing the intern into the life of a surgeon. His finger remained in the hole, deep in her chest, Lauri and Erik sealed together as they were whisked away on the gurney to surgery.

In the waiting room hours later, Erik rubbed his right hand, trying to hasten circulation into his finger. The numbness and tingling edged away.

"Erik, Lauri and I are indebted to you. Do you think she's out of danger now?" Harald, his tie hanging loose, sat with his head in his hands.

"She had a very rare complication, Harald. The tip of the tracheostomy tube had eroded into the carotid artery. Her chest surgery went well. I'm certain she'll be off the respirator in a couple days. I'll give you a call at home tonight."

After giving his friend's shoulders a squeeze, Erik turned to answer his page. It was the prison director from the district jail attached to the D.C. General Hospital.

"Hello, Doctor Landon. Hear you're on call for sickbay over here. I got a middle-aged Hispanic with some abdominal pain. Probably from the wonderful food, but rules require an MD's check."

"Oh, shit."

"Sir?"

"Sorry. I'll come right over. Who and where?"

"Name's José Gomez. Cell block Two-West, number fourteen. The warden is expecting you. No hurry, but tonight sometime. Thanks."

After Erik presented his ID, the guard, eyebrows knitting together as he swung a noisy key chain, guided the doctor through a steel gateway and into the second floor cell block. The iron door clanged shut, the noise reverberating through a collage of sounds along the chilly corridor. Erik heard the scraping of tin dinner dishes, a tangle of rock and country music, and conversations in various degrees of indifference and insult. The heels of Erik and the officer clicked on cement.

The sergeant herded Erik toward cell number fourteen. A double-bunk, a toilet with no seat, and odors of urine and cigarettes greeted the young doctor. One convict, a short man of Hispanic extraction, looked up as the cell door slammed shut, incarcerating bolts cracking home.

The guard remained at the barred doorway. "The rest o' yez shaddap if yez knows wots good fer yez."

"I understand you have some stomach problems? I'm Doctor Landon. How are you feeling now?" Erik pulled a stethoscope from his white coat pocket.

"Hi, Doc. I have stomach ulcers, and these goons here keep insisting on feeding me spicy food. So I'm from Mexico originally. But I got to stay away from the hot stuff now."

After a brief exam, Erik concluded that José was right. A diet order and some medicine was all that was required.

Erik took a closer look at his surroundings. As darkness gathered outside, blue-white beams from an alabaster moon spilled around the bars of the grated window, painting shadows of crosspieces on a concrete brick canvas. A filigree of clouds floated across the bright face of this crystal globe while Erik tried to gain some perspective on his fellow man's situation.

José, a pleasant and agile fellow, related how he had held up a grocery store to get food for his family. He had been jailed for a month, still awaiting his trial.

"How do you like my buddy?" asked José in a friendly, affable voice.

Erik's eyes followed the direction of José's arm. It pointed to a flickering moth ascending a gray wall, the scene illuminated by the silver lunar wash. Erik's aimless gaze locked onto the tiny, winged creature as curiosity held him in its grip.

"She's been with me since I first entered this delightful resort. Comes and goes. I don't hurt her, 'n she don't bother me. I call her Luna."

"Luna?" Erik looked on in bemusement.

"*Si*. Like today, it was a full moon out when I first came here. I read up some. Nothing else to do here. So I named her after the Roman moon goddess, Luna." He spoke in a pleasant Spanish accent. His black hair was combed neatly back, the trimmed mustache dancing, accenting a handsome face.

Erik found himself caught off guard by the intelligent discourse from José and rather liked him now.

José Gomez, welcoming his trapped audience, continued. "Borrowed a book on butterflies 'n moths. The guard will let us read if we don't screw up. So I got this here encyclopedia, see. My friend is a moth, a lunar moth, I think. Neat, huh? Check the picture? Don't you agree?"

Erik nodded. The creature was pale-green with a long projection on each hind wing. Yellow rings on its wings gave startling depth to the picture. As moths go, it had considerably more beauty and character than most he had seen.

"Bet you thought she was a butterfly. Well, it says here," asserted José pointing at opened pages, his Latin hands gesticulating in a portentous manner, "that luna once was the designation for silver in medieval alchemy. That's 'cause the Romans thought the moon 'peared silvery and named it Luna. Same in Spanish. These moths fly at nighttime…dancing before the moon.

"The next time someone calls you a loon or a lunatic, that's where it comes from." He laughed as he snapped the tome shut. "Some people believe that the full moon affects your mind. You believe that stuff?"

"Not really…" But somehow, Erik did not say it with conviction. "Best not to go looking for trouble," he replied.

"Ahh, true enough. She will find you."

Erik's inquisitive mind drifted. He gazed at the tableau — a dainty, fluttering insect rappelling to-and-fro against a backdrop of gray brickwork. The thespian, a graceful Lepidoptera of the evening, hesitated and then flew to the metallic mirror above the sink. It's reflected Daedalean shape made an indelible trace in Erik's memory bank.

José. Lunar moth. Silver moon.

A few weeks later, Erik tumbled into bed after assisting on an emergency appendectomy. He lay on his bunk, staring at the wall as soft strains of "Spanish Eyes" floated in from a record player in the next room of the intern's quarters. A warm breeze whispered into the curtains, causing them to undulate, sending ripples of silvery moonlight dancing on the floor.

Nearby lay scattered pieces of Erik's friend and companion, Oliver, a disarticulated, dry skull. Erik had decided to become a brain surgeon after his forthcoming two years of army duty, and he wanted to talk with his brother about the momentous decision. Elated and excited, Erik snatched up the phone and called Holyoke, Massachusetts.

"Sorry to wake you up, Jeffry. But I just had to tell my favorite brother. I'm going into neurosurgery."

"Hi, Erik. Gosh, I'm really happy for you," Jeffry replied. But Erik thought he sounded strangely depressed.

"Remember when you got your head cracked in Edina?"

"How could I forget, Erik? Harald's skate blade, and your shirt."

"Well, I've been thinking...that's what got me hooked on the brain. You know...seeing your skull 'n all."

Jeffry's excitement did not match Erik's that spring of 1962. Erik pressed his brother, asking him if something was wrong. Jeffry finally admitted that he lay in the clutches of a shattered love affair. Indeed, something more profound than life itself had possessed the man. It had begun two years earlier in the autumn of 1960.

Holyoke, October 1960.

The American populace was about to elect John Fitzgerald Kennedy to the presidency. And Chubby Checker was causing an international dance craze with his recording of "The Twist."

Jeffry had finished his English major and language studies at Trinity College in Hartford. Desire and natural talent led him into the field of English literature. He completed his doctoral studies at the University of Minnesota, following which he accepted an instructorship in literature at Holyoke College. His enthusiasm for the English and American classics was infectious, resulting in his popularity with flocks of eager students. Though he carried a Ph.D., Jeffry preferred the title Mister rather than Doctor.

After classes, Jeffry released his pent-up energy by working out in the weight-lifting room of the gymnasium. By now, an enormous shock of light-brown hair trailed back into a tight ponytail, a handsomely plaited queue which distinguished the twenty-six year old man. Jeffry wore a polo shirt with 'Save Our Trees' imprinted on the back. He strolled down a flagstone path between ivy-covered dorms, feeling independent and refreshed by the brisk autumn air, a chewed red pencil still stuck behind his ear.

"Hi, Mr. Landon. I loved your discussion of Ben Jonson's work today." Emily, wearing oversized spectacles, exuded her usual excitement.

The young scholar turned to face two women running up behind him. "Good afternoon, Emily. I'm on my way for a work-out at the gym." He paused. "Who is your friend? I don't believe we've met."

"Oh, I'm so sorry. Mr. Landon, this is Helga Baumann. She's an exchange student from Germany. And my roommate. Helga, meet Mr. Landon, our favorite English lit teacher."

"I'm pleased to meet you, Miss Baumann. Welcome to America," greeted Jeffry, extending his right hand. He saw a fine scar on her forearm as she acknowledged his geniality with a strong grip. A dainty religious cross dangled from her golden wristlet.

"Thank you, Mr. Landon. I've seen you around but never had the opportunity to meet you personally." She gazed about. "I do love this enchanting campus." The young woman with shoulder-length blond hair brushed aside a natural wave eclipsing part of her forehead.

Her intense, blue eyes sparkled against a radiantly tanned face. A canvas tote-bag hung from her left shoulder. She was dressed casually in a green, scooped-neck tank top and faded blue denims.

Transfixed, Jeffry tried to tear his eyes from the newcomer. "I don't detect much of a German accent. Where did you learn English?" he asked.

"Mostly in private schools. Then I spent two college years at Cambridge in England. Also a few summers vacationing in Florida. Do you speak any German?"

"No. Only college level French. My brother, Erik, does, but I guess I've been too parochial regarding other languages. Can you converse in many foreign tongues?"

"Several." A coy smile formed around Helga's spellbinding features. "I have an aptitude for languages and speak five fairly well." She shifted her book-bag. "I'm heading for the gym also. I like to weight-lift and exercise when time permits."

"Yes, Mr. Landon," interjected Emily. "Don't challenge her to arm-wrestling. She's quite the athlete."

Jeffry glanced back toward Helga, now noticing sinewy muscles hidden by tanned, velvet skin.

"Why don't you join me, Miss Baumann? You too, Emily, if you like?"

Emily laughed, "I'm not into muscle building and karate like Helga. Anyway, I have a handsome date tonight. Have to run. 'Bye."

"Please call me Helga, Mr. Landon. I would be pleased to accompany you. My tights are in the gym locker, so I can go directly there."

"Fine…Helga." A touch of tentativeness. He waved at the other student. "See you in class on Wednesday, Emily."

Jeffry and Helga ambled beneath a vine-covered walk-way, dry leaves crackling under leather soles. Helga brushed another lock of hair from her cheek.

Jeffry felt her staring at him, at his left eye. He saw her shudder as bright rays of the afternoon sun glanced off a dormitory window. Or maybe it was the scent of nearby burning leaves.

"Are you okay, Helga? You look a bit pale. Uh…that's an old ice hockey injury." He touched his eyebrow.

"Oh. Sorry. Just got a little dizzy. I'm fine now. Where…where is your home?" A troubled smile had replaced her rapt expression.

"Minnesota. In a suburb near Minneapolis. Do you know where that is?" Jeffry swiped at a vine branch.

"Yes, near Canada. Maybe I'll visit there someday. Scandinavians settled that area didn't they?"

"True. My brother and I come from Swedish stock on our mother's side. Our father was half English and half Polish. And you? Strictly German?"

She hesitated. "Uhh...yes. From Mainz. If you ever visit there you must meet my family."

"Here's the gymnasium. After changing, I'll join you in the exercise area."

"Okay!" She already was skipping away.

He stared after her while listening to the scrape of the caretaker's rake gathering dried leaves together, preparing to fire the next pile.

After changing, Jeffry, in blue shorts and matching open-neck sport shirt, trotted into the large room. He detected a rustle from overhead and glanced up. Jeffry beheld an extraordinary sight, a formidably lithe figure in blue and yellow tights, its owner climbing hand-over-hand along a rope hanging from the three-story ceiling. A ballerina in space. Helga's taut legs, stretched out into a third dimension, pointed outward towards infinity. From the distant ceiling of the gym she called down.

"Mr. Landon, it's quite a sight from up here." Her words bounced off beige, cemented walls.

"Where did you learn to do that so well?" the mesmerized man yelled upward as he backed away.

"Rock climbing in the Alps. My favorite place was near Davos."

With alacrity Helga wrapped the rope around one leg, let go with her hands, and swung out into space.

"Holy shit! What is she doing?" Jeffry murmured, the man galvanized and speechless. He gaped upward, the ponytail touching his upper back.

Helga arched backward and twirled slowly, a moon encircling her earth. A narrow abdomen stretched out, gathering upward and outward, expanding into a feminine apparition that forced Jeffry to stop breathing. The figure was a blend of beauty and latent power. Jeffry's plan to lift weights that evening vaporized like a droplet of water on a fired stove.

Months passed as Helga and Jeffry became inseparable lovers. And then came the March winds.

Jeffry stirred, awakening from a dream cast in Braille. For the first time in recent memory he felt blissfully relaxed, basking in the sheer moment of it. A faint scent of perfume reminded him as the pleasant thought of Helga's caresses stirred him once again. The luminous red glow of the alarm clock, shaving slender slices from the present, rolled through the hour of four, well past the turn of the night. Jeffry stretched, extending his shoulders and arms as he gazed at Helga, and softly sang, "Beautiful dreamer, waken to me..."

Shimmering light from a street lamp washed over the pillow, a feathered cushion sculptured in relief with blond hair. Helga's naked body next to him shifted, and Jeffry felt a surge of affection. A strange emanation seemed to enfold her, like a mystic vapor, and he knew it must be love. Their autumn encounter seemed to have been serendipity, yet something more commanding than his own will held him within her unyielding magnetic field.

Since returning from her ski holiday in Switzerland, Helga and Jeffry drew closer and closer together, he the instructor in school, she the teacher outside of class. Each treasured the other's warmth and touch. Now, watching her chest expand and relax, he remained mesmerized by her gentle breathing.

Then it started again—her erratic respirations, sudden inhalations, a tempest within her becoming more frequent as weeks passed. The more committed they were to each other, the worse it got.

Beads of perspiration skimmed over her face and shoulders. Fists, now clenched in defense, struck out, pounding unseen objects, first the right, then the left, back and forth. Jeffry thought he saw a focused fury. Or was it fear? Of what? The woman spoke unintelligible and cryptic words, uttered in a foreign tongue he could not fathom. Jeffry struggled to configure these elements of change, but he was witnessing a cerebral code well beyond his ken.

He felt paralyzed, unable to intercede. *The voice. It's like a child speaking. What is she saying?*

Something within was shredding this young Amazon. Jeffry could not decipher the phenomenon as Helga's form altered from that of a tall, athletic body into a shivering, fetal posture. "Helga" was the only word he could understand. "Hel...Helga," she cried while brushing the air with her left hand, her supplication a stuttering, anguished appeal for help. Helga's sobs cut into Jeffry like a blade as penitence and sorrow streamed down her cheeks.

"Helga, darling, wake up. It's okay. Please. I love you!"

Jeffry tried to hold her, to fold her into his arms. But her wounded heart lashed out, pushing him away with her left hand, the right arm now motionless.

Soon Helga drifted back into a less tortured slumber, time less remote, respirations easing, her sinuous limbs relaxing. He swept strands of damp hair from a face etched in fear.

"Hold me, Jeffry. Hold me close, my love. I am so scared. I need you. God sent you to me. Don't leave me again. Please, not again," she pleaded as if from another world, the tormented body shaking as she clung with desperation to her lover.

"I'll always be here for you, my love," he whispered truthfully, not understanding the meaning of her words, unable to unlock the mystery within a mystery. He felt himself balancing on the brink of dangerous intimacy — as if he were a paleontologist digging up fossils, a most hazardous undertaking.

With darkness still pressing down, plump, round raindrops began to fall outside. Slowly at first, then pattering and sizzling against the window glass. The night wind picked up, peals of thunder rolling over a distant, malevolent firmament. Jeffry held Helga tightly in his arms, but the closer he cleaved to her, the faster she seemed to slip away.

Without explanation, his lover left America and returned to her European homeland.

Part II

9

Switzerland, Sunday, June 6, 1971.

One telephone call had set the Chiasso agenda in motion. A phone message to Helga, yet she possessed no memory of it. She sat quietly in the back seat of the silver Bentley, the car driven by a large man with a bullet-shaped head. Trees and farmhouses, blurred images, flashed by.

"Hermann, please slow down. Time is on our side. Caution must be also." Helga put the finishing touches to her make-up.

"As you wish." He let the auto drift down from its 150 kilometers per hour. She saw him glance at her canvas bag.

"Hermann, do you know this Martino LaVeccia? Can he be trusted?"

"He is one of us, Fraülein Baumann."

The answer was sufficient. Even though she did not know who or what the ultimate "us" represented. *Partition the knowledge. Safer. And "us" pays me well*, she observed.

THE THUNDERBIRD COVENANT

Chiasso, Monday, June 7.

A pristine Monday morn, butterflies flitting about, welcomed the swarthy man outside his home. A raven, perched on a telephone line, looked down on Martino LaVecchia. The man and the bird both grinned as he waved good-bye to Melita, Martino's pretty wife standing in the doorway of their clapboard bungalow, calico curtains flapping in the breeze.

An elderly lady, watering potted bright-yellow tulips on the wooden porch, nodded at her son, Martino, then blew a kiss. Her granddaughter of seven summers, long black hair trailing, laughed with glee, attempting to catch a blue-striped butterfly in her hands. Antonietta, gamboling over patches of grass and flowers, just missed the insect and fell headlong into the green hedge fringing the yard. The cheerful girl picked herself up and dashed on.

Martino, a slender middle-aged man with a Mediterranean tan and a black blade of a mustache, hesitated and then hurried along the damp, narrow streets of his hamlet, the heels of his polished boots clattering on eroded Chiasso cobblestone. A dark green, corduroy jacket draped loosely over stooped shoulders. Only the moisture of his palms betrayed intense anxiety. He spent little time in Chiasso, his home village near Italy. Herr Doktor Johann Niemeier compensated him well for transport services in Zürich and the night-time courier activities beyond Trieste Hospital. But then he met Angelo and Riccardo.

Martino learned that the Mafia had discovered he was an employee of some mysterious organization threatening the Mafia stranglehold on European narcotic distribution. Both Angelo Tinnelli and his half-brother, Riccardo, had been assigned by Sicily to search out information so the Family could act with dispatch. The inroad had to be cut off. Immediately. At any cost.

A virile, young Frenchman from Marseille, drunk from passion and alcohol, had filled a corpulent, Mafia-paid prostitute with semen and stories. Disconnected tales of highly pure heroin and dead bodies. The French youth knew so little of substance that, before he died, money, threats, and torture disclosed only one name within this faceless society. The gasping, now toothless mouth spit out blood and the words, *La Vecchia of Chiasso*.

This history drove Angelo and Riccardo to change tactics, to befriend Martino LaVecchia. Within days, Martino heard offers of one-half million Swiss francs for information leading to the nameless alliance. Their last meeting had occurred four days ago at a small restaurant in Zumikon, a village near Zürich. With hesitant interest, Martino permitted the brothers to close in, his own instructions received from a higher, invisible, and soulless governance.

Zumikon, Thursday, June 3.

The discussion had taken place over lunch, Italian accented by Sicilian dialect.

"Aahhh, Martino. Do you need more money? Perhaps we can negotiate a settlement?" spewed Riccardo, swarthy, short, thin, his black sideburns twisting toward a wide mouth. A toupee carpeted frontal balding.

"Yes, my friend. And if you join our Family, there is no limit on your good fortunes." The half-brother, Angelo, framed his white teeth with a broad smile under a luxuriant, brown mustache. His mastodonic body leaned toward the prey, shifting eyes bespeaking evil intent.

LaVecchia, having reported the efforts of Riccardo and Angelo to his superiors, recalled the explicit instructions, mandates with a strange twist. *Deliver the name of Helga Baumann. Tell your new friends that this Helga will meet them at a small cabin on Mount Generosa near Chiasso. They should look for a peasant woman with blond hair.*

Martino had exhaled a silent profanity as he left Niemeier's office in Zürich. *What the shit is going on? Those mafioso guys mean business. After Riccardo and Angelo finish fucking her ass, she'll be left as pickings for the scavaging hawks. Then the Tinnelli thugs will come back for me.* His bowel quivered, tightened.

Still Martino feared the Herr Doktor and his shadowy colleagues even more, knowing that refusing the former Nazi would be tantamount to denying Satan himself. Cold shivers raked his body, anal muscles coiling into spasm after discharging a fine fecal droplet. Martino removed his ambulance driver's cap, laid it on the checkered tablecloth, and wiped a perspiring brow.

"Warm, Martino? Nervous?" sneered the thin man playing with the table knife, spinning the blade on its long axis.

"No...well, maybe a bit. I don't like being forced into this position..." Martino's voice trailed off.

The waitress, a bored brunette with a ski-slope nose, served steaming bowls of pasta and garlic bread, tall steins of beer, and blue flowers in a vase. She set them down, the glasses rattling together in contralto. Pleasant Swiss mountain music and mouth-watering scents of spices wafted through the air, contrasting with the eerie quality of expectancy seeping through Martino.

"I...I'm just a driver, but at night I pick up electronically secured parcels and bring them to Marseille. Look, I don't know who these people are. I just do what I'm told and deliver the packages. That's what they pay me for."

Martino's mustache twitched, his heart hammering within a constricted chest.

"Just where do you obtain these so-called packages?" growled Angelo. He leaned toward Martino, Angelo's bulbous eyes clapped on the courier.

Martino flinched. "They're waiting for me at a mortuary, uh...the Braun Funeral Home in Zürich. A girl...real nice blonde...hands me the package and five-thousand francs. I don't know the guys she works for." The lying eyes avoided Angelo's stare. "I told her she could make big money if she helped you boys out with some info. She seemed interested, but she's scared and don't want to be seen talking to you."

"Yeh? So where's she want to meet?" The query, the sound projecting like sandpaper, was garbled by the pasta sucked into Riccardo's throat. The slits of the questioner's eyes focused on Martino.

Martino shot a worried glance at his watch as nearby cathedral bells rang twice. He looked up.

"In the mountains near my home in Chiasso. A small cottage. Away from any prying eyes. This Helga used to ski near there in the winter, so she knows it well. Here's a map." Martino's hand pushed a penciled drawing to Riccardo. "A dirt road leads off the highway, up to the cabin. Some old lady sometimes stays there when her cows are in summer grazing."

Martino's eyelids blinked and fluttered while the Mafia henchmen digested the information.

"Okay, okay. We'll meet with...what's the broad's name?" snarled Angelo, guzzling beer, his voice wheezing.

"Helga. Helga Baumann."

"Baumann? Sounds German. Don't like Germans. They fucked up Italy real good when Hitler and Mussolini were around." Angelo stared at the map, his eyes tracking the lines.

"I don't know her nationality. But she's damn good looking," retorted Martino. "She must know who the big guys are. Pay her well and keep it quiet. It'll be worth your while."

"Yeh, we'll take real good care of her. Blonde? Alone, huh? When do we meet this…this broad at the cabin?" Riccardo cast a wink at Angelo.

"In four days," said Martino. "Bring a lot of cash. She's expensive."

Angelo pushed his chair back with a grating noise, reared up and stretched. He grabbed the blue flowers in his gnarled fist, crushed the petals and stems, and watched them drop one by one to the scuffed linoleum.

"That's what will happen to you and this Helga if you're fucking with us. She comes alone. In four days you meet us in Chiasso at nine in the morning and show us this mountain road. So you got family there, huh? I bet your wife and daughter are real pretty…and in good health? Melita and Antonietta, isn't it?"

"Yeh, sure. Just keep them out of this. Meet you? Why? I got to stay on the job."

"Just be there," commanded the Mafia enforcer, his words vitriolic. "Understand?"

"Okay, okay. I'll wait at the Ristorante Medaglione."

Martino stood up, another anxious droplet staining his boxer shorts. As he stretched his elbows backward, Riccardo spied something under the arm.

"What's that, Martino?" he demanded.

"What?"

"That mark on your goddamn left arm." He pointed and then spat tobacco juice into a flowerpot.

"This? Just a tattoo."

"Angelo, look at this. It's the same fucking tattoo we saw on that French weasel in Marseille. Now that's a real coincidence or what?"

"Probably we went to the same parlor. So what?" He shrugged away the perturbing query.

"Nothing. Kind of weird, though." He grabbed LaVeccia's arm, locked his frowning eyes on the winged portrait, and then twisted away. "I'll get the check. See you in four days, Martino. And you fucking be there."

10

Chiasso, Monday morning.

Helga looked up from the wineglass she was wiping as Martino, hands in pockets, entered the Ristorante Medaglione. Helga, dressed in a waitress uniform, and the barkeep were sitting on stools and laughing over some ribald comment. Martino gazed about the otherwise empty room, shuffled to the corner table, and disposed himself onto an ashwood chair. Helga noticed that the table annoyed him, its one leg standing a bit longer than the others, the cracked top wobbling.

"Just coffee, please."

"Italian?" Helga hollered from across the room.

"Italian. Sugar."

Beads of perspiration trickled down the nape of his neck, each drop sending tiny shock waves into the spine. Waiting knitted seconds into long minutes while he ground his teeth together. Fifteen minutes crept by. Helga saw Martino's eye spot the tiny golden cross on her wristlet as she served the steaming, black java in a miniature white mug.

"Lovely day," she chirped. Blue highlights danced away from the unnatural sheen of her raven wig. Helga, in disguise, smiled, her expression beguiling, the perfume cajoling.

"You must be new here? Leona ill?"

"Visiting relatives at the lake. I'm filling in. Coffee okay?" As the smiling waitress leaned over to straighten the table cloth, she felt Martino's restless eyes wandering over the swell of her breasts.

"Uh, sure. Excellent."

"Good. If you need more, just ask." Helga glided away, her fluid blue and gold skirt revealing the captivating motion of her hips.

Martino began to speak. "That's a pretty bracelet you're wearing. May I…"

"Martino! Ahh, my good friend, Martino LaVeccia. It's such a pleasure to see you again. Are you daydreaming?" Riccardo's greeting speared LaVecchia, whose wishful thinking exploded.

Angelo and Riccardo grabbed two straight-backed chairs, bronze-tipped legs scraping over the slatted wooden floor. They straddled their seats, flanking Martino, all the while laughing at an obscene joke, their mood expansive. Helga suddenly reappeared, almost as if cued, her radar painting the newcomers.

"Fresh coffee, gentlemen?" She pitched a subtle grin, the corners of her mouth rolling downward. Mixed signals. Contempt laced with curiosity.

Angelo turned and stared at her, his jaded eyes widening. "Coffee? Sure, same for my friend." He looked the beauty up and down, galvanized by the apparition. "What's your name, honey?"

"Christina. My friends call me Tina." A sweet, sensuous voice. Indulgent, red lips beckoned, smiled. A wet tongue licked her upper lip. Deep marine eyes, iconoscopes, wild and piercing, darted from Angelo to

Riccardo and back. Feline eyes veiled in secrecy. Computing eyes receiving and processing information with a fine exactness.

Her eyes served two hidden masters. Halina and the Herr Doktor.

Helga inhaled deeply, forcing apart the cleavage. Occult signals. The brothers seemed to accept them without scrutiny, their higher centers unable — or not willing — to unscramble the code. Helga tracked the tremble of excitement in Angelo's hands. And the thrust in Riccardo's crotch, lust tightly muzzled.

She paused as they surveyed her body, then tossed her hair back in mock disgust while sauntering back toward the coffee bar.

"I saw her first, Rico," whispered the larger gangster, ignoring Martino. Angelo tapped a Turkish Sobranie on the table before lighting the cigarette.

"Okay, Angelo, okay. But after your fun at the cabin, you'll be too worn out for anything tonight." Riccardo paused and turned to the third man. "Martino, after coffee you come along with us to the gravel road. We'll travel on by ourselves. Then meet us here at dusk. Understand. No tricks."

"Got it, Riccardo. I'll be here."

Helga returned with two more mugs of black java. "The cups are very hot. Anything else?" Twin blue orbs, ringed by black eyeliner, peered through the men.

Angelo leered at the tantalizing soubrette. "Uh... when do you get off, Tina?" He flipped his gaudy tie back and forth.

"I'm working late. About nine this evening." She caught a glimpse of leather and gunmetal against Angelo's white shirt.

"I'll be back with my friends. Tonight how about you and me having a couple drinks together?" He twisted the rings on his fingers.

Helga, scorn masked by lips crawling into a smile, pressed her left hand on his forearm, squeezing, raising the hairs on Angelo's skin, the other hand smoothing down the tie against his barrel chest. Helga felt Angelo's heartbeat accelerate as her seductive contact lengthened. "We'll see, Angelo. We'll see." *Sicilian offal!* Revolted by his squalid garlic breath, she released her grip.

The three men finished their coffee and strolled outside. Helga stood at the doorway and pretended to clean a window.

"Hey, Rico, how did she know my name?" A slight stutter in his voice as he tossed the tobacco butt against gravel stones.

"Shit, Angelo, you just look like an angel... Hell, she probably heard us talking. Let's get the fuck out of here."

Helga watched their unsteady feet stump toward a red Maserati. Then, inside, she gathered up the coffee cups as the side door to the café closed with a concluding rattle. Worried, Martino also exited, heading back toward his home.

Helga's eyes abruptly changed. Like those of a black panther stalking her prey. The alluring smile altered, still with the architecture of pleasantry, but more like that of a surgeon who had performed a masterful operation.

She slipped into the ladies washroom and stripped away her disguise. Aristocratic fingers wiped off the mascara. She snatched the hairpiece and stuffed it inside a satchel. Blond hair rolled over her shoulders, the ends dancing on sublime skin — unblemished except for a long, thin white line on her right forearm, the restless scar, like ice in summer and fire in winter, trying to make her recall its origin. But memory flowed in a destructive fashion, splintered debris in a rearview mirror.

Helga rubbed the mystical flaw, grappling to open the steel gates of her mind. *Where did that come from?* A serial number flashed by, then evaporated with its undercurrent of anxiety. For a moment her brow furrowed, eyes searching the edges of a hiatus in faraway memory. Her secret remained safely hidden, locked away from prying eyes, even her own.

The colorful skirt tumbled to the floor. Helga struck the taped padding off her abdomen and released the black bra strap. Firm, unsuckled breasts fell slightly to their natural pose, freedom compelling Helga to inhale an audible sigh of relief.

Der Spiegel. The mirror. The shapely image in the full-length, silvered glass reflected a narrow, muscular abdomen tapering downward, flaring into a maiden's pelvis. Magnetic groins flowed toward a soft and willowy forest descending over the mons, into the hidden valley of dangerous delights. She reflected on the many incubi wandering into her treasure cove, into a tight embrace, the man thrusting, begging for more and more. Lust and pain twisting into a black emotion. Anoxic orgasm. Death. With each kill, Helga became more blooded, more dangerous.

She winced, *It's happening again. I can't stop it!* The Prussian command. The steel gaff, flickering sunlight glinting from the submerged metal, had hauled a forgotten child once again from the amniotic depths of creation, closer, ever closer toward a fragile, wind-rippled surface. *Die Sonne geht immer auf.* The unremembered telephonic whisper, the sun always rises.

Helga, wandering in a reverie, gazed at the face in the looking glass, the portrait staring back at her. *Who are you?* the reflecting image demanded.

"I am Hal...Helga," a part of her answered aloud. Helga laughed to herself as her lips formed a flirtatious grin, but the image did not smile back, one a black thespian imprisoned in glass, the other its white spectator. Like a photographic negative.

Where did you come from? the other self charged.

Helga blinked as the brief question leaped from her shadow in silver and flew through the deeper substrates of her searching mind. "Mainz...yes, Mainz."

The answer filtered under protest along fortified cortical connections and into a protected awareness. Helga was a voyeur peeking back into time.

What are you? challenged the mirrored likeness, the past and present locked in mortal combat.

The inquisition threatened sanity, forcing the question to be thrown back. "What are *you?*" shrieked the perspiring creature facing the mirror.

Helga reached up, unwittingly pulling blond hair back behind her head, and the mirrored image performed likewise. *Ein Pferdeschwanz.* A ponytail. Like Jeffry. The moving portrait blurred. The deep-set, hazel eyes of her former lover were staring back at her. *I am Jeffry.* Thunderclouds formed in the pupils, sheets of lightening illuminating a red background. "The Merry Widow Waltz," unbidden, slipped over the gray walls.

"I...I asked wha...what, not who." Fear and anger had replaced Helga's coy expression, the woman stiffening against herself.

The scathing apparition retorted, *I am your opposite self. I am Jeffry. Look beyond Jeffry.* The deformed eyelid in the looking glass mocked her without mercy.

Helga, her breathing suspended, dropped her hair and the persistent icon did likewise, the hazel eyes fading, the music collapsing. The battle for mastery ended without a winner, the firefight suspended until another day.

Skittish and still perspiring, Helga whirled away, struggling to replace her bra and panties.

Relief and determination displaced anxiety as she resumed dressing. Levis, a woolen shirt, and hiking boots. Steady breathing returned. She shook her head, matted locks and troubled thoughts flying way. Then Helga

The Thunderbird Covenant

coiled her hair beneath a green beret. A black leather bag hung from a shoulder strap under her left arm. She closed her eyes and journeyed briefly back to her Kyoto instructor before exiting the restroom.

"Antonio, here is the rest of your promised reward. Thank you for permitting me to serve the customers. I'll return tonight…if you want me." Helga was back in control.

The cheerful bartender, savoring the memory of last evening's wonders, snatched the crisp lira waving in memorable fingers. "If tonight is anything like last evening, you can be a permanent hire." He shook with excitement.

Her voice dropped an octave. "Remember," she winked, "if you keep this quiet, I shan't tell anyone either…especially your wife." A seductive smile crossed her face while she brushed a strand of hair from her cheek.

"I understand. Absolutely. See you tonight. *Ciao*."

Helga strode over to the kitchen behind the bar and aimed for the refrigerator. The hand of Halina retrieved a plastic pouch from the cold air and placed it in the black leather case.

Outside, a whirr of crickets greeted Helga as she stepped toward a rented Audi, slamming the car door after her. Overhead, a white fireball spun higher in the heavens, well above the mountains. Early morning mists had slipped away, and nearby church bells announced the hour with ten thunderous peels echoing off the valley walls, like the heavy hammer of God signaling the fiery diadem below.

Helga slapped the Audi into gear and gunned the motor over macadam, up the hillside, beyond the village, into the scent of forested pines. Gravel and pine needles spit from the rear wheels, plumes of dust following as the car clawed its way up, the road transforming into twin ruts of gray dirt and pressed grass. Daffodils and edelweiss dropped away in the background.

The thought of pressing her exotic skills toward another fatal ending triggered a hint of dampness in her laced panties. She toyed with her thoughts. *Three assassinations.* Her perineal muscles contracted with anticipation. The confrontation would be subtle. The attack, brutal. *Leave Martino alone. He is one of us,* she had been told. Helga studied her vision. *But the two called Angelo and Riccardo, the two revolting Sicilian brothers, they must be terminated, liquidated without prejudice. And that bartender with the overactive, little appendage...he will play his final, thrilling scene.*

Helga laughed uproariously, thinking, *what a trick he was!* Tears washed down her cheeks, one hand holding her sides, recalling the hilarity of that moment. *A riot in bed. He thought he was mister macho, his drunken body clowning around the room. Kept flagging his little prick, trying to make the record books at...how did he say it?...cleaning out the tubes. That jerk should have been a high-wire jester.* Helga's chortles quieted, and then she sighed. *Still...wish I didn't have to kill the bar keep...rather liked him, so young and cute. Yet, there must be no traces left.*

The tree line fell below the narrow road hair-pinning skyward up the steep mountain. Lively Swiss music from the radio played to her ears, Helga's index fingers tapping with the rhythm of the melody. The tune slipped into a military cadence and her hands gripped the wheel, the tightening muscles in her arms straining in contemplation. *I put just enough in their coffee.*

Today's weaponry—the art of illusion, shadowy seduction, and a samurai's shaft. Her Asian instructors had taught her well. Too well. Powerful muscular reflexes programmed as if by computer, acting in milliseconds. Lethal reactions against two creatures from Hell and one seeker of thrills. A cautious pursuit. A violent intent.

But first the illusion.

11

Mount Generosa.

Sounds from a nearby creek, braids of water gurgling, rushing, and splashing against stone and gravel, echoed against titian slabs and slate-colored buttresses of rock, fortresses jutting away in angular attack formation. Goliathan peaks, home to ancient glaciers, stood point-guard over the steeply slanted walls of sepia and ashen hues, ramparts lining the emerald-green valleys.

The brilliant, scarlet-red heath from the Alpine dwarf shrub flowed in reckless fashion around pitted boulders harboring flakes of yellow moss. Rare stands of pine trees, low scrub bushes and patches of snow clung to the crags and crevasses of rocks, life struggling under a fluorescent-blue sky.

Helga trekked along the path leading away from the mountain creek. The lone figure hesitated, squinted, and then circled around some scree, her head bowed into the whistling wind. She adjusted a black shawl wrapped over secured locks and then forged onward. The path inclined upward toward a remote cabin, a rude and squat hut two-hundred paces further ahead. She had left her small herd of cows and two mules grazing within earshot of this rural cottage, a mountain haven constructed from the gray stone of ancient glacial deposits.

Groaning and cursing aloud with each step, Helga, having fabricated a highlander's bucolic identity, steadied herself against a stout walking stick slightly bent, a gnarled archery bow. Brisk winds slapped her woolen skirt around the heavy staff, impeding her progress as if warning her to desist.

The slouched woman halted to mimic a gasp for breath, Helga's throat rattling with sputum. A wire-thin necklace of titanium braided with silver hung from her neck, two large wooden crosses dangling piously in front from the two ends of the incomplete neckband.

The rustic figure approached the shelter. Using her staff, Helga thumped and thwacked on the round-topped pinewood door. No answer. She jarred the door open and stepped inside, heels on creaking flooring. Chinks of sunlight filtered through dust-stained windows and into musty air, muting dark shadows under a timbered ceiling.

Helga cocked an eye, tracking subtle signs. Since her reconnoiter three days earlier, chairs had been straightened. The bed cover no longer lay askew and throw-rugs seemed too regimented on the splintered, rough-planked floor. Her adversary, looking for traps, had found none. Helga turned on her heel, proceeding back outside, settling into a shadowed porch bench, the bright sun behind her. The lioness of the mountain waited, kinetic reflexes idling. Motionless. Listening. Breathing. Kyoto. Then she saw movement.

"Hello," she hollered. "I've been waiting for you."

Two men were circling granite moraines heaped with pebble stones. They didn't answer. Cowbells and tumbling creek water were the only sounds, except for labored breathing from the Sicilians.

The two thugs approached, the sun glinting off .22 caliber Bernardelli barrels. She pushed herself up from the seat as they drew near. And watched. They were Mafia, brutal territorial carnivores. Sworn to their brotherhood, their Family. One of them stumbled, then caught himself.

"We're lookin' to meet a dame named Helga," shouted Angelo in Italian. He slowed his lumbering step, halting a hammer-throw from the woman. A cloud crossed the sun, shadows becoming vague and formless.

"I am called Helga." She coughed and wheezed. "Where is your car?"

Angelo ignored the question. "You alone?"

"Of course. And you brought the money?"

"Ten-thousand francs. Must be more than you make in five years." Angelo patted a small duffel bag.

"Angelo, she doesn't look like she knows much. I think we're on a wild goose chase," whispered Riccardo out the corner of his mouth.

"We'll find out," growled the half brother, still wheezing from the hike.

"Why don't you nice gentlemen come inside. It's warmer out of the wind." She winked while leaning against her stave.

"First, I'm making sure you're not carrying any weapons. Stay where you are and keep your hands away from your side."

"Sure, come on over," Helga replied to Angelo while smiling at Riccardo. "The only gun I've ever seen is my grandfather's shotgun. Uses it for quail hunting. You ever shot quail…?"

While Riccardo held the pistol, Angelo shouldered his firearm and moved up. He patted her ragged clothing with his hands, ignoring the irritating prattle.

"Hey, you don't need to feel every inch of my body," she squealed.

"Hold still and spread your fucking legs." Angelo's coarse hands, the backs covered with coils of body fleece, pushed upward along the inside of her thighs, reaching her crotch. The billowing skirt buffeted his face, and he drew back, shrugging off a brief second of formless fear.

"I guess she's okay, Rico. Let's go inside." Angelo lifted a hand to shade the sun. "You first, lady."

He shoved her through the rustic doorway, into the center of the single-room hovel. As their boot heels struck the timbered flooring, the Helga's eyes spun downward, fastening on the black leather boots.

Sieg heil…! A child's fist gripped the longbow. Helga fought for inner balance, the brittle edge of attention on her Chiasso assignment, her liquid core firmly anchored to a nonexistent death camp. Then she focused. *No…! Information… Control… Kyoto…* But infantile rage, a choking fury, demanded revenge. The flames of Birkenau licked upward, engulfing Hali's brain, threatening to erupt. She squeezed her eyelids together, concentrating on the oriental teacher, on the metaphysical. Kyoto. *Breathe deeply, Helga. Stop crucifying yourself.* And then, quietly, *Put your child back in a safe place. Asleep on her tatami.*

Helga blinked and looked up, recoiling at the Sicilians as she recovered from her spell, venomous, subsurface loathing redirected, an invisible leash holding her in check.

The woman leaned on the walking stick, Helga's body tense but motionless. Her eyes narrowed. "Martino claimed that you desired information. About my employers."

Her recovering voice reflected fright, her left hand with spread fingers touching, covering the base of her throat, eyes widening with feigned anxiety, the warrior ceding ground.

"If you work in Zürich, how come you're dressed like that?" Riccardo demanded to know. He scratched his head, wondering why the voice seemed vaguely familiar.

"My aunt lives near here. Often I escape to the mountains for holiday. It's restful. Few people. And I dare not let my employers suspect I'm meeting anyone. Could lose my job…or worse."

Helga fixed Riccardo with her chilling, unblinking stare. He glanced away as she asked, "Exactly what do you want to know? And please point that thing elsewhere."

Heightened alertness replaced the façade of trepidation, her iron grip on the walking stick constricting.

"We came to find out who provides the packages you deliver to Martino. What's in them? Where's their destination in Marseille?"

"Where's the cash? I wasn't born yesterday," she scoffed, affecting greater assertiveness with calculating equilibrium, Italian with Sicilian dialect.

Angelo smiled, his yellowed teeth locked together. "Sure honey. Sure. It's in this carry-bag. Come on over and take a look."

Helga shuffled across the room as Riccardo slipped behind her. The screeching of shifting oak planks interlaced with whistling bursts of air currents rattling window panes. As she reached out, Angelo yanked the bag away, guffawing.

"You dumb broad. First you tell us what we want to know."

Angelo grabbed her right wrist in a brutal grip, forcing it back. Helga, teeth clenched, buckled her knees to lessen the pain.

"That's just the beginning, bitch. Who's your goddamn boss?"

He bent Helga's arm further back, driving her knees to the ground, the walking stick clattering to the floor. She could smell the foul sweat peeling off Angelo, his chest wheezing.

"Hold her other goddamn arm, Rico."

Riccardo pushed his gun under a high leather belt and latched on to her left limb. He ripped her shawl away, throwing it on the bed.

"Please, I'll tell you what I know. You promised to pay me," she whimpered, the sniveling a masquerade.

"Goddamn fucking right you'll tell us. Give us names. Who runs the show? Where are they?" spat Angelo. "Yoke her Rico."

Riccardo seized both of her arms, fastening them behind her back. Her hair flew into his face as Angelo punched her in the ribs and tore the woolen skirt from her waist. Helga inhaled from the pain. The furious queen-bee held back the disturbed insects in her nest, the shrill buzzing in the hive crescendoing.

"Take a gander at that, Rico. What a body." Helga's torso twisted as he forced off her hiking boots and stockings.

"Don't do this! His name is Schmidt. Herr Thomas Schmidt," she claimed, weaving her lie into a fabric of truth. "That's all I know. He doesn't tell me what's in the packages. His name is Schmidt. Please!"

"Schmidt, huh? Where does he hang out?"

Angelo, panting, snapped the bra off her breasts, pointed nipples sending him into a frenzy.

"Tie her up Rico. Tie each wrist to separate legs of the bed. Then go outside and keep watch. The details of her employer can wait."

Riccardo yanked down a curtain cord as Angelo leveled a stiletto at Helga's throat. Riccardo bound her wrists to iron stanchions underpinning the wooden bedstead,

Helga's arms now spread-eagled above her head, her body on the wooden floor.

"Get the fuck out of here, Rico. Drink in some mountain air outside."

Riccardo laughed, pulled out his semi-automatic, and clumped out the front door, ash-gray dust spilling from the cuffs of his pants. He dropped down on the bench and began polishing the Bernardelli with an oily rag from his back pocket, the half-brother coveting the sounds of rape. The Alpine wind rose, its low skirl a backdrop to a symphony of creek water, cowbells, and muffled cries.

Inside, Angelo, now on his knees, loosened his belt and dropped the heavy trousers, the bronze buckle clanging to the floor. "Hold still, you little cock-sucker. This won't hurt much. Shit, I think your going to like it."

Helga's writhing body convoluted into a lodestone pulling at the Sicilian's feverish groin, his hormonal toxins rampaging.

"Which hole do you want it in, woman?" he roared, laughing, drooling at the corner of his slanted mouth.

Helga gripped the cord around her wrists and counseled, *You choose, my friend. Neither gives light at the end.*

"Spread those peasant legs of yours if you don't want this blade a skewer in your stomach."

Helga gasped as the tip of Angelo's thin dagger drew blood from the taunt skin of her abdomen, splinters in the wooden floor lacerating her back. Her legs separated, muscles tensing, eyes closed. Angelo pushed her knees up and drove a calloused finger between her legs. Helga groaned, lashing her head side-to-side, the pain only hardening a deadly resolve.

"Please don't hurt me! Oh, God! Someone help me!"

Angelo spit on his hardened prick and plunged full into her vagina, Helga's shrieking firing uncontrolled lust. She now let him wholly inside, her smooth muscles coiling around the incubus, and began to move her hips, inviting his fermenting shaft to greater dimensions. The chameleon's mutation was so imperceptible that Angelo, in his orgasmic frenzy, never sensed the transformation, her own volatile shaft penetrating deeper into Angelo's brain, the hunter now the hunted.

"Angelo," the savage succuba screamed. "Angelo!" She baited as he slammed his pelvis hard against hers, grinding, driving toward the impending climax.

"Oh, God, this feels good," he hissed, heaving breaths demanding more oxygen, his red, bulbous eyes squeezing shut, the knife chattering across the floor. His groping hands grasped the sides of her pelvis, the he-animal kneeling at the edge of a tornado.

Helga toyed with him, waiting for his primal orgasm, her eyes in an electric-blue flame, now fixed on his sadistic grin.

She tightly flexed her hips, inviting Angelo to thrust deeper, her perspiring and sinewy thighs now in front of his barrel chest. Helga's tempered forelegs extended as she rocked with the androgenic force of his irreversible drive.

Helga gripped the legs of the trembling bed while her buttocks rose off the floor, grim determination replacing feigned terror. *Keep fucking this bitch, Angelo*. The pressure of Angelo's movements intensified as he hurtled blindly through the celestial portal into a terrible Hell, lost inside the fire-breathing she-monster.

Your competition pays better, Angelo. "Come on, Ang! Fuck me, baby!" she screeched, her sibilant words driving him towards his execution, the Phoenix, having thrown down the gauntlet years ago, now rising from flaring embers into a fiery maelstrom.

His body tensed, convulsed, jerking savagely in a terminal climax. She could feel his pulsating throb as he arched backwards in a mindless ecstasy.

Now! Helga, thunderbolts flashing from stormy orbs of ice, locked her thighs and forelegs in position, her entire body an unsprung bow. Like whips cracking under the force of powerfully focused muscles and unleashed hatred, the legs of little Hali exploded upward with a terrible fury. Heels, driven by massively detonated energy once contained, rifled like a slingshot, exploding with hair-raising ferocity against her victim's targeted jaw. The seismic shock of the projectiles snapped Angelo's head backward, the spine deep inside his neck splintering in two with a single audible crack.

Angelo's shell-shocked limbs collapsed, limp and fatally paralyzed. The once proud penis stood erect, yet no longer under control. Rapid respirations abruptly ceased, the struggling heart still beating, pushing Mafioso blood through a conscious brain. The immobilized Sicilian listed like a scuttled ship and then tumbled onto her, succumbing to the greater succuba, his eyes bulging and purple with ghostly fear. His contorted face rolled into crimson, then blue, oxygen seeping away as he struggled to lift his head.

Angelo, unable to breathe, could make no sound.

She blew him a kiss. "Good night, my sweet angel. Choose your playmate more carefully next time."

Helga closed her serpentine eyes, her own climax taking charge of the beast within her. The woman's orgasmic crescendo swiftly mounted as the man's life ebbed away, spiraling out of existence. Sculptured Amazonian muscles tensed, thunder roaring through the heavenly body, lightening ripping into a corrupted soul, *Donner und Blitzen*, fired and then muted in vehement retribution.

Within minutes, his heart quivered and then all activity drew down to closure. Helga opened her eyes, the flaming blue now a serene azure.

She shivered, stretched, smiled. Sleep would be more peaceful. For now. The scent, the mirage of burnt flesh and charred bones faded, though the air remained heavy with the heat of battle.

"Riccardo, help! Get him off me. I think he had a heart attack."

Riccardo slammed open the cottage door. "You finished, Angelo? How was she?"

"Get this thing away. I can't breathe. I think he died on me," Helga pleaded.

"Oh, shit. Angelo. Wake up. Angelo! Wake up!"

Riccardo grabbed the lifeless mannequin by its boots and pulled him out of Helga, Angelo's head bobbing on his flaccid neck, the face hewed into a funereal black.

"Cut me loose, Rico. Please."

Riccardo looked at the lifeless form of Angelo, then at Helga. Unsure of what to do, he slipped out the pistol lodged behind his belt and leveled it at her.

"Don't move, bitch. You 'n me are going outside. Taking you to the boss. He'll know what to do."

"Boss? What boss? Shit, aren't you your own master, Rico? Where are you from?"

"Shut up, lady."

He growled a brutal oath, grabbed the knife off the floor, and sliced loose her bonds.

"I ought to screw you, too, and then shoot your fucking brains out. Damn! Angelo, wake up!" He kicked his partner's deformed corpse. The dead and sightless eyes remained frost-glazed.

Helga rubbed her wrists and sat up on the floor. Her breasts leaped into Riccardo's consciousness, causing the brutish crotch of his pants to swell again. Devoid of logical thought, he dropped to his knees, his head swirling with lust, high altitude and the methaqualone in his coffee. While holding the gun in his right hand, he reached out with his left to squeeze Helga's breast. She edged away.

"Please, Riccardo. Leave me alone. Where is your car?"

Yet Helga made no attempt to cover the curves of her bosom as retracted claws pulled her shimmering blond hair back, breasts projecting upwards. Practiced fingers dropped to grip the pious wooden crosses of the necklace as Riccardo, his mind robbed of reason, lunged towards desire. The sunlight from the window slammed into his eyes.

Helga spread her arms, stretching the skin of baiting breasts, and the necklace whipped away, the cruciform weights snapping apart. The sound was like that of a rifle crack. In one deadly motion the wire coiled around Riccardo's neck. With enormous strength and agility, Helga drew the wooden crosses together, closing the noose, inflicting inanimate pain. White-hot and incandescent. Riccardo flailed out with both arms, but with each raging movement the unrelenting loop of primal hatred tightened.

His eyes over the edge of panic, fear replacing arrogance, death no longer held at bay, Riccardo sprang forward, staggering and dragging Helga with him. A karate kick to his right hand sent the gun skittering across the floor. In desperation he lurched toward the sidearm, but the piranha grip constricted. He twisted his body, slamming her naked torso full-length against the mattress.

Helga locked her legs around the post of the bed, her limbs now grappling irons in an indomitable scissor-cut, at the same time drawing the noose. She hauled in his convulsing body, his face against hers. Oxygen leaked from his bubbling lungs as he fought one last battle, a useless frenzy to shake her loose. But the wire sank further into the hemorrhaging neck. Riccardo's head, teetering towards decapitation, pivoted to one side, slitted eyelids dropping over terrified eyes.

His toupee, loosed from adhesive, fell to the bed cover, highlights reflected from the man's scalp.

Helga froze. *You aren't Riccardo. Who the fuck are you?* She saw a jowled face with a sunburned complexion and thick eyeglasses, arterial streaks magnified on oscillating orbs. Helga still dangerously hard-wired to a forgotten past, drove to unleash her final, deadly venom. But then she blinked and the image, amidst a distant waltz, faded as conscious reason took charge.

Helga inched the life-threatening crosses apart, allowing Riccardo to suck in some air.

"Hold still, Riccardo. One false move and it will be your last." The tense muscles of her limbs undulated under wet skin, moving like those of a raging panther toying with its prey, waiting for the kill.

She let life back into his body. His lungs expanded, straining to draw in oxygen, his jaw falling slack with fear and disbelief.

"Now, Riccardo, my obscene bastard. Tell this bitch who your chief is. Who sent you to Martino? Catch your breath and talk to me. Easy…don't move, or your neck will break like Angelo's did."

Hearing her last words, Riccardo's eyes snapped wide open. Spitting blood onto the bed sheets, he uttered the words, "Mafia…Sicily. Benito, Benito Dumonte."

"Dumonte? Your master? Where is he now?"

"Yes…yes, he sent us to Martino."

"I asked you where he is." She tightened the bloodied wire.

"Near here. Somewhere. Please, don't kill me," he begged in choking gasps.

Helga released her scissor-grip on the bedpost, ignoring the wounds on her own abdomen and back. Dragging Riccardo by his neck, the man stumbling on weakened legs, she picked up the frayed curtain-cord.

"Arms around the bedpost, Rico." Her venomous eyes shot terror into a weakening core, the heart of a dangling marionette manipulated from the sinister wooden crosses of the master puppeteer. Helga held the choke-wire with one hand and bound his hands together with the other, then releasing the tourniquet.

She cast a chilling smile. "Well, lover boy. So you want to play?"

Helga's fingers crawled like a crab over Riccardo's crotch and ripped apart his trouser buttons, slipping by a limp appendage, grabbing terrified testicles, squeezing. A loose button tumbled and rolled over the floor.

"Is this what you and Angelo had in mind? Come on, Rico, where's the mafioso hard-on?"

He gasped, hard shocks belting his groin. "Please…"

"Benito Dumonte, huh? Well, Mister Dumonte. We have some bait for you." She patted his retracted balls and released her grip.

Helga clothed herself in the peasant dress. A devious Cheshire grin crept across her face as Riccardo scanned every movement with riveted eyes, his evil mind recoiling.

With cold determination she snapped up her walking stick, drew a roll of stout filament from her pocket, and strung the weapon with the braided nylon cord. Muscles strained as Helga bent the bow into a lethal weapon. She snapped several steel-tipped arrows out of a quiver hanging by the fireplace. Helga eyed the arrowheads and then Riccardo, dipped the points into a plastic bottle from her pocket, and capped the container. She waved the arrow at Riccardo, and his knees turned to putty.

The sun settled lower in the western sky behind the cabin. She took Angelo's blade from the floor, briefly poised it over Riccardo's left eye, and then dropped it downward to slice free his bonds.

"Run to your car, Rico. That's what you wanted, didn't you?" She leaned on the bent walking stick, her breathing deeper, thighs tightening.

"Go on, Rico. Out the door. Run for your life. See if you can beat this peasant's arrow. After all, I'm only a bitch. Isn't that what your dead brother claimed? I'm offering you a chance. That's more than you were willing to give me."

He paused, unsure of his choices. "Get out, or I'll finish you here!" she screamed like a wounded, feral cat, electric intensity radiating.

Riccardo stumbled through the portal, blood trailing in rivulets down his panic-stricken body. His boots scarcely touched the ground as he fled the unleashed assassin.

"Help me!" he shouted, his screams bouncing in scrambled Italian from canyon walls. "Shoot her! Stop her!"

Two men appeared from behind shadows of gray boulders one hundred yards away. They saw Riccardo running toward them in halting, erratic strides, one hand holding up his pants. The cabin door lay ajar, the sunlight behind, the passageway dark. Unable to decipher Riccardo's garbled pleading, they sprinted toward their friend, hands on loaded carbines.

Suddenly, Riccardo lurched and dropped to the ground, his skull crashing on rocks lining the bubbling mountain stream. Helga cocked an ear to the sounds of running feet and splashing water.

The two men waded across the shallow waters and approached their comrade, a single arrow in his back, a ribbon of blood trailing. As they advanced within fifty meters from the cabin, Helga lifted the longbow armed a second time with a curare-tipped arrow. She pulled the braided nylon to its maximum stretch, the arrow's notch securely imbedded. Weapon and body as one, she released the feathered missile. The projectile tore with deadly aim, traveling in a whisper through the cold afternoon air. A third shaft followed in swift pursuit.

Helga hauled Angelo's corpse from the cabin, an Alpine abattoir in lengthening shades. She searched the pockets of the four inert men and loaded each body crosswise upon one of the two mules, two limp torsos per animal. Then she bound wrists to ankles after extracting the arrows.

"Sorry, boys," she said to the mules. "I expected only two loads for you, not four." They brayed as she slapped them on their backsides, and the mules clopped back down the trail.

An orange disc of fire descended in the sky, slipping into a sanguine red, casting irregular shadows on the broken terrain. Fading sapphire tones slid further through the heavens, heralding the return of twilight. The solitary assassin brought her quarry down to the lowlands. Helga would leave Martino to clean up the refuse and report her success.

12

The next day.

Martino watched from a distance, fearful of getting too close. The police had placed barricades to prevent onlookers from entering the Ristorante Medaglione. Early this morning the owner had discovered the young bar keep lying naked on a couch in the back room. Dead.

An early morning fog crawled around the upturned coat collar protecting Martino's neck. His heart stopped beating for a second, jolted by a familiar voice greeting him from behind.

"Good morning, Martino." A cheerful woman hailed him. "What's happening?"

"Oh, hello, Tina. You startled me. The police are here. Antonio died last night. No obvious injuries. They say his face appeared ghastly."

"Paralyzed. Couldn't breathe. Curare will do that," she replied in a matter-of-fact tone.

"Christ, what do you mean," he hissed, spinning to face her.

"Here is another 'package for Marseille.' Toss it to my sponsor. He has paid me well for this."

"You...you're Helga!" His stunned eyes tried to search through the woman's mascara and rouge.

"A pleasure to meet you again, Martino." A sardonic grin flickered across her face. "There are four dead men from the cabin. I've described their location on a map among the items in this sack. The contents of their pockets and all the information I could extract are filed in this bundle also. Do not lose it." She handed him a tote-bag. "And you may keep the 10,000 francs inside."

Antonio and the four Mafioso, flotsam and jetsam bobbing in the wake of Helga's deadly force, had succumbed to an invisible power whose true signature defied understanding.

The tall, imperious woman flashed a cold smile, turned on her heel, and moved regally toward her silver Bentley, powerful engines idling. Reflections from the sky, light clouds chasing eastward, painted strange, twisting patterns in the depths of the fender's polish. A uniformed driver stepped out, saluted, and swung open the back door. Helga waved at Martino and disappeared into darkness, the rear door closing behind her. The Bentley rolled through narrow streets, precision machinery then accelerating northward to Lugano.

Martino clutched the duffel bag as he stared after the motorcar and its enigmatic passenger, waiting until they vanished from sight. Then he cut toward a public phone and dialed Zürich.

"*Herr Doktor Niemeier, bitte.*"

At the Trieste Hospital in Zürich Doctor Johann Niemeier, cloaked in a surgeon's long white coat of pressed respectability, replaced the Victorian receiver on his office phone. Fingering a gold watch chain, he turned toward two men sitting and waiting expectantly before his expansive desk. Thick walls decorated with oriental trappings muted the disquieting sights, sounds, and smells of a busy metropolitan medical center in Zürich. Trieste Hospital.

One of the elderly men spoke first in German. "What news from Martino, Johann?" The thin, stooped shoulders of the Polish engineer pressed forward, agitated, bone-colored eyes in reptilian focus, feverish, flicking around the study. "Was our protagonist successful?"

"Performing beyond all expectations, an awesome product of Prussian ingenuity. Not only did she dispose of four curiosity seekers but also my Helga dispatched the bar keep. No one can trace the killings to us..." His eyes squeezed into slits. "That is, no one except Helga, of course."

Niemeier hesitated, steepling his fingers, stretching a spasmodic smile at the brilliant success of his domination—*Die Sonne geht immer auf.* "I think our Sicilian friends have lost the scent."

"Excellent! Herr Dietz will be pleased," replied Jerzy Sierpinski, hardened nails methodically scratching his dead-white, scaly skin.

"Martino LaVecchia is bringing the belongings of Helga's victims. We should raise his salary also. What do you think, Jerzy?" the rotund Niemeier asked, twitching his sleeves until a good inch of cuff showed.

Sierpinski, the engineer who worked at Cumaves AG in Zürich since leaving Poland, stood up. Thin blue lips muttered as he paced back and forth. "I agree. He is our most trusted courier," responded the surgeon's former foe, returning to his seat.

Niemeier watched the vulturine neck of Sierpinski crane forward, leaving winged shoulder blades behind. Patches of long white hair fringed his balding head. Deep frown lines sliced his face, aqueous eyes draining from shadowy sockets. Shadows from Auschwitz.

"Good. I will so instruct Jørgen Busche in Copenhagen." Niemeier removed the thick eyeglasses and wiped his bald crown.

The surgeon rotated his swivel chair to face another presence. "And how is my Helga behaving from your standpoint as a father, Heinz, my good friend? Any signs of mental instability?"

Heinz Baumann, the third man in the room, older now but still a bull out of uniform, his neck straining at the collar, moved uneasily in his straight-back chair. "No, no...except..."

"Yes, yes, what is it?" Niemeier raised an eyebrow, the cold pupil focusing on the man from Mainz.

"She has her dreams...her nightmares. More often now. She won't speak to me about them. Helga tells my sister, Anna, however." Baumann shook his burdened face, the skin tremoring as if too loosely drawn upon it. "Frankly, the whole thing is troubling me. If she should ever find out..."

Baumann's voice trailed off, leaving a pregnant hesitation in the air. His saturnine visage twitched on the left while the bulging lids of his thyrotoxic eyes drooped to avoid the surgeon's unnerving gaze, the Kommandant worn down by the sheer power of Niemeier's personality.

Niemeier, his face remaining impassive, ignored the premonition of the former Nazi *SS* commander. Instead, eyes shifting, he turned back to the hawk-like engineer.

"Jerzy, how is your secretary at Cumaves working out? Do you still successfully monitor Suzanne's communications with her former husband? An absolute stroke of luck...having her return to Zürich and apply for her old position." He replaced his spectacles, the glass magnifying movements of arteriole-streaked whites of his eyes.

"We have learned little about either Swedish or Danish intelligence. Still, there is no hint they have any knowledge of our activities. After the Ljunggren divorce,

Internal Security in Stockholm relieved Bjørn Ljunggren of all assignments, except shuffling papers in Copenhagen. Suzanne and Bjørn talk of their deceased son, Christian. The weather. Her new job. Not much else."

"I must run to the operating room. Herr Sierpinski, you and I will meet tomorrow at Cumaves. In your research laboratory. Herr Dietz will update us on the advancement of our project. You will be pleasantly surprised." The two men nodded in conspiratorial agreement and then filed out the door, each moving in different directions.

The third man, former Kommandant Heinz Baumann, treading with a cane to support his large frame, exited Trieste, the walking stick tap, tap, tapping on the marble floor. He stood on the massive portico, searching about the steps while waiting for a taxi to bring him to the Zürich railroad station. Searching for answers.

Baumann shivered, pondering his debt in the next world. *My God, I am wealthy beyond my wildest dreams. But at what price?* A glacial chill infected his spine from the unspeakable memory of two murderous table-top toys, one emerald green, the other ruby red—1943. *And for engineering such a super-Aryan, Himmler himself awarded me the silver medal. God in Heaven, now our creation is my beloved daughter, yet not truly of my blood, of German blood. Polish blood congealing into ice!*

He opened his wallet, his eyes wandering over the photo of a blond girl on horseback. Baumann felt a strange rush of paternal affection. A taxi horn, honking loudly, jolted him back to the present.

13

Copenhagen, Wednesday, August 25, 1971.

The telephone rang in couplets, jarring the early morning solitude. Helga's long arm blindly extended, her fingers grabbing the receiver. Half asleep, she listened, her mind slipping into a trance upon hearing *"Die Sonne geht immer auf."* And then, "Meet Herr Jørgen Busche today. Usual time and place. Follow his every command. *Auf Wiedersehen*, my little Halina."

Helga hung up and blinked. She assumed that the alarm clock had awakened her but wondered why her hand was resting on the phone. She tugged a feather-down pillow over her head and stretched legs and memories, hoping to twist over and slide back into much needed sleep. Instead, an urge to see her Copenhagen contact drove her into action.

"Scheisse!" Helga groaned. Shit!

She headed for the shower, the woman clutching her chest, wishing that the libertines of her life were toothless.

Humming to herself, Helga toweled her hair dry and laced her body with a private brand of a lanolin-based skin moisturizer. Her roommate had already departed for work and left a pot of hot coffee on the stove. Helga drank it black and then dressed while listening to the weather report, her trenchant mind on pressing duties. A perfectionist, she did not wish to be late for work.

More important was the matter of the twelve-thirty appointment. She had another job to do. Helga asked no questions. Her contract required it so. Under no circumstances could she miss this engagement.

Helga departed 30302 Anders Henrikensgada, Apartment 2A, and walked into bright daylight. She surveyed the traffic rolling by and hailed a taxi, the Saab skidding to a stop. Today would be no ordinary day. Helga was not an ordinary woman.

Helga folded the *Wall Street Journal* with its interesting feature on the State Department and Lance Masters. Looking out the taxi window, she dreamily watched towering trees and stately houses flashing by. Then a traffic light. Red switching to green. Helga shuddered and diverted her gaze toward the heavens. The weather bordered on schizophrenia, mares' tails streaming happily across the sky, yet the air hanging ominously still over her part of the earth.

To pass the time, Helga hummed "The Blue Danube Waltz." Eyelids blinked, her thoughts shifting to a postcard and a world she had left years ago, a faraway place called America.

14

Washington, Tuesday, August 24, 1971.

Harald found himself revved up, in a hurry. Stafford had called an urgent conference at BNDD.

This summer day fired up the nation's air conditioned capitol. The early morning showers, recently sprinkled over the city, boiled off the sidewalks and rooftops, driving a haze into the already oppressive air. Harald, listening to strains of Stravinsky, swung his BMW over a puddle of tar and into the parking lot under his office building. He dashed between closing elevator doors, faced the one-way mirror hiding a TV camera, and keyed in the fourth floor. Ping, ping, ping.

"Mr. Johnson, the Director is preparing to start the meeting," announced Stafford's secretary, Martha Farnsworth. A concerned look had replaced her usual pleasant smile. She was fifty-two years old, contentedly married, and indispensable to the section.

"Thank you, Martha. I'll pop right in."

"Also, your friend, Doctor Landon, called. Wanted to know if you would join him at the sports club for a workout."

He grinned. "Please tell him thanks, but I'm tied up."

Harald, with an eagerness born of innate curiosity, took long rapid strides further down the corridor, hesitated as ash gray eyes shot down to his wristwatch, and then entered the oak paneled conference room. Navy-blue, rubberized drapes closed out the inquisitive sunlight. High level personnel from two Bureaus of the Justice Department—the Federal Bureau of Investigation and the Bureau of Narcotics and Dangerous Drugs—occupied Naugahyde cushioned chairs. Also present—the Central Intelligence Agency from Langley. Harald suspected that the gravity of the assembly had to do with the recent influx of narcotics onto the streets of east and west coastal cities.

"Sit over here, Harald." Stafford waved toward an empty seat.

After someone served coffee and donuts, an assistant slid open the door of a paneled cabinet, exposing a bank of electronic maps televised in the far wall, their cursors flashing. Excepting a few coughs and muted whispers, silence hung in the air, the mood somber, tense.

Harald liked and respected Tim Stafford, Director of the Bureau of Narcotics. This imposing man had climbed through the ranks as a tough in-house fighter, brooking no failure in himself or anyone under him, inspiring rather than manipulating. Today, with his tie loosened and shirt sleeves rolled up, Stafford was determined to bring the entire might of his Bureau to bear against a monstrous fungus infecting his country, his America. Intelligent reasoning had failed to ferret out the cancer. More was needed. Much more.

From the other end of the table, Agent Terry Caldwell nodded at Harald. Terry had just completed his situation précis with martial brevity before Stafford drew everyone's eyes.

Standing erect, neck muscles tense, hands fastened behind his back, the Director addressed the audience, his tone commanding. "You are all now up to speed regarding the massive flood of highly concentrated heroin into the United States. We estimate this most recent surge hit the streets two weeks ago. So far no one, and I mean no one, has been able to place the source or the methods of shipment. Our undercover agents in known Mafia-type and subversive societies have heard zip...except that most of the same organizations are forfeiting a significant percentage of the market. And they don't like it."

He searched the eyes of everyone present, inhaled deeply through his nostrils, and resumed. The audience was rapt, listening.

"Our only lead so far is a dead man, a foreign sailor by the name of Tony Salucci. Remember that name.

"A couple of days ago, he hit the bottle at a local bar near the New York City docks, and the braggadocio claimed he knew about some new technique of bringing in smack. He did so at his peril. A couple of our more notorious underworld boys nailed him, invited him to an off-shore yacht, and tortured the poor bastard without mercy. He disclosed little of substance except that the powder was transshipped from Europe. Salucci died. One of our own undercover people sat in on the council and relayed the info on to us."

"Any *corpus delicti*?" asked Joseph Smith, CIA. The tall, rugged and wiry man from Chicago held a thoughtful gaze toward the inset ceiling lamps.

"Yup. On the ocean beach near Atlantic City. Found swollen and barely recognizable from the bruises and water. He died by drowning in fresh water. Not sea water. The unfortunate chap's lungs contained diluted urine, presumably from a toilet bowl. This Anthony Salucci had no prior record in the USA or Canada. I'll project slides and distribute photo copies to field agents."

THE THUNDERBIRD COVENANT

Stafford flicked a switch under the table and a cleft opened up in the far ceiling, a humming sound announcing the descent of a silver screen. The lights and televised maps dimmed as a white beam hurled its portrait of death. A naked male torso, detritus from the grim reaper's gluttony.

Harald had witnessed death often. He still did not like it. The artist instinct forced him to analyze all features. Interpretative analysis. He never forgot a face. He'd remember this one. A cruel mouth frozen between mottled, fleshy cheeks. Black muttonchops.

Above the left elbow, on the inner side of the arm...a strange tattoo. Like a Rorschach ink blot, marked Harald in silence, his eyebrows knitting together, eyesight focused, attention heightened.

"What's this red and green thingamajig on his arm?" he queried after approaching the screen. He swept away a fleeting sense of panic.

"Don't know, Harald. It will be your mission to find out. Several tattoo experts reviewed it. No one recognized this particular style. Sort of like a bat or manta ray, maybe? One colleague compared it to the thunderbird of North American Indian mythology — suppose to personify lightening, thunder, and rain. It may be unimportant. Or a remote clue. Check out this close-up shot."

The projector clicked in a new slide. Now the tattoo appeared like a holographic mask suspended in space, a coat-of-arms with the initials SSV emblazoned beneath. Harald heard himself suddenly inhale as if he had, for a millisecond, witnessed the unlimited depths of evil. A new dimension.

Stafford, still standing, rolled his shoulders back and swiveled to face the wiry BNDD agent with a crewcut. "Now, Terry, fill us in on your follow-up."

Terry had been working alongside the New York police and the FBI for the past week on the new heroin affliction. The projector snapped off, blanking the image as the lunar screen lifted skyward. The geographical charts brightened again. Terry targeted his light pointer, flashing the tight, red laser dot on the series of global maps.

"As you all know, in the past, the vast majority of our heroin has traveled by way of South and Central America, Asia, or Southern Europe. The amount passing through Northern Europe has been nil. Salucci came off the Greek registered ship *Salamis*. Her last port of call was Copenhagen. It's our only lead…or a red herring."

"Ladies and Gentlemen," Stafford punctuated, marshaling far-flung intelligence, the parts failing to cohere. "Although this is our basket, I've asked the CIA to assist where possible." He cut his eyes to Joseph Smith. "At least they're informed and one of their overseas contacts may come through.

"This heinous situation is unique, disturbing. First, the amount and purity of the heroin boggles my mind. Second, the foreign distribution point, Northern Europe, is unique. Third, the culprits are bypassing some very angry underworld organizations, including the Mafia and spin-offs. Fourth, the method of entry remains a mystery, escaping both standard and extraordinary inspection processes.

"Fifth, the USA and Taiwan are the only countries known to be recipients of these special packages. It smacks of a vile conspiracy to undermine our free society. The situation is urgent. Time, short. We will keep all of you posted. In the meantime, Agent Johnson will activate his team into twenty-four hour duty. Harald, come into my office now. Let's move on this."

He paused, recognizing a raised hand.

"Terry?"

"Boss, remember that other body found in the water three months ago?"

"I don't follow you."

"Ed Piccollo's wife. Hauled out of the Potomac. You thought back then it was a drug cartel hit."

"Jesus!" Stafford closed his eyes. He and Ed had been close friends.

Late that same afternoon Harald took off for New York City's La Guardia Airport. Before transferring to Kennedy and his KLM jet for Copenhagen, he paid a visit to the Manhattan morgue where Salucci's body had been transferred. To inspect Tony's remains. Nothing new. The tattoo seemed faded on wax-like, corrugated skin.

Harald, artist and photographer, shot a close-up photograph of the small icon. At the New York office, he developed the film and produced a series of enlargements. He could make neither head nor tail of the image. The initials SSV stood in tiny print at the base of the figure. Each light and dark pixel, standing alone or taken together, produced indecipherable clues. Converging together on film they formed an image, a picture without meaning when viewed out of context. A giant pixel on a cosmic screen.

"Damn, I haven't the slightest idea where to start looking," Harald muttered to himself while taxiing to the airport. He had this gnawing and uncomfortable feeling that the tattoo would find him first.

Harald boarded the jet launching him out of Kennedy, eastward to uncover the first key to the enigmatic portrait. Into Copenhagen to rendezvous with his deep-cover counterpart. Bjørn Ljunggren. This Swedish citizen was working with the Danish government. Stafford had contacted Bjørn, well known to Tim, because the Swede had operated in counter-espionage inside several narcotic organizations throughout Europe and Asia. Electronics and electro-optic surveillance was his particular expertise.

While speeding on wings over the North Atlantic, Harald turned his attention to the bewildering photograph cupped in his hand. *An eagle...butterfly...manta ray?* A flowing series of remote possibilities sailed before his judgment. *A leaf...ink blot...bat?* Twin tails and symmetrically placed wings, feathered limbs seducing the unwary, accursed fins warning Harald away. He closed his eyes, searching for an illusive connection, even a small tincture of information.

15

Copenhagen, Wednesday, August 25, 1971, 12:30 P.M.

Jørgen Busche, working underground in Denmark, signed the bank drafts made out to Helga. This man with spider-web connections was her conduit to a powerful organization, a society specializing in obtaining information and selling risky services on an international scale.

There existed insidious and unknown controls, and Helga was kept in the dark. Yet she was handsomely rewarded, on special retainer to Jørgen's syndicate. An added monthly income of thirty-thousand dollars, deposited in Zürich, was a sufficient price to barter her soul, Busche concluded, though he doubted she had one.

This byzantine broker sat alone, perched on the low stone wall surrounding a courtyard and enclosing an outdoor restaurant of the Hotel København. The warm air was changing, rising, tugging at the Danish flag across the avenue, carrying aloft the scent of spices and the salty tang of the sea.

His complexion—Mediterranean. Short. Paunchy. Nearly bald. Black sideburns took a sharp angle toward loose jowls. Fifty-eight years of age. Smartly dressed.

Busche slid off the stonework and returned to his table. Today, his stomach churned, molars gnawing at the mucosa of his right cheek, for he had new reasons for Helga's talents. Personal reasons, but she was not to know. Fed selected facts only, Helga remained a puppet of seditious units within nations to be narcotized, annihilated from within.

"And now. An unspeakable blunder," he hissed to the wind. "An alcoholic fumble in New York. Dear God...Tony Salucci of all people." He crossed himself. "And I, in the long run, inherit the responsibility." Unequivocal countermeasures were needed, indeed demanded, by the tribunal—Cut off the antagonist without delay. Helga, an experienced professional, again would be their uncanny protagonist.

Busche coughed down the last drop of warm beer as Helga arrived. The eyes of Jørgen Busche tracked his spymaster, his hired assassin of ice-cool intelligence, as she stepped from the taxi. The Baltic Sea breezes pulled quixotically at the skirt of her gray cashmere suit, its owner moving with elegant economy.

Helga wore a pearl gray blouse with tie. A pair of hushed, gray suede shoes, pointed toes, high spiked heels. Complementary hues. Strong feminine curves building to a provocative architecture. The extraordinary power of rippling muscle and sinew hidden under fabric, beneath soft, silky skin. Pearl earrings surrounded by dazzling diamonds.

Long blond hair fastened on one side. Opera length pearls across visually palpable breasts, the terminal necklace hanging in empty space. On the right wrist, a gift from Aunt Anna, a thin gold chain supporting a tiny gold cross, a crucifix, a dainty amulet hanging in pious contradiction—to stave off the evil within. Like Helga's vestments, a prismatic personality of many chameleonic shades.

Helga approached him, and he sat riveted—indeed, awed. She was a silhouette in mendacity, controlled by something terribly inscrutable, antediluvian. A wary animal, dimensions he could not map.

His instructions—termination to be delayed until completion of all three phases. Helga, a hardened professional, was too valuable a resource for now. After that, assignment back to Switzerland. One of the three had prescribed her quietus to be executed under a controlled delamination. *Controlled delamination!* Busche could only guess at what that meant. His gut recoiled as he glanced down at the table. *But why?* he brooded. *They must have far more than bullets planned for her.*

Approaching, Helga nodded at her contact. She thought he seemed different. Not his usual gallant greeting.

"Hmmm...good afternoon, Miss Baumann...our lovely Helga." Busche, his true face masked by a courtly smile, stood up and extended a moist hand. "What a delightful pleasure to see you again. Would you like some food? Or something to drink, perhaps?"

"Coffee and smoked salmon, Jørgen. Thank you."

The waitress, wearing a snug uniform, jotted down their requests, shoved her pencil into the slot of an order pad and departed, Busche's cynical eyes following.

He removed his glasses and dabbed his perspiring forehead on the right. A bullet during the World War II had sliced sympathetic nerves in his neck, a drooping left eyelid resulting. His collar, pinned behind a solid tie, eclipsed the scar. Busche, shifting uncomfortably in the oakwood chair, pivoted back toward Helga.

She felt small gusts of bronchial wind from his lips as he leaned closer to her ear. "Miss Baumann, there is a Swede, a Bjørn Ljunggren, employed by the Danish government in Copenhagen. In the past, he has worked undercover to expose narcotic traffic. My illustrious customers wish to discover his role in Denmark. Their sources in Zürich have already learned that his code name is Falkon..."

He leaned away, as if to assess Helga's response but witnessing only a burst of demonic intensity in her eyes. "This Ljunggren is to encounter someone from the United States, a man or woman identified only as Neptune. My clients also wish to determine who this Neptune is and the purpose of their meeting. Cast out your net once again, Miss Baumann. See what manner of fish or fowl you can haul in."

Busche leaned over the side of his chair to fetch an alligator satchel off the floor. He withdrew a manila folder and presented Helga with a dossier. She grasped the three-page document and thoughtfully fanned her face before placing it under her handbag.

"Don't make any copies. Phosphorus dipped papers," he noted.

"What is so important about their meeting together?" wondered Helga aloud in an almost detached fashion. "How did you learn of this Ljunggren?"

His voice slipped into a lower register, the thick, tight lips barely moving. "Please, it is better you do not know, Miss Baumann."

His muttonchops bristled as he quickly looked about and then resumed. "Neptune is due to arrive sometime this week. You performed admirably...very admirably... in the Georgetown affair last May...as well as in Chiasso more recently." A mechanical smile oscillated from cheek to cheek. "Do as well in this, and we shall extend your stipend by twenty percent. Be cautious. Falkon did not survive this long by happenstance."

The waitress returned with additional coffee, but Busche waved her away with a flick of his wrist. He removed his suit jacket, hanging it on the back of his chair. The breeze waxed humid, his short-sleeved polyester shirt, wet with nervous perspiration, clinging to his skin. Helga spotted an unusual tattoo inside his left arm. *Must have been in the military*, she deduced, making a mental note.

After a brief chat about the weather, Helga gripped and held fast to Busche's moist hand, the unnerving feminine gaze probing shadowy caverns beyond masculine pupils as she bade adieu. She turned, beckoned to the waiting taxi, and climbed in. Helga was due to return to her daytime vocation as assistant manager of the Falkoner Centret, a nucleus for various national and international meetings.

Concerned, Helga stared at the file folder, weighing the theater, pondering her role. *What the shit is going on? The entire discussion was too short, too brittle. Too…cautious.* She glanced back at the disappearing contact. *You had better not be fucking with me, Jørgen, my sweet.*

While cruising across town in the cab, dispassionate eyes read the profile data on the forty-seven year old Falkon, Helga's middle finger unconsciously tapping the vinyl windowsill, tapping to a rhythm from the past. The similarity of the names, Falkoner and Falkon, appeared to be coincidental.

Then she scrutinized the attached portrait of Falkon. Short. Slight. Brown hair. Early frontal balding. Mustache. Brown eyes. Average male dress. Elevator shoes. Wedding ring.

"Photograph must be months old," she murmured.

Another mission had been assigned, unseen forces set in motion, moral indictments not a consideration—at least not now. With fingers pressed together in a cloistral arch, Helga closed her eyes. She wondered who Bjørn really was.

16

Copenhagen, Wednesday, August 25, 1971.

Bjørn Ljunggren had not yet recovered from the emotional anguish of his separation from Suzanne. It had flattened him like a boulder rolling down a mountain slope, the man caught in a box canyon at the end of the reel. The Swede understood he was drinking too much, but alcohol tranquillized his sleepless nights and the all-consuming solitude.

Bjørn understood that Suzanne, lonely and lovely Suzanne, had needed more attention than his assignments would allow after the death of their son, Christian. Following the divorce, she had repaired to Berne and thence to Zürich, becoming a secretary for Cumaves, a prestigious electronics firm in Zürich. She took back her Swiss maiden name, Suzanne Mullineaux, while struggling to forget the man she dearly loved.

He was expected at the home of Helen Baker, the U.S. Ambassador to Denmark. This evening she was throwing another lavish party for the NATO Command. The gala affair would attract many international patrons. Mrs.

Baker had held this diplomatic position for several years, and her festive balls were seasonal highlights.

With restless energy Bjørn, dashing in his summer blue suit and matching vest, motored up in a spanking new Volvo, braking to a halt on the ellipse before the white portico and its fluted stone columns. An array of floodlights lit up the blue and white striped canopy, flanking hedges standing at attention.

After the Marine corporal parked Ljunggren's car, Ambassador Baker, wearing a gracious smile, greeted the Swedish operative in the vestibule. She had snow-white hair coiled with amber beads and wore a teal evening dress. Following a polite but brief conversation, she led him into the drawing room and introduced the agent to a colonel of the American Air Force.

Bjørn felt surrounded by a noisy humanity, rank and rabble separated by nods of approval or rebuke, faces masks of politeness. In spite of all the excitement, he did not want to be there. But orders from higher up had directed his presence.

The starched colonel was a type A personality from the cut of his jacket to the break of his trousers. This desk warrior oozed exquisite politeness as if attempting, with elaborate ceremony, to elbow his way up in the world. Washing through his third martini, he barked with enthusiasm about the new tennis courts at the Danish Officers Club. All the while, he canted his head to one side or the other, depending on which hand held the vodka and vermouth.

Bjørn refused an offer for Stolichnaya on ice, deftly excusing himself. He cut through clusters of tactful chuckles and ribald laughter, avoiding the compressed grips and limpid handshakes. In the background, a U.S. Marine Band played "I Never Promised You a Rose Garden."

A woman, dressed in a tan chemise, its collar disappearing under brunette locks, emerged from a gaggle of guests and engaged Bjørn in idle conversation. Bjørn had met her before. Swedish Intelligence.

"Falkon is expected in the drawing room, end of the hall, next floor up. Return this to Neptune. It belongs to an associate." A golden cigarette case.

The girl stared at her contact before darting back into the crowd. Bjørn snatched up a piece of Italian cheese, savored the rich taste, and then cruised up the carpeted stairs. He rapped on the heavy wooden door, the vibrations muffled by deep-pile carpeting and folded drapes.

"Please come in." A deep, male voice.

The door clicked as Bjørn turned the solid brass handle. He warily poked his head in and then entered. He faced Harald, whose index finger was tapping an attaché case. To the right sat Ambassador Baker in a white antique armchair. The lady, her bearing aristocratic and firm, stood and again offered her hand, introducing Bjørn, code-named Falkon, to Harald Johnson, Neptune. Falkon handed over the golden compact. Bjørn, encountering Harald's penetrating, thundercloud eyes, diverted his gaze toward the lady.

"Please, let us make ourselves comfortable at the coffee table." The Ambassador retook possession of her chair and ushered the two men toward the couch.

"My instructions come from Washington and Copenhagen," she continued while fitting reading glasses to her nose. "I am furnishing each of you with a brief resumé on the other. Read them here, then destroy the papers in the fireplace.

"We hope, but do not assume, that Harald Johnson's assignment in Copenhagen is unknown to others. Mr. Johnson will be residing at the Hotel Mercur on Vester Farimagsgade. We have been informed that you, Mr. Johnson, are in Europe posing as an American employee of International Telephone while attending the telecommunications conference at the Falkoner Centret.

"My role in this operation ceases here. Mr. Ljunggren, Agent Johnson will fill you in on the details. I bid farewell...and good luck to both of you."

A moment of unsettled silence followed. Each returned to his seat, Bjørn emitting a hollow, nervous cough. The sterile room had already been searched and swept for bugs.

Bjørn looked about at the rich furniture upholstered in artistic brocade, lit by lamps of hand-blown glass casting light from the ceiling. Fashionable appointments. A Chippendale lowboy on cabrioles in one corner, a grand piano in the other.

Harald and Bjørn studied the files and then burned them, terminal smoke drifting upward from the fireplace. After light talk of European football and politics, Harald summarized the meeting he had with Stafford and colleagues at BNDD. He handed Bjørn photographs of Anthony Salucci and the tattoo, wallet-size and blow-ups.

"Tim Stafford and I go way back. Worked together in Stockholm years ago," said Ljunggren as he studied the portrait. "Rather odd. This sailor...from the steamer, Salamis, you say?"

"Make any sense to you, Bjørn? Note the initials SSV at the bottom of the design."

"I've not seen this before. If your heroin is coming from Copenhagen, I should be able to get some info on that. Very strange... For the opiate to show up in large quantities both in San Francisco and in New York City is unusual and, I should think, risky for the peddlers. That doubles their chances of being caught."

Bjørn analyzed further, his mind searching out parallels. "For this to occur in two or more places without the entry method being discovered requires at least two salient facts. One, the delivery technique or vehicle is unique but very likely being duplicated. Two, not only does the organization pulling this off have no foreign undercover agents inside, its members possess a means of mutual identification that precludes strangers from getting too close."

Harald and Bjørn abruptly turned, dilated pupils glued to the blow-up on the tattoo, both minds locking onto a remote key, as if the answer were staring in their faces. They just had not known how to frame the question.

"What do you think?" queried Harald, watching Bjørn drum the film with his fingers.

"You might have something. Maybe, maybe not. One thing is for sure. A satisfactory duplicate can't be made from a dead man's skin. A society of this size and orchestration would have many electro-optic methods of confirming the authenticity of such a mark. At the very least, we should analyze the actual skin containing the tattoo. Human nature being what it is, the image is symbolic of something. A goal, a mascot, a common enemy or friend, a purpose..."

"We'll get our Washington lab working on the tattoo, its chemistry, detectability, et cetera. In the meantime, I'll search out whatever information we can glean from New York and San Francisco customs."

"Let me nose around the local immigration office and check with my underworld contacts in Copenhagen. How about meeting in two days on the steps of the Town Hall at nearby Frederiksberg? At 1800 hours?" suggested Bjørn as he slipped one of the photographs into his wallet.

"You're on. I wouldn't flash that photo around yet. It may turn into a death warrant. If I need you sooner, I'll contact you through the Ambassador's phone number."

Falkon departed first. One half hour later, Neptune left for the U.S. Embassy to send an urgent, late evening, coded message to Stafford. Tony Salucci would have to be exhumed, the left arm reexamined, the tattooed skin excised for chemical analysis. Harald grabbed a cab for the Hotel Mercur. He registered and handed over his passport.

"Our bellman will escort you to your suite. Your passport will follow within the hour. Thank you, sir." An effusive smile grew on the clerk's face while an overhead lamp, a ceiling fan revolving beneath it, reflected in four-quarter time off his apical bald pate. Then his dentures clicked, "And have a very pleasant stay in our country."

In his room, Harald, exhausted from his trip, flopped down on the bed. He was missing his wife, Lauri. He stretched out, toeing off heated shoes as compressed time zones slipped westward over the Atlantic. Time registered a quarter day earlier on America's east coast.

New York City, Wednesday, August 25.

As soon as Stafford reviewed the decoded request from Denmark, mandated orders were cut. Retrieve the body of Anthony Salucci. The command carried top priority, state authorities cooperating, red tape sliced within the hour by judicial edict. At nine that same evening, New York time, grave-diggers breached the tomb and raised a rococo-styled, mahogany coffin under the watchful eyes of the Justice Department and the New York State Police. Terry Caldwell presided.

"Jesus, Caldwell. Who put up the cash for this casket? Someone paid a bundle to bury this creep," whistled a police captain.

"Don't know, Hoss." Terry shook his head. "It was handled by the mortuary."

Smells of pungent loam and freshly turned sod mixed with the clicks and rings of darting night insects. The moon cast a wake of alabaster over eerie intentions. Terry nervously unbolted and forced up the lid. The odor of chemicals and decay assaulted their nostrils.

Anxious hands directed flashlights into the depths of Tony's eternal resting place. Whips of light, searching for answers, sliced through musty shadows. Salucci's wax-white face reflected a gelatinous and ghostly image. And then...

"Holy shit!" gasped Caldwell, every muscle in his raw gut constricting, an electric charge sizzling up his spine. "Everyone, comb the goddamn grounds. Footprints, tools, anything... Jesus!"

Terry vaulted out from the crypt, dashed for his car, and flashed a coded intelligence to Washington.

Stafford's eyes, numb in disbelief, focused on the deciphered revelation—*Body exhumed. Left arm missing. Extracted at the shoulder. Someone...or something preceded us.*

Stafford murmured, "So Neptune was right. What next?"

Another elusive piece of the puzzle, nearly within their grasp, had slipped away, iridescent soap bubbles in the wake, the controlled search spinning erratically out of control. Hands behind his back, the Director of BNDD gazed out the window, weighing the evidence, now merely smudged fingerprints. *Buried intact inside a cheap government-ration coffin. And now resting with only three limbs inside rich mahogany, rococo engraved. Who? How? Why, for Christ sake?*

He grabbed the telephone receiver, squeezing it for answers, and rang up a transatlantic call to Copenhagen. He had to warn Harald and Bjørn.

17

Copenhagen, Thursday, August 26, 1971.

This evening, Bjørn wended his way to the Restaurant Claudius, his habit of late. He did not like habits. They were like addictions providing a pattern of weakness for enemies to track. But he had not been working on any special project—at least not until yesterday. Ljunggren's superiors had placed him 'on hold,' giving him administrative duties only until the emotional instability of the divorce would no longer pose a liability.

Now a foreign state required his special expertise. He sensed no particular danger, the heroin problem a conundrum for the far-away United States. *Not for Denmark*, he concluded. *This unfathomable business about Salucci? Too farfetched.* Bjørn, casting caution behind him while a picture of a tattoo simmered in his wallet, turned from the sidewalk and entered the crowded restaurant, loud music, raucous laughter, and flushed faces greeting the guest.

The quaint, lively inn stood just off Vester Farimagsgade, near the Hotel Mercur. Dangerously free of worry, Bjørn sailed into the colorful, two-story building, a swell of warmth replacing the frigid night air. Dance music from the second floor massaged his ears as the hope of finding Karla again quickened his pace and his heartbeat. He buzzed up the narrow, wooden staircase, squeezing past a few girls trawling the passageway.

At the top of the stairs a fetching, thinly clad damsel, platinum blond hair leaping in piquant wavelets like an enchanting waterfall, exchanged Bjørn's money for a ticket, her capricious hand lingering in his, honeyed scents hovering about the young woman. Her dress was a candy-apple red. Bjørn handed her Danish kroner, hesitated, and then walked straight-away into the festive ballroom.

The arm on the timepiece ticked toward nine-thirty, the five-piece combo from London playing a medley of pieces, presently "Yellow River." Bjørn, purring and nodding to the beat of the music while inhaling scents of universal temptation, hummed the melody as he walked to the crowded bar. He ordered up a gin and tonic. Gay laughter, provocative dancing, and spirited conversation in a multitude of tongues filled the chamber. Handsomely dressed men and women exchanged glances and then danced or drank, an occasional couple pairing up, touching and smiling and touching again, strolling arm-in-arm toward the exit, mystery and seduction softening the gap between reality and fantasy.

Bjørn's eyes swept the room. A fine haze of stratified, undulating smoke and flashing beams fired from swirling crystals. Blended aromas of perfume, cigarettes, and marijuana, no longer just a trace. Psychedelic memories.

Starched collars, black light. Warm hands, soft cheeks.

Bjørn sipped his solace of Tanqueray and tonic. The scintillating music continued, the unrelenting beat, beat, beat commanding a willing mind and a consenting body.

Bjørn's dancing eyes suddenly snared the red-headed coquette with whom he had spent a previous evening in abandoned copulation. The mere sight of her heated up the Swede's blood. He smiled and lifted both his glass and stiffening intentions in her direction. Karla responded with a flirtatious grin, the skirt in supple leather sauntering up to him. Neon lighting pulsed over her freckled cheeks. One of her green eyes dropped a lid with long lashes. Another woman, chatting and giggling, accompanied Karla.

"Good evening, Bjørn. How are you this evening?" Sparkling eyes. An infectious, lilting voice.

"Fine, thank you, Karla. A bit tired, perhaps." Bjørn bantered, "You...uh...kept me up most of the night."

Karla twittered, lifted generous breasts with her cupped hands, and then turned to her companion. "Helga, this is Bjørn. He works for a newspaper in Stockholm. Bjørn, please meet my very good friend, Helga."

"My pleasure, Helga. May I buy you two a drink?"

"No thank you," chirped Karla, rolling her emerald greens. "I have a client waiting for me over there. Very wealthy." she chortled while rubbing thumb and forefinger together. "Perhaps Helga might?"

"I'd love to...I mean if I'm not imposing on you," the blonde replied with practiced grace. Their eyes, his, chestnut brown, and hers, azure blue, locked together for a second. Helga glanced demurely away, deflecting Bjørn's early-warning radar.

The Swede inhaled, a reflex response, and asked her preference.

"Tanqueray and tonic... What newspaper do you work for...uh, may I call you Bjørn?" A seductive smile and possessing voice infiltrated ambiguous defenses, seizing his imagination as Helga fiddled with a bronze button on her garment.

"Please do. I work the foreign correspondent desk for *Svenska Dagbladet*. Covering the telecommunications conference at Falkoner Centret." Bjørn was captivated by her mystic beauty.

"How exciting! I'm an assistant manager there. We must have lunch together sometime. I know the chef personally. You would absolutely love it." She flashed coquettish glances, subtle scrutinies covering a fierce light fixing on her target.

"Sounds nice. How would I find you?" Her scent hauled him into her net. Suzanne's perfume.

"Just call the main office and ask for Helga Baumann. Everyone there knows me." She would not release him from her magnetic stare, the tip of her tongue playing within the twilight of parted lips.

Enthralled, his heart skipped a beat as he tempered animal thoughts. "I work out of our local office here. I...uh...need another drink. You, too?"

His palms were moist with anticipation, his stomach constricting with unconscious dissuasion.

"Oh no, not yet. I get too giddy. Oh, I'm so excited...a real newspaper man! I've never met one socially." Helga played her role, the coy smile expanding, eyes flashing, processing.

Bjørn, losing the battle to limit his cocktails, carved a path back towards the bar. He wanted to see more of this girl. His glance propelled sideways, watching Helga powder her nose, his eyes feeding off this woman haloed by pulsating backlight.

Bjørn felt a heated, primal urge stirring inside, rapidly rising, ignoring the body language of a beautiful but lethal lioness approaching estrus. Helga, in black satin, swayed her disquieting hips, firm buttocks and seductive pelvis trailing, weaving with the muffled beat of the music. Passion relieving panic. Emotion supplanting wisdom. Helga replacing Suzanne.

She cast a furtive glance in his direction. He felt his body respond, slipping headlong into the intense plasma field of sorcery as the high priestess from Poland stirred her ancient, infantile potions. A part of Bjørn desperately wanted what she had to offer.

He returned and begged Helga for a dance. Her nostrils flared. She obliged, seductive warmth drawing, pulling him closer until he found himself peering into the twin abyss of paralyzing eyes. Her lithe body electrified the man as he felt the minstrel music, a life force, flowing from Helga directly into him. They drifted closer together, Bjørn desperate for affection. The night began to take on a pattern all its own.

"Bjørn, where did you learn to dance so well? I love it when you hold me close." Hot, moist whispers tugged at his right ear. It could have been the ear of a German border guard.

"Oh, I...I took some lessons at school in Sweden. Suzanne...uh, my former wife...liked to dance," Bjørn replied, his heartbeat accelerating, corpora cavernosa expanding.

"Bjørn, why don't you come over to my apartment? It's really quite comfortable. The bed is so soft and large. I'll rub your shoulders and...and, well...I'm a fantastic masseuse. You do seem a bit tense." Helga's eyes stared deeply into his, excavating, reaching into a reluctant soul.

"Sure. Sounds good to me." His mustache rose up on one side. *Lord, is she for real?* "I suppose you charge a lot."

"Hmm, we can discuss that in the taxi. If you change your mind, it's okay." A pout replaced her furtive look. "But then, I would be awfully disappointed."

Helga drew him close to her, almost too close, almost forgetting to shroud her powerful musculature in a magnetic field of charm and beauty, murmuring, "Bjørn, darling, let's forget the fee. I want you to fuck me tonight..."

Jesus! His heart, in full gallop, skidded against its cage.

Helga injected methaqualone into his last drink. Never tasting the bitterness, he lost sense of proportion, zoned, slurred speech and glazed eyes telling her that the potent tranquilizers had seeped through his bloodstream. She led Bjørn into a cab, his body swaying like a sailor stepping ashore. The dissonant, cold snap in the air, striking his face, startled him.

The taxi roared away as her stroking hand, claws retracted, rested on his thigh, the tension in his trousers building. Barely perceptible caresses. Melting whispers.

Watching the couple leave, another figure sitting at the dark end of the bar was making a close study of the scene. Patrons saw only the outline of a large man wearing a modern waistcoat. Niemeier dipped his chin and checked a ponderous gold timepiece hanging from a twenty-one karat chain, the tether ringing a protruding belly. He checked a cuticle and then tossed three coins onto the hardwood counter top, the metal discs clinking against his empty beer stein. Still embodied as a brain surgeon, the devil incarnate walked toward a telephone booth, his subterranean power wielded from stratified shadows—

18

Helga led Bjørn up the marble steps of her lair, past the double doorway set in ornate bronze and glass, and into the anteroom of the luxurious apartment. Her roommate was entertaining a customer in another suite. Dim lighting, pulsating music, and muted squeals crept out from under another closed door.

She brought him to her parlor, where a polished Bachstein piano graced one corner. On top was a crystal vase with scarlet zinnia flanking blue sage. Oriental Tabriz carpets, finely woven in wool and silk of intermingling colors, blanketed the wood-blocked hardwood floor. A pair of nineteenth-century gilt chairs with blue plush upholstery stood sentinel under a Qum prayer rug. A finely upholstered and pillowed divan stretched along the another wall, an intricately carved mahogany and glass coffee table before it. The scent of night-blooming jasmine arose from a burning incense candle on the glass.

Helga turned on a Judy Collins record, "Send in the Clowns," a favorite of Bjørn and Suzanne. She helped Bjørn off with his jacket, guiding the acquiescent man to the couch. In her bedroom, she changed into a nightgown and dabbed on more of Suzanne's favorite fragrance. Helga returned to the parlor and drew him to her, rubbing his temples, making the Swedish agent feel warm and viscous. She pressed her lips against his while her hand stroked the cotton trousers stretching between his legs. She knew that he was too numb to respond further.

"Bjørn, I love you, I want you," she whispered. Her incantational powers pressed him further into amniotic waters. She stood back and watched him sail through gin and methaqualone, into the arms of Morpheus. Then, for a split second, she felt a twinge of shame, even anger at something within her. She wanted to run away and hide from the evil. But only for a split second.

Helga did not try to waken him or examine his pockets. When he awoke Friday morning, he must not discover anything awry. She wanted him to trust her. Helga needed to extract information. Halina would command much more. The riptide and the undertow, working at cross-purposes, nipped playfully at the heels of Achilles, both his and hers.

The predator, with a smile of chilling contempt playing over her lips, slipped off her gown, leaned over, and kissed the soft swell below his belt. *Sleep peacefully, my friend. On the morrow we have far to go.* She snapped off the lights, stole away from the dozing agent, and crawled into her bed, her nakedness slipping between silken sheets. She drew the brocaded down cover over and nodded off, soft music gliding through the background. Quiet hours passed in the still night.

The mantel clock, striking three, sparked a change in the game. Helga, with fits and starts, began to wrench in bed, clinging to her pillow. Her breathing became erratic, her eyes rolling under closed lids. Distant images, frozen relics ricochetted off the boundaries of her mind, a renitent undertow again sucking thought back into a time banished from conscious recall. Like the distant drumroll of a funeral cortege, the beat, beat, beat of her heart heralded Helga's procession back into the darkness of a bottomless pit.

In a paralytic sleep, she could not run from the creature. *There it is again. Ss...stay away! Go away!* The giant beetle from Birkenau, its shape devolving into a death's-head image, crept closer to Halina. Its jaws opened like the insect of Kafka, "The Merry Widow" spinning louder and louder. Suddenly, the scarabaeus with black, chitinous wings splintered, dissolving in columns of fire and smoke. Twisting legs and twisted souls.

Screams. *Matka Boska!* From where? *Where are y...y...you?* her lips stuttered in Polish, the unconscious vision tearing into a forgotten shame, the past and present intimately knotted, yet light years apart. A bleeding, disembodied eye floated in midair. Then, as suddenly as the portal had swung open, the window to her corridor of Hell slammed shut, the thunder leaving two hearts still beating, the larger lying starboard to the line of sanity, the other aport. The one with a hand on the mainsheet in stormy seas. The smaller with an even stronger grip on the tiller. Helga controlled the velocity. Halina, the bearing.

Both heard Papa's footsteps from across space and time.

Helga bolted upright in bed, the taunt muscles under her drenched skin straining at the bone. Strands of wet hair fell like tiny snakes of the Medusa, clinging to her face. The lurid nightmare, recurring again. More frequently now—as if something terrible was about to surface. It was always like this prior to the kill.

With trepidation, she remembered how a psychologist in Holyoke had sought to unearth the key—*The beetle is a ceramic scarab, a talisman, a symbol of the soul.* Yet for Helga it was still a beetle, a horrible, menacing beetle. She never could move beyond that, the gray walls too high to rappel up and over, barbed wire and broken mirrors lying in wait on the other side.

"Stop!" Helga shrieked.

Bjørn, still senseless, twitched faintly.

Birkenau's offspring snapped on the lights and shaky fingers flipped aged, fragile pages in the German Bible gifted to her by Aunt Anna. Inner terror receded as she focused on the inconsistent parable, a part of her seeking a spiritual longitude and latitude, a stable compass, the other driving toward a terrible vengeance. Halina dissolved as Helga's internal gyroscope restabilized. Helga, digging deeply inside herself for elusive moral strength, was back in tenuous check once more.

"God, why hast thou forsaken me? *Why?*" A single treasure spilled from azure blues onto the pious pages, spreading outward from the point of impact. "I weep. See what I have become." She clutched her head, fingernails drawing slivers of blood from her scalp. Helga, alone in the world, closed the Book. And wept.

19

Copenhagen, Friday, August 27, 1971.

Absent his fabulous femme fatale, Bjørn awoke on the parlor couch at nine the next morning. He shook his pounding head, trying to focus on the slippery present. His clothes were rumpled but intact.

"What a bore I must have been," he muttered aloud. Bjørn checked his pockets and wallet with ID. All was in order. The magnetic seal on his wallet and key case had not been cracked. He surveyed his environment more clearly now, inspecting the subtly garish apartment. Nothing otherwise unusual. He vaguely recalled Helga mentioning a roommate living there.

Bjørn trailed the scent of fresh Colombian coffee to the kitchen. In the dinette, he read Helga's note penned in flowing script on hand-marbled paper —

> Bjørn! Inga (my roommate) and I have gone to work. Call me at lunchtime. I'll take you up on your offer to go dancing again tonight (Inga is visiting her parents in Düsseldorf this weekend). I made some coffee for you.
> Fondly, Helga.

He ran a finger over *Helga Baumann* in raised gold lettering at the top. Bjørn, squinting his eyes, could not remember making the date. He recalled little of the events in her apartment. And that frightened him.

The Scandinavian counterintelligence agent taxied through traffic to the Swedish newspaper office and checked in. No messages. *Call Suzanne in Zürich* — the thought puzzled him, a mixture of confusing imperatives giving silent instructions. Dangerous melancholia.

He stared longingly at a photograph of a small boy in his wallet, his throat aching, blanketing an emotional storm. Ever since his son, Christian, died, Bjørn's life had slipped into a honeycomb of dead ends.

He wiped his eye, cleared a husky throat, and asked the secretary to come in and take a message. She was cleared for top secret work.

> *Subject.* Helga Baumann. Falkoner Centret employee. Institute code five-one-one search. Top priority. Use channel two for response.

The secretary encoded the message and delivered it into the computer for immediate transmission to Danish Intelligence. She also took the handwritten note Helga had left by the coffee. Bjørn had to meet Harald later in the day, but a part of him wished he never had taken on this assignment.

At quarter to six in the evening Harald, impatient, tapping his foot on the loose gravel, continued reading *The Guardian*, though his thoughts were embroiled in other matters. He was leaning against a pillar on the fountained square facing the Fredricksberg Town Hall and listening to the coos of pigeons, feathered gladiators fighting for morsels of bread thrown from passersby. Two mongrel dogs stopped barking and chasing one another to cast a curious look at the American. A parade band sounded from the distance, martial music, muffled trumpets. The coppery sun swung lower in the sky, scattered cirrus clouds drifting by.

At six o'clock, Bjørn stepped from his Volvo and walked toward Harald. The Swedish agent snapped off bits of crackers for the pigeons. He was confident that anyone tailing him had been eluded.

Harald informed Bjørn about the missing arm.

"Jesus, Harald. This sounds like an old-fashioned werewolf tale. We're running out of clues." Bjørn fumbled with his lighter and then lit up a cigarette, the flame singing its tip. His eyebrows rose a millimeter as he clicked the Ronson shut.

"I know, I know." Harald tapped Bjørn's chest with the rolled London newspaper and then tucked *The Guardian* in his briefcase. "You look tired, Bjørn. Up until the wee hours last night?"

Bjørn dropped his eyes a fraction and described his recent activities, including the previous evening's excursions and today's lunch with Helga. The information on Helga had come through. Nothing very suspicious. A known prostitute who often entertained wealthy businessmen and visiting dignitaries. Polish, German, and American background. Schooling at Holyoke College.

"I'm going to see her tonight. She may practice the world's oldest profession, but that is the worst that can be said of her. Danish Intelligence is quite thorough. It was the same for Karla...uh...another friend...sort of like Helga." He coughed and studied his fingernails.

Harald, shooting an accusatory glance, hesitated and then replied, "Well, be careful, Bjørn. Let's not be too incautious... I have an old friend teaching English at Holyoke College in Massachusetts. Jeffry Landon. It wouldn't hurt if I ring him up and see if he recalls a Helga Baumann."

Bjørn was irritated. "Damn. You're really reaching, Harald." The Swede shot his cigarette toward the water fountain, the cylinder bouncing off a brick and emitting sprays of sparks, its red point ending in a wet hiss. Blinded with masculine indestructibility, he trotted back to his Volvo, driving off to re-enter the world of Falkon.

Harald listened to the decrescendo of the car disappearing in the distance. The dogs resumed their noisy chase, and the band music grew louder as the parade approached the square. Oompah, oompah, oompahpah.

Harald signaled for a taxi. He had to make a transatlantic phone call.

Holyoke College.

Jeffry had just finished lunch and was strolling down the hall while discussing a folk epic with two of his students.

"...and the old English word, *Beowulf,* probably is a metaphorical name for 'bear.' If you..."

"Oh, Mr. Landon. There is a telephone call coming in for you. From overseas. The college operator is transferring it to us now."

Jeffry's breathless secretary had just run up.

"Thanks, Vickie."

Jeffry proceeded into his office. The phone rang. Something told him not to respond. It rang again, demanding to be answered. His hand, feeling a weight upon it, uncradled the receiver.

"Mr. Landon, please," requested the overseas operator, her foreign accent spiked with crackles of static.

"Speaking."

"Go ahead, Copenhagen."

"Hello, Jeffry? This is Harald...Harald Johnson."

"Harald? Well for cryin' out loud! Hey, buddy, I gather you're not in the good old USA. What's up?" Jeffry sat up straight in his chair, a big grin splitting his face.

"Can't go into that now. Sorry to bother you, but I need help with an urgent problem. You were teaching at Holyoke in 1960 or thereabouts, weren't you?"

"Eleven years ago…yup. My first year as an instructor. Why?" He doodled with his red pencil, drawing wavelets of birds in a sky.

"Do you recall a student by the name of Helga Baumann?"

A pregnant pause as a fusillade of balled-up memories wiggled back to life, Jeffry's heart lurching in his chest. An unexpected resurrection of the past. His finger stiffened, fracturing the pencil tip against the pad of yellow paper.

"Jeffry, can you hear me? Do you remember such a woman? An exchange student from Germany. About twenty-one years old then."

"Sorry. Of course. Most everyone here at that time would know her… Same year Kennedy won the presidency. She was a couple of years older than her classmates and a brilliant student. Spoke several languages." His thoughts rolled back through a suddenly condensed time span.

Harald hesitated. "Had she been involved with any unusual organizations? You know, Jeffry, communist or fascist groups, Mafia types, anything?"

"No, I'm certain she wasn't. She had German parents who were quite wealthy. She loved to ski…usually took holidays off and flew to the Swiss Alps. Had many friends among the students but no close attachments. Belonged to some clubs…archery, fencing, karate."

"Karate?"

"Yeh. Black belt. Remarkable strength and agility."

"Where did she usually travel in Switzerland?"

"Somewhere in the Engadin Valley, not far from St. Moritz. She had an aunt or some relative there. In fact, I recall her trying to teach me Romansch."

"Teach what?" queried Harald after the split second delay in transmission.

"Romansch. A derivation of Latin spoken in sections of eastern Switzerland. I sure would like to visit that part of the world some day."

"Thanks, Jeffry. If you think of anything, leave a message at my Washington desk."

"Certainly will. Uh…why the interest in Helga?"

"One of our staff seems to be infatuated with her. Just a security precaution… By the way, what's new with Erik? I haven't heard from him for a few weeks."

"He's up to his eyeballs in work. I'll tell him you said hi."

"Well, give him my best. The three of us must go skiing together again. Let's make it Utah next winter."

"Okay, Harald. You're on." Jeffry hesitated. "Hmm …one other thing you should know, your being my friend and all."

"What's that?"

Jeffry closed his eyes and sighed. "Remember when I fell in love a few years back. Erik knew, but I didn't publicize the fact."

"Sure. I tried to get you and your lady friend to go skiing in Colorado with Lauri and me, but you couldn't get away. Oh, you mean…"

"Yup. That was Helga."

Jeffry settled the receiver down, his stomach roiling in turmoil. He stared at the afternoon sun. It was already evening in Europe.

Helga. How could he forget. He could not imagine her name coming back out of the past after all these years. Undercurrents from a brief but intense love affair. Mixed feelings tempered the remembrance. *Hold me, Jeffry. Hold me close. I am so scared. I need you. Don't leave me again.* He gazed at his nervous hand tapping the desk top. *'Again?' What did she mean by that?*

But *she* had left *him*. It was she who broke up the relationship. Then why, he wondered, did he feel this faint blend of reignited passion and dreaded excitement? The structure in his world unraveled slightly, submerged memories no longer dormant. The impression of her head on the pillow next to his was still there.

Jeffry rummaged through his desk. Books, drawings, and well-thumbed manuscripts were stacked everywhere, a paper amphitheater surrounding the man.

"Damnation. Where is it?" Jeffry exclaimed to no one.

He yanked out the right bottom drawer and flipped it upside down on the rug. "Ahah. There." A poem she had written in English class and presented to Jeffry. "And what's this? A postcard from Zuoz. All these years... I'd forgotten. Christmas, 1960."

The photograph portrayed a Swiss village winter street scene. On the other side of the memento —

> Dearest Jeffry, the skiing is heavenly. Wish you were here. I love the Raggedy Ann and Andy dolls you gave me. They're fantastic! Don't forget to pick me up at the airport. Hugs and kisses! Oodles of love! Your Helga.

He read it again. And again. He touched his cheek with the photo, recalling how she adored those dolls.

Jeffry knew Helga added superlatives for effect. She had a way about her. *Well, it worked,* he reflected. *I did pick her up at the airport. And all she could talk about was her dream mountain. Some strange name. 'Motta' something? Near a town with two different names. Can't remember.*

He slipped the postcard and poem into his breast pocket and walked to the restroom. He combed his hair and refashioned the ponytail. School bells rang for class. *Where are you now, my mysterious love?* he wondered.

20

Copenhagen, Friday evening.

On the other side of the Atlantic Ocean a distant carillon tolled eight o'clock. With gay abandon, Helga and Bjørn strolled hand-in-hand through the Tivoli Amusement Park. She felt Bjørn clasp her fingers in a desperate embrace as if to prevent the escape of another love. Halina's hand bound his in a more sinister grip.

"Bjørn, let's jump on the Ferris wheel now. I've never been so happy or had so much fun in years."

Helga tilted over and planted a mischievous kiss on his cheek. Bjørn handed over two coupons for the ride and they climbed on. She edged over, their knees touching, and nuzzled his ear with a wet tongue. Scintillating music and light perfume ebbed and flowed with each turn of the great wheel.

"Helga, isn't this great?"

"Hmm…best ever." She grasped the back of his head and pressed her lips onto his, burrowing in while the prodigious rondure spun them skyward. He slid his arm around her, and then she laid her head against his shoulder. At the summit of their ascent they found themselves caught between the city lights shimmering below and celestial stars twinkling above. The giant toy continued a slow rotation on its massive horizontal axis.

Helga pitched her head upwards, pressed curious hands to Bjørn's cheeks, and gazed with hunger into his brown eyes. She felt heated, damp, the excitement building.

"I just love your mustache, Bjørn. I think I'm really getting to like this newspaperman." Helga stroked the finely groomed brush on his upper lip. She sensed Bjørn's body bending in submission.

After the ride, the improbable lovers, each led by a different star, wandered close together through the picturesque park. Under the cool summer-night air, lights dazzled on a bubbling fountain. Tree limbs fanned the sky, their branches quivering as a refreshing breeze rose.

"Step right up and strike the gong, my good sir," challenged a carnival man, his painted face grinning at the couple. "Show the young lady how strong you are." He held up a huge mallet.

"Helga, I'll bet I can make that ball knock the top off the meter." Bjørn pulled her toward the game, its scale of flashing lights and tempting chimes rising toward the stars.

The laughing circus jack lifted the hammer, playfully tapped the green knob on the ground, and held the handle toward Bjørn.

Helga's hand suddenly squeezed Bjørn's, an iron grip of fear rolling through her. "No, Bjørn! No! Please let's go on."

Puzzled, Bjørn saluted the game-man as Helga tugged at her target's sleeve, drawing him away from the red-faced beast with edge-thickened spectacles. The clown turned away and cajoled another couple wandering by.

Bjørn's arm wrapped around her waist, the sound of his footfall dampening the chatter from her spiked heels. Then she turned toward him.

"Oh, Bjørn, I know a heavenly dance hall. It's absolutely fantastic. One cannot get in unless you're invited or a member of the club. But I know the doorman. And you dance so divinely. Oh, *do* come on."

"Karla never told me about the place. Sounds interesting."

A masquerade of love, Helga's hand pulled seductively at his.

They hailed a cab, and she provided the address to the driver. The TransEuropa Club. When they alighted, Bjørn and Helga were surrounded by a wealthy residential neighborhood. Black wrought-iron fences enclosed enormous mansions and sedate, upper-class apartments. Lacing her arm through his, Helga gaily steered him toward a giant iron gate covered with ivy. With a demure smile, she spoke to the senatorial doorman who bowed and waved them through the imposing portal.

The couple walked into the gray-stone building, strolling arm-in-arm down a long, slightly curving, ornate hall, the floor lavishly carpeted. On either side lighted, glass-encased insets in the wall contained enchanting specimens of expensive furs, oriental tapestries, and seductive paintings. As they neared the end of the hall, captivating music and the din of excited voices curled up from a stairway.

Helga's cool fingers fastened to Bjørn's perspiring hand while they descended the twisting staircase. At the end, a small man dressed in a tuxedo bowed at the waist and opened the brass-lined double door. "Welcome, Miss Baumann. Evening, sir."

Bjørn, his mouth agape, glanced at his date as they entered the dance hall. "Jesus, Helga. You must have some powerful connections."

Sparkling crystal chandeliers, intersprinkled with garlands of fresh flowers, festooned the ballroom. Glittering shafts of multicolored lights speared layers of cigarette smoke. The light haze floated above polished oakwood flooring and its marble penumbra. On the far side of the hall, an eighteen-piece band was playing lively music in brocaded melodies. The finely-dressed, both saints and sinners, a phantasmagoria of nationalities and colors, reveled and danced to the enchanting music, a thrilling scene of labyrinthine activity.

"Come on, Bjørn, darling. Buy me a gin and tonic," Helga coaxed. "I'm dying for one."

"Your wish is my command," he assured. And then he whispered in her ear, "And your tits are driving me crazy."

A smile crossed her lips, their ends rolling downward. Suzanne's perfume and the opiate of reason stretched deeper. As she replaced Suzanne, Halina replaced Helga, the inner spider binding the outer arachnid in her own twisting gossamer.

After a long swallow of gin and tonic, Bjørn spirited Helga toward the dance arena. The "Blue Danube Waltz," her favorite tune, rippled across the floor. She hummed the melody as they moved with nimble grace, spinning through the happy crowd. She closed her eyes, indeed feeling happy—until the reality of her assignment once more held sway.

Then, the disguised beat of her demonic dirge intensified, like a scorpion deploying a carefully orchestrated pincer attack. Helga's eyes flashed excitement, athletic curves pivoting this way and that. Nostrils taut, her body radiated the magnetic heat of a Greek siren into his loins. She knew that the weakening moral censor within him was attempting to navigate toward safer shoals.

She slipped the tranquilizer into Bjørn's third drink. Then, during a slow dance Helga pulled him wondrously close to her. She felt his body quiver within her iron grip. She could taste his blood, the anticipation arousing Helga's other self to even higher levels of voracity, her respirations increasing.

Placing her undulating hands behind him, surrounding and gripping his buttocks, she suddenly clamped Bjørn's pelvis against hers, his penis already full, pressing, pushing hard into her fabric.

"Helga..."

"Oooh...Bjørn, baby. Your cock is knocking at my door and driving me deliciously insane!"

She swayed her hips in harmony from side to side, caressing, stimulating, pulling. Helga spoke softly, her deadly sweet voice packaging his mind, her tongue penetrating into the man's very soul.

"Bjørn, darling. It's so warm here. Let's find our way home. Hmm?" Halina, peering from behind the mask of Helga, commanded both as if they were one, her eyes of yesteryear darkening with stifled, imprisoned rage.

Another taxi drove them to her apartment. By one o'clock in the morning, Bjørn was a slave to the passions of his possessor. Helga helped him scale the steps to her lair. She coaxed him beyond the sitting room and into her bed chamber. He stumbled, striking the armoire before lurching onto her bed. She unbuttoned and removed his outer clothing, placing these, almost reverently, on a credenza by the far wall. Yellow light from the street lamp filtered through sheet drapes tied back with brass shell clamps.

"May I bring you anything, my love...anything at all?" Vaginal moisture redoubled.

"No, darling. I'll be okay. Just drank too much, I guess," he murmured.

Helga's nipples tightened, her pulse quickening. Yet, while she manipulated Bjørn, Helga remained unaware of the insidious but remote processes governing her. Both marionettes, the man and the woman had skidded headlong into the same rabbit hole.

Bjørn, glassy-eyed, blinked and then gazed at saccharine splendor, her curves pulsating in and out of focus.

Helga slipped into a black silk negligée, naked underneath, silk and skin fusing into one. She knew that Bjørn recognized the scent—Suzanne's perfume, but his mind was too fuzzy to acknowledge the inconsistency, the trap now sprung. He could not escape.

Neither could she.

Strains of "Send in the Clowns" filtered through the background. The matador in lace carried a small leather container from the refrigerator to her boudoir.

Like a high priestess, she hummed the music while stripping away Bjørn's undergarments. He struggled to assist her, but his limbs, intoxicated with the unrelenting balm, refused. She guided him into a cozy bathrobe and propped him half sitting against fluffed pillows.

Helga lifted Bjørn's wallet and withdrew the portrait of his son, Christian. She taped it onto a small photographic frame and placed it on the bed stand.

"Bjørn, here is a nice Tanqueray and tonic. Come, I don't want to drink alone."

"Had...had too much already, love. Maybe just one."

Helga, now undaunted in her quest, sloughed off her skin, the silky lace falling in a sigh onto the Sarouk carpet. Her nude body, illuminated by flickering candlelights, glowed unblemished, except for a fine, almost invisible scar on her right forearm. Her tresses tumbled in golden waves, graceful feminine curves undulating as the sleek panther circled the bed.

Soft pubic hair swept below the mons veneris. The swell of her breasts, kindling desire, fell slightly—again seizing, diverting Bjørn's misty eyes toward taut, pink nipples. Helga, a nude avenger, sat on the bed and leaned over, her hair dancing on his chest.

Bjørn jerked slightly, Helga sucking on his nipples, first one, then the other. She pulled with sensuous lips, rubbing with her darting tongue, the vanguard in a highly dangerous foreplay. The marriage of Quaalude and alcohol, patiently tarrying for the final act of consummation, had weighted down his limbs. In tortured motions he struggled to grasp her bare flesh, his arms raising inch by painful inch off the silk bed sheet, then tumbling back to the brocaded coverlet as the rolling battalion of a feminine force delivered archipallic vibrations, shivering and pulsing into the male torso. For Helga, failure was not an option.

Helga whispered, "Bjørn, my love, relax, you're much too tired from overwork. Does this help?"

She stroked the sensuous layer of his abdomen, traveling with well practiced fingers, a small child's weapons extended from muscles rippling dangerously under a woman's smooth skin.

"Tell me about your news assignment, my pet. Exciting, or just a bad day?"

"Not too bad," he murmured.

"I really wish you would not work so hard, Bjørn. We need to spend more time together. Besides, I just love being with you, holding you…caressing you."

Helga slid her torrid body down next to Bjørn's, close on his left side. Her left hand stroked his quivering thighs as volatile lips resumed electrifying receptive nipples. Practiced fingers brushed southward, fondling his tense scrotum. A fiery hand then grasped the male scepter, fingers moving rhythmically to and fro, electrostatic visceral energy building and charging seminal condensers, the drumming of hoofbeats rising to a thunder. It was the hand of Halina pulling on a Prussian penis, drawing on iron flesh springing from a sadistic storm-trooper.

"Helga!" he cried.

"Bjørn, I absolutely love your prick." She squeezed harder, her breathing deeper, his more rapid.

"Don't stop. My God, don't stop!" Short, gasping breaths.

Her slave strove to move his vitiated legs apart, the limbs ponderously heavy. Two parts of him were planted in separate worlds.

Helga slowed the stroking motion, his penis, a decorated warrior fully armed for insemination, remaining ripe with lust. She did not want him to come to orgasm yet. Jørgen's command—*First, the name*. Flanking the agent, she kissed his lips teasingly, his drugged eyes unable to focus.

"Bjørn, my handsome devil, you're so exhausted. You really need someone to work with you on your job. Who can help you, Bjørn? Hmm?"

She squeezed the glans, afterburners spiking the cannon as energized sperm cells, feeling stifled and enraged, drove up his heart rate.

"Hhhuuu...ooohhh!" A sudden gasp, a deep gut response. "I'm...I'm okay. I got help. Helga...Helga, why are you slowing down?"

Helga ceased all movement, controlling, watching Bjørn catapult into desperation, his rampaging heart thump, thump, thumping out of control. She knew that her reincarnation of Suzanne now was the powerful epicenter of an earthquake surging through his body and mind. The rising tsunami could not be stopped.

"Who is helping you, Bjørn?" she softly hissed.

Helga slowly increased the rate and depth of the rhythm, Halina's fist striking his pubic bone and then drawing restless skin to the head of the extended phallus. Lessons from a time unremembered had taught her hands how to hold the engorged penis, how far to brush the sensitive corona of its head. The androgenous warrior, Samson, now shorn of his seven locks, lay blinded to the plummet toward Armageddon.

"Bjørn, is Neptune still helping you?" She squeezed again, driving a chill of blue flame through his spine.

"Neptune…Neptune," he choked. The word rocketed home like a thunderclap.

Helga watched closely, the male contender now an infant submerged in a tall, alien world. She knew Bjørn's future was measured in terms of seconds, maybe minutes, where an explosive release was all that he sought, flesh and blood unable to bear it any longer. There was nothing else. Nothing. Violent chasms and pressure ridges were forming, hammering at the door, but the final temblor eluded him. That much she knew from years of experience.

"Yes…Christ! Stop worrying about him…hold me tighter! Don't stop," begged Bjørn. But he was giving a futile supplication to the commanding infant in Helga's skin, for she was his master, the iconoclast of phallic power. She was the feminine retribution to maternal rape and Prussian pedophilia. Her caged eyes, once promising adoration, fell to white-hot anger.

Helga, unmerciful, a perspiring storm gathering in strength and thundering forward in the jousting list, could never stop. Even if she chose to. With resolute pertinacity, the lioness moved up on Halina's knees and pressed Bjørn's willing limbs apart with her other hand. Martial arms flexed his legs and placed a tube of lubricating jelly on the bed next to her.

Helga changed hands, stroking, controlling his flushed genital organ with her right. She knew he had absorbed too much drug and alcohol to ejaculate yet—in spite of his beautiful erection. He needed more help, and the benevolent thrust had arrived.

She covered the middle finger of her left hand with jelly and inserted Halina's surprise into his anus, its startled sphincter tightening in a sudden reflex. Bjørn, in a rapid pant, nearly fainted with bestial ecstasy as Helga penetrated far beyond the forebrain, deeper and deeper into his rectum, then pulling forward to touch, to feel the excited fullness of his prostate gland. With the experience of much practice, the long and gracefully kinetic finger massaged the lobules holding back part of his seminal fluid. Her right hand continued its firm caressing of Bjørn's sensual shaft, masturbating both his penis and his mind, a remote part of her brain once again about to taste the sweet reward, the promised candy to soothe Halina's tiny, hungry stomach.

"Who is Neptune, Bjørn, my baby?" Helga's heart beat faster, another drum-roll before a climax. Undulating muscles of the feline tightened.

Suddenly her hand and the music slowed, only soft gentle strokes keeping him in a ferment. But the drugs yet blocked rhythmic contractions and terminal bliss. Helga repeated the question, "Who...is...Neptune?"

"My God...please..."

She gazed at her mark, now programmed for the inevitable clash of mounting sexual ecstasy and rapidly approaching panic. She increased her magnetic movement and began sucking on his penis, her mouth, a muzzle closing over its frightened head, her tongue massaging, removing fear as soothing honey-blond hair splashed forward over a writhing abdomen.

Incarnadine lips demanded again, "Bjørn, my love, give...me...Neptune's...name. His name!"

Bjørn shut his eyelids and screamed, mouth gaping, yet there was no sound.

Helga asked once more, her deadly patience unrelenting. She knew his body demanded the orgasm or it would suffocate, dying a thousand deaths. He was spiraling headlong into an ungoverned, sexual panic as her trap, now sprung, drove torrents of blood upon his heart.

Bjørn's voice was now a muted echo. "Damn you...faster, deeper! Oh, sweet Jesus! Please, help me!"

"Who...is...Neptune?"

"Harald...Harald Johnson," he cried, his wild and tearful eyes searching for his deceased angel, for Suzanne.

"Who does he work for, Bjørn? Who is it?"

"United States...How did you know about...?" He panted and seven times slammed his head side to side on the pillow. "Bureau of Narc..." Bjørn's muscles abruptly seizing, he shrieked, "Oh, Gu...Gah...Gahhddd..."

Bjørn came, a bittersweet ending, his flesh throbbing, erupting, overflowing with molten lava. His body convulsed in spite of the drugs. He would answer no more questions.

Helga, focusing curiously on the stream of semen, shuddered briefly at the malignant and hateful sign of the unremembered Birkenau inseminator. Her finger felt the rhythmical, prolonged contractions of a storm trooper's anal sphincter, the after-shock of a violent release. Helga's dispassionate hand then reached into the black leather case. She heard him moan as the needle of death pierced his left thigh.

The male fly, now bound up in Halina's spider web and isolated from all humanity, gasped only once.

With his last sigh, Helga swooned, her limbs flexing, internal detonations triggering prolonged and fiercely undulating vaginal compressions as her fingers pressed onto the charged clitoris. Every sinew quivered, her spine arching backward, eyes squeezed shut. Her body glistened with wavelets of icy perspiration. Then the climax ebbed.

The scarab of Helga's nightmares disappeared, and the snap of jackboots silenced. The stench of burnt flesh evaporated and the terrifying "Merry Widow Waltz" faded, lingering behind a fortified escarpment of cerebral neurons.

Minutes later, Helga stood up. With steadfast efficiency, she unfolded Bjørn's clothes and redressed the lifeless mannequin. She picked up Bjørn's leather billfold. Helga's fingers replaced the portrait of little Christian after wiping away fingerprints. As she did so, another photograph tumbled from the wallet to the floor. She seized it, inhaling audibly. *A picture of the same mark I saw on Jørgen's left arm.*

Helga stiffened. *Neptune isn't after one of Jørgen's clients. He threatens Jørgen himself. And even Lance Masters.* Her mouth went dry.

No! No! No! — A silent scream, the revelation staggering. It was she who had manipulated Bjørn. But who — or what labyrinthine power controlled her? A mortal danger had raised its ugly head. Had this been her final command performance?

She knew that Busche's nefarious society left nothing to chance when its own members were menaced. A brutal intelligence awakened within her. *They have always known I could lead others to the society. 'The killer must be placed under negative surveillance and eliminated by a remote executioner.' An unwritten commandment. This was not the same as Chiasso. This involves Federal Agents!* An unseen hostile force from an unexpected quarter, a shroud lifting to reveal a new and shadowy dimension as death compressed the chamber.

Helga, still damp from Halina's orgy of sex and murder, stunned from the discovery of her own impending doom, fought to regain a semblance of self-discipline. She placed the fatal photograph within her own snakeskin bag and reached for the phone, dialing a local number. Twenty minutes later, Bjørn's body was hauled away in an ambulance sent by Jørgen Busche. Her job was completed. She had delivered the name, and the Falkon was executed.

Helga returned to the telephone. Desperate fingers dialed the number.

"Hello, Swissair? When is your next flight to Geneva? I require a reservation for one. My name? Hensell...Tanya Hensell." Her voice was tight, fire-blue eyes now rolled into orbs of ice. She would not go by Swissair. She was certain her phone was tapped.

Helga parted the window drapes. She tensed. The street didn't look right. Helga walked to the bathroom mirror and imagined herself as a crippled grandmother. She opened her jars of theatrical paint.

Helga thought she merely feared for her life. Yet, beyond awareness, she sensed a more foreboding compulsion, a child named Halina trembling before Dante's inferno and a doctor with edge thickened glasses.

21

Fredericksburg, Virginia. Sunday, August 29, 1971.

At four o'clock, Terry Caldwell, suited in black pinstripe and cowboy boots, arrived in time for a final farewell to Marty Campbell. Terry and Marty had been close friends, graduating together from the University of Virginia. Terry, his torso a thin knot of gristle and guts under a Marine's buzz cut, had developed into a brilliant, hard-nosed narcotics agent. The jovial and rotund Campbell, a young business executive for Rockwell International, had been consulting with Cumaves AG. The respected and prestigious electronics company specialized in communications systems near Zürich, Switzerland.

Terry heard the sad tale from Margaret Campbell, the mother of the deceased. Upon returning from a tour of the Rhine River at Schaffhausen, a dense fog engulfed Marty's car, resulting in a disastrous automobile collision outside the town of Winterthur. In Zürich, he was attended by a private neurosurgeon at the Trieste Hospital and required surgery to evacuate a large blood clot compressing the brain. Two weeks later, he died. The family had arranged for return of the body to be buried next to his wife, a victim of viral encephalitis. They had no children. The burial was delayed until Sunday, the only time Terry could be present.

While viewing the lifeless body, Terry marveled how the staff of the funeral home, with cosmetic assistance, had retouched Marty's features, casting him in a lifelike image immobilized merely by the weight of death. His cordovan brown hair, preserved by nurses after shaving the head three weeks previously, had been reconstructed so as to obscure the surgical burr hole incision.

Now, after an eulogy, the pallbearers lowered the remains of Marty into his grave, from sunlight to darkness, the soul having long since risen. The chirps and warbles of a few birds flying aloft and the creaking of tired pulleys traveled across the lush green fields. Margaret cried softly. She had lost her husband, her daughter-in-law, and now her only son. Terry, his head bowed, placed a strong arm around Margaret's shoulders as the reverend cast a handful of earth over the casket—"ashes to ashes, dust to dust..."

22

Copenhagen.

Harald walked out of the city morgue. Passersby had spotted Bjørn floating in one of the canals. Examination at autopsy disclosed evidence of alcohol, methaqualone, and pancuronium, a curare-like chemical employed by anesthesiologists to paralyzed muscles during surgery under controlled ventilation. Bjørn died from asphyxia. The coroner had located a needle track in his left thigh, next to the femoral vein. Harald knew that pancuronium bromide required storage by refrigeration to prevent decomposition.

Harald assumed the elusive, underworld narcotic organization, recently code-named Thunderbird by BNDD, had found out that Stafford's task force was tracking evidence leading to the Society. But the trail faded on rocky ground. Helga had vanished from the face of the earth.

Upon returning to the U.S. Embassy in Copenhagen, Harald telephoned Director Stafford. After filling him in on the events in Denmark, Harald concluded, "Our only lead to Thunderbird is Helga. Tim, I'm going to ask Danish Intelligence to search their files of embarkation points in Copenhagen. Perhaps this Helga has left some telltale tracks.

"In the meantime, there exists one man I know who has actually seen her. However, a few years have passed, and I don't know if he would be willing to help. Professor Jeffry Landon teaches English at Holyoke College."

"Harald, in secrecy our President has declared this fucking narcotic situation a major menace to our country. It worsens by the day. Death rates from overdosage are climbing. Millions of dollars in U.S. currency are flowing out of our country. Our own sources here are clueless."

"Okay if I fly to Massachusetts and chat with Jeffry?"

"We'll do better than that. Send him to Washington. I'll ask the President to speak with him in person. Our leader is taking a lot of heat. The goddamn newspapers are asking embarrassing questions, and he cannot divulge the entire truth without breaching national security."

"Will do. By the way, Tim, do you recall a Doctor Landon?"

"Erik Landon? Sure do. Nice guy. Helped us round out the medical aspects on the Piccollo file. Any relation?"

"They're brothers."

"Some coincidence, Harald."

"Maybe... Maybe not."

"How so?"

"Tim, something is bothering me. How often do we see cases involving curare-type drugs? Almost never. Yet suddenly we got Piccollo and Ljunggren."

"That's a tenuous thread, Harald. And it stretches three thousand miles. Jeffry's former Holyoke student assassinating Erik's DOA case in Washington, and then our Swede operative in Copenhagen. Still, I suppose it won't hurt to get State running a search on a May 1971 entry visa for your Helga. Oh, do you have Jeffry Landon's phone number available?"

Harald gave Stafford further data on Jeffry. "That ought to do it, Tim. You might also let Jeffry's dean know that we'll secure Landon's salary and pay all expenses while he is acting as Special Consultant in Linguistics to the Department of Justice. On my way home I'll stop off in New York City and chat with Customs."

"Right. This office will arrange for our meeting in three days. You had best shoot back here today if possible. I'll get on the phone to Landon."

Holyoke. Sunday, September 5.

The day about to close, Jeffry Landon continued grading student papers lying on his desk at home, the chewed red pencil working overtime. Numerous files and books lay scattered about, reflecting the teacher's halfhearted attempt to prepare the next day's lectures. Jeffry yawned and then jumped up to draw the blind. The afternoon sun reflecting off a nearby glass cabinet bothered him. The telephone rang, interrupting the monotonous ticking of a wall clock.

"Hello."

"Mr. Landon?"

"Speaking."

"This is Tim Stafford, Director of the Bureau of Narcotics in Washington. Sorry to bother you on a Sunday. I believe you know Harald Johnson?"

Jeffry hesitated, twisting the phone cord with his fingers. "Yes, sir. I've known Harald for many years."

"He is one of my senior agents in the Bureau. We have urgent need of your valuable aid in a…shall we say…a highly confidential matter. Harald is flying in late tonight. If possible, we would like to meet with you here at eight A.M. this next Wednesday. Could you arrange to join us?"

Jeffry paused, concerned about his academic duties. He glanced down at his Seiko, as if the timepiece would provide a reasonable solution.

Stafford interrupted his thought. "The President of the United States and I would be most grateful if you could attend. We are faced with a matter of national sensitivity. I cannot delve into details now."

"The President. Of course, I'll be there. I'll need to make arrangements for my teaching assignments."

"We've already cleared this with your Dean. The Department of Justice will pay all expenses. My secretary has reserved a room for you this coming Tuesday at the Roosevelt."

"I'll begin getting my things in order."

"It would be best if you communicate neither this conversation nor the purpose of your trip to anyone. You can reach me through Harald's telephone. Many thanks. You have no idea how your role will affect the lives of hundreds, perhaps thousands of our young citizens. Until two days hence, then."

A small, but persistent, knot welled up in Jeffry's stomach as he tried to fathom the depth of his suddenly expanding role. *In what?* he wondered. His hazel eyes squinted, tracking the receiver as he cradled it. *How can I communicate the purpose to anyone? I don't know it. Can this have anything to do with Helga again? Absurd, yet...* His thoughts slipped back in time. *Oh, Helga, I truly loved you once. That was so long ago.*

23

St. Moritz, Switzerland.

Helga peered out between the curtains. She felt a swell of relief when she saw her aunt coming up the street, the walkway lined with colorful trees of autumn.

Helga's Aunt Anna, a pleasant and lively widow, owned a jewelry shop in the village of St. Moritz. Heinz Baumann, a former Kommandant in the Nazi army, was her brother. Helga's eyes tracked Anna Baumann as she strode with brisk steps toward the fashionable storefront, a brown wood and white stucco building abutting one of the narrow side-streets. This stately woman of seventy years unlocked the front door after brushing dried leaves off her fur coat. A nearby church bell chimed out the time of nine in the morning.

"Oh, dear. I must have left the heat on all night," Anna muttered aloud. A shadow moved out from behind a closet door. "Who's there?"

"Hello, Auntie. I turned the heat up earlier. Sorry to surprise you." Helga looked out the doorway to see if anyone had followed the lady. "I've missed seeing you."

"Helga! Oh, my Helga, what in God's Heaven are you doing here?" cried the alarmed lady. "The whole world is searching for you. What have you done? What is going on? I don't even recognize you. Brown hair, business suit, eyeglasses, dark make-up."

"It is better you don't know, dear Auntie. I used my old key to get into your shop. I hope you don't mind." Helga sat down at a corner table.

"I fear for you, my child. Not for this old woman. Strangers come and ask for you. A man calls on the telephone and says he is your uncle and has a message for you. Claims he must talk to you on the phone. In person. Helga, your only uncle is dead. My husband is buried in the graveyard."

Helga shuddered, not knowing why. An unconscious obscuration deep inside her understood only too well. The sorcerer from Spiegelgrund. *Die Sonne geht immer auf.* Coral snakes posing as telephones.

"Your parents are worried sick. My brother, Heinz, calls from Mainz. He wants to know if I have seen you. You must tell him you're safe," pleaded Anna.

Helga saw agitation roil through her aunt, the older woman now struggling beyond her depth.

"I can't speak to father…or anyone. And I won't stay but a few more hours. I must disappear, and I need your help. I trust you more than my own parents, more than *anyone*. Please. I'm desperate." Helga felt trapped in a time warp, her chest constricting, her mind grappling to focus.

"*Mein Liebschen*, of course I'll help. I've loved you so ever since my brother and his wife adopted you. Come to the back room where we can talk. And I have something I've been meaning to give you. A couple of old photographs. I'll lock the door."

The Thunderbird Covenant

"First, accompany me to the churchyard, to the cemetery. I'll tell you my plan as we walk." Helga had to gain Aunt Anna over to her purpose.

At the church the two ladies climbed the flagstone to the graveyard. Helga led Anna to a plot of land where Anna's husband was buried.

24

New York City. Monday, September 6, 1971.

Harald trotted up the steps, two at a time, and entered the spartan offices of U.S. Customs. After a brief discussion with the receptionist, she escorted him to a nearby room. Harald introduced himself and sat down after the officer pointed to an oak chair.

At the other side of the desk perched Theodore Burns on the edge of his seat, fussily tapping his knuckles with a letter opener and swiveling slightly side to side. Contrary clumps of chalk-white hair disclosed beds of transplantation dotting the scalp. Speaking with annoying emphasis, his demeanor bordered on arrogance.

"Mr. Johnson, I've been briefed on the nature and reason for your visit. I appreciate the need for security. Yes, yes, indeed. I must tell you, however, that I've spoken with many, many people from your office several times already. Several times. I have no suggestions yet nor anything new to report. Indeed, nothing."

He repeatedly clicked his blue ball-point pen while compressing thin, colorless lips.

"I understand, Mr. Burns. Might I speak with one of your officers on duty at Kennedy Airport? And also someone at the docks? Perhaps I could elicit a few ideas."

Officer Burns, shooting to his feet, torso in a modified military bearing, ten stiffened fingers spread on the edge of his desk, abruptly acceded. "Get in touch with Marvin Cheverly at Kennedy. He is in charge there. Yes, indeed."

Harald thanked him and departed, listening to the dry rat-a-tat-tat of the harried ball-point.

At Kennedy Airport, Marvin Cheverly, a small, lean man, his russet hair trimmed in a tight crew-cut, side-burns shaved at midcheek level, wore the starched uniform of a U.S. Customs Officer. Harald grabbed his extended hand.

"Burns told me you were coming. He's getting a little flinty from all the pressure out of Washington. Anyway, I understand your position. Please, call me Marvin." He cracked a match with a thumbnail and fired his pipe.

Harald expressed his appreciation and asked the Customs Officer to detail changes made in their search procedure, any unusual findings. Marvin pulled down a wall chart of ongoing operations.

After considerable discussion, he pointed out, "We simply cannot search every nook and cranny of each piece of luggage and shipping crates. We have neither personnel nor time. As it is, our force is working overtime."

Harald waited while Marvin drew on his pipe, released double jets of smoke, and resumed speaking. "Still, if there are shipments of drugs in the amounts you're suggesting, somewhere we should be latching onto supporting evidence. We're not. If heroin of high purity is being ferried in, it would not require much space. However, our usual methods of detection, including dogs trained to sniff it out, have failed to turn up significant quantities. Oh, sure, we pick up some small amounts of impure stuff. You know about that. But that's not what we're after."

"What about cans, crates, and boxes off-loaded from ships and planes?"

"They're all opened, but our canine constables remain unimpressed. We even uncover caskets containing dead bodies. Nothing. Before embarkation and after disembarkation, our officers inspect sealed containers of money, documents, or machinery requiring the presence of a licensed diplomatic courier or government official. Our inspectors rotate positions to prevent one letting such containers through on a regular basis."

"And diplomatic pouches?"

"A customs officer and the appropriate departmental official together open the pouches. Nothing suspicious so far."

"Can the dogs have their identification of odor confused by chemicals?" Harald scratched his head.

"Yes, but not neutralized. The animals still will react to any programmed odor...unless the powder is locked in air tight, especially if it is pure. We unseal such containers or secure them under guard until the contents can be disclosed in our presence."

"You mentioned caskets. Do you breach the coffin and examine the body?"

"Sure do," responded the customs officer. "At the City Morgue. If the corpse is decomposed, we search under protective conditions. Such decay to that point remains uncommon with today's preservatives. The dogs will detect traces of heroin in a cadaver. We x-ray the bodies for sealed packets lying beyond orifices or underlying sutured skin. So far, we've found no evidence for the amount of heroin traffic you've mentioned. Shipping of contraband or drugs in caskets, particularly in dead bodies or false compartments, is an old trick. Doesn't work anymore."

"I would like to arrange for me or a member of our unit to work side-by-side with some of your officers. Perhaps we might pick up a clue."

"Glad to assist," volunteered Cheverly. "Let me know who and when."

"By the way, if you observe this tattoo on anyone in or out of customs, contact me ASAP."

Cheverly studied the curious photograph in Harald's hand and then looked up, his forehead lined. "What's it mean?"

"Maybe you'll solve the riddle for us." The problem tilted ponderously before Harald, like a sheer cliff.

Harald departed Customs and hopped on a flight to Washington National Airport. En-route, he tried to dissect the enigma of a dead sailor's tattoo, now spreading beyond international borders. Thunderbird, a deadly cancer, had to be cut away before further metastases snagged a foothold, threatening mankind. A swift surgical strike would demand meticulous, forward planning. But first, follow the thread. Helga. For that, Harald needed Jeffry.

PART III

25

Washington, Wednesday, September 8, 1971.

*I*n the year 1971, the musical *Jesus Christ Superstar* became a smash hit while President Richard Nixon teetered at the edge of Watergate infamy. U.S. Forces were blockading North Vietnam. Unleashed sex and nudity were forcing reclassification in the movie industry. Crime and corruption, drugs and promiscuity, and lurid tales of the "Washington Wives" were driving the general public to one conclusion—the system was out of control. Amidst this turmoil, the Justice Department reported that nearly half of the nation's major crimes were committed by juveniles, the relationship to drugs all too evident.

At 8:15 A.M., the President met with Tim, Harald, and Jeffry at the White House. After intense exchange at a conference table, the Chief Executive took his leave from the national security chamber. Jeffry guaranteed the President full cooperation. The narcotic agents filled Jeffry in on the events swirling around Thunderbird and the assassin extraordinaire after Jeffry was sworn to secrecy. He would be given a security classification following FBI clearance.

Jeffry remained their only link to Helga, to Thunderbird. BNDD had a few newspaper photographs of the woman when she lived in Mainz, but they were poor in quality and portrayed her in jet-set groupings. Interviews with Herr and Frau Baumann in Mainz failed to elicit any leads, Herr Baumann angered at the intrusion, his wife certain her daughter was not the person governments were seeking—a terrible mistake, she said. Up to now, Helga had been slotted by the Copenhagen constabulary as a highly-paid queen of the tarts, a lady of the night suspected of selling her services to some government employee seeking information.

"Where do we go from here?" Jeffry inquired, sighing and shaking his head. He refused to believe this was the same Helga he had known and bedded years ago.

Harald fielded the question. "Danish Intelligence discovered no evidence of Helga Baumann skipping the country. They did find that a Tanya Hensell boarded a KLM flight from Copenhagen to Geneva eleven days ago. The passport must have been falsified since the real Tanya Hensell, a Dane, has been deceased for three years. The girls would be the same age, thirty-two years, if Hensell were alive. Our fugitive may be in Switzerland or she might have traveled through under another false passport. We've checked for a credit card, telephone, and wire trails. Nothing."

Stafford added, "It is a bit of a mystery why she fled Copenhagen. Although we know Bjørn was cavorting with a known courtesan and we suspect she killed him, we have no solid proof of her culpability. The apartment and her roommate, Inga, were clean. Too clean. Inga denied any knowledge of Helga's friends or activities. Records indicate Inga was in Düsseldorf that weekend."

"Helga must have learned from Ljunggren that the U.S. Justice Department was involved, became frightened, and fled?" suggested Jeffry with reluctance, finding it difficult to accept the concept of Helga's role.

"In her line of work, if she did in fact kill Bjørn, she would not scare easily. Something else precipitated her flight. Something terrifying," guessed Stafford.

"Jeffry, be prepared to leave home on a moment's notice. It may take a some weeks to get you into the field," charged Harald. "I would suggest you begin growing a beard and do whatever you can to prevent even your best friend from recognizing you." His fingers made a scissoring motion at Jeffry's braided pigtail. "I know it's been a few years, but pay close attention to your habits and mannerisms. Time does not erase these. And change your cologne." He sniffed. "By tomorrow you will receive a diplomatic passport in your own name. As soon as your face is bearded and altered, we will photograph you again for a second passport under an assumed title. Our make-up artist will add some significant changes.

"Your code name is Orion, and Helga will be designated Ursa. Thunderbird refers to our underworld narcotics organization. My call sign is Neptune, and Stafford's office will go by Hamlet." explained Agent Johnson. "Any other questions, Jeffry?"

"Not now, but I'm sure I'll think of several after I leave here."

"Okeydoke. By the way, Jeffry, you're not, you know, still carrying a torch for Helga, are you?"

"No...that was ten years ago." Jeffry avoided Harald's gaze.

Stafford stood up to stretch his legs. "We shall deposit one-hundred thousand dollars for you in a U.S. bank account. You may draw on this money for needed expenses, including pertinent entertainment. Because trips to Europe are involved, a like sum will be deposited in Swiss francs at the Swiss Credit Bank in Zürich. Both accounts will be under the names of Jeffry Landon and Brian Trent, your other name. And ownership will be listed under electronic codes only. Tomorrow my office will provide the proper financial forms to fill out."

Jeffry struggled to assimilate all of these new and strange demands, the mutating events rapidly transforming his once-secure life. His photographic memory and morphemic mind helped, but the picture show was moving far too fast.

"In the meantime," resumed Stafford, "the CIA agents in Europe will get a handle on any leads. At that time we'll send for you to locate and identify the quarry, hopefully to obtain hints regarding the nature of her employer. Harald and others of our staff will continue working with Customs.

"By the way, Landon, Harald here introduced me to your brother, Erik. Nice chap. He gave us some medical insight into another bothersome case this last spring."

After shaking hands, Jeffry left and Harald turned to the Director. "Any word from State about a visa for this Helga?"

"No. They deny any match with her name and description. Of course there were no fingerprints at the scene in Georgetown. Probably a wild goose chase."

The next morning Jeffry's shaving kit remained untouched. He paid a visit at Harald's office and received his first diplomatic passport. Then he completed the bank form. On the upper left the bank's name stood blazoned in German, French, Italian, and English —

    Schweizerische Kreditanstalt
    Crédit Suisse
    Credito Svizzero
    Swiss Credit Bank

An account number was already prepared with a credit of Fr. 300,000 for Jeffry P. Landon, Jr., and Brian A. Trent. Orion inscribed both signatures.

Jeffry engaged the next week working with Harald, plunging into crash courses on espionage, theatrical make-over, and the German language. After FBI scrutiny, he received top secret clearance. Harald provided him with both a wallet-size and an enlarged photograph of the red and green tattoo from Anthony Salucci's missing left arm.

Jeffry eyed his friend, Harald. "Orion, the hunter, after Ursa, the bear." He felt like an astronaut seeking a remote star that only a mathematical calculation told him existed. "The bards of ancient Greece tell us that a beautiful nymph, Callisto, had been transformed into a wild creature, a bear doomed to live forever in the sky. Ursa...banished from humankind. But who, or what is Thunderbird?"

"One of our team imagined that the tattoo looked like the thunderbird of American Indians. You know...like on totem poles," explained Harald, tapping the photograph. "We really don't understand its true significance."

Later that day Jeffry walked down the marble steps of BNDD and into the slippery biosphere of Brian Trent, of Orion, a perilous world not of his choosing. Or perhaps it was.

Jeffry shook his head to ward off a feeling, a foreboding experienced before a disaster, the skin of his neck contracting. The figure of a lithe, blond woman climbing hand-over-hand up a rope at Holyoke crystallized in his mind's eye. Jeffry needed to talk to someone, feeling the desperate urge to call his younger brother. He headed into a nearby pay-phone booth, lifted the receiver, and dialed a number in Washington. *Tell no one*, Tim Stafford had instructed. Jeffry's mouth went dry. One ring. His moist hand hesitated and then replaced the receiver. *Not even Erik.*

26

Trieste Hospital, Zürich.

The neurosurgeon glared, twirling his spectacles as he spoke to the two men in his office. "I just got off the phone with Martino LaVeccia less than an hour ago. Neither he nor any of the couriers have seen or heard from Helga. Busche has put all his resources on this problem without success. How on earth did she escape our net?"

"Herr Doktor Niemeier, how much damage can she really do? Our Helga knows nothing regarding the real Ludwig Dietz operation nor is she informed about your SSV," scowled Jørgen Busche.

"Our assassin understands enough," argued Sierpinski, the third man. "She can implicate the American Secretary of State as well as lead the CIA to you, Herr Busche. In turn, your own mortuary branch in Copenhagen and those in other sites, including our own, will be in jeopardy. And I can guarantee the Mafia would pay her well for solid information…in spite of what she did to four of their stooges."

Johann Niemeier buzzed for another round of coffee while studying his knuckles. *She's got more guts than the rest of you put together. I'll give her that.* The slightly-stooped waiter arrived with the silver tray, refilled the cups of Dresden china, and departed, bowing stiffly as he backed away.

Niemeier had other, more ominous, reasons for having Helga returned to Zürich. "We must stretch our net. My Helga cannot escape from us. I personally shall guarantee a reward of a hundred-thousand Swiss francs. She may not have access to the inner workings of our Society, but she possesses something else quite unique."

The neurosurgeon's jowled face suffused into a crimson red, determined fingers nearly cracking the stem of his eyeglass. "She will be found, and I alone shall deal with our Fräulein."

27

Washington, Wednesday, November 17, 1971.

This day Erik had another complicated neurosurgical case at Washington Memorial Hospital. Upon entering the OR, he headed over to a wall board and read the notice: Patient's name, Henrietta Echols. Procedure, Craniotomy for clipping of aneurysm. Surgeons, Landon/Hamilton. Anesthesiologists, Perilli/Chou. Room, Seven.

After changing into his scrub suit, Erik fingered the neck piece Marlene had given him in Vermont—a silver half-moon on a gold chain. It was his good-luck charm. He walked toward Theater Seven, where the anesthesiologists and nurses were preparing the patient for her ordeal.

"Henrietta, you're looking chipper today. We should have you in the Intensive Care Unit by early afternoon."

"Hello, Doctor Landon. Doctor Perilli and I are doing fine. He only had to stick my vein once." The patient lifted her arm with the IV infusion.

Soon she lapsed into a deep sleep with Doctor Perilli and his resident controlling her blood pressure and depth of anesthesia, preventing a premature rupture of the aneurysm, an arterial blister lying under her brain. Angiography had demonstrated that the lesion arose from the bifurcation of the right internal carotid artery. The potentially lethal anomaly had bled once, precipitating her arrival in the emergency room.

After shaving the patient's scalp and positioning her head, Erik clamped a steel three-point skull fixation device through Henrietta's skin, the pins grabbing into the outer layer of the skull and immobilizing her cranium in space.

To the left side of the patient, Doctor Alonzo Perilli and his anesthesiology resident, Doctor Andrew Chou, were recalibrating a blood pressure transducer. On the patient's right stood the neurosurgical resident, Doctor Frank Hamilton, and the the scrub nurse, Margaret Simmonds, RN, in the coveted position of handing to the neurosurgeon. She was arranging surgical instruments on the trays of her covered stainless steel Mayo stands. The Sony TV monitor displayed the magnified surgical field as seen by the surgeon. Nurses tied a clear, sterile plastic drape around the operating microscope and its television camera.

The operating theater settled into a calm ambience, rhythmic beats of the patient's heart harmonizing with the softer, slower cadence of the respirator. A symphony of sounds with soft country-rock music in the background.

"Hey, Stella," Erik quipped to the circulating nurse. "Did you finally make it with that new surgical intern?" He fastened plastic clips on the bleeding scalp edges.

"Doctor Landon...how did you know...uh...I mean no, of course not." Without looking up, she continued counting the sponges, "One, two, three..."

"With a body like yours, how could he resist? Besides, the poor guy has been working so hard, he needs someone like you to take good care of him. Know what I mean?"

A snicker from under the drapes. Perilli, adjusting the halothane gas.

"Better put the patient back to sleep, Alonzo." Erik reflected the scalp flap.

"She's just laughing at your OR humor," chuckled Doctor Perilli.

"OR humor?" scoffed Stella, leaning down to pick up a blood-stained sponge from the floor bucket. "I think you've been sniffing your laughing gas."

"How is the patient's blood pressure?" Erik inquired as he incised the right temporalis muscle, the head fixed in a forty-five degrees leftward rotation.

"The systolic is one-hundred," answered the anesthesiologist. "When you want it lower, let me know and I'll start the nitroprusside drip."

The continuous BP readout on the oscilloscope confirmed vital sign stability, the pulse regular. Bleep, bleep, bleep...

Doctor Chou injected another dose of pancuronium and then adjusted the ventilator.

After picking up an air-powered drill, Erik made two burr holes in the skull. Another high-speed drill and surgical rongeurs interconnected the holes. He reflected the cranial flap, thus opening a window in the skull while Doctor Hamilton and the circulating nurses prepared the 'scope.

The bright room lights were dimmed to near darkness, leaving only the microscope's beam to illuminate the operative field. The assistant observed through a side port of the 'scope. The scrub nurse handed Erik a diamond-tipped drill to shave down a projection of the cranium, the sphenoid wing at the base of the skull, thus clearing away the last bony obstruction to Henrietta's time bomb. The drill emitted a harsh whisper as it wiped away fine layers of bone.

Then Erik cut open and reflected the dura, a tough membrane, thus exposing the living brain. He could feel an eerie iridescence of energy flowing from grayish-pink surface convolutions as vital feeding vessels pulsated, expanding and contracting with each heartbeat, life-giving red blood coursing through. He always thought of the brain as the sanctum sanctorum for the soul during life.

"Begin dropping the blood pressure, Alonzo. We're working our way up the carotid toward the aneurysm."

"Roger."

Erik put out his right hand, into which Margaret placed the bipolar electrocautery forceps. Under magnification, he coagulated a leaking vein near the vital optic nerve controlling Henrietta's sight.

"How's her blood pressure now?"

"Systolic of eighty-five," replied the anesthesiologist.

While working to outflank the enemy, Erik struggled to prevent its rupture during the dissection. The room lapsed into silence, all eyes, except the surgeons', glued to the TV or vital sign monitors.

With gentle microtechnique, Erik separated the frontal and temporal lobes of the brain. "There's the base of the aneurysm." He pointed with his forceps. "Now to isolate the neck and clear away these tiny perforating arteries."

The magnified image of the time bomb pulsated on the monitor, its size expanding and contracting with each heartbeat. Using delicate movements, Erik freed up the aneurysm at the summit of the carotid artery while its swirling blood leaned dangerously against the paper-thin walls.

"Clip, long-narrow, upward curve."

Margaret lifted the miniature weapon off the Mayo tray, placing the clip-holder into Erik's extended right hand. He aimed the clip through the skull aperture, along the sphenoid wing, deep under the brain.

"Blood pressure?"

"Seventy."

"Clipping now."

Under controlled pressure from Erik's thumb and forefinger on the clip-applier, the crucial wings of the clip spread apart, surrounding the aneurysm, then closing, grasping, miniature jaws strangling the serpent's neck.

He withdrew the applier, leaving the clip behind. A sigh of relief swelled through the room as the aneurysm collapsed, the head of the viper now crushed. Erik shot a second clip across the defused waist of the aneurysm, securing its dome. Then her blood pressure was permitted to drift back to normal.

As Erik stitched the dura closed over the brain, he nodded to his resident in training. "Do you know the parts of the sphenoid bone?"

"Yessir. The main body forms the central floor of the skull and encompasses the pituitary gland under the brain. Behind each eye, the sphenoid extends two bony wings laterally, the lesser wing above and its greater wing below. After leaving the brain, the optic nerves dive through canals in the sphenoid."

"The word sphenoid is Greek for 'wedge-shaped.' Have you ever examined it in a disarticulated skull?"

"No, sir."

"Stop by my office and meet Oliver. He's in bits and pieces...a dry skull that's been with me through thick and thin. Study the skull-base anatomy. It's like a jigsaw puzzle."

Out of the clear blue, another image snapped into Erik's memory pad—José's lunar moth. *How strange*, he thought.

Two days later, Erik was pouring a cup of soup for a quick lunch in his office. Henrietta had survived Wednesday's ordeal, awake and in good spirits on this Friday morning's rounds. Having not heard from Jeffry for days, Erik snatched up the telephone and dialed a number in Holyoke.

"Professor Landon's office. May I help you?"

"This is his brother, Doctor Erik Landon. Is the Professor available?" he asked while absent-mindedly doodling a sketch. A lunar moth.

"No. About ten days ago he left for Washington, DC. He has taken a leave of absence. I think the government asked him to consult on some committee or other."

"What's going on?"

"No one knows. Kind of hush-hush. Jeffry, I mean Professor Landon, always let me know where to reach him. But not this time. He's grown a beard. And cut his hair, ponytail and all. Looks rather cute…sort of."

"That's strange. When will he be back?"

"Didn't say. I gather he'll be gone for a few months."

"A few months! He didn't leave any address or phone number?" Erik scratched his head.

"No, Doctor Landon."

"If you hear from him, ask him to call me, please."

"Certainly will. 'Bye."

Erik hung up the phone, balled up the sheet of paper, and tossed the drawing into a waste basket. "That's odd! What the hell is he up to?"

28

Washington, Monday, November 8, 1971.

Jeffry sat fidgeting in the BNDD secretarial parlor, waiting in suspense to meet with Stafford. On a wall plaque next to his door—

Department of Justice
Bureau of Narcotics and Dangerous Drugs
T. Stafford, Director

At dawn, an urgent phone call had startled Jeffry, the Director's assistant requesting his presence in the Bureau Office in Washington by three P.M. Something was up, but the woman would not discuss it on the telephone except to inform Jeffry he should pack for an extended period of absence. Jeffry had his papers, two passports, closely cropped light brown hair, and a trimmed imperial beard nurtured for two months. Silicone injections had restructured his face. An incision of the left vocal cord by laser produced a slightly hoarse voice, its pitch a fraction lower. Mannerisms, such as sticking a chewed pencil behind his ear, were struck down and others replaced.

"Mr. Landon, nice change." She waved toward the door. "Mr. Stafford and Mr. Caldwell are ready. Please follow me."

Two pairs of heels, differing in pitch and frequency, struck the marble flooring as they walked down a sterile hallway and turned into the small conference room. Portraits of former bureau chiefs clung to the walls, the Korean War period separating black-and-white from color images.

"Hello, Landon," greeted Stafford. "Or should I say 'Brian Trent.' Super job. Please meet Terry Caldwell, one of our special agents at BNDD."

Terry gave Jeffry a solid handshake.

"Nice riding boots, Terry."

"I have a spread on the Maryland eastern shore. My family runs western saddle there. Hoss, why don't you and Erik join me in a ride some day?"

"Love to."

The Director motioned Jeffry to a leather chair, coffee and donuts sitting nearby on the octagon-shaped, glass-covered conference table. Tim Stafford, still standing, brought Jeffry up to date.

"We have two new leads." Stafford paced back and forth after refilling his coffee cup. "They are remote, but we must act on them with dispatch. First, one additional country has suffered a noticeable rise in heroin entry. Taiwan, the Republic of China. Your friend, Harald, departed yesterday to check for clues in that Asian country.

"The second break we have involves you. A large sum of money was withdrawn from the Swiss Bank Corporation in Zürich on August 30. One of the CIA agents in Switzerland, Chester Phillips, later verified that the numbered account belonged to a Tanya Hensell, who we believe is Helga Baumann, your Ursa. Hours after the withdrawal the same bank received a stop payment demand on a check that had been deposited in her account. For

72,000 Swiss francs. But the transaction had already cleared."

"Oh, oh. Who made the disbursal?" asked Jeffry.

"Drawn on a local bank in Winterthur, just northeast of Zürich. The account there belonged to Langerstein AG, apparently a business front for some other organization. A company with that name in the area recently closed. The account was terminated a week later. A 'Jørgen Busche' signed the checks. We've failed to locate any such person, but the bank documents had him registered as living in Copenhagen. The address was a P.O. Box, also closed."

"But he would have needed a passport," suggested Jeffry, rapidly digesting the intelligence.

"Absolutely. And in fact, such a Danish passport had been issued to one Jørgen Busche, age fifty-five. The problem, as in our Tanya Hensell's case, is that the real Busche has been dead for four years."

"What do you want me to do?" Jeffry's thumb and forefinger pulled at his beard, a new habit.

Terry leaned back in his chair. "In our search for clues, Hoss, we find that Helga's adopting father had a sister, Anna Baumann. She had married a Swiss by the name of Hirschen and moved to St. Moritz, Switzerland, where they managed a jewelry business. Anna's husband passed away from a heart attack, leaving her the shop and a small fortune. She now uses her maiden name, Baumann.

"As Brian Trent, you are a wealthy tourist interested in a ski vacation in St. Moritz. We have deposited an additional one and a half million Swiss francs in your account at Crédit Suisse...not for lavish spending, but as a credit reference should the occasion arise. Needless to say, we have to trust in your judgment regarding expenses. In addition, here's a card for their automatic cash withdrawal machines."

188

Terry handed him the plastic and a note with a code number to punch into the automatic teller.

"Hoss, we really need you to get a handle on Helga's whereabouts, St. Moritz being the starting point," said Terry. "We suspect she is somewhere in Switzerland. Hopefully you will catch her scent, as it were, or obtain information at her aunt's shop. Without doubt this Helga has altered her appearance and is, perhaps, hiding in the mountains."

Stafford detailed the method of contact with Washington, either Caldwell or Stafford at BNDD receiving all of the messages from Orion to Hamlet. "Insert our electronic scrambler between your lips and the speaker to make your voice unintelligible for any eavesdroppers. The computerized phone in Washington will unscramble the transmission. No reverse scrambling. An acoustic print of your speaking voice fed into the computer will confirm ID."

After handing over a Eurorail pass for trains, Stafford provided Jeffry with the unlisted name, phone number, and Zürich address of Chester Phillips, CIA, Jeffry's initial contact in Zürich. Terry Caldwell advised Jeffry not to take any firearms. Should the need arise, Phillips or colleagues will supply him.

"If I recognize Helga, what then?" queried Jeffry with an air of reluctant courage, pursing his lips as he inhaled.

"Don't let on. Befriend her if necessary, but beware of any companions she keeps. Also, someone is very unhappy that their check cleared her account. Don't get caught between them. If and when you and this Helga connect, inform your CIA contact and our office without delay. We'll take over from there. Do not, and I repeat, absolutely do not take matters into your own hands. Your life will depend on it," warned Stafford.

Jeffry now feared the deeper implications of his commitment, turning back no longer a viable option. It wasn't the task so much as the desire. Helga.

29

Switzerland, Wednesday, November 10, 1971.

Zürich and its surrounding canton. Clean. Punctual. Unfriendly. Crime limited to the scions of wealth and privilege. A masterpiece of banking ingenuity.

Jeffry's plane landed in Switzerland early Wednesday morning. He passed quickly through the green door at Customs. The immigration officer stamped his passport and Jeffry made his way to the street. He caught a bus transporting passengers the eleven kilometers from the airport to the Hauptbahnhof, the main railway station in Zürich. Then by taxi eastward to the Krone Hotel on the Limmatquai. His unpretentious room faced west, overlooking the Limmat River, a blue-black ribbon of water curling southward into the lake. Centuries earlier, the city and its financial centers had been constructed on the northern shore of Zürichsee, or Lake Zürich.

Jeffry registered as Brian Trent. After settling in his room, he telephoned Chester Phillips. No answer. He left the hotel and crossed to the west, traveling by foot into the center of the city. The route took him down narrow streets winding past ancient cathedrals and buildings. He wished to visit awhile, to sightsee, luxuries he could not afford. He had to locate Ursa before Thunderbird did. Find Helga.

The principal thoroughfare was Bahnhofstrasse, or Railroad-Station Street, which Jeffry encountered at Paradeplatz, a busy encircling intersection. He forded the stream of traffic, dodged a tram clattering by, and turned right toward a neo-Gothic structure, the prestigious Crédit Suisse. Jeffry entered the bank and approached the information clerk. Some banal emotion pushed up the corners of her lips as she jotted down his name and picked up the telephone. A thin, swarthy man arrived, a starched smile straining his face. He was swallowed by a fine pin-stripe, the fabric pressed and measured. Italian.

"I am Herr Lugoso. Please come with me, Herr Trent." They shook hands, the Swiss wearing an elegant Piguet timepiece, the American with a sporty Seiko.

He directed Jeffry to the rear of the bank where they stepped into a small elevator. The lift, its walls of stressed oak paneling, swished upward, sliding to an abrupt halt on the fourth floor. Electronic bolts snapped the brass door free and Lugoso ushered Jeffry into a well-appointed suite. A multicolored Isfahan carpeted the floor, antique French tapestries on the walls. A trace of cigar smoke. Air sighed out of a cushion as Jeffry settled down in a leather and rosewood chair. The bank official departed and returned, both hands now clutching a burgundy-red folio.

"Herr Trent, I require your passports for verification. Then your signature." He spread out the documents and pointed to yellow arrows stuck onto onionskin pages.

Jeffry scrawled the name Brian A. Trent.

"Both of your signatures, Herr Trent. Please sign the name Jeffry Landon. Do not be concerned. Such occurrences are common with us. This information is privileged, for our eyes only."

"How did you know?" puzzled Jeffry, handing over the second passport.

"Your government does much official—and unofficial—business with us. Herr Stafford and I are well acquainted. I do not wish to know why you are here, but since the Director approves of your activities with this account, our bank accepts you. Here are your deposit and withdrawal forms.

"When you desire to make a transaction, proceed to the teller's window, *Konto-3*. The clerk at window three has been instructed and shall attend to your requirements without delay."

Before leaving, Jeffry arranged for a safe deposit box to hold his Jeffry Landon passport, the 1960 postcard from Zuoz, a poem Helga once wrote, the photo of the tattoo, and his diary on Holyoke stationary. At window number three he withdrew eighteen-thousand Swiss francs. He located a public telephone and dialed the number given by Stafford.

"Phillips here."

"Ah...good evening, Mr. Phillips. This is Orion. Do you have anything for me?"

A pause. "Been expecting your call. Meet me at the restaurant on Halbinsel Au. Eight tonight. Take one of the large boats ferrying passengers on Lake Zürich."

"Halbinsel Au?"

"Yes. A peninsula at the southwest shore of the lake. Named Au, spelled 'a'-'u' by the locals. They put on some fantastic folk dancing and singing Wednesday nights. Few tourists know about it. Hard for anyone to monitor our conversation in all that noise."

"How will I recognize you?"

"Brown and tan sport coat, brown trousers. Smoking a pipe. After I hand you a wedding ring, inspect it, return it to my left hand."

"What about me?"

"Washington's description. And the ring. Take a table seat by yourself. Close to the band."

Jeffry hung up, scratched his head, and proceeded north on Bahnhofstrasse, passing the Swiss Bank Corporation. After checking out several stores, he acquired a yellow ski jacket over black pants and navy-blue ski boots. He would rent skis at St. Moritz.

Back at the Hotel Krone he asked the desk clerk to telephone St. Moritz and secure a reservation at the Suvretta House, one of the exclusive accommodations in that town. Jeffry pressed a hundred-franc note into the man's hands for his troubles.

Then he handed the clerk a small, crisp stack of three-thousand francs and requested that he arrange deposit for suite availability starting tomorrow night—even though arrival may be delayed a few days. The desk attendant, straightening his shoulders, assured Jeffry all would be in order, earlier indifference sliding into indulgence at the promise of further gratuity.

At six-thirty Jeffry, dodging evening foot traffic, dashed to the green tram, which transported him from his hotel to Bürkliplatz, an intersection at the north end of Lake Zürich. At the dock he purchased a ticket for Halbinsel Au.

By now, the vapor-masked sun had slipped below the horizon, pulling slate-gray light with it. Bellies of southbound clouds reflected metropolitan lights and silver flicks of the sun's lash. The weather was turning frigid, but at its low altitude, Zürich sustained minimal snowfall in spite of extensive accumulation in the high mountains. A hint of blue ice clung to the lake's shores.

While waiting to board, Jeffry watched a scattering of scavenging seagulls flying about, swooping down, screeching in the wind, fighting for crumbs. The birds settled on scarred and withered pilings roped to bobbing dinghies. Sailboats, yachts, and a police launch heaved amiably about the wharf, rising and falling with the waves, hawsers squeaking, stretching and straining, masts clinking in the breeze.

Slipping its mooring lines, the festive launch, with multinational banners flapping in the breeze, ferried Jeffry and fifty-odd passengers toward the port of Au. Shore lights of small villages and homes twinkled through a matte indigo screen as the watercraft sliced southward into dark waves slap, slap, slapping against the hull, a cauldron of black foam boiling at its stern. The narrow streets and granite vaults receded to the north. Then, while holding on to the port gun'l, Jeffry felt a lovely, freckled face girl brush by him, smile, and vanish forward on the deck.

In less than an hour the twin marine diesels revved into reverse and pulled starboard, a faint crunch heard as it docked at a wooden jetty. The invigorated crowd disembarked off the gangplank at Au. Jeffry noticed the faint odor of fish and a nearby accordion playing schottische.

He ascended the steps to a large restaurant attached to the Landgasthof Hotel. Broad bay windows faced the lamp-lit dock. The band music had not yet begun. He entered and the maître d' escorted Jeffry to his table for two.

Joyful customers were filling the spacious and brightly lit room. A band in colorful Swiss ethnic costumes followed, playing captivating music to the bustling crowd. Wine, beer, and merriment flowed as young and old danced with boundless enthusiasm, spinning modern and traditional folk dances to the melodies of the tireless players.

Spinning dreams.

"Orion?" The word jolted Jeffry out of his reverie.

Before him stood a black-haired, middle-aged gentleman, unpressed trousers dangling from suspenders. He was fidgeting with a small object in his hand. This stoop-shouldered presence with a swarthy complexion thrust the wedding band into Jeffry's extended palm. Jeffry examined the ring and delivered it back to the left hand. The quiet agent slipped the band on the fourth finger of his right hand, covering the white telltale circle.

"I am Orion," proclaimed Jeffry. "Please sit down. What can you tell me about Ursa. Any new reports?"

"A beer or two, enjoy the music, and then talk." His eyes flicked about, a cardboard smile raising the ends of a narrow mustache. A waiter approached. "Two dark lagers, please."

After the polished dance floor was cleared, a cheerful couple trotted out onto the stage, the man and woman performing a virtuoso yodeling session to loud cheers. The long Alpine horns followed, trumpeting prolonged, mysterious and sonorous echoes from the Swiss valleys of ages past. Jeffry was edgy, patiently waiting. The band from Glarus promenaded back and struck up a defenders' march.

A petite young woman, brunette, approached. The girl on the boat. Tight, white sweater, sans bra. Embroidered collar and sleeves. A colorful skirt of yellows and orange. The pixie's sunburned, freckled face and deep brown tiger-eyes flashed with fire, laughing as she sauntered up to Jeffry and gaily announced, *"Grüezi!"* the traditional Swiss-German greeting. *"Sie scheinen sehr nett. Tanzen, bitte?"*

Asking Jeffry to dance, she caught him off guard, the man bewildered by the sudden change of the Swiss into jovial, fun-loving people.

"Grüezi," Jeffry responded with an honest grin.

The vivacious woman omitted her name, permitting Jeffry to feel comfortable in his own anonymity. They danced a fast polka, Jeffry momentarily forgetting about his visitor. Then the band played while a vocalist sang in English with a Swiss-German dialect, "Good-bye, Ruby Tuesday…"

"Righteous Brothers?" guessed his perspiring partner, still squeezing both of his hands. The girl chuckled, her smile infectious, and Jeffry's tension leaked away.

Their hands remained locked together, neither rushing away.

"You look a bit familiar. Have we met before?" Jeffry stared at her, feeling unsure. The photo of Marlene in Erik's billfold hid from his recollection.

She ignored the query. "The man at your table is not our Chester Phillips. Use caution."

"But..."

"You are a wonderful dancer." She abruptly turned from the floor, back to her table.

Jeffry, still perspiring and nerves drawn tight at the woman's alert, slipped into his seat. The sport coat of his contact dangled on the empty chair back, a pipe trailing smoke while resting in the cigarette tray. Jeffry's roving eyes latched onto the stranger in suspenders—and so did the brunette's from afar. The man called Phillips was dancing with another girl. He returned, sleeves tightly rolled up, his face showing tiny beads of sweat.

"Phew...too much for me. Wouldn't mind bedding that one tonight," exclaimed the stranger, his features alternating between terse grins and anxious stares. "Now, about your Ursa. Any idea where to begin searching?"

Jeffry gyrated into intense caution, inhaling through fired nostrils. Suddenly, appalled, he sat as if soldered to his chair, his eyes cleaved to the image. The tattoo. Like the one locked in the safe deposit box.

Jeffry's face rolled tight, controlled. Pretending to reach for a napkin, he knocked over a bottle of dark Munich ale and then jumped up as the brew spilled across the checkered tablecloth.

"Oh, shit. Sorry, Phillips. How clumsy of me."

The spirits washed down over Jeffry's pants. Jeffry wiped his trousers with the napkin and excused himself. "Going to clean up in the men's room. Be right back."

His contact watched Jeffry until he disappeared into the crowd. Phillips stretched a frosty smile and ordered up a Heineken.

Jeffry, eyes set, ears sharply attuned, hurried toward a pay phone in the lobby. The brunette dancer was gone. Every few seconds some inebriated woman in heat snagged his arm, drawing him toward the dance floor. In the face of danger, this attention played like a bad dream, slowing him down. Finally, his heart rate slammed into second gear, the life force taking precedence, and he reached the communications bank, anxious digits dialing the local operator.

Seconds ticking away seemed like hours. He asked for an overseas connection to Washington, then inserting a two-inch donut-shaped instrument against the speaker.

"Your message?" Fine, high-pitched static crackled across the line.

"Orion here. Patch me through to Hamlet."

"Yes, sir," replied the woman's matter-of-fact voice. "Tape rolling. Is your phone sterile?"

"I think so." His sweaty hand squeezed the receiver. "Why do you ask?"

"We are tracking a series of unusual, quick disturbances on the oscilloscope. More than standard noise. Frequency too high, too recurrent. Suggest you secure your communication port. Please hold. Hamlet's line is now lit."

"Damnation," muttered Jeffry, suppressing an undercurrent of fear, the turn of events producing a chilling effect on his normally quick mind. He could trust absolutely no one. Feeling like a caged animal he paced back and forth in a narrow circle. He was not about to stick around and inspect for wire taps.

Terry Caldwell answered. Jeffry summarized the encounter.

"Hoss, I'll notify the Company operatives in Zürich. The rest of the team will arrive in Au within the hour."

"The *rest* of the team?"

"We have had an agent tracking you…CIA…woman…name's Marlene. The girl who danced with you. Better be on your way. Use care," admonished Terry. "Your phone is tapped. Your friend has friends. The real Phillips may have been seized by Thunderbird. You will need to move fast, real fast."

She's already contacted Hamlet, he realized. "But they can't understand my transmission. I'm using the scrambler." His moist hand tightened again.

"They can translate mine, and they're taping. Thunderbird must have access to a hostile government computer, which can unscramble the signals within a few hours. If so, this puts a new dimension on the chase. Take no chances, Hoss. Get out. Get out now! Shoot for your next destination."

Jeffry, straining to appear unruffled, returned to the table, pretending to wipe beer from his pants. His eyes scanned the room. *Marlene? Who the hell is she?*

"That country girl must have really excited you. I've ordered you a Heineken." The man called Phillips eyed Jeffry.

The band began to play "Yellow River" and Jeffry replied, "Hey, there's my favorite song. One more dance. Don't drink my beer. I'll be right back."

Jeffry strolled through the crowded room to a nearby maiden combing her auburn hair. Straightaway they were dancing toward the other side of the crowded room where he excused himself, abandoning her, leaving the damsel with an astonished look on her face as he dashed to the brightly lit dock. A low-lying fog was beginning to boil off the agitated waters. Jeffry, now chilled, had left his coat behind.

He offered one-hundred francs to a young man tending the dock. "Where might I rent a boat, a fast water craft? I need someone to take me to Zürich, as soon as possible. It's an emergency."

"If you stay a minute, I'll fetch my cousin. He runs one of the fastest power cruisers on the lake."

Jeffry retreated into the shadows, away from the orange sodium lanterns, waiting, watching tiny shore bugs flitting about the harbor lights. Arms wrapped around himself, he shuddered. *Jesus, something is terribly wrong.*

In ten minutes, the prow broke water, the deck tilting, the two men bouncing over the blackness as the slick powerboat, undaunted twin marine engines roaring and lights blazing into the night, raced over the waves toward Zürich, the loud crash of sliced water spraying outward from the cutter.

"The real Phillips must be dead," Jeffry imparted to the wind. Unanswered questions churned through his mind, grappling to uncover the half-truth, the whole beyond human grasp. Now Jeffry would be wanted by Thunderbird for information, the unseen enemy rising up against the lone American trespasser and already clawing at his heels.

Helga, where in God's name are you? Jeffry's brain screamed. He pulled the skipper's borrowed windbreaker tightly about his body.

The boat docked and Jeffry, apprehensive and perspiring, rushed to his hotel. He packed his belongings, paid the bill in cash, and raced toward his rental car, a burnt-orange Opel. He pulled out of the underground parking facility, tires squealing with a vengeance on the turn, and hurtled south toward the Engadin Valley.

Now late at night, Jeffry's tense hands, searching for stability, clutched the steering wheel as he followed the signs toward Rapperswil, Davos, and finally St. Moritz. All roads remained open, but all were lined with snow of increasing depth.

Twice he peeled off the thoroughfare, watching for suspicious headlights. He saw none. Blackness hid the oppressive overcast, crystalline torrents of sleet, hanging like a sash from the heavens, transforming to fine granules of snow beating against his Opel, crystals mutating to swirls of flakes.

Posing as Brian Trent, Orion, with an unsettled sigh passed the sign announcing 'St. Moritz' at early Thursday morning sunrise, fibers of reason beginning to unravel as he chased after a mysterious woman he had not seen for a decade.

In Zürich the clerk with the one-hundred franc note made his phone call. *"Ja, Herr Sierpinski. Der Orion fahrt bis Sankt Moritz."*

The Krone Hotel evening attendant, a chilling smile worming across his face, replaced the receiver. He folded his map after drawing a red circle around St. Moritz.

30

Washington, Thursday, November 11, 1971, 4:00 P.M.

"Fill me in, Terry." Timothy Stafford studied a blown-up map of Zürich. It was pinned to an easel board.

Terry Caldwell stood in military bearing next to the Director. He was wearing his signature cowboy boots. "On orders, one of the CIA agents had followed Jeffry to Au." He pointed to the peninsula on the map. "Marlene Sternschen...that's her name...pretended to be a dumb country girl and coaxed the imposter, LaVecchia, to dance with her. She doped his beer, and with the assistance of a couple of her associates, helped him into their car."

"Then what?"

"Boss, the Agent Phillips has never been found so far. Our CIA colleagues interrogated LaVecchia quite thoroughly. He denied knowing much about Helga except that someone in his organization wants her found. And terminated."

"Who are his superiors? What organization?"

"Don't know, boss. Guess he had a weak heart." Terry tapped his own chest.

"Oh, horseshit. What the fuck are those guys trying to pull? He would have been more valuable alive than dead. Damn! Well, what do we know? Where is he from?"

"A Swiss, originally from Chiasso on the Italian border. Had a wife and an eight-year-old girl. His family still lives in Chiasso. About four years ago, he moved to Zürich to work as an orderly at Trieste. Also moonlighted as a diener in the hospital morgue and drove a hearse for the Braun Funeral Home."

"What did he know about Phillips?"

"LaVecchia played dumb but seemed terrified to give out any more info. What we now know, they dragged it out of him, bit by bit."

"What do *you* think?" sighed Stafford.

"Lots of pieces are missing, but the CIA discovered that the organization had someone on their payroll working inside Helga's bank. This clerk didn't catch on until after Helga withdrew the money. He must have spotted Phillips making inquiries about Helga...and Thunderbird nailed him. I doubt Phillips divulged much information, otherwise they wouldn't have risked tapping into his telephone line. The rest you know."

"What about the tattoo on LaVecchia?"

"Our guys cut it away and sewed up the arm before leaving his body in a vacant boathouse. Agent Sternschen air-shipped the skin to us in a diplomatic pouch, and our lab guys are analyzing it now. In the meantime, I think we could imprint an identical tattoo on one of our own agents if necessary."

"True, but I'll bet that if one were to compare Salucci's with that from LaVecchia, there would be some telltale differences. The disclosure key has to lie beyond the visible portrait of a bird. Otherwise anyone could fake this image."

"Maybe you're right. I can't believe it's just some cute design."

"I'll keep you posted, boss," replied Terry. "In the meantime, Jeffry has arrived in St. Moritz."

"And Harald?"

"Returning from Taiwan. Nothing concrete yet."

"Still no trace of Helga?"

"Not a whiff, boss."

31

Switzerland.

The Mercedes Benz decelerated and then roared onto the roadway rising toward the Diavolezza, a mountain bordering the Engadin Valley. Tires still managed the steep thoroughfares without snow-chains, though the going was rougher. A single pair of Rossignol skis clung to the overhead bars on the roof. The traveler slowed to a hesitant halt before an information kiosk, curls of blue smoke drifting from its brick chimney. A young man, early twenties, blond hair under a ski cap, gold ringlet in the left ear, approached the blue Mercedes from his hut.

"*Guten Tag.*"

"Good day. What a pleasant morning it is. Could you tell me if the inn has accommodations available?" She removed mirrored sunglasses.

"Most certainly. A few rooms remain available at the lodge, Fräulein…uh…Fräulein…?"

"Tanya, Tanya Kessler." The regal brunette passed the young clerk a hundred franc note.

"The best rooms face the south. I will arrange for a bellhop to meet you at the lodge."

"That will not be required. Please call ahead and ask the manager to reserve an executive suite."

"No problem, Fräulein. If I may be a bit presumptuous, take care to avoid the ski run off to your left when you approach the lower lift. There is a cliff easily missed as you descend."

"Thank you for your concern. I know that trail."

"Pretty wristlet. Real gold?" He glanced at her right arm.

A smile warmed her face. "Twenty-one karat. The cross is eighteen."

"My sister has a similar ornament on her charm bracelet. Well, have a good holiday."

"Thank you. I'll ski here for two days and then test some slopes further down the valley. Today I need rest and relaxation from my teaching assignments." She pressed another one-hundred francs into the young man's hands. "This is for extreme discretion. No one is to disturb me. However, I should be pleased if you would join me for a cocktail at the lodge. Say, eight o'clock tonight? Perhaps you could tell me more about the ski conditions here."

Before he could answer, Helga replaced her sunglasses and stabbed the accelerator with her toe, the auto flying up the asphalt.

After dinner, she sat on a pinewood chair in her room. Skis and poles stood against the wall. She had removed the wig, her blond tresses flowing around her right shoulder. The winter static played a mischievous game with the tips of her hair.

Helga kept staring at the taped envelope. The photographs. Something stayed her hand, as if a hundred-pound weight lay on it. She had no reason to unravel the past. And the future looked grim. She only wanted to hold onto the present, hold onto life. Slowly the knife in her hand slit open the cover. The images blind-sided her, Helga's grip strangling the letter opener.

She stared at the two photos given her by Aunt Anna in St. Moritz. Anna had said that they originally came from a Polish friend, and Anna, finding them in her brother's drawer in Mainz, decided they really belonged to Helga. Anna reported that they were pictures of Helga with her natural Polish parents and her brother before their death from British bombers, prior to Helga's adoption. Helga's whole body shuddered, and she knew not why. One revealed a man, a woman, and a small girl with her blond hair done up in braids. A handsomely dressed family. A second portrait depicted a little girl holding hands with an infant boy. On the back, in Polish, "Happy birthday, Franz!" The first one was blank on its reverse side.

"My real parents? And I have a brother?"

She felt as if the world had suddenly stopped turning, a part of her careening into outer space. Breathing became difficult, and Helga, one hand clutching her strangled throat, threw open a window. A jacket of ice armored her heart, any connection to the ancient past now frozen from memory. Yet she shook, crying torrents of tears, hugging herself with both arms. Even yet she did not know why, and she could not stop until a blessed sleep overtook her.

32

Washington, Friday, November 12, 1971.

*H*arald Johnson had returned from Taipei. Waiting for Tim Stafford and Terry Caldwell, he was alone in the BNDD conference center. While sipping black coffee, he concentrated on the Taiwan implications. *Are both the Marxist and the Maoist giants funneling huge sums of money to process opium in selected centers around the world? What better way to bring democracy to its knees. Simply lobotomize our people with drugs until they don't care.* He needed to separate wheat from chaff, to realign a series of facts, mold them together, and build a coherent portrait, a picture with direction.

He mulled over the recent events implicating Thunderbird. Secretary of State Edward Piccollo assassinated in Georgetown. Ed's wife, overdosed on heroin, found floating in the Potomac. Salucci, a sailor murdered in Atlantic City, the corpse minus a tattooed left arm. Bjørn Ljunggren, Swedish Operative, terminated in Copenhagen—by someone called Helga. CIA Agent Phillips missing in Zürich. LaVeccia of Chiasso, sporting a likeness of

Salucci's tattoo, dies under interrogation. Jeffry now on a dangerous chase in the Swiss Alps.

"Good morning, Harald." Director Stafford pulled down a world map.

Terry followed Stafford into the room and tossed Harald a salute. "Welcome back, Hoss. We've missed you here at BNDD. Any leads in Taiwan?"

The three men focused on the geographic chart. Using multicolored pins, Terry marked it up with known and suspected routes of opium and heroin passage and centers for processing while Harald briefed the other two on his Taiwan trip.

"Think it was a dead end, Harald?" Stafford rapped the island of Taiwan with his pointer.

"Too soon to tell, Tim. I did learn something in Taipei, however remote. If it weren't for the trip, the possibility of a larger political conspiracy wouldn't have occurred to me."

"Quite a reach, Harald," judged Stafford, a recalcitrant convert. "All you got is a hunch. What's your plan now?" Irritated, he kept striking the knuckles of his left hand with the end of an ink pen.

"I'll head for Switzerland, to Chiasso, and have a chat with LaVecchia's wife," replied Harald. "Also, I want that vampire bat tattooed on the inside of my left arm. Might come in handy if I go into deep cover."

"Vampire?"

"Why not? Could be a bat."

"A bat in the belfry, huh? Okay," agreed Stafford. "But remember, if you contact LaVecchia's wife, you'll have to assume that Thunderbird will be close behind.

"Also, we'll inform our CIA friends in Zürich of the change in plans. What about you, Terry? Any ideas?" The Director cut to the man from Maryland.

"Boss, I got an idea I'm working on. Let me study on it and get back to you."

In the back of Terry's mind lurked the death of Marty Campbell, his friend buried in Virginia. He had died in the Trieste Hospital. And LaVecchia had worked at Trieste. Marty's mother had gone to Zürich and stayed with him until he died. Terry had to revisit Margaret Campbell.

Fredericksburg, Virginia, Thursday, November 18.

Sheets of rain buffeted the high-winged aircraft. Terry Caldwell's eyes tracked bright reflections from the wet streets of Fredericksburg below. The commuter plane barreled downward against the pummeling wind and landed, bouncing once on a small airstrip near the town. Terry drove a rented Chevy to the Colonial Park Apartments where he was greeted by Margaret Campbell, a plump, elderly woman exuding an honest vitality. She was delighted to see Terry again and invited him into the front parlor.

"Bad weather today, Margaret."

"Yes, Terry. Typical for this season, I'm afraid. Please have a seat. Coffee? Tea?"

"Tea would be nice." His eyes caught a picture of Marty, the portrait sitting on a piano.

"I'm heating some water. You sounded a bit mysterious on the phone. Is everything okay?" she inquired.

"Margaret, I know you don't wish to talk about Marty's passing. But there is a vital project I'm working on in the Bureau, and I really need your assistance." His eyebrows rose with concern while he pondered a line and limits of query.

"My help? How so?"

"You flew to Zürich after Marty's accident. Please tell me about the hospital in which he was treated."

"Well…oh dear me…well, the Trieste was a modern medical center on the western side of the city. The doctors and nurses were very nice and extremely efficient. I just know Marty received the best of care."

"Do you recall the surgeon's name?"

"Doctor Niemeier, Johann Niemeier. Someone in the business where my son was consulting…let me think… the Cumaves Company. They recommended him.

"And the doctor took excellent care of Marty. They did all they could. He said that Marty died of brain swelling. I…I did not want an autopsy." She sighed and looked at Marty's likeness. "My boy had suffered through too much already. I only wanted Marty home so he could be buried beside his wife. Was I wrong, Terry?"

"No, Margaret, of course not. But the hospital seemed to be a creditable institution?"

"Oh, certainly. It has an excellent reputation in Zürich."

Terry unfolded a map of Zürich. "How was it that the ambulance transferred Marty from the town of Winterthur all the way to Trieste? Looking at this map, I see that Central Hospital is much closer."

"I don't know about those things. Maybe Central had their beds full?"

"Guess I can't think of anything else. Oh, you had no problems transporting Marty back to Virginia. How did you arrange it so quickly?"

"I asked Doctor Niemeier about a good funeral home that could help me avoid delays in transfer, someone who knew about these things. Let me think… No. Actually, it was Doctor Niemeier himself who brought up the subject. Anyway, the nice man was quite helpful and suggested the Braun Funeral Home. He assured me they had connections that would avoid a lot of red tape. And he surely was right. Within two days, Marty was flown by jet to New York City. I would have been at my wit's end without them. It's not easy having just lost your son, but in a strange land…"

Her voice drifted off. A whistle bellowed from the kitchen, and Margaret excused herself to remove the teakettle from the stove. She resumed her composure, returning with two steaming cups.

"Can you describe the surgeon? Was he Swiss?" Terry sipped his hot tea.

"Actually, I think he was German or Austrian. Bald and quite heavy. Wore thick eyeglasses. Seemed to have a sun-burned complexion. Dressed nicely. So kind to me. Nothing unusual except…oh, nothing."

"What is it, Margaret?"

"Well, Terry, women notice little things sometimes…you know, appearances and all. Well, it's silly," she laughed. "But when he walked into the waiting room after surgery, he had his operating clothes on—those green pajama-like things. They didn't fit him very well because he was so large. Anyway, I thought it strange that a distinguished neurosurgeon would have a tattoo. Well, you know what I mean."

Terry lowered his cup halfway down. "Tattoo?" His mind shot into overdrive, locking in on Harald's expanding puzzle.

"It appeared like an eagle or a bat with wings spread—right there on his left arm."

"On the inside above his elbow?" the BNDD agent stammered. He nearly broke the teacup with the tension.

"Why, yes. How did you know, Terry?"

He shot a glance at his watch. "Margaret, I've got to run. You may have been more help than you will ever imagine."

Unable to obtain space on the next scheduled flight back to D.C., Special Agent Caldwell hired a charter flying service. Time was vital, sand at the top of the hourglass sinking at its center.

On the flight back, Terry scanned for signposts. At one end of the world, Harald had stumbled onto possible ideological links, however remote, warriors for mind control pursuing intellectual paralysis. At the other end, Jeffry was tracking a beautiful, enigmatic woman inexplicably tied to the elusive Thunderbird Society. And now an aristocratic neurosurgeon diverting ambulance cases to his medical center. He had to reach Harald.

Upon landing at Washington National Airport, Terry checked the time and placed a call to England, hoping to catch Harald between flights.

London.

Harald took brisk, confident strides into the transit passenger lounge at Heathrow Airport. His Swissair flight to Zürich would depart within the hour.

"Mr. Johnson. Mr. Harald Johnson. Please approach the Swissair counter," blared the loudspeaker.

Harald reported to the airline clerk. A transatlantic call from Washington awaited him. Terry Caldwell. Terry related the information about a Doctor Niemeier at the Trieste Hospital. And the Braun Mortuary.

"Stafford thinks it's a wild goose chase, Hoss, but he's under pressure from higher up. He's willing to pursue it. Can you check them out while you are in Switzerland?" asked Terry.

"Snoop on a Swiss brain surgeon? Uh, come on, Terry."

"You owe me, Harald. I stay at home while you get to see the world."

"Okay, good buddy. The CIA won't like our working in their territory, but they've stepped on our toes enough. After my trip to Chiasso, I'll follow through in Zürich."

"Keep in touch, Hoss."

Harald heard his flight announcement. He trotted toward the departure door, his limp from polio barely noticeable. He scratched his left arm, the itching tattoo an excellent replica. First pursue the connection in Chiasso, then back to Zürich. His longtime friend, Jeffry Landon, would be in St. Moritz by now.

33

The Engadin Valley, Thursday, November 11, 1971, 7:00 A.M.

The clerk at the Suvretta House in St. Moritz looked up from his ledger and smiled at Jeffry. "*Grüezi, darf ich Ihnen helfen?*" Greetings, may I help you?

The elderly clerk appeared so thin that a stiff breeze might topple him. He set his ink pen down with some difficulty, his limbs ravaged by Parkinsonian tremors.

"*Grüezi*. I am Brian Trent. I believe you have a room reserved for me."

"Ah, yes, Herr Trent, but you are rather early. May we store your luggage until the room is cleaned? We will have your accommodation ready at noon." A hesitant, whispery voice.

"Thank you. That will be fine. In the meantime, I shall stroll about the village."

"Very good, *mein Herr*. May we check your passport, please?" He extended a bony, finely shaking hand.

Jeffry felt a bit shaky himself after last night's events at Au.

A valet gathered up Jeffry's leather valise and winter coat and then parked the Opel behind the inn. Jeffry

THE THUNDERBIRD COVENANT

walked into the restaurant for breakfast. He ordered tasty croissants and steaming hot coffee.

After paying the bill, he asked his server if he knew of the Hirschen Jewelry Shop managed by Frau Baumann. While dropping coins into a belted change-purse, the waiter provided directions, taking Jeffry outside and pointing up the street.

Jeffry, listening to the creaks and rattles of early morning shutters opening up, walked several blocks, mingling with townspeople until he approached a small jewelry shop in a building made of stucco and wood. The ancient structure leaned against one of the narrow streets where picturesque buildings lined the byway, except for an occasional strip of sidewalk. Jeffry scanned the avenue and then entered the store, bells jangling against the door.

Inside, the shop was modern and functional, yet warm and comfortable. A thin and well groomed woman approached

"*Guten Tag,*" greeted the pleasant owner, her merry head cocked to one side. Fine lines flanked twinkling sky-blue eyes.

"Good day," answered Jeffry. "May I just look around?"

"Of course. Please take your time. We don't get many customers this early in the morning. Are you on a holiday?" She brushed some lint of her brown tweed jacket and adjusted an ivory comb in her hair.

"Yes. I hope to enjoy some skiing this week."

"We have little snow here in the valley, but on the mountains many of the lifts are open. The peaks have had an early snowfall," commented the kindly woman. Highlights played over her braided silver hair, flowers interwoven.

"Your accent is German...not Swiss is it?"

"I'm originally from Mainz, but the Swiss seem to tolerate me," she replied.

"I should like to stop back this evening if you were not to mind."

"Please, return anytime. Americans are most welcome."

"Hmm.... Is it so obvious that I'm from the United States?" queried Jeffry.

"Your accent and rubber shoe covers give you away," she laughed, gesturing toward his feet. "Most Europeans haven't even heard of them, let alone wear them. They are clever, but distinctly American."

Jeffry, feeling a bit sheepish, gazed at Anna's sturdy brown shoes. Then he opened the door, the jingling bells declaring his departure. Neither Anna nor Jeffry noticed a small microphone bonded to the ceiling light fixture.

A light snowfall had begun, flakes melting on his warm jacket. Feeling self-conscious about the rubbers, he returned to the Suvretta House to catch up on his sleep.

Jeffry arose at six pm, showered, combed his hair and beard, and dressed. He reached back to secure his ponytail but grabbed thin air. Orion chuckled to himself. He proceeded downstairs for a veal dinner and then relaxed over a glass of cherry brandy.

Shortly past seven, he returned to the jewelry store, still open for after-ski patrons. He browsed about until the customers had departed.

"May I assist you? I was about to close my shop."

"Frau Baumann, I have a rather urgent task, and I must speak with you privately about your niece, Helga. Would it be possible?"

Anna's pleasant smile vanished, a look of terror flowing over her alarmed face, features turning brittle. Standing motionless, the startled lady struggled for balance.

"Who are you? Please, I have done nothing! Helga is not here. Why must you ask me these questions?"

"My name is Brian Trent. Your Helga is in terrible danger. I must—absolutely must—find her as soon as possible."

"I do not know where she is. Please leave, Herr Trent." She tripped toward the brim of panic, her voice splintering.

"Helga might be using the name of Tanya Hensell. If I do not locate her before someone else does, she will be killed. She has valuable and extremely dangerous information."

"Would that I could help you," cried the frightened lady. "But you may be the very person seeking to do her harm." Her English strained, now breaking into a heavier German dialect.

She refused to discuss it any further. Jeffry now knew that Anna had seen Helga, feared for her, the stunned reaction giving her away.

"Please, I..."

"*Nein!* You must leave! Now!"

"If you change your mind, please contact me at the Suvretta House. I'm truly sorry to disturb your day," apologized Jeffry, still desperate for a lead.

Jeffry returned to his lodging and contacted Washington at eight-thirty. He inserted his scrambler.

"Orion here. I am certain that Ursa is not in St. Moritz. I am traveling down the valley to check out the skiing there." His mind was on an ancient postcard, a fingerpost in the security box at Crédit Suisse.

"Keep in touch. Use care."

The following day Jeffry employed his plastic bank card to obtain five hundred-franc notes. He discarded his rubbers and purchased a pair of stout, leather boots. After making reservations for the Hotel Crusch Alva, he sped away in his Opel, striking out for Zuoz, an hour's drive northeast through the Engadin Valley.

Three inches of fresh snow had blanketed the ground and brush-stroked the trees. On either side of the road, crowning jewels of glacial ice capped a green cloak of fir along the towering mountain ranges. Traditional cottages and white stucco apartment buildings, a potpourri of ancient and modern, dotted the rolling landscape.

In Zuoz, the picturesque mélange of homes and shops edged the narrow main street. Jeffry swung his Opel up to the front of the Hotel Crusch Alva, to the right of the passageway. The stately architecture shared the compressed thoroughfare with buildings of similar vintage.

During the week, he skied the slopes and took meals at every restaurant, but failed to catch a glimpse of anyone remotely looking like his Helga. At the visitors' center and hotels he inquired for a Tanya Hensell. No such person had registered.

On Friday evening, Jeffry entered the Café Restaurant Walther, a rustic and romantic Swiss inn, an ancient cellar of an Engadin house. Old stone vaulting and thick, medieval walls rose above a granite floor worn with age. He toyed with his quiche Lorraine, feeling despondent at the lack of success, chewing the back of his cheek.

The buxom server, noticing his disconsolate expression, asked, "Gives there a problem with the food?"

"It's nicely done, thank you. I'd favor another glass of your excellent Chablis."

She returned and poured the vintage drink. Jeffry held the crystal aloft before a candle flame, searching for some dramatic insight into the fire of Helga's hermetic enigma. His vanishing blonde kept flitting, unbidden, from the visceral recesses of a haunting memory.

The clear, limpid eyes and tanned cheeks of the curious waitress, red hues contrasted by raven hair clutching her face, caught Jeffry's attention. As did her fragrance of French perfume.

"I see you've been skiing today." He swirled his drink again.

She set her dessert tray down. "Oh, yes. On the Motta Naluns. It's my favorite mountain. Do you know the runs there?"

"The Motta Naluns?" The words sounded familiar.

"Yes. One of the high mountains near Schuls."

"Schuls?"

"A village further down the valley and one of our charming skiing areas. The local people call the town by its Romansch name, Scuol."

"My God, that's it," he exclaimed aloud. Helga's words exploded into conscious memory. ...*A town with two names, Jeffry, darling. Schuls, Scuol. My dream mountain, the Motta Naluns.* Jeffry's mind locked onto a forgotten path, and another pin dropped with a thud into its niche deep inside a padlock's tumbler. His heart, blazing with past memories and future anticipation, lurched forward.

The wide-eyed waitress gasped as he jumped up, threw down a sheath of francs, and rushed into the night air. Jeffry, stalked by the trail of his own footprints, trotted toward his car. He gripped the door handle and looked up.

Starlight plus a sliver of lunar scape, a signet ring in the sky, outlined the shadowed Alpine peaks. Jeffry, gazing down the snowy alley, cast his eyes toward the unseen crossroad of judgement, the village of Scuol, a mysterious hamlet now pulling at him, another encrypt far remote from the Hamlet of BNDD. Frost collected on his beard, a surrealistic chill surging through him as fingers of Kismet lightly stroked the back of his neck, warning him of the monumental perils on the Motta Naluns. An icy digit pressed into his heart, causing one portion of him almost to turn back. The other, dauntless and desperate to find the fiery love he once knew, could no longer be stopped. He pulled open the door of destiny and stepped in.

34

Chiasso, Saturday, November 20, 1971.

Elsewhere in Switzerland, Agent Harald Johnson proceeded from the Zürich Airport direct to the Hauptbahnhof, where he boarded the train which sped Harald from the northern Swiss-German states to the southern Swiss-Italian cantons. The engine, its shrill whistle heralding the express, rolled onward east of resplendent Lake Luzern, southward through the famous Gotthard Tunnel in the Alps, along the edge of Lake Lugano, and into the southern border town of Chiasso.

Melita LaVecchia resided in a humble dwelling on the village outskirts. After an hour of searching and asking directions, Harald motored in his rented Fiat up to her home, a wooden structure surrounded by a picket fence in poor repair. Green paint was peeling from the sides of the house, a shutter hanging awkwardly from its hinge. The calico curtains undulated with wisps of wind. As Harald bounced along the weedy, gravel road, he caught sight of a young woman. Her black hair was twisted into a simple chignon. Dressed in a tattered dress under a green, polka-dotted smock, Melita was sweeping the walkway.

"Good afternoon. Do you speak English?"

Melita shook her head and scurried into the house. In a moment she returned with an elderly lady, whose voluminous white hair was pulled down by a red and white checkered kerchief. They stood on the porch.

"May I help you? I am Melita's mother. I know little English. Learn from American soldiers twenty-five years ago." She wiped her hands on an apron as Antonietta, her grandchild, peeked out from behind the door.

Harald spoke slowly, using the false name listed on one of his passports. "Thank you. My name is Mr. Astrup, and I work with an American newspaper syndicate. I am searching for background material regarding Martino LaVecchia's untimely death."

The mother of Melita translated. The two then turned and shot a look of puzzlement.

Harald proceeded. "Did you know Martino's employer?"

"Martino was hospital worker in Zürich. He send many francs home to Melita."

"Did he ever mention the name of his supervisor?"

The older woman shrugged her shoulders. "No, he never discuss."

"And the circumstances of his death?"

The woman with the checkered kerchief glanced at her daughter, Melita, speaking in Italian. Then she answered, "Robbed and beaten. The police can tell you more. We bury him in Chiasso, behind our Chapel of St. Ignatius." The lady crossed herself.

"I see. What did he do before he went to Zürich?"

"Truck driver."

"Ahh... For whom?"

"Martino never say. He send much money. Now no more." The mother and Melita resumed their discussion in Italian, their hands gesticulating with animated theater.

The older woman gave a broad smile and turned to Harald. "He travel very much. All over country." She waved her arm in a big circle. "Very nice. We get many colorful postcards."

"Postcards?"

"Oh yes, so pretty. Make my Melita feel much important. She show all her friends that Martino such distinguished man. You wish to see?"

"No thank you." Harald was about to say goodbye and then a thought changed his mind.

"The postcards, yes, I would like very much to look at them."

Antonietta's grandmother turned to Melita. After another lively conference, they invited Harald in for coffee at the kitchen table. Harald stepped into the bungalow, floorboards under a threadbare carpet squeaking with each footfall. Light Italian music and the odor of freshly baked bread drifted in from the kitchen. The older woman pushed the window shutters wide open.

Melita proudly brought out her picture cards, treasured remembrances of her Martino. Harald scanned each while sipping the strong coffee, many pictorials filling a small wicker basket. He pulled a map out of his pocket and studied the towns from which they were mailed. He circled all of the sites on his map, then slipped it back into his pocket.

Harald tossed down the last of his coffee and chatted about Chiasso and the weather. Then he bade a pleasant farewell and trotted back to the rental car. A little girl in a flowered dress stood barefoot by a tree and waved at him. Antonietta. The eight-year-old daughter of Melita and Martino. Her face one big innocent smile.

Harald drew open the door of the Fiat, his actions followed by the eyes of a stranger, a slouched hat pulled down low as he conversed with a woman in the shadows of a nearby market.

The train to Zürich hurtled northward, skirting Lake Lugano along the east shore. Harald watched a deepening sunset reflecting off the still waters, two fireballs appearing to melt into one another. As his body swayed with the rhythm of the car, he turned from the window and reopened the map, its edges curling inward. A world reduced to two dimensions. The circle-marks trailed from Zürich toward Lugano and on past Chiasso into Italy. Then appeared Como, Milano, and Genova. His fingertip traced and retraced the telltale clues, tracking into southern France along the Mediterranean Sea—Nice, Cannes, ending at Marseille. *Marseille.* He pursed his lips while tapping the city with his pen.

As he folded the map, the train lurched, screeching to a halt at the Lugano station just north of the lake. He heard the pitch of excited voices. Local gendarmerie, visibly armed, boarded the passenger cars and scrutinized the passports and ID of everyone on board. An officer threw open the door of Harald's first class compartment which he shared with the elderly, French speaking couple facing him. The backup corporal fingered a MAT-49 submachine gun at the ready.

"*Pässe, bitte!*" The three handed over their passports.

"What's happening?" Harald shoved the map into his pocket.

"We are seeking the killer of a young woman and her elderly mother in Chiasso. We have reason to believe he is on this train." The captain glanced over his shoulder at the rigid corporal and then back to one of the passports.

"*Meurtre?*" exclaimed the lady.

"Yes, Madame. Two very brutal murders. The suspect is an American, a Harald Johnson. Sorry to speak ill of one of your countrymen, Mr. Astrup," apologized the officer as he returned their documents, "but these women were viciously beaten and tortured. A most gruesome sight. Only their child escaped into the woods."

"How did you get the man's name?" queried Neptune, his pulse racing. He tapped his thigh with a pen.

"An unidentified phone call to the police station. Good day, sir."

"*Sacré bleu*," whispered the old Frenchman, his cadaverous, rutted face twisting at the mouth, the butt of an unlit cigarette balancing on a liver-colored lip. "Such a man on this train."

His lady, fading into a sepulchral pallor, painted lips aghast, shuddered, both staring at the American. Harald felt as if a knife were being sharpened in the darkness.

Upon arriving in Zürich on Saturday, Neptune placed a transatlantic call from the U.S. Consulate to Hamlet at BNDD.

"There is no question that Thunderbird has had your name since Copenhagen," Stafford said to Harald. "They know you are in Europe."

"After Martino LaVecchia's death, they suspected one of us would visit the wife and were lying in wait near the house. Then they murdered Melita and her mother to inflame the people and police. Once given a name, my name, I would be hunted by the police throughout Europe. I'm surprised they did not make an attempt on my life."

"Harald, with you alive and a target of Interpol, our efforts against Thunderbird can be hampered, if not stopped. I'm sure this underworld society will follow up with an accusation by telephone that the American CIA also were responsible for the murder of Melita's husband in Zürich. An in-depth examination by the Swiss National Police could be quite embarrassing."

"I suspect LaVecchia, a bearer of money and narcotics, drove the truck between Zürich and Marseille. Tim, see if you can find out about unusual narcotic activities in the Marseille environs."

"Will do. You had better head back home. We're operating in the dark, and you're exposed. The risk is too great," warned Stafford.

"Right. First, I'll mail the map to you by diplomatic courier, then check out the Trieste Hospital and Braun Funeral Home. Shouldn't take more than a day. Terry believes a lead may show up."

"Still think there is some connection?" asked Stafford.

"Don't you?"

"You're convincing me."

"Any word from Orion?" asked Harald, concerned about his friend.

"Earlier today he arrived in Scuol, a little town at the lower end of the Engadin Valley. He thinks Ursa is near there."

"We should have kept him out of this."

"Maybe. He's got grit, I'll give him that."

35

Scuol, Sunday, November 20, 1971.

Yesterday, Jeffry had registered at the Hotel Engadinerhof. He roused to the ring of an early wake-up call. Following a continental breakfast, he rented skis and rode the first gondola up the cable on the Motta Naluns. Following the night's blizzard, the evergreens below him displayed a new sheath of snow, their pine smell permeating the air.

As the crimson gondola shot above the timberline, Jeffry looked southward across the valley. The sun had climbed above the peaks, the morning torch casting a silvery glow over the land. At the higher elevations his cable car swayed like a cradle in the gentle breeze. At the summit of the lift the car edged into its berth, bumpers nudging and skidding along the welcoming guard rails.

The skiers, dressed in winter garments with a riot of colors, jostled to the rampway and exited on the Motta Naluns. Gaiety and laughter intermingled with the harsh drum of plastic boots on steel ramps. Skis rattled against each other until the thud-thud of each ski hit the snow in readiness for flight.

Jeffry, anxious to head for the slopes, instead trekked toward the restaurant, his boots scrunching in the dry snow. Inside the mountain haven he pulled out a log-hewn chair at a corner table with an advantageous viewpoint, waiting for Ursa, for Helga, his almost forgotten lover, for something not quite tangible.

He sipped hot chocolate, his restless hazel eyes searching through moving throngs of skiers. He studied the implications. *When I spot Helga, then what? Thunderbird won't be far behind. That's what Stafford wants. Helga is just a means to an end. Bait to interdict the flow of heroin.*

A man and a woman, indistinguishable from the other patrons, settled in a booth not far from Jeffry's table. Appearing as winter vacationers enjoying each other's society, they had trailed Jeffry from St. Moritz to Scuol. They were not in a hurry, but they were deadly.

The killers seeking the lady assassin did not know the reasons for their assignment, nor did they care. The triumvirate had given instructions. Helga must be stopped. She would be interrogated and then delaminated. In Zürich.

36

Washington, D.C., Sunday, November 21, 1971.

The jarring ring of the telephone pried Stafford from a hammerlock hold on sleep. His wife hauled the pillow over her head when Timothy slapped the nightstand twice before fingering the receiver.

"Hello?"

"Tim, this is Terry. Sorry to disturb you so early in the morning. The lab techs have hit on something. You'd better hear this."

"What have you got?" The Bureau chief pushed himself up, swinging his feet over the edge of the king-size bed. He rubbed his feet on the carpet to stimulate wakefulness.

"One of the men assigned to the project of assaying the tattoo from LaVecchia's arm worked extra time this weekend. As you know, the typical pigments were confirmed several days ago. One chemical had eluded analysis. They narrowed the possibilities down and found the culprit today," explained Terry.

"Well? If you don't hurry up and tell me, I'll reach through this wire and strangle your damn neck."

"Thorium...Thorium dioxide."

"Thorium? What does that mean for us?"

"Boss, it's radioactive...gives off ionizing radiation."

"Radioactive. Holy shit! That's it! A Geiger counter or x-ray film will verify a real Thunderbird agent."

The Director, now standing and checking the luminous dial of his watch, paused. "How come the tattoo doesn't affect the arm?"

"The radioactivity is mild," Terry replied. "Its long-term effect on skin is some scarring and a remote possibility of cancer. I don't think it concerns these people where megabucks are involved."

"Reach Harald ASAP. We've got to let him know."

Tim looked at his sleeping wife, blew her a kiss, and rushed to pull on his clothes. A lead ingot of uncertainty pressed into his gullet.

The hotel clerk in Zürich notified Terry that Mr. Astrup had already left for the day.

Zürich, Sunday morning, November 21.

Harald awoke with a start. He had registered at the Sheraton Hotel, not far from the Trieste Medical Center. The Braun Funeral Home occupied the same neighborhood, adjacent to the *Friedhof Grünfeld*, the Greenfield Cemetery.

Mottled skies, intermittent drizzle, and fog confirmed the Zürich forecast. Harald strolled eastward along the thoroughfare known as Albisriederstrasse. On his left were Albisrieder Street, its number three tram route, and a loose collection of buildings, including the Braun Funeral Home. On his right, the Grünfeld Cemetery displaying serrated ranks of tombstones. Several freshly dug graves, covered by a fine layer of wet snow, interrupted otherwise flat ground. Broken branches and wet flagstone pathways drew erratic forms on the white canvas.

The mouth of one gravesite lay agape, a mound of freshly turned dirt and sod rolled up nearby, as if expecting soon to blanket the deceased. A marble gravestone, speckled slate in color, hovered slightly askew at one end.

Harald listened to the sounds of an occasional tram, cathedral bells, and his own footfall, with a slight limp while the BNDD agent ambled down the walkway. A nine-millimeter Pietro Beretta was snapped in black leather under his windbreaker. Trees spiking the air dissolved and reappeared in the miasma of swirling mist as he approached the sooted, red-bricked *Krematorium Grünfeld*.

Not everyone was resting on the Sabbath. Uneasiness, a discordant tune, infected him. A thin column of dark smoke curled in a helix from the brick chimney above the cremation chamber and then floated toward the undercover agent. A hearse with the name "Braun" scripted on its side idled in the shadows of an adjacent alley.

The gates of the silent grounds stood half open in a ferruginous grin, beckoning. Harald, appearing as a casual visitor, entered and snaked his way amongst the flowers and fir trees. In spite of the insufferable gloom, curiosity drew him toward the new gravesite, a copse of chestnuts keeping the upright stone marker company. The moist air wrapped around his neck, warning him away as each quaking leaf underfoot accelerated the blood backward toward his heart. He imagined a sinkhole at the ready to swallow him up. *Harald, what the fuck is the matter with you. It's only a graveyard, and you've seen many. Get a grip!*

But a nervous hand fingered the automatic pistol in its holster as he peered into the open grave, a growing, invisible dread cloaking his skin, a primitive chill from the crypt seeping into his chest. Then he saw the marker, the headstone giving form to a terrible, thickening fear. His hand froze on the gun butt. Uncanny. The name on the prophetic rock —

Harald Johnson
1934 - 1971

Suddenly he felt it. Cool and hard. Probably round. Pressing the base of his skull from behind. Cold sweat dripped down the skin of his back and thighs, his muscles knotting up. He knew that if he moved, even a millimeter, the gun barrel would explode. He heard the breathing.

"*Grüezi*, Herr Johnson!" A familiar tongue behind him shattered the reptilian stillness, the words dispatched through a frozen mist, wrenching the sanctity of the dead. "We have been expecting you. Be so kind as to remove your hand slowly...very slowly from inside your jacket and turn around. *Now*, if you please. Two other weapons are aimed at your heart."

Harald, his bones convolving into ice, drew his hand back out and faced the man. A cadaverous, elderly man dressed as a caretaker in overalls. In profile, his countenance appeared to be that of a rodent holding a large pistol. Harald's eyes were playing tricks on him. He had seen that haunting face before — *the old Frenchman on the train from Chiasso.*

"You! But how...?"

"Please join us, Herr Johnson." Two fingers embracing a half-smoked cigarette, his hand beckoned toward the fog-shrouded incineration chamber. "We always take such illustrious visitors as you on a personal tour. You shall find it quite informative." Ridges of skin undulated across the chalky face of Pierre Montaut.

Two surly lieutenants with Lugers aimed at Harald's chest flanked their ghostly leader. Their gun hands waved Harald toward the charnel house, secured inside by armed Thunderbird guards. They entered a large freight elevator that descended underground, into the bowels of the earth. Harsh screeching and scritching echoes. A rumble at the bottom. Steel doors cracking open into a long hallway leading under the street. Metallic footsteps ricocheting against bare walls. They proceeded deeper and deeper into the mildewed catacomb.

Harald looked about, marking his bearing. *This must be a secret passageway northward to the Braun Funeral Home, on the opposite side of Albisriederstrasse.* The rumble of an overhead tram filled the dank space, the sound felt more by his bones than his ears.

On his right a steel door slid open with a harsh whisper following the quadruple thuds of heavy electronic bolts. Frohmut, the shorter and strangest of the servile henchmen, shoved Harald into a massive subterranean chamber.

Harald blinked, his eyes wobbling, straining, adjusting to the bright shimmer of the fluorescent lights. The air, ozone-tinged, tasted almost metallic. A malignant, sulphurous odor prickled his nostrils while an intense, hollow coldness touched the skin. In the center of the illuminated room a modern surgical operating table, stainless steel Mayo stands with instrument trays, and anesthetic gas tanks greeted the reluctant visitor.

Harald glanced up and gasped at the awesome sight suspending before him. Between overhead spotlights hung a strange, intimidating instrument. Heavy ceiling cables connected to pulleys supported the large device, a futuristic apparatus, its core of glass tubing—as much as five feet in length, perhaps two inches in diameter. A separate coil of thin glass tubing and steel framework wrapped around the inner core.

A low-pitched hum with intermittent fine static spun outwards. Thickly insulated electric wires and tubing exited one side and dove into an electronic control panel located at one end of the room. Mists of cold fumes from liquid nitrogen coils percolated down to the floor and crawled along the ground, sliding toward heavy demijohns filled with chemicals.

The skin of Harald's palms pricked with sweat.

"How nice to finally meet you, Herr Johnson. You did not really expect to breach such complex security, did you?"

The dubious greeting came from a heavy-set, bald man whose thick eyeglasses set his sunburned complexion in relief. The spectacles exploded the globes, giving them a startled look. He was stuffing the shirt of a green surgical scrub suit into cotton pants stretched between his ballooned buttocks and a powerful paunch. Harald's scanning gray eyes snapped onto the Thunderbird insignia tattooed on the surgeon's left arm. *SSV. This must be Niemeier. Terry was right!*

A dry tongue clung to the roof of Harald's mouth, his skin glacial one minute, igneous the next.

"We have been waiting for you, Herr Johnson, ever since you left Copenhagen. We knew that Astrup and Johnson in the American Justice Department were one in the same, though the Swiss police did not. You didn't meet our beloved Helga, did you? Pity. Her tactics identified your name and alerted us to the increasing risk of discovery." A malevolent smile rolled over the lips of the surgeon. "A risk soon to be put to the test!"

The master of tyranny turned toward the two muscular subordinates, Thunderbird swains now gowned in scrub suits. "Hermann. Frohmut. Strap him in the chair. We shall find out how much he does know," snarled Niemeier in German, his voice dictatorial, manic.

Satan's acolytes, neck and arm circumferences exceeding their cap sizes, nodded, then pinned Harald in a brutal grasp. They secured both wrists behind his back, shoulder ligaments tearing, their strength making it pointless to struggle as pain boiled more sweat from his every pore. The obedient vultures removed Harald's jacket, gun, and shirt. A racing heart betrayed a stalwart resignation.

"Well, well, well," carped Niemeier, the pitch of his voice rising as he latched on to Harald's arm. "Your tattoo matches mine. So you were thinking of infiltrating our organization? A good likeness, but..."

He picked up a flat electronic instrument, flicked a switch, and shoved it against Harald's tattoo. Silence. Then he pressed it next to his, the metal device now emitting a harsh, staccato noise. Niemeier, his jaw muscles involuntarily working, dug his fingers into Harald's left limb.

"Ahh...you see, my friend. A flaw in your plan. You were not so clever after all." He spun toward Hermann. *"Die Nadel!"* The needle!

Niemeier drove an intravenous line into Harald's restrained right arm, protective moats now breached as the advanced guard of sedating solutes charged through vessels, outflanking cerebral nerve cells. The prisoner struggled to focus his eyes, but the overhead lights and leaning faces dissolved into a blurry luminescence. Initial terror splashed into the soothing oils of detached feelings, mind and body separating from one another. The burden of proximity to the afterlife melted away as the drug continued seeping into his core, time and place reeling beyond the present.

Harald's stone gray eyes trailed his detached body as it was carried to the operating table. Three metal points pierced his skin and pinioned the elevated skull, his head now immobilized.

Harald heard his own voice answer repeated questions, but he had little of substance to divulge. Thunderbird already knew of Jeffry in Scuol. Niemeier merely confirmed that the American Department of Justice was searching, trawling through dangerous waters with Helga as their lure. Harald did not know where Helga was.

The surgeon injected lidocaine into Harald's scalp after parting the hair. A scalpel incised a distance of three centimeters on both sides of the midline, down to the white skull. The liquid dripping down his neck felt warm. Shrill drilling sounds. Two small openings in the brain case. Harald struggled, but the three-point skull clamp attached to the operating table shackled him in an iron vise. Vibrations echoed across his head, the sound waves careening from bone to bone.

Suddenly, the terrible noise ceased, and the attendants engaged the huge instrument hanging patiently from the ceiling. Pulleys spun and the electronic tube hovered closer and closer, sliding to a halt over Harald's head. Once in position, the device emitted a high-pitched hungry whine, powering up as Pierre Montaut fed in electrons from the control panel. Encircling coils glowed with green, flickering iridescence.

Harald squeezed his eyes closed, whispering, "Good-bye, Lauri, my love."

"*Los!*" thundered Niemeier. On with it! His perspiring face kindled into a fiery scarlet.

A brilliant, blue-green light beam knifed through the air, into the burr hole, a plume of hissing smoke exploding in reverse thrust from Harald's dissolving brain. Arms and legs, straining at their bonds, convulsed out of control. Paralysis stormed through the prisoner's limbs, Harald lapsing into a terminal, unconscious state.

"*Strom!*" demanded the surgeon. More electric power! His black pupils widened with bursts of an evil excitement, of surging Prussian adrenalin as overhead lights flickered, the laser device sucking in massive quanta of electrical energy.

The lance of light accelerated in intensity. Harald's body arched backward in one final spasm, his spine rising, bending, curving above the table. Both arms suddenly extended and curled inward, his legs jolted into ironwood rigidity. At the end, all strength gave way as the light in Harald's eyes dulled, the final flare of life fading, then extinguished.

"*Ja*, Herr Johnson. Now you will work for us... *Fertig*." Finished.

The javelin of high-energy photons collapsed with a sibilant swoosh, followed by the screeching, thunderous clap of a dying vacuum. The surgeon, perspiring as his own rush of epinephrin also imploded, turned and beckoned to Hermann and Frohmut.

Above ground, Marlene Sternschen strolled by the Braun Funeral Home but observed nothing unusual—except the front bay window, dark and moody, a large square eye staring at her. The CIA agent had received the communiqué from Terry Caldwell.

A green tram thundered by, the rumble of steel rolling on steel soon fading. Marlene observed the Braun hearse across the street at the red brick crematorium. Harald was nowhere in sight. She walked the dark and lonely avenue between the mortuary and Trieste Hospital. Upon returning, passing by the crematorium, the sudden dimming of street lights startled her. She waited until midnight before reporting back to Hamlet. Harald had vanished.

37

The Motta Naluns, Wednesday, November 24, 1971.

Jeffry suspended respirations, gooseflesh rising up as his heartbeat slammed into hyperdrive. *Helga! God, it must be her…has to be her!*

His eyes narrowed, tightly aimed at the newcomer. Tense fingers nearly fractured the edge of his chair, hands fastened with a grip steeled for a committed purpose. The heart rate quieted into a resolute and solid cadence.

The Alpine Siren, garbed in a skier's haute couture of blue and gold, strode into the restaurant. Fräulein Helga Baumann slapped a multicolored ski cap against her thigh, knocking off crystals of snow. Her black ski boots were half unlatched. Though she was brunette—or perhaps closer to a sandy brown with camouflaged make-up expertly applied, Jeffry's heart instantly recognized the woman. His stomach convulsed into knots, emotions surging this way and that, like a tailless kite whipping about in a strong wind. A tender, faraway longing resurfaced. He had waited nearly four days—or had it been ten years. His eyes were focused on expanding memories from the past, memories now walking closer and closer.

Jeffry clicked on the microphone hidden under his sweater. It transmitted voices to a tape recorder in his fanny pack. And also betrayed his heartbeat.

She stepped in line behind other skiers waiting for food and drink. Jeffry slipped into the queue, watching as she purchased hot wine and a Danish roll. The wonderful smile. The elegant poise. The commanding grace.

Jeffry ordered up a fresh cup of coffee. As she turned to find a seat, he lurched sideways, bumping her arm holding the wine glass, causing the heated spirits to tumble over her tray.

"Oh, how clumsy of me. Uh...*es tut mir leid*," apologized Jeffry. I am sorry.

"Oooh! That's hot!" She brushed her jacket and then looked up. Her cerulean-blue eyes peered at the man, casting a quizzical blink. "I speak English. The wine will wash off with mineral water."

"Please, let me buy another for you."

Jeffry purchased a glass and carried it to her table.

"May I join you?" he asked.

"My pleasure. American, are you not?"

"Yes, my name is Brian Trent. Vacationing from Washington, D.C. And you?"

"Tanya Kessler. *Aus*...uh...from Zürich." She put forth her hand, which he shook after a brief hesitation, the seconds in slow-motion time. "The snow is unusually good for November. So I'm on a short holiday."

"You speak excellent English...nearly without a Swiss accent." He stroked his beard.

"Thank you. Language studies is a favorite pastime for me. I teach English at the Inter-Community School near Zürich, in a little town called Zumikon." Her gentle and soft words, like the French music in the background, plucked at his trembling heartstrings.

"Are you going to ski anymore today?" queried Jeffry, pressing the tension from his temples with stretched finger tips.

A small wrinkle of confusion played over the bridge of Helga's nose. "Sorry. What was your question?"

"Uh, are you hitting the slopes again?"

"Once more down the fall line. Then catch a trail into Scuol. Why don't you join me, Brian?" She smiled and touched his descending hand. "I might even let you buy me dinner tonight."

Jeffry, squeezing his eyelids together, sensed the Helga he once knew—charming, seductive with artistic manipulation.

Jeffry unclosed his eyes, endeavoring to behold the true woman, but seeing only the penumbra. "It's a deal. Let's go. In case we get separated, where are you staying?"

"At the Belvedere, Room 128," she replied, naming the most expensive hotel in Scuol. "We can enjoy a lovely dinner there. And their wine is out of this world. Oh, Brian, I can't wait."

"Neither can I...Tanya."

Jeffry and Helga, Orion and Ursa, departed the mountain café and headed toward their skis parked by the chalet. Ursa snapped closed the buckles of her boots, waved, and pushed off toward a double-black diamond trail, Orion, with intensifying vigor, catapulting over the mountain after her.

Halina had recognized an image of her father immediately. Helga sensed only a burning pain in the pit of her stomach.

At the same time, another couple, two Thunderbird agents, slipped away from their secluded table.

"Doch. Sie ist die Helga!"

"Ja, Zimmer 128."

The Thunderbird Covenant

At dinner that evening, Jeffry watched candlelight flicker shadowy patterns across Helga's mercurial face. The intervening years had added grace to someone already blessed with the accouterments of womanhood. The statuesque figure was garbed in a patterned, low-cut, green sweater above fitted, white after-ski pants. A gold and blue lace scarf, so carefully embroidered that one could count every stitch, encircled her midriff.

Their table, covered with a damask cloth, was a discreet distance from the quartet playing light dinner music. Helga had ordered veal scaloppini and red Burgundy for two. The solicitous waiter was enormously pleased to help in the selection—especially after she complimented him in fluent Romansch.

"Such efficiency. You are obviously a master of the cuisine. And so young and handsome. I shall be sure to remind the manager how valuable you are to this establishment." Her smile, captivating.

The waiter, missing the hint of mockery, agreed, making certain that her table had fresh flowers from the greenhouse. Soon, the four strolling minstrels wandered by to serenade the couple. Jeffry, marveling at her extraordinary command, pondered his next step. His orders were clear and explicit. *If and when you and this Helga connect, inform your CIA contact and our office without delay. We will take over from there.* Consummation of these orders was ambiguous, even onerous.

The musicians completed a beautiful Italian love song, bowed to the couple, and then launched into an enchanting waltz, "The Merry Widow." With passionate conviction, their strings climbed towards the penultimate crescendo, sweeping the patrons into a summit of human felicity—all except for one.

Jeffry saw Helga's face abruptly twist and blanch. She dropped her dinner knife, the silver clattering to her plate, and spun around in her chair. The wine glass shattered on the oakwood floor. "Stop! Stop it! No! Nnn...*Nein!*" she screamed, like a terrified Gaelic banshee.

The startled troubadours lifted their bows, a dead hush hanging in the room, only the sound of a few nervous coughs cutting through the stillness.

Tense minutes passed as Jeffry and a waiter picked up the shards of glass.

"I...I'm truly sorry. I don't know what came over me," she said to herself as much as to Jeffry and the musicians, the lady blinking away the anomaly. Finally, "Do you know the 'Blue Danube Waltz?'"

Gradually the chattering voices and music strings restored a semblance of normalcy. Halina again returned the mask of Helga, who beamed at Jeffry as if nothing had ever happened.

The evening slipped by too swiftly for Jeffry, the dancing exciting, pleasantly distracting. Yet he felt as if he were crawling further and further through a wobbly fourth dimension, wine and anxiety churning through chilled veins. Into *terra incognita*.

Helga was toying with her chocolate mousse when she glanced up and again smiled. Perhaps it was but a gleam. Two aristocratic fingers rested against her chin. She lapsed into uncharacteristic silence. And then—

"Would you like to sleep with me tonight, Brian?"

His gut seized up at the unexpected invitation to sexual encounter. Struggling to parry the assassin's unforeseen insertion behind the lines of combat, Jeffry stammered, "I...uh...I hardly know you. Besides I'm... I'm...married. And I..."

His body and mind screamed out, *Yes, oh God, yes!* The lesson of the Bjørn episode had forewarned him otherwise.

Jeffry felt white-hot inside, iron chains beginning to melt. Memories recaptured. Sensual memories. His pulse quickened. He didn't like being manipulated, forcing his wandering eyes away from full breasts stretching the defining fabric of her sweater. Remote passion rekindling, detonating charges under walls protecting a deeper love.

He sensed Helga watching his eyes, searching. Under camouflage, Halina scanned again and blinked. And blinked once more.

"I was thinking of getting up very early tomorrow," continued Jeffry truthfully, light perspiration painting a sheen on his forehead. "I've made friends with one of the mountain patrols, and he has promised to allow me some early morning skiing before the public arrives." Her stillness was unnerving. "Snow is predicted for tonight, and I'm very anxious to schuss in fresh powder."

With a gesture of quiet impatience, Helga placed her hand on his thigh and murmured, "Oh, Brian. I won't keep you up late. At least come to my room for some brandy. I need someone to talk to. I've been so terribly bored." Behind the tablecloth the provocative hand of Halina nestled against his leg, pushing reason from Jeffry's consciousness.

"Let me take the check. Brandy sounds good." Orion accepted the dangerous compromise. The art of deception. The theater. The final sophistry. He was no longer sure who was the hunter, and who, the hunted.

From the table next to theirs another man and woman, pretending to be engrossed in themselves and laughing gaily, donned their jackets and walked outside. They chatted in Swiss-German slipping into Italian. A light snowfall had already begun.

Ursa enlaced her arm in his, leaning slightly against her former lover. The perfume dulled his forebrain, a familiar and seductive scent caressing deeper yearnings.

At her room, Helga passed Jeffry the key. He unlatched the door to her well-appointed suite, soft lights illuminating Victorian furniture and Persian rugs inside. A floral arrangement, Birds of Paradise and cattails, contrasted on a coffee table. Flames in the fireplace made the room especially companionable. Helga blew a kiss his way and then excused herself, walking toward the bed chamber. The brass key tumbled to the carpet. He fetched it back, then laid her latchkey on the end table.

"Pour yourself a bit of brandy, love. I'll return in a few minutes." She waved imperial fingers toward a crystal decanter. Jeffry drew in a deep breath and then closed his eyes after catching a glimpse of the turned-down feather bed, the chamber door open halfway.

He nudged the metal against his chest. Earlier he had checked the body mike, the electronics transmitting faithfully to the recording unit in his room. The idea of monitoring their conversation began to bother him. What if her fingers traveled too far?

He inhaled a whiff of the brandy and then poured the spirits into two snifters, setting Helga's glass next to the key. Jeffry turned to the window and stared out at the snow swept mountains. Sanity screamed out, *Run...run!* The snowfall thickened, distant cottage lights now barely seen. Memories of Holyoke, the Raggedy Ann and Andy on her birthday, of...

"Jeffry!" A supernatural shriek. "*Jeffry!*"

Electrified, gasping, he whirled around. The real Helga. Only this time she was not smiling, her unruffled brunette hair now an intense cascading blonde. She sat in a silk brocaded chair, holding a silenced Ruger Blackhawk, the .44 Magnum targeting his chest, fine lines radiating from eyes of a female diamond-back.

38

"Welcome to Scuol, Jeffry. It's been a long time," Helga screeched between clenched teeth. She could not believe what she saw. Did God or Satan send him?

Jeffry dropped his goblet, the glass smashing on polished hardwood, and tripped backward toward the frosted window.

"Sit down, Jeffry. Sss...sit down and tell me what's going on," exploded Helga, her face etched in anger, a wrath laced with fear. "My God, what's happening? Why are you here? They even got to you?"

"How...Jesus! How did you recognize me, Helga?" He perched on the edge of the couch but kept his hands in full view.

"I didn't at first. You seemed vaguely familiar. Yet years later, no ponytail, and with a beard...yes...yes, you could have fooled even me. Your face is different, your voice changed, deeper. Then I watched your eyes." She shuddered to herself. "That's what gave you away, Jeffry," she replied as her own fire-blues narrowed, tearing into the perilous revelation.

"My eyes?"

"Yes, the fine ss...scar in your left eyelid. I knew only one other man who had a similar mark. Professor Jeffry Landon, an English scholar at Holyoke College." She hesitated, distilling the impact of her discovery. "Tell me, Jeffry, are you truly married?"

"No," sighed Jeffry, his eyes focused on her weapon, his lips barely moving. "I...well, I never found the right woman. Not after you, Helga."

"Who were the couple sitting next to us tonight?" The timbre of her voice intensified.

"Couple? I didn't notice. What do you mean?"

"They were watching us at dinner. And at the restaurant on the mountain. Who are they?" she blazed.

Her gun hand quivered, the past and present on a dangerous collision course once more.

"Helga, I don't know them. You're imagining things. Dammit, do you have to point that weapon at me?"

"Who sent you?" she screamed. "Why are you here? Do you work for them, for Jørgen? Tell me now!" *Please, Jeffry, don't do this to me.*

"Good God, Helga, calm down. I don't work for your Jørgen Busche. I operate undercover for the United States Government. That couple may belong to Thunderbird. If so, they indeed want you dead. I may be the only one who can help you. Please, please listen to what I have to say."

Helga lowered her gun hand, like a cunning and vicious animal now trapped, choosing the lesser danger. She knew Jeffry was right, Jeffry, the only man—the only man in her world—that she ever truly once loved and trusted.

"What do you *really* want of me, Jeffry? I'm so tired of hiding. Is it sex, money, assassination? Surely not love." *I cannot be worth that.*

Anxiety and desperation were taking command as the new reality set in. Somewhere deep inside the cynical woman, moral law demanded retribution, the death of one in the other world—of the invisible Halina, of the child reborn into Helga herself. Or neither would ever be free.

Then, with a sigh of near-defeat she asked, "And what do you mean, Thunderbird?"

Jeffry, telling her all he knew in hopes she would fill in the gaps, begged her to cooperate with BNDD and seek protection. She attempted to maintain her composure, yet each revelation cracked it looser. She watched as he jotted notes down on a small wire-bound booklet.

"But don't you see, I don't even know Busche except to receive instructions." Helga, becoming more desperate, endeavored to learn the truth—if there were a truth—about her own invisible source control. "He arranged the payments, but I don't know who or what his organization is."

"Have you ever noted a strange tattoo that looks like a bird with its wings spread?" Jeffry was staring at the Birds of Paradise.

"Yes, yes. Jørgen has one on his left arm." She nodded her head and pointed to a similar unblemished area on her own raised limb.

"Helga, how did you meet this Jørgen Busche?"

"I was introduced to him by one of my former employers in Germany, a Herr Ludwig Dietz. Dietz owns a number of funeral homes around the world. The main office is in Berlin."

"Do Busche and Dietz work together?"

"I never thought so, but now I'm not so sure." Her tension softened.

"Did Ludwig Dietz ever have a tattoo like Busche's?"

"I never saw Dietz' upper arm."

"In which cities did he have establishments? And why?"

Helga described Dietz' reputation for cutting red tape to deliver dead relatives in foreign lands across international borders. She listed the cities for him.

Jeffry sat on the couch and surveyed his notes. "I see you have Zürich as one of his centers. Would I find Dietz in the phone book?"

"No. His connection in Zürich is with the Braun Funeral Home. When I worked for him, there was much correspondence with Zürich. Also with a nearby Swiss company in Winterthur called Langerstein."

"Langerstein?"

"Yes. I think he was part owner."

"That is our first definite connection. A Jørgen Busche signed the check made out to you. The account in a Winterthur bank was under the company name, Langerstein AG."

"Yes, I know." She paused and then her eyes snapped open as tenuous recognition flooded her face. "That means that it is Dietz himself that may be running things. Busche was his intermediary with me and others. The head of your Thunderbird may be Dietz. And he knows I have an aunt in St. Moritz. They must have followed you from there. Oh, Jeffry, none of this makes sense to me."

"What is his connection with the narcotic problem? Why did they have you kill Bjørn? And why did they need to know who Neptune was?"

Helga was silent, averting her face, suppressing Copenhagen, two sides to her personality in conflict, violence and compassion athwart. She had been programmed—beginning in 1943, the horrors of Auschwitz hiding behind synapses fortified by inhibitory recruitments secured in Spiegelgrund, in Vienna. Halina's Armageddon had come and gone, but Helga was not to know. She would neither recall nor recognize her good doctor Niemeier, healer of "the unfit and unwell" at Spiegelgrund.

She trembled as remorse and anger collided, the gun dropping to the piled carpet. Jeffry went to her and pulled her close to him, holding her shaking body close against his own, soothing a child's inner terror. "I don't know, Jeffry. God help me, I truly don't know."

Synaptic control wavered as past recollection fought to surface, vengeance crying out. But unconscious reflections of electric shocks to her own body twenty-eight years ago resealed escape. The child, Halina, now terribly alone on the steppes of purgatory, knew what evil she had done to her mother and father, the horrendous guilt concealed deep inside a complex cerebral abyss. Even the hideous Nazi guard, naked except for his jackboots, had been part of the diabolical Pavlovian experiment to establish rule, to enslave Halina under Prussian phallic sovereignty.

Helga wept, not understanding that her cries were muffled screams for forgotten parents crucified under the SS Death's Head at Birkenau, and for little Halina bent to Herr Doktor's will at Spiegelgrund.

Jeffry pulled her to the sofa and poured some more brandy, her hand, moving like a robot, accepting the drink. Soon Helga's tremors ceased and, drying her eyes with Jeffry's handkerchief, she edged back into the reconstruction of a history as she knew it.

"Dietz was an expert at transporting live bodies in caskets through the iron curtain. Why not heroin also?" she envisioned, trying to re-create her part of the enigma.

"The customs officers have searched caskets, even to the extent of reopening autopsied bodies. Nothing."

"I don't know. Dietz is a very clever man. If anyone could do it, he could."

She struggled in thought for a moment while retrieving her silenced Blackhawk and placing it on the mantel, Jeffry tracking every motion.

"Jeffry, there may be a connection with your Secretary of State, Lance Masters."

"Masters?" Jeffry shot a quizzical glance at Helga.

She fetched a briefcase from a wall safe and pulled out a tape cassette, handing it to Jeffry. She felt almost glad of his reappearance, of the closeness, thinking to herself, *Jeffry, is this really you.*

Helga explained, "I...I overheard Masters make this phone call before he was promoted. An overseas call to Busche. The code name of your Secretary of State was John Tempest. You keep this. It may come in useful."

She passed Jeffry the tape, briefly holding his hand in tender confusion.

"How do you know this, Helga?"

She hesitated and then, in a tight voice, "Because it was I who assassinated Edward Piccollo."

"Oh my God."

Both lapsed into stillness at the unintended and staggering revelation. The puzzle expanded and contracted at the same time, like the celestial universe, the cosmic black hole sucking Helga and Jeffry together, inward ever faster, plunging them into a void without boundaries, human logic becoming frayed.

The man and the woman, their moist eyes meeting in unspoken communication, once tenderly in love many years ago, gazed in fear at one another, their hands clasped together, each wondering how they could have altered the course of their now distant love, their once shared life.

She tried to stabilize the conversation and take rein of her senses. "Whatever happened to your brother, to Erik?" A fleeting smile passed on softening lips. "I remember how much fun the three of us had when we went to the football game at your alma mater."

"Practicing neurosurgery in Washington. Still the same Erik. Always working too hard."

But she did not hear him. Jeffry, suspending pursuit of the enigma, peered curiously at her. "Helga, you look like you've seen a ghost."

She slurred her words, her speech thickening, stuttering, the alcohol and disturbed subconscious strata disconnecting rational thought. The couple faced each other, Jeffry again squeezing her hands.

Helga, pale with panic, blinked. She stared through Jeffry, her crippled eyes trying to bat away the tears, the conflicting events, the raw strife tearing at her inside, the festering wounds. But the ice-hockey scar in his left eyelid sliced away at reason, the threads of the umbilical cord tying her to the present unraveling. The rope she had climbed in Holyoke slipped away, the kaleidoscopic plummet earthward pulling her past the gray walls of Auschwitz, her vertigo accelerating.

"J…Jef…Jeffry, what's happening to me?" she choked. "Your left eye, Jeffry. What are you doing to me? Sss…Stop! Oh, God in Heaven, help me!"

An incinerated beetle, chitinous, black wings still thrashing, flashed through her field of vision, her left hand lashing out into thin air. The scarab, the stained soul of little Hali, was burning in a private, agonizing hell, searing flames erupting within her brain, the terrifying headaches blinding. "The Merry Widow Waltz," its ebony disc spinning out of control, screamed from long ago. Her brain wide awake, yet dreaming.

"Go away! Ge…get out!" she begged.

Jeffry flinched and said, "Helga, I'm not here to hurt you. Please calm down."

Leather jackboots snapped their heels together, rifle shots in subterranean caverns. Shock therapy in Spiegelgrund. *Not again*, she begged an unseen force.

"*Halt! Bitte, nicht mmm…mehr!*" Stop! Please, no more! Her voice was changing, stuttering, devolving into that of a German child.

Jeffry backed away, out of his element. Helga's nightmares years ago in Holyoke. He could do little then, and he could do nothing now.

She opened her clenched eyelids, rivulets of scorching tears tumbling down terrified cheeks. She recognized Jeffry's face only as a blur, a blurred image from the past. The gray walls were cracking. A four-year-old child, tenuously spliced to the present, lay maimed on the other side. Helga struggled to breathe as her mind traveled beyond Jeffry, beyond the black, barbed-wire fences. Red, red rain. Green rivers in a deluge. They blanketed Jeffry's distorted image while the stench of '43 flooded her nostrils.

Stop the red! her brain screamed. "Stop the rrr...red! Ss...sst...stop it!" She pounded imaginary buttons, flashing emerald and ruby crystals on the coffee table.

"What red, Helga? Where?" pleaded Jeffry, grabbing her thrashing hand, his voice desperate.

A relentless human magnet from the remote past pulled her toward him again, toward his eyes, his sharp, deep set, hazel eyes. An ancestor residing therein, time out of mind. Portraits of the past. Beyond Holyoke. Beyond Mainz. Vienna...and something even beyond that. A mirror...

The eye. *Papa, your eye!* "Your lef...left eye! I...I didn't mean it! The ba...bad men tricked mmm...me!

"*Matka Boska!*" Halina screamed in Polish. And screamed again. Then a great wracking wail as human sanity, at the brink of an emotional crevasse, crumbled, dropping away in enormous chunks.

Jeffry, witnessing a visceral fracture, slapped Helga's face with such forcefulness her head jerked rightward. And a wire snapped from the microphone. The shrieking suddenly ceased as the gates of hell slammed together, tectonic plates shifting back again, isolating the primal storm with a terrible rattle in her head, the smells, sights, and sounds of the killing ground rapidly slipping away, only the sting to her flushed cheek remaining.

The waltz faded, the sound of the swastika slipping back behind the amygdala of her brain.

The woman reborn in Auschwitz looked up at Jeffry. Far, far beyond his face. Pleading. "I'm so tired. Please let me sleep, Jeffry. Please...no more questions...need to sleep..." *Unbrake my heart, my darling Jeffry.*

Jeffry lovingly, gently carried Helga's nearly catatonic body toward the waiting feather bed, her words slipping away.

Suddenly, she strained him to her bosom with one convulsive grasp, crying, "Jeffry, I am so scared. Can you still love me? After the insanely horrible things I did to you? I need you back. Please...please forgive me. Please tt...take me back." It was as if she were speaking to someone else. "I don't know how to find God's ff...forgiveness. How to wa...wash the stain away. You are my only hope. Jeffry, help me. *Wo ist mm...meinen Pferdeschwanz?*" Where is my ponytail?

A sudden current of intense feeling flowed between them, her lungs delivering a quivering gasp as he laid her on the quilt. He watched her breathing, Helga now collapsing into suspended sleep, mumbling, German sliding into Polish. He kissed her cheek, shuddered, and left her room, a soft click as he closed and locked the door behind him. Confusion and moisture filled his eyes. He left the key to her chamber behind on the bedroom dresser, reflected in the looking glass.

39

As Jeffry walked down the hallway toward his room, the full meaning of her cryptic disclosures kept spearing him with delayed jolts, shocks loosening reason in his stunned mind. He had not been privileged to know Helga's past, the volatile chemistry of her driving compulsion to right a wrong inflicted beyond the time of both. Yet he sensed that he stood on the brink of a revelation, unable to visualize the form of it.

Jeffry proceeded to his room and pulled the broken mike from his chest. He phoned Hamlet in Washington, D.C. and played his recorded conversation with Helga. Then the tape of Lance Masters.

"Wow, a big fish. Hot damn, Hoss. We may be onto something solid now," exclaimed Terry. "Call me tomorrow night." He hesitated. "We have lost contact with your close friend, Neptune. We may need you to help us out."

"He's very resourceful. I'm confident he will resurface. What about Ursa?"

"I know you have been hurt, Orion. Sorry for putting you through this. You've done all you can. But stay away from her or you'll be dead too. She can take care of herself."

"But I promised her protection. And you could tell she was close to losing her grip."

"Let it rest, Hoss. Should she come to one of our consulates or embassies, we'll have to arrest her. The FBI will want her for the assassination of Ed Piccollo. Go skiing tomorrow and relax. Keep a low profile. Call me tomorrow night. Your job is finished, Hoss. The CIA will take over."

Jeffry hung up and attempted to marshal his thoughts, his objective changing. Now he had two commanders—BNDD and his heart. He didn't like leaving Helga alone. It was an hour past midnight. He had to get up very early to meet the ski patrol.

Sleep overtook Jeffry as his Helga, his resurrected love, paced back and forth in his mind. He was not yet fully conscious of the depth of his feelings, the need to see her again frightening, furious, and enduring.

Thursday, November 25.

The alarm clock sang, then clattered at six. Jeffry peeked out the window, the sky devastatingly clear. He could detect faint streaks of morning sunlight. Shadows still filled the southern ski slope of the Engadin Valley, holding on until the fireball crawled above the craggy peaks.

Jeffry stretched his arms, showered, and donned his ski suit. A half hour later, thunderclaps of exploding howitzer shells echoed up and down the valley as they dislodged loose snow in avalanche-prone slopes. The cannons quieted. A call to Helga's hotel room. No answer. He thought she must still be sleeping.

Jeffry skipped breakfast, grabbed his skis, and headed for the gondola swinging from its cables. He waited for one of the ski patrols.

"Giovanni. Giovanni Molinari," hollered Jeffry. "I'm over here."

He had met Molinari at the Romansch restaurant on the Motta Naluns. This ski patroller had invited Jeffry to schuss the early morning deep powder. They both boarded the gondola in Scuol and ascended toward the top.

"What is that box hanging from your neck, Giovanni?" Jeffry nodded toward the instrument.

"A radio transmitter. Patrols carry it in case trouble arises. Then their comrades can locate the disabled man or woman. It's especially useful during avalanche control."

"Have you ever been caught in one, in a snow avalanche, I mean?"

"Thankfully, no. Survival is unlikely. If you're not crushed to death by the force of the snow, timber, and rocks, you will most likely die of suffocation."

"Isn't there some air under the snow?"

"Yes. Some. But the snow packs around you so tight that you cannot even move your diaphragm to breath. But no need to worry today. It's a fine morning. And we're almost at the end of this lift run."

As the gondola docked, Molinari signaled, "If you are going to the top, we'll separate here. The Motta Naluns is my patrol area. Have a good run. *Ciao*." Jeffry vanished among the trees as the patroller picked up his radio.

After exiting the gondola and snapping into his skis, Jeffry slid downward and laterally toward the nearby ski lift high up on the Alpine mountain. A series of lifts brought Jeffry up another massif, the pinnacle of the Piz Champatsch. At the very top of the world, he paused to gaze at three snow-covered countries.

"Switzerland, Austria, and Italy. I'll never forget this view as long as I live." He took a deep breath and then side-slipped into an accelerating descent back towards Scuol.

The rays of the sun snared the silhouette of Jeffry against lofty, white slopes. Only a soft ripple sounded when ski hit snow, the whisper louder as Jeffry executed a quick downhill jump-turn toward a clump of trees, white crystals spraying away from his feet. Slight movement in the forest caught his eye. He twisted back again, ski edges knifing with precision.

He tried to push the world's problems from his mind. Having partially severed the Gordian knot, Jeffry felt, however, a bittersweet success, a sense of disquieting pride. Ursa had been trapped, instructions given.

Yet something was terribly wrong. It gnawed at him. He desperately needed to see, to hold Helga again. He could not help it, an invisible chain tying him fast. He would go to her as soon as he reached the valley floor. Nothing—not the Bureau, the CIA, the Mafia, or the elusive Thunderbird—would stop his clasping the woman he hopelessly loved. Common sense told him he was crazy, absolutely insane to return. But his heart pleaded otherwise, a passionate grip and obsessed determination choking the ski poles. Chance had rekindled protected embers. Jeffry was still thunderously in love.

The slope steepened. Jeffry swerved, leaning into the mountain, hugging the Motta Naluns. Another twist of his body avoided a beckoning ledge of rock. The air, thin and cold.

A distant cannon fired, the report rocketing through the valley.

Toward the north ridge, the retort of a muffled explosion. Silence. Then the eerie rumbling. A mountain of snow moving down from above. The main thrust of the ensuing avalanche tore into the direction of his eastward path, the west cut off by the top of a steep escarpment. Jeffry suddenly was skiing the knife-edge of terror. Stone, ice, and snow careened downward, about to ensnare the one man who could have saved Helga.

40

Helga found herself awakened by the rolling thunder of an avalanche. She stirred, pushed herself up off the bed sheets, and shook the cobwebs from her head. Her hand, squeezing the receiver, snatched up the telephone and dialed St. Moritz.

"Aunt Anna, I was so afraid you wouldn't be at home. It is time. Please, do as we planned." Her voice, tired yet taut, projected an invisible burden, its edges worn away by dueling contenders leaving only scorched earth in its wake.

"I was afraid this would happen sooner than we thought. Dear Helga, of course I'll help."

"There's something else, Auntie. I'm hopelessly in love again. And I don't know what to do about that. His name is Jeffry. Oh, God, I need him back." She wept, unable to subdue her feelings, a child consuming the core within. "I met him at Holyoke College, where we were lovers, yet I knew him long before that—before a time I can't remember. That is what fr…frightens me."

Helga, swept by disparate emotions, cried again, trusting in her aged Aunt, telling her about the past and renewed longing for Jeffry. The protective jacket of ice about her heart started to thaw, a raw circle in her chest now burning, yet its torment a strange and singular sweetness.

"My Helga, if your Jeffry feels the same, perhaps there is hope and..."

"Please pr...pray for me, Aunt Anna."

"I shall beg God's love and forgiveness for you. We must talk more when we meet, Helga. I'm on my way." Anna clicked off the line.

Helga replaced the receiver and stared out the still-frosted window, the spiritual gravity of her violet-blues deepening, twin obsidian points tracking flakes of falling snow. Suddenly, her memories of Jeffry and Erik, her struggle to discard the unrelenting past were snapped away by a rap on the door.

She knew it was time, her brain pounding. *It's begun. They're here...I must do it. I've got to be free.*

Rap...rap...rap.

"Yes, who's there?" Her voice was tight, lips barely moving.

"The maid and busboy. Sorry for the disturbance, Fräulein. We're here to clean your room and change your bed."

"Just a moment. Let me put a gown on."

Helga covered herself with a terry-cloth bathrobe and thrust the Blackhawk, still muted with a silencer, into the deep pocket. Safety off. She unlatched the hall door.

"Please, tidy up the front parlor first. I'll be changing in the bedroom."

She recognized the faces of the two, now dressed in hotel uniforms. The maid entered the suite, the man behind. Helga's sharp eyes trailed as he pushed a canvas, four-wheeled handcart stuffed with a mound of dirty linen. The maid, chattering away, piled fresh sheets and towels on the couch.

"Leonardo and I will be only a minute," apologized the maid, her smile brittle, blond hair laced into a tight plait.

Helga turned back toward the bathroom, slipped in, and closed the door on yesteryear, preparing for a fire storm in the not-too-distant future. The centurion stiffened into a razor-sharp barb of concentration, a bow about to be strung, staring into the looking glass, into an invisible past twisting into prologue.

Part IV

A Place in Zürich

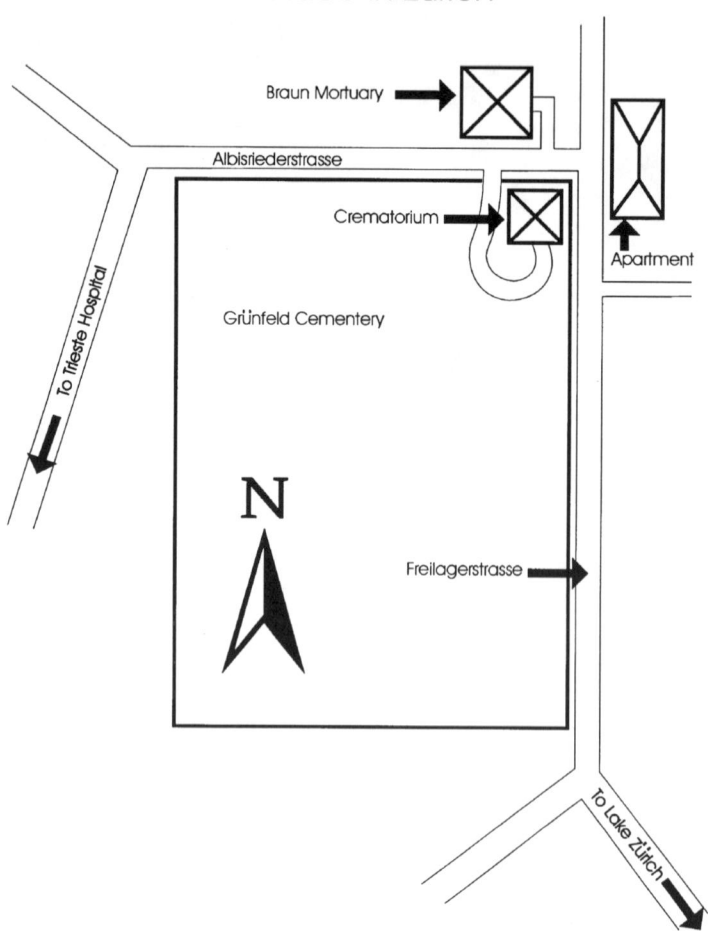

Braun Mortuary

Albisriederstrasse

Crematorium

Apartment

To Trieste Hospital

Grünfeld Cementery

N

Freilagerstrasse

To Lake Zürich

41

Washington, Friday, November 26, 1971.

Tim Stafford slammed a top-secret file against the glass-covered conference table, the report like a rifle-crack, a dozen BNDD, FBI, and CIA personnel looking on. Loose neckties, snapping suspenders, and grim countenances showed thickening frustration. Shifting, semi-erudite frowns. Clicking cigarette lighters. Black coffee. Red eyes.

"Damnation," exploded the BNDD Director. "No word from Harald, and Jeffry is gone. Buried in an avalanche. What the hell is going on?

"LaVecchia's family killed and we're accused of making the hits. Now word comes in that a Tanya Kessler, our Helga, is shot in her hotel room. And some Italian guy found dead in a clothes hamper." The dark eyes of Stafford strafed the gathering and then aimed at Caldwell. "Terry, I want an explanation," his bass voice boomed, fingers drumming on the table top.

Terry heaved a sigh. "Boss, you know as much as I do. From a legal standpoint, we can't search the Braun Funeral Home in Zürich, and it's too secure for covert insertions. Marlene and Joseph are doing the best they can. We're investigating possible links between Dietz and other cities...especially New York and San Francisco.

"Customs is monitoring the entry of coffins and dead bodies from overseas. But they need a little more to go on. They x-ray every corpse. Nothing. The dogs smell zip. How can one stash that much heroin inside a torso that's never been cut or autopsied? If Dietz is involved, the funeral and coffin business is just a cover. And the CIA in Germany have been unable to nail down this Dietz guy."

Terry paced the floor, bounced his eyes off the Director again, and asserted, "We have alerted the French authorities. They are investigating the possibility that an opium-to-heroin processing plant exists in Marseille. So far, they have failed to produce anything substantial...only an underground rumor of a surge in Turkish opium flooding the back alleys."

"More than a rumor," Stafford chipped in. "A French gun boat just intercepted an impressive shipment of Turkish powder in the Gulf of Lyon."

He cruised over to a blown-up photo clipped to an easel. "Take a gander at the map Harald mailed from Zürich and the world map. Marseille...Zürich...New York. But why Zürich?" Tim's pointer slapped the enlarged snapshot as if trying to slice the problem into manageable pieces.

Terry stood and fired a suggestion. "Tim, let's assume that Marseille employs a new technique to concentrate Turkish opium. They still need concealment and transportation over the ocean, which perhaps is the reason for a Zürich station.

"Movement across French, Italian, and Swiss boundaries to and from Zürich would be no problem. Too many sites facilitating unseen passage. Even at their customs stations, how often have you seen even the most diligent officer there look for secret compartments or use dogs to sniff out narcotics? Almost never. Yet entry of this magnitude into the USA? The usual trafficking methods would have turned up something by now. The key is in Zürich."

"Thunderbird's attempts to arrest surveillance suggest that we're a gnat's eyelash from the target," allowed Stafford. "They know we're getting close, but close to what?"

Terry opened his mouth to speak. "Tim, let's…"

"Mr. Stafford, please, it's urgent!" Martha, breathless and agitated, her face chalk white, stormed into the conference chamber.

"Martha, what's going on? This meeting is for our ears only."

"I'm sorry, sir. Mr. Burns, the Chief Customs Officer in New York City, is on the phone. He said it is most imperative. It's about Harald…Mr. Johnson." She caught her breath while wringing her hands. "The blinking line, sir."

"I'll take it in here. Thank you, Martha. I'll call if I need you."

He clicked on the speaker phone, everyone leaning forward in rapt attention.

"Stafford here with my team. We're all listening."

"You must come to New York at once. Yes, yes…at once. One of our customs men, Marvin Cheverly, was inspecting a coffin that just arrived by jet from Zürich. The dead American is supposed to be a Mr. Gerald Baskin, according to the passport. From Trenton, New Jersey. Marvin first recognized a tattoo on the cadaver's left arm and then looked at his face. He says, well, he says it isn't Baskin."

"Well, who the hell is it?" Stafford was losing patience.

"The corpse is one of your agents, sir. One of your agents, yes, yes, indeed. It's your Harald Johnson!"

"Good God!" the Director gasped. "We'll fly out within the hour."

"Our team will be waiting. Indeed, we will." They could hear Burns fussily tap, tap, tapping his knuckles with a letter opener before clicking off the line, as if his regimented mind were poorly coping with an altered routine at New York Customs.

Everyone in Washington sat in stunned silence, all eyes riveted on the speaker phone.

Caldwell cracked the tension. "Tim, shall I tell his wife, Lauri?"

"Not yet. Wait until I return from New York," replied the Director, his attention on blurred faces mirrored in the glass-topped table. Nothing would add up. There were encircling coils of enigma, one defocusing as another took its place, a three-dimensional chess game.

Stafford buzzed Martha and over the intercom said, "Please get Doctor Erik Landon on the phone for me."

Despondent, Erik stared out the office window. Word had arrived late this morning that Jeffry had been killed in a skiing accident. He did not understand. *No word from my brother, and suddenly Agent Caldwell of the Justice Department phones. Tells me Jeffry had been vacationing in Switzerland and now is dead! An avalanche!*

Erik was preparing to fly to Zürich where the body lay and make the identification at the canton morgue and arrange transport home. First, he needed to call Minnesota and tell their mother the horrible news. But he felt immobilized, stuck on an island, time flowing past like a river in flood as he attempted to shift the focus of his well-planned life.

The intercom buzzed.

"Doctor Landon?"

"Yes?"

"There is a Director Stafford on the phone. From the Justice Department. The gentleman would like to talk to you...on line two."

"Thank you, Jennifer. Hello, this is Doctor Landon."

"Doctor, Tim Stafford here. Bureau of Narcotics. You might recall our last visit together...after Ed Piccollo's death."

"Yes sir. What can I do for you?"

"We have a rather urgent problem. It concerns your brother in a way. And maybe the Piccollo case also. Could you meet with us at the New York City morgue late this afternoon?"

"Is Jeffry there already?"

"No. I'm not at liberty to explain over the phone."

"I was leaving to fly to Zürich and get Jeffry, but I can re-arrange that. I'll be in New York no later than three this afternoon."

"Much appreciated. We'll await you at the chief coroner's office in Manhattan."

For a minute Erik listened to the dial tone. Mystified, he wondered what Jeffry really had to do with Justice. Had he been in some trouble? Erik asked his secretary to cancel the Zürich flight for now and jot down the address of the New York City Central Morgue. After arranging for patient coverage, he caught the Eastern shuttle.

Office of the Chief Medical Examiner, Manhattan.

Erik's taxi barreled along the East River and stopped in front of a dated edifice, part of the complex of buildings at the New York University Medical Center.

"Doctor Landon, meet Doctor Randolph Crowley, Chief of Pathology and Forensic Medicine here. On your left, Officer Theodore Burns of U.S. Customs, and his associate, Marvin Cheverly. And you might recall Terry Caldwell, one of our Special Agents whom you met last spring, after Ed Piccollo's assassination." Stafford introduced Erik to the group, following which Burns hastily escaped and left Cheverly to represent their office.

Stafford cleared his throat. "The reason for your presence goes far beyond an unfortunate skiing accident. In fact, it was no chance event. We have reason to believe that Jeffry was deliberately killed." Stafford paused. Erik felt his jaw go slack.

Terry, sensing Erik's pain and discomfiture, rushed to suggest, "Tim, maybe we should…"

But the Director continued as if locked into a script. "The same avalanche also buried a ski patrol. You see, the treacherous snow-slide followed firing of a cannon in the Alps above the Swiss village of Scuol. Jeffry was working with us as a Special Agent *pro-tem* on a mission of great importance to the Federal Government. The night before he died, your brother contacted us and reported that he had successfully, and rather brilliantly, I might add, achieved our initial objective.

"Caldwell here ordered him to stand fast until the next day and then phone Washington for further instructions. In the meantime, the CIA headed for Scuol, arriving too late." Stafford glanced at Terry, then back to Erik. "During that interim, your brother arranged for some early morning deep powder skiing. He had obtained permission from a ski patrol by the name of Giovanni Molinari." A moment of silence followed.

"And?" Erik leaned forward.

"No such person worked there."

"*Murdered!* I can't believe it. Jeffry, the English Instructor…an agent?" Erik shook his head in disbelief. "And what has all this to do with me now?"

"The United States Army once gave you top secret clearance during your laser research at Walter Reed and at Redstone," fired Stafford. "I'm therefore going to swear you to secrecy and detail the events. You are positioned to provide immense assistance."

"Of course," Erik acknowledged, still shaken, "but I can't imagine how."

"First, we would like you to join us and inspect another dead body in the morgue. We would value your professional opinion as a neurosurgeon. Be forewarned. In spite of your surgical experience, this may be a bit of a shock to you. For reasons of security, we've sealed off the morgue to other personnel this afternoon."

"I see. Well, lead on."

After a brief swearing-in ceremony, Doctor Crowley led the way to the elevator. En route they filed by several men in dark suits, armed BNDD agents. The group passed a door labeled, "Evidence Room," a repository of testimony to morbid causes of death in years past.

In the cold room, harsh fluorescent strips painted a white glow across worn linoleum. The normally busy chamber had an eerie stillness about it, on pans, a half dozen cadavers lying in various stages of disrepair. In the light their skin glowed a ghastly hue. On one wall sat a bank of gray file cabinets, white labels slotted in front. The dispassionate pathologist pulled out a manila envelope, crossed to the center of the morgue where a bank of refrigerated crypts stood, and rolled out a stainless-steel drawer upon which lay another sheeted corpse. Stafford and the others looked on with grim countenances, strangers intruding on the smell of formaldehyde.

Erik felt as if Stafford, in part, was testing his stamina and resolve for another purpose.

Long rubber gloves grabbed the cloth cover, drawing the sheet down. Erik inhaled through clenched teeth, blood draining from his face as the medical examiner stepped back.

"Harald...Harald! How on earth?" Erik shook his head, trying to erase the image. He cringed at the sight, wanting to rouse his friend and shout, *Run, Harald! Run from this house of death before the rubber-aprons get you.* Erik held his breath. *Hurry, Harald!* But his friend didn't move as Erik's eyes welled up, a strange tattoo blurring on Harald's arm.

His head spinning at the shock, Erik forced myself to sit on a nearby stool, his hands holding his head. "Harald, Jeffry and I were the closest of buddies, even schoolmates at one time. Well, you knew that. My God, what happened, Mr. Stafford? Who did this?"

"Doctor Crowley has provided us with a conference room upstairs. Come and I'll relate a remarkable history about heroin, a tattoo, and a singular espionage agent called Helga Baumann, Ed Piccollo's assassin. We need all the assistance we can get. But first..."

Erik thought the BNDD were playing tricks on him. "You mean Helga, my brother's former girlfriend? Assassin?"

Tim ignored the query. "...but first, please examine the head of the deceased. Doctor Crowley has noted an incision. In your capacity as a brain surgeon, can you render an opinion?"

Erik sighed and wiped his eyes. Crowley handed him a pair of thick rubber gloves. Ribbons of nausea ripped through Erik's gut upon lifting up the head of his dead playmate of years past, objectivity slipping further away.

"It...uh...must have been made by a knife. Healed solid...at least the edges are well approximated. Maybe you'll find more at autopsy." He pressed on the cold, rubbery skin, but the body remained silent.

Erik was about to lower the head when a blemish caught his eye. "Also, there appears to be a small stab wound here in front of the left ear...and another puncture behind the ear."

The four men leaned closer as Erik inspected the other side.

"And a third above the right ear. Odd, very odd. They are identical to marks left by a skull fixation apparatus, like that we use to immobilize the head during brain surgery. Do you have any idea what happened?"

"No. X-ray studies of the skull revealed nothing obvious," scowled Stafford. "Come and I'll fill you in on what we have reconstructed so far."

"Harald never had a tattoo. How did he come by that one on his left arm?" Erik wondered aloud.

"That's part of a recent chapter in Harald's life," said Terry. "We'll explain upstairs."

"You all go ahead. I'll begin the autopsy," suggested Crowley.

The sun had made its way westward by the time Erik heard the entire story, a history he grasped with much difficulty. Dimpled light slanted through the office windows, falling on his hands, his thumb and forefinger holding the picture of the strange tattoo. Salucci's. Erik fixed his gaze on the image.

"So it contained thorium dioxide. Very clever," noted Erik. "Neurosurgeons once injected the same stuff into arteries many years ago for x-ray angiography…until it was found to cause liver cancer. We called it Thorotrast back then."

Erik paused. The picture held a strange fascination for him.

"Reminds me of a moth…a lunar moth I once saw crawling up a jail wall." He scrolled back in time. "There is something else about it that is very familiar. Damnation! Can't place it. Hmm."

A lady's voice over an intercom interrupted. "Doctor Crowley would like everyone back at the necropsy."

They returned to the pit and assembled around Harald's rigid body, the disemboweled package resting on a special gurney, a long stainless-steel pan. A black rubber block pillowed his head. Doctor Crowley had removed the entrails for a detailed examination. The empty abdomen and chest gaped open. Erik turned away from the gelid torso. Crowley, gowned in a surgical scrub suit, a plastic apron, and rubber boots, ceased dictating notes into a microphone.

"Nothing unusual in the viscera except a few gallstones. The spinal cord suggests evidence of his childhood poliomyelitis. We're about to inspect the brain. I share your pain, Doctor Landon, but I thought you would wish to be present." Crowley waved them over.

Pungent perfumes of formalin, lysed fat, early organic decay. Erik recalled many hours dissecting cadavers in medical school and assisting at autopsies, but those were lessons in objectivity. The body might have been a "ruptured aneurysm" or a "coronary occlusion." Not an emotional attachment with a human name. Not "Harald." Erik's throat tightened.

Crowley's diener incised the stiff blue-and-white scalp side to side and stretched the soft tissues forward over the frozen face, backward over the occiput. The room wobbled, and Erik pinched himself to overcome a feeling of faintness. A hole less than an inch in diameter revealed itself in the skull on either side of the midline, a hard plastic substance filling the apertures. The medical examiner removed the acrylic and excised the skin edges of the original wounds for analysis.

"Appears like methyl methacrylate," Erik observed. "Surgeons use it to fill in skull defects, though rarely for such small openings."

An orthopedic vibrating saw cut into the side of the skull-bone, whining, scattering bone dust as it sliced in a circular manner around the equator, leaving a V-notch in front for refitting. Like the top of a jack-o'-lantern carved from a pumpkin. The diener raised the liberated skull cap and placed it upside down — an ancient Norse goblet resting on its pedestal. As the dural membrane fell away, everyone, riveted, stared into Harald's brain case.

"It's empty!" choked Stafford in disbelief. "There... there is no brain!"

Collective breathing ceased as they leaned under the spotlights, searching the cavernous stillness, the skull base lined only by a pool of dried blood.

"Harald! What have they done to you?" screamed Erik. His fingers gripped the edges of the metal table, holding on to a mooring — any anchor in the real world — or at least, in his.

Then he shied away, trying to think of the corpse as a thing, a shell. But this same anencephalic torso had once built tree forts, fished for walleyes, and played ice hockey with him. On Minnehaha Creek. *Skoal...Skooaal!* shrieked and echoed at Erik from the distant past.

Marvin Cheverly sat down and rested his head in cupped hands. The strain was getting to him also.

Doctor Crowley had invited Cheverly, Stafford, Caldwell and Erik over to his home for the evening. Everyone gathered in Crowley's study. They all felt the need for a stiff drink. Erik sensed that emotional stabilization had began to elude Timothy. He was the one who had authorized Harald's assignment. He had sought out Bjørn in Copenhagen, Bjørn Ljunggren his former colleague of years past. His orders sent Jeffry to Scuol. And now he was asking Erik for help as narcotic deaths piled up on the streets of America.

Terry Caldwell, a solid man Erik was learning to trust and admire, remained in command of incisive reasoning, however troubling. The agent with sharp, blue eyes rubbed his buzz-cut. He sat stirring two fingers of Jack Daniels-on-rocks and took a measured sip.

Terry glanced up. "At my request, Harald, after leaving Chiasso, had been seeking information on a Doctor Johann Niemeier. This Niemeier must be involved somehow. We know he is on the staff at the Trieste Hospital and consults with the Braun Funeral Home." He thought a minute while he clinked swirling ice cubes against his cocktail glass, tiny glaciers bouncing about in pale amber. "He performed brain surgery on a close friend of mine following an auto accident in Switzerland. We've got to exhume the body of Marty Campbell in Virginia."

Stafford nodded in agreement.

Erik was still numb at the sight of Harald. And now he had to go to identify his brother's mangled body in Zürich. Looking Stafford in the eye, he asserted, "I don't know what happened to Jeffry and to Harald, but I intend to find out. I will do it alone or with your help, Tim."

"Of course," answered Stafford, a Valkyrie losing the chess game. "We'll support you one-hundred percent. We need each other. The heroin...it must be tied in with Niemeier. Did you meet him the year you were in Zürich?"

"No. The Trieste is a well known private hospital. I had heard of Niemeier...an excellent reputation. Quite wealthy. Traveled a lot. I find it difficult to believe he is corrupt. I can obtain an introduction through my neurosurgical friends at the Zürich Central Hospital."

"If you could get into his office, you should be able to plant a bugging device. The CIA there will help you with that. I must warn you of the perils. Our action is on foreign soil, and there may be little we can do to protect you."

"I understand, sir. Sounds like I'm on the team."

"Done. I'll get final clearance. Should be okayed by the end of tomorrow."

Terry interjected. "Boss, I'm flying to Fredericksburg. Got to examine Campbell's body." His wiry six-foot frame shot up.

"And I should have some more info on Harald's autopsy very soon," advised Crowley.

Stafford added, "Cheverly and I will brief Burns on our findings and re-evaluate the protocol for examination of the head of a corpse at Customs. In the meantime, I can't emphasize strongly enough the need for secrecy. These findings and the apparent role of our illustrious Lance Masters must not leave this room."

When Erik asked why the body had been taken from Kennedy Airport to the morgue in Manhattan rather than Queens, Stafford said that it was Cheverly's idea—after learning that the receiving mortuary had a Queens address. Stafford suspected that the Queens funeral home might have contacts in the Queens morgue. Everyone agreed to return to Crowley's office the next evening, Saturday, at five.

Washington, Friday evening.

Erik tried to define reasonable clues while taking the Amtrak back to the capitol, but emotion crowded out logic. He was in a tide of despair. On the way home, he stopped by his office to check for messages. The lights still glowed inside.

He found his partner, Henry Madigen, and their surgical resident, Frank Hamilton, sitting at a table and studying the two dry skulls nicknamed Yorick and Oliver. Oliver, disarticulated at the suture lines, lay about in disjointed pieces, a human moraine heaped on oakwood. Doctor Madigen was pointing to a photograph in a textbook, *Advanced Radiographic Anatomy of the Skull*.

"Hi, Henry. Doctor Hamilton, you ought to have that committed to memory by now. How are Oliver and Yorick?"

"Never better. Doctor Madigen was showing me his approach to a tumor on the sphenoid wing. A meningioma scheduled for Monday. Rounds ended late."

"Sorry to hear about your brother's accident, Erik." Madigen stood and stretched. "When are you flying to Switzerland?"

"In a day or two. Some rather urgent business popped up. I need to stay a bit longer in Zürich if it's alright with you."

"Of course. We'll take care of your patients."

Doctor Hamilton lifted a piece of dry bone up to the light.

"Remember in the operating room, when you asked me to describe the sphenoid, Doctor Landon?"

Erik did not answer, his eyes locked onto the ossified remnant of Oliver. Mysterious facsimiles marshaled his thoughts, the strength of the parallels increasing as he seized the object and rotated it. He stopped when the view from behind matched the portrait in his mind. *José's lunar moth...vampire bat...thunderbird?... It's none of these. The tattoo is a symbol of that keystone wedged into the base of the skull! A replica of the sphenoid bone. The skull base.*

Erik knew then that Terry Caldwell was right. The neurosurgeon at Trieste was the link. And the narcotic distribution center had to be in Zürich. But why? A prominent brain surgeon tied in with a transporter of coffins, of dead bodies?

"Erik? Are you alright?"

"Uh, yeh... May I take a peak at your book, Henry? I'll bring it right back."

"Of course. We're finished anyway. I'm bushed."

After retrieving a camera from his desk, Erik photographed the sphenoid, the keystone, a skeleton key, a clue to the meaning of the tattoo and its initials — *SSV*.

42

New York City, Saturday, November 27, 1971.

As scheduled, the meeting took place in Doctor Crowley's office at five. Both customs officers were present. Stafford initiated the discussion.

"I have the President's okay and FBI clearance for you, Erik. Do you have a passport?"

"Yes."

"Excellent. Justice will cover all expenses. You will have a dedicated phone number in Washington, and I'll let you know how to contact our CIA people in Zürich. You'll be working with Agent Sternschen. She's originally European, but now a U.S. citizen. Her associate operative is Joseph Smith." The Director turned toward Agent Caldwell. "Terry, what did you find?"

"The local judge in Virginia refused to give an order for exhumation of the body. I'm afraid it will take a week for the legal wheels to turn there, boss. Our judicial section will make a formal request."

Stafford then faced Erik. "Any ideas?"

"Let me show you something interesting." Everyone gathered around. Using the pathologist's Caramate projector, Erik shot his slides onto opaque glass, illustrating the sphenoid bone and the tattoo. "The symbol would tie in with the skull, the brain. With Niemeier."

The Director whistled and turned to Agent Caldwell. "So that's it. My apologies for doubting you, Terry."

"I would like to have the thorium dioxide tattoo knitted into my skin." Erik tapped his left arm. "Should I insert myself into the Braun Funeral Home, it will be very helpful...even critical. They don't know me. And if they recognized all their people, they would not need that insignia on their arm."

"We'll arrange for it to be done Monday. Can you come to Washington then and leave for Zürich on Tuesday?"

"Yes, sir. I'll be there."

"Doctor Crowley, what news from your front?" asked Stafford.

"Doctor Landon's syllogistic aim was correct, in part. The plastic was, indeed, methyl methacrylate. Of interest, it contained just enough barium to make the acrylic isodense with skull bone when examined by radiography. In other words, an ordinary x-ray film would fail to reveal any intrusion."

"To hide the openings, no doubt," reasoned Tim. "It would appear that our adversary has some serious medical talent."

"In addition, your mysterious Thunderbird operator sealed Johnson's scalp incision with a known tissue adhesive...probably a cyanoacrylate. We're still working on that. Since it lay behind the hairline, a casual examination would miss the incision. Something peculiar though."

"What's that, Doctor?" Stafford's thick eyebrows rose and fell.

"There were, in fact, two incisions, both sealed with tissue glue. One lay so close to the other that the naked eye would miss it. We nailed it under the microscope."

"Did the heart stop before or after the knife cut the skin?" Erik asked the pathologist.

"They made one incision several minutes before blood flow ceased. We saw subcutaneous blood cells. The other breach occurred following death, without any reaction."

Erik sensed that the implication had been there, but the correct inference, however nebulous, only now began to take form. They had been looking for black on white, not seeing the white on black.

"Well...is everyone thinking what I'm thinking?" Officer Burns punctured the brutal silence, the starch in his trousers slackening.

"The heroin comes inside the skulls of the dead bodies!" exclaimed Terry.

"Harald solved our case and never knew it," asserted the Director. "If it weren't for Harald's earlier visit to you Customs boys, he would have passed through as Gerald Baskin. Nice work, Cheverly."

"Gentlemen, this magnitude of financial power and technical cunning derives from more than just greed," reasoned Terry. "There has to be an ideology, a philosophy, a cult, another meaning. By logical extension there has to be another key. Harald had warned, look beyond Taipei."

"Genesis control," Stafford countered. "Hiding behind a tattoo."

"What now, boss?" Terry was anxious to get moving.

"Fill in the vacuum. Erik joins up with the CIA in Zürich to set up a meeting with this Niemeier. I'll notify the Company's operatives in Zürich and Marseille. You follow up on your case in Fredericksburg. Customs will examine the heads of all bodies coming in...with the help of the medical examiner."

Stafford rubbed his chin. "Also, without alerting the new Secretary, I need to chat with some of my friends in the State Department. How can a body under an assumed name get into the USA?"

"There cannot possibly be enough returning dead U.S. citizens to account for all this heroin...even with such high purity allowing storage in compact spaces." Terry, gritting his teeth, approached Harald, or what once was Harald. He peered into the empty skull cavity again and shook his head in confoundment.

"And how was the brain extracted and replaced by heroin?" Erik puzzled. "Where is the drug that Harald must have been carrying? How was it removed? There are only two small holes in the skull."

Crowley clasped his hands behind his back as he paced the floor. "Remember, we saw two incisions under the microscope. One about the time of death and one long after. Our mysterious vampire reached into Harald's body after its arrival in U.S. Customs but before our examination. Someone with connections in State found that the deceased could not be claimed immediately in Queens. That same person gained entry to the Manhattan City Morgue."

"What was the delivery address? There must have been a funeral home," marked Terry.

"Consigned to Priestley & Dietz in the Queens," responded Officer Cheverly.

"We'll check them out. Dietz...that name was on the tape from Jeffry Landon." Tim jotted a note on a pad. "Undoubtedly one of Thunderbird's many far-flung enterprises. Ship the remains on to the mortuary."

"But they'll know we've autopsied Harald's body," surmised Terry. "They shall realize we suspect something."

"Not if you give them *another* Gerald Baskin," observed Crowley. "Two can play at this game. Send them one of our John Doe's. We have a sleeper in our ice box. Just make that skin incision and glue it shut.

"The local morticians don't know what Harald looks like. You can alter the passport without any trouble. They're not going to open the skull. They already have the heroin. If the culprits see no autopsy was done, they will believe they pulled one over on us. Whoever took out the heroin and replaced the plastic did it in the dark with flashlights. And even in the light, I doubt that, in their haste, they bothered to look at Harald's face. All Thunderbird wants now is a body to burn and bury."

"What do you think, Terry?" asked Stafford.

"Got nothing to lose."

The Director turned to Erik. "Tomorrow let's discuss the details of your assignment. You'll need to sign some legal papers and we will update the CIA.

43

Zürich, Wednesday, December 1, 1971.

Erik rang the doorbell of Number Twelve on Freilagerstrasse and stamped his feet onto a mat in the outer hallway. The lady operative opened the door, her face a singularly massive smile.

"Good evening, Doctor," she greeted as Erik entered the large foyer.

"Agent Sternschen?" Erik blinked at an apparition from his past.

"Marlene. Yes, please do come in. It's chilly in the hallway."

Erik sensed her struggling to stifle excitement in her voice, formality melting away.

"I'm Erik Landon. I was instructed to meet you here at eight. Hope I'm on time. I…uh, have we met before?" He felt embarrassed, at a disadvantage. He couldn't help staring at her and still hadn't caught on.

"Actually you are fifteen years late." The words, unintended, tumbled out.

"I'm sorry, I thought…"

"Oh, you're quite on time, Doctor. Please join me in the library. First, let me have your hat and coat. Place your rubbers by the door. May I offer you some brandy?" Her genuine smile and air of disarming grace set him at ease as she added, "I wondered if you would remember me. The last time we met I had long hair, fifteen years ago. In college."

Erik hesitated. "Marlene...Marlene Ferguson? The girl I danced with and...? In German School...in Vermont?"

He felt a blush and then remembered his orders. "Oh! Here is the letter from Hamlet. I...uh...believe you were expecting it in the mail." The code-phrase.

He felt pleasantly stunned. *Marlene?* Strange feelings clashed within after losing Harald and Jeffry, then chance, or a higher power, suddenly throwing Marlene back into the equation—like a warm bonfire on a chilly day.

The lovely intelligence agent grasped the brown envelope, tore it in half twice, and returned the pieces, contact now made. She took his coat.

"It's a small world, Doctor Landon, Erik. Yes, when I beheld your picture and the name on our intel file, I could hardly believe my good fortune. Everything happened so fast." She laughed, large brown eyes sparkling. "When we get time, you must tell me all that's happened to you since we met at Middlebury College. I know the cold details from your dossier, but there must be much more to account for your being here. And I shall clarify my last name, Sternschen."

Erik stared at the vivacious woman of thirty-five years. Slender and willowy. Beautiful and blessed with soft, dark brown hair, now close cropped with natural waves and curls, the ends flipping inwards. Serious freckles still dotted her cheeks, scrunching together when she laughed.

Marlene was explaining that she had leased her two-story townhouse apartment on the eastern side of the street, Freilagerstrasse, near the northeastern corner of the cemetery known as Friedhof Grünfeld. Freilagerstrasse ran along the eastern side of the Grünfeld Cemetery and intersected Albisriederstrasse, this avenue a northern boundary of the graveyard. Looking westward out the second-floor window, she obtained a good view of both the crematorium building across the street, diagonally to the left, and the Braun Funeral Home cater-corner across the intersection to her right.

Through local connections, she found a clerical job in the emergency room of the Trieste Hospital. Marlene, keeping a low profile, soon passed unnoticed as a neighborhood background figure walking from her apartment to the hospital. Her route to the infirmary led her westward down Albisriederstrasse between the crematorium on the south side and the Braun Funeral Home north of the street.

Marlene turned toward the sideboard and brought out glasses and a bottle of cognac. Erik recognized her faint perfume as dormant memories resurfaced.

"Not very fancy, but it's Courvoisier. Joseph does not drink. I like a sip now and then." She sparkled, like her earrings.

"Joseph?" Erik looked around the sparse room, noting volumes of shelved books and several comfortable reading chairs. No windows.

"Yes. He is the agent-in-charge here."

"And where is this Joseph?" Erik glanced about again.

"Come. Bring your drink with you."

Marlene opened a door from the library to a large, dimly lit front parlor. An amazing electro-optic fortress greeted Erik. This startling inner sanctum hummed with sophisticated computer and audiovisual activity, cascades of electronic tones softly warbling. Moving green lines and bouncing orange dots. The smell of tight security.

"Wow. Rather fancy digs, Marlene."

Erik saw that Joseph was running checks on his surveillance equipment, making a correction in the power-deck of one of three TV monitors. Aside from four straight-back chairs about a plain cherrywood table, fully carpeted flooring treated with a web of sound-proofing, and a comfortable leather-and-fabric couch, the room contained an astonishing array of electronic instrumentation. Joseph jumped up and turned toward them.

"Doctor Landon, this is Joseph Smith. Joseph, Erik Landon will be working closely with us on the Thunderbird case. It was his brother, Jeffry, who was killed in Scuol," declared Marlene.

Joseph extended a firm handshake. "Sorry to hear about that, Doctor Landon. Jeffry provided enormous help by discovering links between Busche, Dietz, and Thunderbird. We're stringing the pieces of the puzzle together for Mr. Stafford."

Lines of service to his country creased the chiseled face of Agent Smith, a fifty-four-year-old veteran of the CIA. Erik immediately liked this thin, tall, and lanky man from Chicago.

Erik thanked Joseph for his concern. "I tried to identify Jeffry at the morgue today. All features were altered by plastic surgery, dyed hair, and the crush of boulders. The police failed to find any I.D." He hesitated, staring at a bobbing fluorescent dot. "But it must be him. The coroner has taken hair and teeth samples along with fingerprints, where possible. Needless to say, I engaged someone other than Braun to arrange shipment. We'll bury him next to our father in Minnesota."

Marlene, changing the subject, preferring a more appropriate moment to comment on Au, offered, "More cognac, Erik? May I call you Erik once again? We work very closely together here."

"I'll pass on the cognac, Marlene. And Erik it is." He paused, grappling with his own feelings, attempting to separate grief from joy, Jeffry from Marlene. "By the way, Stafford has assigned me a second passport with my pseudonym, Samuel Lock. Wouldn't want Thunderbird to recognize the Landon title. My code-name for communications is Taurus."

Marlene frowned. "Sounds like a name game, but it can become deadly."

Looking about, not knowing quite how to confront his past with Marlene, Erik asked, "What are you doing with all this equipment, Joseph?"

Joseph told how he monitored the mortuary as well as the cemetery and its crematorium. Due to the awkward sighting angle, only the front bay window of the funeral parlor could be seen from their flat. However, Joseph's expertise was electronic surveillance.

Earlier in the week, Joseph, dressed in the gray uniform of a tram-line repairman, had scaled up one of the posts carrying power for the tram on Albisriederstrasse. Joseph faced northward toward Braun, a stately mansion with peaked gables. An infrared sensory device, previously bolted outside his apartment window and connected to a radio transender, would detect reflected infrared radiation and frequency changes. He toted the radio receiver with attached earphones on his belt.

From the crossbeams high above the street, this man from Central Intelligence had angled a disguised infrared laser gun toward the Braun window, its photons ricochetting toward their rented duplex townhouse. He siphoned off electrical current in the tram line to power the device. Joseph then modified the angle of the laser beam until his earphones detected the energy reflected off the mortuary window. A high-pitched signal from the remote infrared receiver hummed in the earphones at that moment.

Upon returning to the flat, he adjusted the sensor for optimum reception.

Joseph explained how sounds inside the funeral home caused a minuscule vibration in the window pane. This oscillation changed the reflected frequency of the invisible light beam in proportion to the frequencies of the acoustic waves, the Doppler phenomenon permitting Joseph to indirectly monitor conversation inside the building.

A curious observer outside the apartment would fail to see the undercover agents on the other side of the coated windowpane.

Joseph rolled his shoulders back with a hint of pride. "...then this photo-detector amplifies the infrared signal which, in turn, is fed into the loudspeaker, tape deck, and this oscilloscope. We obtain our energy level off the scope and feed it into this minicomputer. The system is quite accurate, unless we have a dense fog or a pouring rainfall.

"Also, we have employed TV systems to detect normal light energy alterations and infrared changes for nighttime surveillance. As you can imagine, there is a lot of taxpayer's money invested here."

"And that?" Erik pointed to another phalanx of equipment.

"To detect electromagnetic radiation and fluxes in electrical current. I stowed it in our van and drove around the funeral home and crematorium. We...Marlene and I...discovered evidence of highly sophisticated security alarms and surveillance traps...not unlike those surrounding the Russian Embassy in Washington. Furthermore, our electronic snoops revealed extensive electrical power going by cable under Albisriederstrasse, between those two buildings." He pointed at the street with the tram line. "As if some form of creature feeding on thunderbolts of electrons dwelt underground there."

"Shh...listen." Marlene put a finger to her lips. "Voices from the funeral home. Sounds like a family discussion."

"Remarkable," Erik exclaimed. "And those words actually originate from there?"

"Sure do," replied Joseph, launching keystrokes into a computer. "Uninformative so far. We've failed to detect any audio signals from remote rooms, and the telephone, unfortunately, is secured elsewhere."

"What about the crematorium?" Erik nodded leftward toward the structure.

"We have not seen any activity at that red-bricked building, and window space is nil. It also has a seamless electronic envelope."

"Marlene, have you learned anything at the hospital?" Erik turned to the quiet woman standing behind. He felt eye contact rapidly closing space and time between them.

She paused, and then, "The ambulance drivers transport most of their head injuries to Trieste...even those with accidents closer to Central Hospital. Erik, I'm sure Niemeier has arranged something. Even more interesting is a conversation I overheard between two general surgeons. They were complaining that since this neurosurgeon took over the care of head injuries, the death rate has tripled."

"Any connection with Braun?"

"Without question. All of the doctor's unfortunate non-survivors are packed off to Braun unless the relatives complain." Looking out the window, she waved toward the more northern building on her right. "And many of the deceased locals are buried across the street from Braun."

Erik followed her gaze leftward and pondered for a moment. "Have autopsies been performed?"

"No," answered Marlene. "They're costly, rarely considered necessary in this country, and Niemeier would discourage the idea of cutting open a loved one."

Joseph conceded, "At present, the worst that can be said of Niemeier is that, from his connections with Braun, he is feathering his nest with money made from dying patients. If we tried now and failed to find evidence of traffic in narcotics, he would up and relocate to another country.

"We must move with extreme caution. Soon our forces will execute simultaneous hits here and in Marseille, Mainz, Copenhagen, and the United States. The CIA, Customs, Justice, and people like you, Erik, are working together, climbing the face of an icy cliff, inch by slippery inch, as it were." His features tensed. "If one of us slips, the rest shall lose everything."

Marlene added, "For the time being, we are gathering intelligence. Stafford is coordinating the campaign. Even our CIA Director in Washington now agrees. We must move forward, but with extreme care.

"Erik, do you think you could consult with your friend at the Central Hospital and encourage him to introduce you as Doctor Samuel Lock to Niemeier?"

"I'll visit the med center tomorrow. Professor Gunther Roellein is the chief. And a tough cookie, but if I approach him right, he will help."

"In the meantime," suggested Joseph, "we have a short time to reconnoiter. I'll be doing much of that here. For the next two days Marlene will work undercover at Trieste. Erik, you try to gain access to Niemeier." Joseph sat down and fiddled with the gain on a transducer. "Tomorrow evening you might take Marlene out to dinner. On Company expense, of course. She needs some diversion."

"Absolutely not, Joseph," Marlene exclaimed. "Company rules forbid it."

But Erik noticed her eyelids dropped, a blush rising to her face.

"To be truthful, I would enjoy the companionship again, Marlene," Erik responded, rather hoping she would accede. "And besides, I'm not a paid employee of the CIA."

"Well...it would be nice." She bit her lip, but a smile crept through. "Where are you staying, Erik?"

"The Hotel Poly. Under my assumed name. May I pick you up here in my Volkswagen tomorrow evening, say at seven?"

44

Zürich, Thursday, December 2, 1971.

The following day, Erik returned from his visit with Professor Rollein at Central. At seven the same evening he entered the foyer of Apartment Twelve, hesitating to speak, thinking he was addressing another woman. Marlene winked at him as she hummed a merry melody. She was adjusting a black, interlacing belt around her thin waist and over a dark green, shaded wool skirt. White satin blouse. Brown leather and muslin vest. Champagne-colored silk stockings. An elegant collar of seed pearls about the neck. Two sets of pearl earrings, dangling.

"Marlene?"

"It's only been a day since we again met, Erik," she answered with a twinge of humor and her megawatt smile.

"Say, you're something else!"

"Something else?"

"I mean you…you're beautiful. That is…even more so than in Vermont. I uh…." He felt himself stumbling over his words.

She laughed. "Oh, please come in and keep me company me in the front room. I've already poured a glass of sherry for us. Was your day fruitful?" She led the way into Joseph's lair.

They were greeted by electronic audio and visual signals—soft beeps and slightly fractured, moving green lines.

"Hello, Joseph! Yes, Marlene, I am to meet Niemeier on Monday at noon. Rollein arranged an introduction for me."

"Super. In the morning, I'll cable Stafford and bring him up to date. Nothing new from Trieste," she disclosed as her eyes tracked his.

"Speaking of Trieste, Roellein was surprised and quite ticked off about head injuries bypassing Central Hospital."

"I did make a point of speaking with a couple of the ambulance drivers," replied Marlene. "Even had to turn down a date with one. That same person had the tattoo on his left arm. It's obvious that Niemeier's organization is in control even before the patient reaches the hospital."

"We're still left with another enigma," noted Joseph. "First, the numbers of American citizens dying in Europe, let alone in Switzerland, would not provide sufficient cranial space, as it were, for the amount of narcotics involved. Second, dead Swiss or European countrymen can't be admitted to the USA. American compatriots like Harald Johnson or Martin Campbell might be ideal for their purposes, but there aren't sufficient numbers."

"Marlene, can you take enough time off to check the past year's death certificates at the cantonal building? You might discover some clues there," Erik suggested.

"Good idea. I'll do it tomorrow morning."

"Anything new at the Braun parlor?" Erik pulled his gaze from Marlene, addressing Joseph.

"Nothing so far."

Marlene jumped up. "Come on Erik. A promise is a promise. I know a fantastic little restaurant on the Limmatquai."

After Erik assisted Marlene with her tan suede coat, she fastened her belt and looked up, flashing a coy smile. A lovely butterfly leaving her cocoon. Erik sensed her excitement mixed with his, as if they were going on a first date. He thought of a childhood tryst in Edina and chuckled as he closed the front door.

Driving eastward, they crossed the Sihl River and then the Limmat.

"What were you laughing at, Erik?"

"Well...you just remind me of a girl I knew when I was in junior high school."

"Junior high school! I look like a thirteen-year-old?"

"Hell, no. I mean I was excited about taking her out, and I feel the same about you."

"Oh, I can see we'll have a fun evening," joshed Marlene as she drifted toward him, tilting her head to his shoulder. Soft brown tiger-eyes conveyed an even deeper closeness.

"I see you have two earrings piercing your ears now. What happened to the third?"

"You would remember that. Actually, I had four at one time in my growing up phase," she rejoined with a smirk.

Erik laughed, feeling in a good mood.

"Still unhitched, I'm told," Marlene ventured, looking at his left hand.

"Few close calls...but I never married. And you? Aren't you originally from Scotland?"

"Oh, it's a bit complicated. After World War II, my Scottish parents moved from Edinburgh to Mönchaltorf, a small hamlet near Zurich. That's where I learned to speak Swiss-German. After my stint at Middlebury College in Vermont, I obtained U.S. citizenship, a masters degree at American University in Washington, and applied for employment with the Central Intelligence Agency."

They rode in silence and then she added, "Since we last met, I wed an attorney in Washington. His family name was Sternschen. After two years we split up. Had different agendas to our lives." Marlene pointed toward bright lights across the misty water. "There's a parking facility just beyond the bridge."

Upon crossing the Bahnhof Bridge above the Limmat, Erik swung the Volkswagen into an indoor parking garage. In spite of the winter season, scores of locals and visitors had invaded the streets to shop and sightsee. The Limmatquai ran along the eastern side of the river, the street lined with well preserved buildings remodeled for the tourist trade. The shops, cabarets, guild-houses, and narrow streets tempted passersby with a dazzling array of traditional wares. The quaint locale held fond memories for Erik, his favorite part of Zürich opening up before him once again.

Hand-in-hand, they wandered down the byways, wishing time would slow down, each enjoying making the other happy. Both laughed, chatting about old times as Marlene and Erik snaked their way among the milling throngs of multi-linguistic people. A violinist was treading the cobblestones and playing a brisk tune.

Erik stopped at a small shop and purchased a yellow rose. She blushed as he pinned it to her vest, above her bosom. Long, sweeping eyelashes threw shadows on her face. Marlene kissed him tenderly on the cheek, and he felt a vibrant response to spontaneous intimacy.

Swiss folk music spilled from one of the small restaurants on the Limmat, swelling and receding each time a customer opened the door.

"Let's go in. It sounds heavenly," entreated Marlene, pulling Erik's hand.

The Thunderbird Covenant

Arms interlaced, they wound their way in through the crowd and settled at a cozy table. A four-piece band made up of men dressed in traditional Appenzell costumes saluted the newcomers. The merry quartet, red-faced and perspiring, never ceased performing in song, except for the theatrical reading of requests and the sipping of warm beer. Erik and Marlene drew up their chairs as the audience clapped and stomped their feet to the joyful four-quarter tune.

Marlene, speaking perfect Swiss-German, ordered two flagons of beer, spaghetti, and meatballs. Two huge platters returned, and Erik found it difficult to believe his eyes as his diminutive date polished off her entire plateful.

Speaking in the local dialect, she hailed the minstrel leader, requesting the unforgettable "La Montanara." That brought on cheers and nods of approval from the crowd as the lusty accordionist sang of soulful memories and personal challenges within the beautiful Swiss mountains. A moving lyric with special meaning, tears glistening the eyes of the hardened men, young and old. Toast after toast was raised with beer steins clinking, and Erik felt as if the Alpine winds truly were blowing through the inn.

Later they walked the small, age-worn, cobblestone streets, the sounds of accordion and Alpine horn music fading. They approached the Predigerkirche, an ancient church fortified by centuries of Christian devotion and stonework. Only a few visitors were strolling about the courtyard. "I haven't had so much fun in years, Marlene." Erik squeezed her hand. "Let's do something together Saturday night."

"I must give Joseph a rest at surveillance Saturday. Why don't you join me at the apartment, and I'll prepare a fantastic dinner."

"Sounds great. You can count on me."

They dallied, listening to two lovers speaking in Italian as another couple drifted by.

"Erik, I've been so busy. Yet I'm still...lonely. Have you any idea how often I've thought of you. When we went separate ways after college, I never felt quite the same again."

She turned to walk further when, on impulse, Erik clasped her hands in his. A provocative stirring swept over him, a revived love expanding the envelope encompassing their mutual passion. Eyes of granite-blue and tiger-brown locked together in unspoken communication.

Marlene smiled, and then, standing on tiptoes, whispered in his ear, "Oh Erik, to hell with the rules. Kiss me. Now. Please kiss me again."

The lamplight cast a shadow on her dimples. It seemed the most natural thing in the world — to embrace, to kiss. Erik knew they were falling in love again after all these years.

Saturday, December 4.

After a morning at the Landesmuseum, Erik reconnoitered the Trieste Medical Center, learning the lay of the land. He returned to the Hotel Poly by three.

"Any messages?"

"*Nein*, Herr Doktor," the clerk clucked in a sharp tongue, her lids blinking snappishly over half-glasses. A beautiful face spoiled by a serrated demeanor.

"May I have the key to my room?"

Erik cleaned up for the evening, a hot shower sweeping and firing his skin. Anxious to see Marlene again, he was humming a tune while shaving. He could not chase her out of his mind, the lovely flower already cemented between the pages of memory, deep roots resprouting, taking a firmer hold each hour. He felt different, his obsession with patient care now on vacation, a refreshing breeze blowing.

After jumping onto one of the trams, Erik arrived at the Freilagerstrasse townhouse and a radiant and cheerful Marlene greeted him. She turned out in a revealing light moss-green blouse. Form-fitting, pine-green, satin slacks. Tan sandals. An alluring beauty.

"If you don't kiss me, I'll think Thursday night by the church was just for fun," teased Marlene as she took his hat.

Feeling the intenseness in her svelte architecture, Erik set down two wine bottles and pulled her body against him. She tilted her head back and stood on her toes, warm, volatile lips melting into his. Their hearts retreated to a stable thump-thump when she stepped back to regain equilibrium.

"Just think, Erik. I have you all to myself tonight. I sent Joseph to see the *Nutcracker Suite*. It just opened and he loves the ballet."

"Doesn't he have a family?"

"His wife and the children were killed years ago. I don't know the circumstances, but he's been a loner ever since."

"Oh, I'm sorry."

"He'll sleep in his own next door loft tonight and return tomorrow. He carries a bell-boy, and I can reach him in an emergency. Please make yourself comfortable while I stash the wine away."

"Didn't know what you planned for dinner, so I brought both red and white." Erik pointed at the two bottles on white linen covering the mahogany end table.

"Oh, thank you. Let's have the chardonnay as soon as it's chilled. It will go with my hors d'oeuvres. Then the sauvignon at dinner. I have my own special way to make veal. Hope you like it.

"Now you play spy for a while, Erik, and look out the window. Joseph's toys haven't detected anything out of the ordinary. Niemeier has been neither seen nor heard yet."

"And I suppose you understand all this electronic stuff? What if something goes wrong?"

Marlene flushed with a trace of anger.

"The CIA has trained me well, Doctor. Not to worry. I can take them apart and put the pieces back together again. Joseph knows that, but they are his pets and I don't disturb them unless necessary. Call me if you hear something suspicious. And don't push that self destruct button," she warned and pointed, half in jest, half in earnest as she walked to the kitchen.

Feeling a bit put in his place, Erik sighed and settled on the interwoven coverlet, over a firmly cushioned sofa. The loudspeaker remained silent, except for an occasional footfall outside the Braun front window or a number three tram rolling by. Streaking shades of rainbow colors, flowing from red to violet, rushed to catch the disappearing sun outside, lengthening the cemetery shadows. The twilight illuminated several graves, freshly covered.

Marlene popped in from the kitchen.

"Learn anything from the death certificates?" Erik asked.

She grimaced and curled up on the far end of the couch, savoring her white wine.

"I had difficulty obtaining permission to look at them. I informed the courthouse clerk that I was carrying out a research project on automobile deaths in the area. He finally relented, my Swiss-German convincing him, I suppose. I reviewed the files for both last year and this. The numbers of auto accidents were about the same according to their motor vehicle records, but there was a noticeable increase in mortality — not at the scene, but later."

"Let me guess. Nearly all the deaths were at Trieste, and most were Niemeier's patients."

"A number of them were at the hospital, but the majority were not primary head injuries. At any rate, you're close because most were consigned to the Braun Funeral Home and interred at Grünfeld," acknowledged Marlene.

"And if people like Martino LaVecchia worked there as orderlies, they would be in a position to offer 'friendly' advice to bereaved relatives regarding a reputable funeral home."

"Exactly. But being buried at Grünfeld would be a dead end in more ways than one. How does that help our narcotic problem?" Marlene took another sip.

"I don't know yet. Do you have the names of all of the deceased in the area?"

"Sure do. I jotted them down along with the listed cause of death, the hospital, the doctor signing the death certificate, and the mortuary. All in German. I'll send copies to Stafford."

A moment of silence was interrupted by the loudspeaker reflecting the screech of a car stopping. A stranger stepped out and carried a package to the side door of the Braun Funeral Home. He swiped an electronic device by the rear door handle and disappeared inside.

Then over Joseph's loudspeaker shot the stranger's words. *"Noch ein Geschenk aus Marseille. Montag gibt es Arbeit für Niemeier."*

The voice retreated after a second man answered in muffled French.

"A present from Marseille. On Monday Niemeier has work to do," repeated Marlene, intent, listening for clues. "I can't make out the other man. Joseph can replay it with computer analysis."

"Must be a shipment of heroin from the Marseille plant." Erik surveyed the scene in front of Braun.

Soon the courier departed. A door slammed shut and the loudspeaker went dormant.

Marlene jumped up and fetched two glasses of chilled vintage.

"Thanks, Marlene." Erik grasped his wineglass. "I know you CIA types can't talk much, but at least tell me enough about you, so I can believe you're more than just a recurring figment of my imagination. What is your favorite pastime now?"

"I still love to ice skate. Was runner-up for the Olympic figure skating try-outs during my teenage years. I practice whenever I get the chance. You used to skate a lot, as I recall?"

"And I still love it. We must go together in Zürich before I return home."

"But first, darling, we shall eat dinner."

Marlene prepared a small table for two, the smell of the cooking making Erik's mouth water. As she retreated back to the kitchen, he marveled at shapely buttocks moving in tight satin. The vision, a catalyst to a pleasant urge returning.

Cool it, Erik, he thought. *She's gorgeous but don't get too involved again.* He knew it was already too late.

Near the end of the feast, Marlene switched the tape, and "Hang on Sloopy" danced throughout the air. She ferried in two cups of hot coffee-amaretto on a carafe. Facing one another on the couch, they sat cross-legged, sipped coffee, and stared once again into each other's eyes—with a different kind of hunger.

"Marlene, when this is all over, I'd like you to come to America again and meet my mother. You'd like her. She's still living in Minnesota."

"Of course I will, Erik. In the meantime, we're under presidential orders. In my work, life can be cut short. I have to find my happiness in moments like this."

Marlene hesitated, gazing at a ticking clock on the mantel, her feelings seeming to flow back at full ebb. Her glowing brown eyes, clear and earnest. Tiger-eyes of liquid gold.

Erik put down his coffee and drew her now familiar hands close to his chest. He brushed a lock of hair from her cheek, and she glanced downward. Erik sensed the want, the conflict in her.

"My darling, Marlene. Let me stay the night. I'll make no conditions."

"Hmm…"

"That sounded like a yes. So, where do I sleep?"

She leaned forward and kissed him, the sheer energy of her heated body arousing a desire deep within his.

"You can stay, but I have one proviso."

"What's that?"

"I made the dinner. You do the dishes." She leaned back and flashed a cheeky wink.

After an ardent embrace, tongues enmeshing, lungs expanding, firm breasts pressing through soft velour, Marlene rolled off the couch onto the floor and leaped up.

"While you're busy in the kitchen, I'm going to change into something less confining. Now make a good effort or you'll just have to do the china over again," she teased while running her finger down the front of his shirt and stopping just short of the belt buckle, his heart throbbing and swelling.

Fifteen minutes later Marlene returned to the kitchen as Erik stashed the last of the plates to dry. Melodious strains of "The Girl From Ipanema" trailed behind her.

"My, aren't we domestic. Might just keep you around for a while."

Erik spun around, nearly dropping a steaming chinaware saucer. Before him stood a stunning apparition of femininity silhouetted in the doorway.

The beaming woman, her body in delicate profile, cast a fiery sheen, a halo of pure energy. A Nile-blue negligée over soft, glowing skin, a luminosity of love. Pink nipples, erect, projecting from well-formed breasts, the sexual tension electrifying. A trim waist expanding into a maidenly pelvis. A small woman in extraordinary physical shape, musculature rippling as she danced gracefully across the room, whirling into his arms, incredible heat pouring off, like fire raging through combustible dry wood.

Drinking in her beauty, Erik dropped the dish towel as they enmeshed in a passionate embrace. An embrace that had waited fifteen years, the gulf of time melting away.

"Hold me, Doctor Landon. Oh, Erik." Then with an anxious sigh she released him, drawing him into a chamber illuminated only by two flickering candles. "Leave the door open...for the...uh...loudspeaker," she fumbled, squeezing his hand.

She pulled him close, her arms about his neck. While holding Erik's gaze with hers, her hands moved down to unbutton his shirt. Somehow the rest of his clothes tumbled to the rug, followed by Marlene's gown. In the grip of a Vermont love renewed, they rolled onto the bed, their arms entwined.

"Darling, you kept the neck piece I gave you." She gazed at the tiny silver moon.

"Of course. And your picture in my wallet." Erik brushed her forehead with his lips.

"Oh, Erik!"

Her fingertips floated over his face, stroking his eyelids closed, lingering at his cheeks. The static was so charged that Erik feared to breathe. She took his hands in hers, ever so gently, and blew a warm breeze against his lids, right, then left, again and again. He tried to swallow, but his throat would not move. She put his fingers to the sides of her neck and, still blinded, Erik lightly touched her skin, exploring her earlobes, her temples, her forehead.

He kissed her cheek, whispering, "Marlene, you cannot believe how much I've missed you."

"Lust or love, handsome?" Erik felt her fingers wandering south.

"Hmm. Both. Careful, I might lose total control."

"That's the idea, dear doctor."

Her soft hands embraced his penis, now recharged to new heights, her eager fingers not yet moving. Immense, bronze eyes glittering in the candlelight.

"I'm impressed! Do you get that way by doing dishes or playing ice hockey?" Then Marlene leaped up on her knees and wrapped eager arms around his neck. "Hmm?" She mischievously rubbed his nose with hers.

"Falling under the spell of ladies in Central Intelligence," Erik chided, draping his arms over hers.

Erik searched her eyes, finding jeweled droplets of both joy and sorrow welling up, inherent beauty radiating from within. He drew her into his arms, and they laid their heads on the pillows, misty eyes staring at the ceiling. Hands clasped together.

"Marlene, my darling, your beauty takes my breath away. And I've fallen in love with *you*, not the memory of you. I don't want to lose you. Somehow we are going to complete our assignments in Zürich and meet again—and not in secrecy."

He turned and drew her molten torso close, pressing his aroused flesh hard against her tummy, the throbbing reaching up as two bodies melted into one. His lips on hers, she opened her mouth, receiving his tongue, hers probing every nook and cranny. They were enfolded in each other, committed without fully understanding. A wildly sensual déjà vu.

"My God, how I've missed your touch, Marlene." Ripples of ardor rose to squalls of furious ecstasy.

"Oh, Erik, kiss my nipples again. You make me feel so good. It's been too, too long."

She ran lithe fingers through his hair, an impetuous wildfire surging once more as his lips and tongue kissed and tugged, warm hands massaging firm breasts. At first, a light touch.

A sensual magnet pulled his left hand downward, masculine fingers swimming over her abdomen, thighs, and hips. Marlene's legs separated, urging him to release the mounting tension within.

His hand moved slowly at first, wanting to please, stimulating desire with gentle persuasion. And then faster as she pressed her fingers onto his. Erik sensed her exquisite passion billowing upward through her demanding, now rigid torso as she gasped, her body accepting, commanding their electric contact, completing a reborn circuit. Her topaz eyes squeezed shut as she bit her lower lip, Marlene's whole being shuddering, then launching into a continuous crescendo of blissful rapture.

"Erik...Errriik!" Her body arched backwards in one clitoral explosion of joy, her hands now gripping at the headboard, Erik's fingers feeling her sensual wetness. "Hold me, my love," she panted. "Hold me."

With a loving tenderness Erik hugged her, kissing her cheeks and forehead. He kissed the tears from her eyes.

"Oh, Erik, I see a thousand exploding stars moving beyond a velvet horizon."

He leaned over and nibbled the side of her neck. "I love you, Marlene." His head was spinning with desire.

"Darling, this is even better than lying on pine needles in Vermont," she sighed, massaging his scalp, guiding his head downward.

Once again his lips surrounded an aroused nipple, and she shivered, squeezing, pressing the back of his head. The connection was tempestuous, and another whimper of euphoria bolted through her lips. Marlene gasped—short, rapid breaths of an erotic ferment.

Erik rolled over, sitting up behind her, tilting her head back and sideways to meet his searching lips. He knew she could feel him, now struggling to withhold emission, pushing against her back. His arms around her sides, a surgeon's fingers fondled succulent breasts, his eager mouth kissing her parted lips and probing tongue. Marlene's pelvis writhed and twisted, tempered legs crossing and uncrossing, chest and abdomen heaving.

Again, he kissed Marlene and cupped her breasts as her hands skated beyond her mons veneris, seeking heightened sexual pleasure, willing her sculptured legs to separate further. Her breathing accelerated, and the muscles of her lithe body quivered and tightened. Marlene moaned louder, and louder until she could no longer contain herself as torrid waves of orgasm rocketed through.

Then her breathing calmed and Erik gently laid her head down.

"Doctor Landon, you do such therapeutic wonders for my vital signs," she cooed. "Do we have to wait another fifteen years?" She fingered the silver moon hanging from his gold necklace, the small icon tangled in the hairs of his chest.

"Marlene, I can't wait another fifteen seconds."

She blossomed a knowing smile and drew him over on top of her. "Come inside me, Erik. I need you inside me. Now, Erik. Not fifteen years from now."

She spread her legs apart, riding astride, guiding, wiggling, thrusting her pelvis onto his stamen of love, her wet vagina enveloping, accepting, holding him fast, libidinous fingers grasping his buttocks.

"My God, what a man! Fuck me hard, Erik! Don't stop! Don't ever stop!" Vulvar contacts detonated, triggering the rippling and quaking of vaginal muscles, the undulating constriction of pelvic sphincters surrounding, kneading solid and sensitized flesh.

"Oooh, I love your prick. Fuck me, Erik, fuck me! I love it!" Short rapid whispers in his ear.

"Marlene, I adore you. Oh God, I need to come so bad now!"

Erik drove faster and faster, her fierce pelvic movements matching his. As he hurtled toward release, she strengthened the grip of her pelvic muscles. He could no longer hold back, uncontrollable contractions spiraling through. Marlene, blissfully conscious of the climactic event, his sperm feeding into her, convulsed headlong into the apex of another powerful orgasm. She screamed in ravished delight, biting her arm to muffle her shrieks, cleaving Erik against her with her legs about his back. He melted into her, a vibrant love holding them fast.

Then, while the clock ticked on, they plunged headlong into exhaustion, catching their breath as the minutes passed by, a tender union engendered.

"Erik?" She sighed a rosy glow of contentment.

"Yes, my darling?"

"Thank you for your gift of love."

"I need you, Marlene. Tomorrow and forever."

"Erik?"

"Yes, my sweet?"

She brushed his hair. "Did you really like my cooking?"

In wonderment, Erik grinned, thinking of the Milky Way in the Vermont mountain skies. The candle flickered out as a new day began.

45

St. Moritz, Sunday, December 5, 1971.

Erik had discussed his idea with Marlene and Joseph. Visit Anna Baumann at her jewelry shop in St. Moritz. He would sorely miss staying close to Marlene, yet some additional clues regarding the Thunderbird Covenant lay hidden along Jeffry's trail. It would entail a Sunday's excursion into the Engadin Valley.

Crisp, clear weather embraced the countryside. Radiant beams of sun collided with crystals of snow and scattered into the forested landscape. The wheels of Erik's Volkswagen sedan spiraled along narrow roads winding into the Engadin. In the valley, his eyes chased after the cross-country skiers, moving dots along the landscape of the lowland, as they raced in wintry competition.

On the road to St. Moritz, Erik studied his situation. He attempted to stratify his thoughts. Heroin. He was a healer, not an intelligence officer. He needed to employ a surgeon's logic, not a secret agent's strategy. Cunning, not caliber. He intended to find the killers of Jeffry and Harald. *And what of this Helga?* he wondered. *How had she fit into this?*

His car entered the narrow streets of St. Moritz where panes of shop fronts reflected sparkles from murals of frost. He pulled over at a quaint restaurant to seek directions.

"*Grüezi, Fräulein.*"

"*Grüezi wohl.* May I help you," the comely waitress greeted in Swiss German.

"I am looking for the Hirschen Jewelry Shop. Would you be so kind as to direct me?"

"It's Sunday. Frau Baumann is at home and won't do business today." She turned toward a shelf, pursuing a cobweb with her dust brush.

"It's important that I speak with Frau Baumann. Perhaps you could tell me where she lives?"

"Most likely she is attending church. If you wish to try her home, travel two kilometers north on this road. Turn right at the Sankt Moritz Gasthaus. Her house is the only one on the left. A short stretch." The cobweb fell to her attack.

"Thank you for your help. Good day."

Erik, feeling a trace of ambivalence, returned to his Volkswagen and drove on. After parking on the snowy hill, he approached the front portal and tapped the black, wrought-iron knocker. It looked like the beak and head of a raven.

The elderly woman who appeared at the door was dressed in church finery, bundled in a fur coat. Her lovely head lay nestled between the corners of an upturned collar. She blinked and then squinted at the bright sunlight before her.

"May I help you?"

"Frau Baumann?"

"Yes?"

"My name is Doctor Erik Landon. Might I ask you a few questions about my brother, Jeffry. You knew him as

Brian Trent." Erik paused. "He visited you shortly before he and your niece were killed."

She edged the door closed. "Please go away."

"You were one of the last persons to see my brother before he found Helga in Scuol. I won't stay long."

She hesitated and then with tired resignation replied, "Yes…yes we both lost a loved one that tragic day. Please come in. I'll fetch some hot coffee for us."

After entering the front hall, she took off her coat and beckoned Erik toward an Afghan covered chair in the parlor. Church music traveled at a hushed volume from another room. He sat down, and the lady returned with two cups of aromatic café au lait. She settled on a Venetian love seat. Erik noted her aristocratic bearing, her pleasant features withstanding the wear of time.

"Sugar?"

"No thank you." He cradled his coffee and examined the rising steam.

"You do not resemble your brother a bit, Doctor Landon. His voice was hoarse. His hair appeared lighter, the face fuller. Something about his eyes…?"

"A scar in the left eyelid, a childhood injury. Perhaps that was what you saw?"

"Yes, that's it. Herr Trent…your brother, Jeffry, seemed in a hurry, and I couldn't help him. I truly did not know where to find Helga at that time." Her coffee cup shook slightly, rattling in its saucer.

"Were there any other visitors seeking your niece?"

"No…no one. The police have questioned me many times. What a terrible thing." Her agitation increased. "Four people dying that awful day."

"Four? I don't understand."

"The avalanche buried your brother, as you know. Newspapers reported another skier caught in the slide, but his body was never found."

"That leaves two. Helga was one?"

Anna gave a sigh of pain. "I was the first person to find Helga following her murder. After your brother came upon her in Scuol, she telephoned me in St. Moritz the next morning. My niece begged me to come and help her disappear. Helga's voice was teetering on the edge of panic. She admitted to me then that she still loved her Jeffry...yes, I knew Brian Trent must have been a false name. I think she would have done anything to get your brother back again.

"I drove to Scuol as fast as I could. The roads were slick. When she failed to answer the door, the hotel manager let me in. Helga was lying dead on the floor, you see. She had been shot," Anna cried, crossing herself.

"And the..."

"Doctor, my Helga was the closest person to me. I loved her so very much. I'll never forgive myself for not reaching her sooner." Anna wiped her eyes and glanced down at her apron.

"And the fourth?" Erik asked, puzzled as he drained his coffee.

"That evening the laundry staff uncovered a dead man at the bottom of a hamper filled with hotel linen. They say one bullet pierced his head. He came from Italy—at least that is what the police claimed. They never solved the murders, but the detectives suspected that the same person who killed him also murdered my Helga."

"I'm very sorry. I imagine Helga was buried in Mainz?"

"No...no, she was put to rest in our local churchyard. I can show you if you like." Anna slipped over the brink of tears, her words carried by soft, lamenting halftones.

"I would like that. Before we go, do you have any idea why Helga was running away?" Something was amiss, but he could not lay his finger on it.

The tempo of the hymn rose and then fell into a more solemn cadence. After a long silence, Anna turned toward a wooden icon of the Virgin Mary. The Mother of Jesus stood on a small marble pedestal — as if to forgive and protect the strange ornament above her, an enigmatic symbol of a duel between retribution and forgiveness, a necklace suspended against the white, stucco wall.

The lady walked over to the Madonna, the fingertips of Anna's left hand in a nostalgic gesture touching the pious figurine, the other hastily forming the sign of the cross.

"Though really her aunt, I was both mother and friend to Helga. Yes, she had adopting parents. My brother, Heinz, was her father. But she felt distant to them for reasons fathomed only by God. She always came to me with her problems. Never to her parents. More coffee? Some sweets, Doctor?"

"No, thank you." Erik remained staring at the necklace.

"She was merely four years old when I first saw this frail Polish child. Heinz brought her home from some agency during the awful war. My brother's wife, Ingrid, wanted a baby, and she could not have one of her own. Helga's real parents were killed during an air raid attack from English bombers. Such wretched days. Over the years our little Helga grew into a beautiful and wonderful young woman."

Erik waited while Anna thought back in time. She gave a nervous twist to a lock of her hair. "Then the dreams, the nightmares. She became a different person after she left Mainz. Something dreadful lived inside her, eating away, little by little. Tearing at her heart.

"She traveled frequently, always searching for answers, for happiness. Seeking the key to...how do you say it...unlock Pandora's box. She was determined to do it without help.

"But the path toward such an exorcism kept eluding her, my Helga dying just after stumbling onto one of those clues to her past. Doctor Landon, your brother held that key and never knew it. I really believe that my Helga, so fearful of close intimacy, still deeply loved her Jeffry...and only Jeffry...with such extraordinary passion. She was crying as she told me so on the phone." Anna buried her head in her arms, sorrow overtaking a shaking body.

"Why don't we take some flowers to Helga's grave," Erik gently suggested. "I didn't mean to cause you this much pain." Rocking between sadness and agony, his own throat ached for his brother. And, strangely, a little even for Helga.

"I'm alright, Doctor Landon. Yes, flowers would be nice, but the floral boutique is closed on Sunday. Maybe I'll bring a cross to lay on her grave. She had this odd necklace with two wooden crosspieces. Yes, that's what I'll bring."

From the shrine she lifted the neck piece, titanium braided with silver, and two Christian crucifixes. Two parts of love both bound yet severed by a leash of hatred, a chasm of hell. Nearby church bells announced the morning service.

46

New York City, Wednesday, December 1, 1971.

While Marlene, Joseph, and Erik walked on dangerous turf in Switzerland, the Bureau of Narcotics continued working hand-in-hand with Customs in the United States. The phone rang in the Office of Theodore Burns. Officer Burns hung up and lit out for Kennedy Airport. Another cadaver. As he marched into the room, he greeted Marvin Cheverly, who was pressing fingerprints and snapping photographs.

"Name is Sterling Mason, Mr. Burns. Has the same incision behind the hairline as Agent Johnson. Shipped over on a Consolidated Airway charter flight and consigned to Priestley & Dietz in Queens. Passport appears valid."

Burns' eyes washed over an obese corpse, rolls of purple falling from the belly.

"Doctor Landon had recommended a CAT scan unit. Is it available?" Burns triple-clicked his ballpoint.

"Yes, sir. Within the hour we will transport the item to the county hospital. The techs will scan the head, no questions asked. All arranged at the highest levels."

"Call me when you're finished. Then forward our 'Sterling Mason' via routine channels to the funeral home. I'll call Stafford as soon as I hear from you, Marvin." Burns yanked a loose thread from his starched shirt and hurried away.

Washington, Same Day.

Stafford had been in daily contact with Zürich as new intelligence unfolded. With mixed feelings, he had little to say about Helga and her aunt. Though BNDD had lost a witness against Lance Masters, Stafford was spared the hassles of extraditing her for trial in America. Yet he had this gnawing feeling that Helga's ghost was lurking in the shadows of Europe, like cigarette smoke waiting to be inhaled.

He was irate that the State Department continued to stonewall his efforts to gain info regarding illegal passports. And he could not go directly to Lance Masters. Now another body had slipped into Customs, and he needed Terry's expertise.

"Terry, come into my office. We received some news from New York."

Terry hustled in and grabbed the seat nearest the desk.

"Afternoon, boss. What's up?"

The Director, squinting in thought, swiveled in his captain's chair. "Burns called. Another package from Zürich...named Sterling Mason. They're forwarding the photographs and fingerprints. See if our CIA friends in Switzerland can scare up a real I.D."

"Same condition as Harald?"

"Yeh. They scanned the head. The usual skull x-ray did not show any holes in the skull, but the CAT scan sure did."

"CAT scan?"

"It's one of those special x-ray machines that can identify structures inside the body. Means 'computerized axial tomography,' I'm told. Anyway, our hunch was right on target. Someone had replaced his brain with something else. Guess you know what that something else is."

"Heroin."

"Can't prove it without removing some. So I asked Crowley for help. He...."

The intercom buzzed.

"Yes?"

"Mr. Stafford, Doctor Randolph Crowley, forensic pathologist, on line four," reported Martha.

Timothy punched the loudspeaker button.

"Hello, Randy. You're on speaker phone. Come up with anything?"

"Sure did. I passed a long needle through the cheek and base of the skull, into a small opening, the foramen ovale. A bit tricky in a rigid cadaver, but we got a tiny morsel of what you wanted. It's the big H alright. Our assay revealed ninety-eight percent purity."

"Ninety-eight percent?"

"Yeh, your 'Bird must have some high-tech labs."

"Terrific work. Leave any marks?"

"Not so you'd notice. Customs is preparing to ship the body on to Priestley & Dietz."

"Wonder how they do it?" marveled Stafford. "How do they get the brain out through two small holes and replace it with heroin? And so quickly."

"The ancient Egyptians had clever techniques of removing the brains of their pharaohs prior to burial in the pyramids. Given enough time in a warm climate, enzymes in the dead brain autolyzed it into a cerebral soup. The priests extracted the liquefied brain of the monarch through the nose. Used some crude type of spoon or syringe and drove it through the thin cribriform plate at the skull base," recalled Doctor Crowley. "Maybe Erik will come up with answers about your 'high priest' in Zürich. I'll be in touch."

"So long, Randy, and thanks."

Stafford turned to Agent Caldwell.

"Well, that's where we are, Terry."

"Remember my friend, Campbell, buried in Virginia?"

"Yes?"

"Exhumed yesterday. Don Martin was present. Campbell had never had an autopsy, but his goddamn brain was…like…not there."

"Shit. Hope you didn't tell his mother."

"No. She's had enough grief. But I'll have to give her some explanation for the disinterment."

Tim Stafford shot to his feet. "Terry, I want you to go underground for a while. We're not getting any help from State on methods of forging passports and illegal entry."

"Want me to do a little snooping?"

"We've given you a new moniker, Peter Swicker, once a Mafia type. Our G-men took him out six months ago during an attempted arrest. I'll give you the details later. Your assignment: obtain two illegal U.S. passports…and you're willing to pay well for it. See what contacts you can scare up. There is something rotten in Denmark. And in the District of Columbia."

"Peter Swicker, huh? What am I trying to get back into the USA?"

"An illegal alien from Europe. And Terry?"

"Yeh?"

"Agent Don Martin will be tailing you."

Terry let his beard grow, in a few days cultivating an itching, reddish-tan stubble. He wore old, loose clothing, which flapped on his wiry frame, and rented a run-down garret near the railroad station. He learned from an underworld informant that an Ezra Thomas might be helpful — for the right price.

Ezra often hung out at a tavern just off Pennsylvania Avenue. Terry wandered into the Tell-Tail Bar and Grill and ordered up a Schlitz. Yellow light flowed weakly through the blue haze of the parlor. A jukebox, flashing in a kaleidoscope of colors, spun out hard-rock music for lounging clientele.

"Seen Ezra around?" sniffed Terry, wiping his nose with a cloth.

"Who wants him?" replied the bartender, a stained apron hanging from a protruding belly, his gaze fastened on his arthritic knuckles.

"I got business with him," Terry coughed. He hefted the glass of fine bubbles swirling, building up to a foam on a sea of amber brew.

"What kind?" The man looked up.

Terry sniffed again and threw a twenty dollar bill on the counter.

"Comes in at five on Thursdays. Stick around."

Soon after the hour a stocky black man, sporting flashy threads and diamond rings, sauntered into the lounge, flanked by two well-endowed girls, one white and one black. They drew up chairs and settled down at a window table.

"Hey, Ez. This white dude here wants to chat."

Terry shuffled over and yanked out the fourth chair.

"Name's Swicker. Heard you might help me."

Ezra shrugged and sent his two molls up to the bar.

"Depends on what you want 'n how much you're payin'," he wheezed, squinting at the intruder. "Now I can get you one o' them broads over there. That black one in the green jump suit...the one with the tits...man can she fuck. But if you're looking for weird tastes, my friend, it'll cost you."

Ezra grinned from ear to ear, a gold tooth gleaming. He fingered a diamond tie stick set in relief by an expensive checkered suit.

"Have in mind getting a couple passports. Jimmy sent me."

"Passports?" Ezra hissed in a whisper, glancing around the room. "Hey, man, you got that kind of bread?" He spread his thick hands as if to show off the rings.

Terry threw down five bills, a hundred-dollars each, one slipping off the table top to the linoleum as Ezra sucked in his breath. Ezra then ran his tongue along the left upper molars, protruding his cheek as he considered the transaction.

"That's all I got on me," said Terry. "So don't have your boys nail me outside. There's a shit-load more if we can do business."

"You know Jimmy, huh? I'm checkin' you out. If you're the fuzz, man, you're as good as dead. You got photographs for the passports?" He snatched up the loose greenbacks and pocketed the money after counting it, then picked his gums with a lavender toothpick.

Terry handed him two pairs of Kodachromes, one of himself and one of another face.

"I need one for me. My age and address are on the back of my picture. My buddy's in Europe, and I want to bring him back with me."

"Man, yours is easy. Cost you only three grand. Your friend's might be a problem. An extra six thou'. Be here this time tomorrow. I'll have the passports. You get the cash."

"Shit, that's a lot of bread for a couple pieces of paper. Make it five," cracked Terry as he leaned back in his squeaking chair, speculating, *He must have hard-wire connections if he can do it so cheap.*

"I got expenses. Nine big ones or forget it." Ezra gulped a mouthful of beer. "Check with me here tomorrow. No one's gonna touch you."

"I'll be here." Terry stood up.

"For another five-hundred, I can get you one fantastic piece of ass tonight. You know…two of those specialty girls. Soft bed. Sensuous music. Lilac cream. Heavenly massage…four hands…twenty fingers…all over. Pills, if you want."

"Just the passports, thanks."

The jukebox flipped over a new platter—"Got along without you before I met you, gonna get along without you now…"

Terry pushed himself up from the chair, back legs scraping as he did so, walked up to the bar, and pinched the well-endowed green jump suit. He choked on the heavy perfume. From the weight of her handbag, he guessed she carried Ezra's artillery. She pivoted and winked at Terry as he hopped up on a leather bar stool next to her.

"Hey, Lily, if he ain't payin', he ain't touchin'. Git over here," hollered Ezra, twisting his cigarette into a beer can.

An hour dragged by. Ezra Thomas and his inebriated lady friends left, doorway bells jingling. An aged-appearing barfly with a slouched hat, a ragged sweater, oil-stained, and mismatched baggy pants lurched from his stool and also departed. Martin had made contact.

Terry threw down the last of his beer and headed out into the winter twilight, turning to walk east. A blue Cadillac, bristling with antennae and its motor purring, almost growling, rolled up beside him. The black beauty in the jump suit leaned out the window, lyrics of "Yellow Submarine" escaping, heavy breasts garnishing the frame. Sable hair hung like waterfalls twisting to her shoulders. She was alone. A Lucky Strike bounced on her lips as she talked.

"Mistuh Swicker, Ezra say if you want your passports, you have to spend the night with *me*. He don't want you out of my sight." She studied him, as if analyzing for unknown purposes.

Terry, chary of hidden intentions, hesitated.

"Come now. Ezra—he is just one cautious man. He don't want you talkin' to no one that might get him in trouble. Leastwise not till he checks you out and gets his bread. Come on, you 'n me can have some kind of fun tonight. For what you're payin', Ezra wants special care taken of you." The woman flipped the cigarette against the curb and ran a wet tongue along painted lips. Cherry red.

"Sure, baby. Sure. No problem." His beard itched.

Terry jumped into the front seat but close to the passenger window, the perfume, cigarette brume, and body heat stifling. The Cadillac lurched and then sped northward up Sixteenth Street while Lily prattled on, occasionally slapping the man's thigh or punching buttons for a new music tape. In a half hour she turned left into a residential neighborhood near the Maryland line.

"I canceled all my engagements tonight, honey. Just for you." Lily giggled and blew him a kiss while lighting another Lucky.

The vehicle swung into a driveway lined with trimmed hedges and pulled into the four-car garage of a fashionable, three-story colonial. Brick and wood siding.

"How do you like my pad? Not bad, huh. Now you can see how Ezra takes care of his girls."

Terry stepped out, and they entered the kitchen from the garage. Servants, armed, were tending routine household affairs. A serenade of soft rock music in the background.

"Evenin', Miss Lily. Evenin' suh."

"Evenin', Jones. Please inform my lovely sister we have a special customer tonight. Fix him what he likes to drink while I take my shower. Give him a shower, too. He needs it." She wrinkled her nose. "And pick through his duds for any wires."

"Yes, Miss Lily."

Terry was baffled, but he had to play the game. He showered and shaved, leaving a goatee. Jones tossed him some clean threads and directed Terry to the living room, where he sat down in a curved, velvet couch. Jones, dressed smartly in a butler's uniform, including tails, poured a scotch and soda. The shapely sisters strolled in and settled down on either side of their guest. Terry felt strange, overheated perhaps. Maybe the scotch? Or the brace of black beauties.

"Well, saints 'n sinners! Ain't Mistuh Swicker just the cutest white dude you've ever seen, Mary? Ezra…he says we're to give him our most special attention. And Ezra don't take kindly to such distinguished company bein' denied any creature comforts." Lily spoke in an excited voice, eyes of black opal flashing. A revealing white bodice clutched soft brown skin.

Mary, dressed in a tight leather skirt and a see-through orange blouse, squeezed close to Terry, her practiced fingers stroking his arm. Foreplay before a pantheon of pleasures, Terry in a slipstream of indecision, already tripping over hormonal depth charges. He swallowed his Cutty Sark, the potion burning away apprehension.

"After dinner, Mistuh Swicker, Lily and me will want to know your special tastes so we can provide a most appropriate dessert with uncommon but scrumptious sweets, don't we Lily."

Lily answered by resting her hand on his upper thigh, spidery fingers crawling over his crotch, leaning into a stretching zipper. She trilled wet kissing sounds as Mary unbuttoned the top of his shirt.

"Mary, I do believe I detect a noticeable rise in this man. Appears we should serve hors d'oeuvres before the main meal."

Terry reached for another whiskey. The telephone rang as he felt his zipper slowly running astray.

Saturday, December 4.

"Where the hell have you been, Terry?" demanded Stafford. "We've been trying to reach you at your room. We didn't know if you were alive or dead, goddammit!" He waved Terry over to the empty, cane-backed chair near his desk. "Coffee?"

"No thanks, Tim."

Terry summarized the previous thirty-six hours. He had been released by Ezra, who had waited outside the Riggs Bank while Terry obtained the money. Only then did Terry receive his two passports—one for Peter Swicker, the other in the name of a Lee McIntyre. Terry tossed the documents onto the green blotter.

Stafford picked up and analyzed one of the passports while pacing the carpet. "Where did that name, McIntyre, come from? Any ideas?"

"No," replied Terry. "I'll track it down. In order for such a passport to be good...and this one has a three-year-old number...there must have been a real Lee McIntyre somewhere. Just requires an alteration in the photograph and a forged signature under the stamp."

"Hmm... Don Martin followed your Ezra Thomas to the home of our illustrious Secretary of State, believe it or not. We'll have to tread softly. If he's truly a part of the narcotics problem, he might have received sensitive information through some of our joint conferences. Helga's tape is rather incriminating, but it might have been doctored."

"On the otherhand, boss, Masters may be just getting some extra cash by providing resources to alter passports. Let me nose around. I have some friends in State who have no love for the Secretary."

"Okay," replied Stafford. "My efforts at State hit a brick wall. Monday give me full written particulars of 'Peter Swicker' for the files. You can omit some of the details with Lily and Mary, though."

Terry kept a straight face. "Thanks. See you Monday." He jumped up and turned towards the door.

"Something else, Terry. The CIA in Zürich sent us considerable information on the good Doctor Niemeier." He tapped his index finger on a shelved portfolio. "Most of it was not helpful. Born in Germany. Former resident in psychiatry at a mental hospital in Vienna—Spiegel-something. Then studied surgery in Berlin before the war. Has a Nazi background. Later he entered neurosurgery. They're checking into all of that. Last spring he did take a long vacation…in Hong Kong."

"The 'Bird's claws reach further than we thought."

"We have the appropriate mortuaries in New York, Hong Kong and 'Frisco under surveillance now. But we don't want to launch a strike until all parts of the riddle are assembled."

"What about Ezra and his operation?"

"We'll leave him alone for the time being."

"Yeh, I guess he is small fry compared to Masters."

"One final piece of info." Stafford walked toward the double-paned window and stared at the traffic below.

"What's that?"

"With their usual attention to detail, the CIA stumbled on to an interesting notation in one of the World War II documents on Niemeier. Came from Russian files relating to their taking of Auschwitz in '45. When he was the surgeon-in-charge at Auschwitz, guess who his commander was?"

"I've no idea, boss."

"Kommandant Heinz Baumann...Helga's father!"

"Jesus!"

"Both were tried at Nuremberg for war crimes, but a strange thing happened. One of the few surviving Polish prisoners...name was Jerzy Sierpinski...testified on their behalf. They only served a couple years in prison and then were released."

Stunned, Terry shut the Director's door and returned to his office at BNDD. He closed his tired eyes, elbows pressing on the desk, fingers massaging aching temples as he reflected. *Helga's father, the Nazi Kommandant? What was, or is, Niemeier to her? A faulty connection?* He laid his hands back down on the desk, fingers spreading, stretching. *Helga's daddy...? Damn.*

Monday, December 6, 4:00 P.M.

"Boss, I chased down the name of Lee McIntyre, the one on the passport forged by Ezra's friends," reported Terry. He had entered Stafford's office.

"Is it for real?"

"Yes and no, Tim. He died of a heart attack in Madison, Wisconsin, two years ago. There is a valid passport number for him. The same one that's imprinted on the falsified certificate."

"So that's how it's done. Masters or someone working for him snags an obituary list from various U.S. cities. Their computers tell them which of the deceased had a recent passport, and Thunderbird simply uses an identical document with a new photograph. And that becomes the passport for the returning dead 'American.' It could only happen if someone at State manipulated the computer files, keeping the original American corpse 'alive.'"

The intercom interrupted. "A CIA transatlantic call for you, Mr. Stafford. Been chopped. Going through the unscrambler now. I.D. verified. Tape rolling. Switch to channel three, fourth bank."

"I'll take it. Thank you, Martha... And thanks for the apple pie. You're a marvelous cook."

Stafford punched code numbers into a computer and hit the loudspeaker button, answering, "Hamlet here."

"Zürich." The electronics stretched the voice of Joseph Smith into a metallic crackle. "As per request, I searched out the data on your 'Sterling Mason,' the corpulent body with heroin shipped through New York Customs. My friendly Swiss contacts here checked out the photograph and prints. Sterling Mason he is not. His real moniker is Frederick Hoffmann, a Swiss railroad conductor. Died from a stroke.

"The Trieste docs treated Hoffmann, and he expired two weeks later. At Niemeier's recommendation, the family shipped the corpse to Braun. The mortuary buried him across the street, or at least a grave sits there with the name, Hoffmann, tagged on it." Joseph paused. "I'll bet my last Swiss franc that the tomb is empty. Except for one or two homeless ghouls."

"You've been an enormous help, Zürich. We have enough evidence officially to bring in the Swiss police as soon as Taurus is finished. What's his status?" Tim was worried.

"He went to make contact today," reported Joseph. "It's late in the evening here, and we've had no word. He was to call in at five."

"Oh, Christ. Trouble. We better run our time-line up. Let's see... Today is Monday evening. We will coordinate simultaneous strikes in Hong Kong, San Francisco, New York, Washington..." Tim's eyes tracked an electronic wall map. "…Marseille, Mainz, Berlin, Copenhagen, and Zürich for two days hence. Wednesday at 18:00, Zürich time-zone. Any objections?"

"No sir. We can move anytime. We'll need the Swiss police if we want to stay out of trouble."

"They'll be there. I'll have them contact you tomorrow. Look for a Major Reiter. He owes me a couple."

"What about Taurus?" asked Joseph.

The Director looked at Terry and swallowed hard. "Keep your surveillance up on Braun. We can't help him without knowing where he is. Pray he's okay."

"I'll tell Marlene. She'll take it rather hard. I think she kind of likes him. They knew each other a few years back."

"Shit. That's all we need. Okay. Good luck."

Stafford snapped off the speaker phone. "Terry, you've been wanting to see more of Europe. I want you to wing it to Zürich tonight and have a down-to-earth chat with my old friend, Major Roland Reiter. Zürich Division, Swiss National Police. We'll arrange for an Air Force jet. Get the strike-team in Zürich set for Wednesday. In the meantime I'll get things moving here. Martha?"

"Yes, sir?"

"Call the Bureau of Vital Statistics and see if a Sterling Mason expired somewhere in America in the past five years."

"Will do."

"Do you see it now, Terry?"

"Yup. There must be a lot of empty graves in Grünfeld. The Swiss aren't going to believe this."

"It will be your job to convince them. The sands of time are close to running out, so get cracking." Stafford glanced at his Rolex. "I better brief the President about Lance Masters. Wouldn't want to embarrass our Chief Executive."

Terry rushed out to prepare for his flight to Zürich. He mentally reviewed Joseph's communication, troubled. *What the fuck is going on with Erik?*

47

Trieste Hospital, Zürich, Monday, December 6, 1971.

Erik followed Niemeier's receptionist into the study.

"Good afternoon, Doctor Lock. My good friend, Professor Roellein, spoke very highly of you. Very highly, to be sure." He rose and stuck out a pudgy hand which Erik grasped. Erik detected a humorless smile stretching across Niemeier's face, distorting lipid like Spandex. His vibrating eyes were lusterless, disturbing.

"A pleasure to meet you, Doctor Niemeier. I hope I'm not interrupting our day," Erik replied.

"Quite the contrary. *Bitte, nehmen Sie einen Platz*…uh, please take a seat." He motioned Erik toward a leather chair after closing double French doors, a rattling of the panes trailing.

Erik's eyes skimmed over the executive suite. Niemeier's spacious office, with wainscoting of dark oak on beige walls, occupied a corner of the top wing at Trieste. The smell of polished hardwood rose up from a floor of inlaid wooden strips.

Erik watched the bespectacled man shoe-horn himself into a high-back chair, behind a mahogany stretch-desk. Two Tiffany lamps bracketed the surgeon's image. His sunburned visage appeared leathery, aged, his ocular gyrations magnified by the edge-thickened glasses. Behind the German doctor handsomely dressed rows of hide-bound medical journals stood at attention, their ostentatious spines serving more to impress the visitors, Erik guessed, than to bind a useful source of information. Tasselated ropes and velveteen drapes hung in royal fashion at frosted windows.

A tailored, three-piece pin-stripe clothed the owner's portly frame. Recessed ceiling lights reflected the sheen of the doctor's silver-blue lines of fabric, generating a feeling of regal, almost religious eminence. Decorating his chest, a row of caduceus-scored penlights and gold-plated pens against medical white had replaced the silver medals and iron cross on military brown. Bifocals straddled the end of a damp nose, his forefinger habitually pushing them back up.

"I am fascinated by your work with induced hibernation of the nervous system," Erik finessed. "With much interest I studied your article in *The Journal of Experimental Techniques*."

"Is that so? And why such concern?" Niemeier tugged at his starched shirt collar and then flicked a speck of dust off the sleeve. The surgeon tilted his head back and peered down the side of his nose, scrutinizing Erik.

"We have been mastering some clinical research on the use of barbiturates for cerebral protection. While visiting Professor Roellein in Zürich, I thought I would take the opportunity to discuss your findings with you first hand."

"I'm quite flattered, indeed," chortled Niemeier, his jowled face reflecting a titanic ego. "I have some business today with the Cumaves Company. Why don't you come along with me, Doctor Lock. En route, I'll review my personal theories with you. But first, I must check on one of my critical patients."

He scooted his chair back, grunted, and stood up.

"I would be delighted." Erik fingered the magnetic box in his pocket.

Unable to attach the electronic bug, he followed Niemeier as they exited the office. After excusing himself for a moment to use the toilet facilities, Erik scribbled a hasty note on paper toweling and stuck it into his pocket.

On the surgical ward Niemeier demonstrated several neurosurgical cases. They stopped outside of one room. The patient's name pasted on the door — Louis Valentini.

"This poor man suffered a devastating motorcycle accident. We tried to save him, but his cerebral damage was too great. Brain dead." Niemeier paused and shook his head in an affected manner. "What a tragedy. Soon we shall terminate the respirator. If you don't mind waiting in the walkway, let me speak in private with his family." He rubbed his bifocals with a handkerchief.

Erik lingered nearby in the hall. The muffled German voices of Niemeier and another man, laced with spikes of anger, filtered under the closed door. Niemeier hissed instructions to have the patient's face photographed as soon as the endotracheal tube was removed and then prepare for transfer to Braun at seven that night. The family would be no problem.

"*Ja, Alles in Ordnung, Herr Doktor.*"

The door swung open, and Niemeier, adjusting his glass frames, approached. "Come. We'll leave by the Emergency Room. My driver has our automobile standing by."

Marlene pivoted in the chair behind her desk as she watched Erik and Niemeier depart through the ER. Erik dropped the piece of paper from his hand. She snatched up the note and read it to herself. "Unable to place device. We're going to Cumaves Company now. See you at five."

She lifted the phone receiver and called Joseph Smith, pretending to be conversing with an ambulance driver.

"What do you think is going on?" she wondered, fearful of concealed strategies.

"Haven't a clue. What business would the subject have with an electronic company?"

"Perhaps the doctor will achieve a diagnosis."

Cumaves AG, Monday afternoon.

Erik accompanied Niemeier into a glass and steel building surrounded by iron fencing and security cameras. Niemeier marched up to the receptionist and trumpeted their arrival.

"Ja, Herr Doktor. Herr Sierpinski has been expecting you. Come with me, if you please."

Erik had to give up his passport. They signed on the register and followed her to an electronic research laboratory. Scripted on the door—*Achtung! Laser Strahlung!* Attention! Laser Radiation!

"We may proceed inside," she announced. "The warning light is off."

Niemeier introduced Erik to the engineer. After they shook hands, Sierpinski removed a laboratory coat, rolled down his shirt sleeves, and donned a jacket. Erik's eyes clapped onto Sierpinski's tattoo, the green and red icon, the wings of the sphenoid.

What a strange looking man, observed Erik. Sierpinski's pupils receded into tiny dots, the eyes narrowing, fighting off Erik's inquisitive gaze. He was elderly. A slight man. Stoop shouldered. Quiet in voice and manner. Obsequious grin. A false, fawning attitude. Disposed to hold his hands in a praying construct. Wintry gray-blue eyes dancing, darting about, never addressing his colleagues. An aquiline head projecting from a stretched neck, an ostrich looking first one way and then the other. The collar of his tweed coat which hung loosely on a spare frame, falling away from the withered neck. His mottled hair turning white.

The presence of Erik seemed to irritate the engineer. "Herr Doktor Niemeier, perhaps my secretary might show Doctor Lock about while we discuss our business in private."

Niemeier grunted approval, and Sierpinski steered Erik next door to his office.

"Fräulein Mullineaux, please be so kind as to inform this American gentleman, Doctor Lock, about our research institution…our non-sensitive areas of interest. We'll be quite occupied for an hour." Sierpinski spoke in rapid German with a Polish accent, the voice shrill and raspy.

"I would be happy to, sir." She turned toward Erik and shifted to English. "Doctor, may I offer you freshly brewed coffee?"

The heels of Niemeier and Sierpinski faded down the hallway, becoming distant clicks.

Erik faced a young, black-haired woman wearing eyeglasses. She had a plain, yet comely and expressive face devoid of make-up. He made a special point of checking for a tattoo on her arm. None existed. *Suzanne Mullineaux* appeared on her nameplate.

"The coffee smells wonderful. I would love some. Without cream or sugar," Erik replied.

"Please take a chair. Have you been here before, doctor?"

She smiled, removed her spectacles, and stepped toward the coffee pot. He sensed a blend of warmth and grace radiating from her—yet a faint strain of melancholy hovered about.

"No. I understand this is an electronic company."

"Yes, indeed. We supply electro-optic mechanisms for communication systems, particularly for aircraft. Hence our name, Cumaves. Most of our work is classified."

"Cumaves?"

"Yes…it's Latin for 'with the birds.'"

The image of the avian tattoo flashed through Erik's mind, snapping into the framework of an unfinished puzzle.

"I see… How would that help a neurosurgeon like Doctor Niemeier?"

"We are involved in many other electronic and related research missions. Herr Sierpinski specializes in laser systems. He and Doctor Niemeier have been working together for several years on experimental projects. I don't know the details since they are classified."

"You speak with a French accent. You're not from Zürich?"

"Oh, no. From Lausanne…in the French part of Switzerland. I've worked here for a few months. My previous husband used to carry out research at Cumaves. I needed a job, and my friends here helped me obtain my previous secretarial position here. I'm most grateful." She handed him a cup of coffee and replaced her eyeglasses.

"Was your husband an engineer?"

"Yes and no. Bjørn began as a mathematician, switched to electronic engineering, and later worked for the Swedish and Danish governments. He is dead now."

"I'm sorry. Didn't mean to pry," apologized Erik.

"That's alright. I…we divorced prior to that time, anyway."

"Bjørn? That's not a Swiss name."

"No," replied Suzanne. "He was a Swede. After our separation, I took my maiden name back. His family title was Ljunggren."

"Ljunggren? Bjørn Ljunggren!" Erik's jaw dropped in astonishment.

"Yes…what's the matter, Doctor Lock? You look surprised."

Erik straddled a moat of indecision. *Tell Suzanne or not?* She did not work for Thunderbird, and she could be a tremendous help to Hamlet. Was she emotionally stable? Could she handle it? Time was crucial and little remained.

After soul-searching hesitation, he resolved to divulge the manner in which Niemeier and Sierpinski were responsible for the death of Bjørn—and his own brother, Jeffry. Erik saw the coffee cup in her hand decelerate, freezing in space.

Suzanne slipped her glasses off and wiped tears from shell-shocked eyes.

"Dear God, I know I should have gone to his burial. I just couldn't. I could not bring myself to go." She turned and picked up a photo from her desk. A portrait of a small blond boy. "First Christian. Then Bjørn. I loved them both so very much. Have you any children, Herr Doktor?"

"No, I've not yet been so blessed."

She hesitated for awhile, as if waiting for pain in her throat to recede, and then resumed. "Niemeier and Sierpinski. It doesn't make sense to me. They knew I was once married to Bjørn, and even offered me this position here. My Lord, I don't know how I can help. But it would be the least I could do for Bjørn."

Erik omitted details about the heroin aspects, though Suzanne knew that Bjørn's specialty had been narcotic undercover surveillance. Erik asked her to call a special telephone number, notify 'Joseph' that Doctor Samuel

Lock had been there, and inform him that a Jerzy Sierpinski at Cumaves worked with Niemeier.

The door shot open, jarring the tension in the air.

"Fräulein Mullineaux, what is the matter?" inquired Sierpinski stiffly as he and Niemeier swept in.

"It's something in the air, sir. I'll be alright." Her nervous fingers rolled a pencil back and forth.

"Come, Doctor Lock. I'll drive you back to your hotel, and we can talk some more," suggested Niemeier. "I trust you found your time here stimulating. You didn't drink your coffee?"

Leaving Suzanne alone, the men filed out of the office, progressing down the aseptic, neon tunnel of modern ingenuity, passing photos of rockets, laser beams, sun spots, and atomic substations.

As they departed, Erik knew he was leaving a woman distressed.

Suzanne turned from the door and stared out the window, the request almost a command — *call Joseph*. She had finally found some semblance of peace but now felt her very being torn asunder. *Call Joseph*. Espionage lay beyond her depth, yet she was resolute in her determination to help Bjørn even now. Her role was simple — *call Joseph*. Simple, yet a struggle to reach for the telephone.

At the Hotel Poly, Erik stepped out of Niemeier's Mercedes Benz and thanked him for his time. The scarlet sun dove below the horizon, indigo thrusting upward in the east and chasing the Mercedes.

Erik was determined to witness the final rites of Louis Valentini, whose fate Niemeier had already plotted. Erik had to find out what had happened to Harald. A short thirty minutes remained to race back across town to Trieste. He paused on the front steps of the hotel, his eyes trailing the rear lights of the Mercedes until they dissolved in darkness. Then he hopped on a tram, striking out westward back across town, planning to insert himself inside the funeral home somehow. He watched the dancing red and white beacons of moving vehicles, a part of his mind on Marlene, another on Suzanne.

Inside Trieste, Erik spotted a long, white coat suspended on a rack. He threw it on and walked with an air of authority toward the surgical ward, nodding to a group of chatting nurses passing in the opposite direction. After snapping up a patient's chart from the nursing station, he approached Valentini's room just as the lifeless body, wrapped in linen sheets, rolled on a metal gurney toward the lift. A muscular orderly, dressed in surgical whites, propelled the stretcher. Close behind, Erik cleared his throat and pretended to review notes on the chart while entering the freight elevator with them.

The conveyance rattled, descending to the ground floor. Erik glanced up, noting the Thunderbird insignia on the man's arm. The attendant bypassed the hospital morgue and wheeled the cloaked corpse directly to a hearse, the vehicle idling under flickering, acerbic orange lights at a rear loading dock. Steeling his nerve, Erik seized a nearby iron wedge used to open wooden crates and slipped the weight into the pocket of his coat.

After loading the lifeless form into the hearse, Niemeier's henchman strapped it down as Erik hid behind shipping containers stenciled "Radiation Equipment." At that moment he leaped into the rear of the hearse, shoe leather striking the floor with a thud.

"*Was machen Sie denn?*" spit the driver. What are you doing?

The felon's hand reached under his coat, unholstering his pistol. Erik lunged, heaving the metal wedge, its base hammering the man on the head, red stains sweeping down from a fractured skull. He plunged against the stretcher and folded to the floor of the vehicle. Arms and legs quivered, and then quiet respirations followed, congealing drops of blood matting his hair. Erik pushed the Luger under the front seat.

After peering outside, Erik closed the back doors and exchanged clothes with the unconscious man. Voices of two security guards passed by and dissolved. He bound the orderly with coarse twine retrieved from the loading ramp. After hoisting the limp torso onto the gurney that had carried Valentini, Erik covered the Thunderbird operative with a sheet and rolled him back into the hospital.

After a brief greeting, *"Guten Abend,"* to a janitor scrubbing the floor, Erik delivered the victim into the basement morgue half-way down the hall, the courier of dead bodies and heroin to terminate in a refrigerated drawer. Then Erik returned, leaped into the hearse, and drove into the dusk, away from towering glass and granite, toward shadows of the Braun Funeral Home. He was determined to get at the bottom of the mystery, the evil that caused the terrible deaths of Jeffry and Harald.

The machine sped eastward on Albisriederstrasse, and then Erik swung to the left, into the Braun driveway. He rapped on the side door. The peephole blinked, like the nictitating membrane of an owl.

"I've brought Valentini," Erik announced in German, peering about for signs of security devices.

The door swung open.

"Who are you? Where is Rolf?" demanded Niemeier's hatchet man, the eyes sallow, smoky and deep-set. His orbits glared from sockets like dim sconces in a dark tomb. The cigarette glued to his lower lip delivered a screen of smoke.

"I'm new — from England. Busche sent me to learn the ropes. Rolf had business with some whore. And you are…?"

"Pierre Montaut, of course. I'll deal later with that idiot, Rolf. The delivery goes to the crematorium." A knarled, tremoring finger aimed at the silent monolith across the street. "I will join you there."

Shaking his head with irritation, Erik returned to the hearse. After a tram rumbled past, he threw the vehicle into gear, then wheeled it across the tracks and pavement. And on through the cemetery gates. He parked under a lamp, its tungsten filament casting a sour-yellow glow, painting the red brick crematory a burnt orange. Erik shuddered at the repository of embered bones, a repelling phalanx of tilting shadows rising like a black, petrified temple.

Wondering if Marlene and Joseph were watching, Erik shoved open the back doors of the hearse. Montaut, assisted by two stooges of contrasting heights, transported the body by gurney into the strange edifice.

"So you are here to learn the ropes? Herr Doktor Niemeier failed to notify us. Come, let us proceed downstairs." He glared while motioning his arm toward the freight lift.

Five men, one without a heartbeat, boarded the elevator which descended with eccentric fits and starts, deep through layers of earth and stone, the air turning musty. After a sudden jolt, the steel doors creaked open. The four propelled the gurney and the remains of Valentini northward along a dimly lit corridor, passing an armed Thunderbird guard who joined their group. Footsteps resonated, wall to wall. At another entrance, halfway down the hallway, they stopped and turned to the right.

Montaut squeezed his smoking butt between thumb and forefinger and then leaned against a protruding three-inch button. Two ponderous metal doors opened, grating as they slid apart. With heightened alertness, Erik trailed the assemblage into an underground operating theater, the air here no longer damp but dry and chilled. The walls swallowed sounds, in sharp contrast to the ambiance of the tunnel. He took rapid mental notes as Thunderbird minions rolled the cadaver onto the operating table.

Montaut snatched up an instrument and studied Erik's frame, then spoke in German.

"Well now, if you are not Rolf, then who, pray, are you?" His pallid eyes stared through Erik. Two henchmen moved up.

"Bruce Perrone," Erik fired without hesitation. "Rolf will return tomorrow."

"I trust you have identification, Herr Perrone."

Erik felt their scrutiny as he rolled up his sleeve until the tattoo revealed itself. The old man's hand grabbed Erik's forearm, and he pushed an electronic instrument against the skin, a brisk staccato snapping through the air.

"Very good, Herr Perrone. Herr Doktor Niemeier will arrive shortly. His engineer is coming with him to repair a small short circuit in our machine." Montaut stabbed his thumb toward the ominous creature clinging to the ceiling.

Erik spotted a spiral staircase at the far corner of the room. The metal stairway ascended through a dark opening overhead. Gas lines, water conduits, and electrical cables snaked through the crawl space, between the hanging ceiling and the top of the room. His eyes darted back to the glass and metal monster. He had seen a smaller version of a similar device during his medical experiments with the U.S. Army laser unit.

Suddenly, with a shiver, he understood. *An argon laser! The searing beam of blue and green can melt and vaporize the brain, the resulting liquid and gaseous residue easily siphoned away.*

Having not yet reported his own research, he intended to verify his findings with further studies. Erik couldn't believe it. *Niemeier had done so on the human brain! Through two small holes in the skull Niemeier is able to annihilate each side of the brain, dead or alive. Harald's brain still had been alive.* Erik did not want to meet the same odious fate.

His eyes snapped back to Montaut. "I shall be missed at the hospital if I don't return immediately."

"Very well. Hermann, accompany Herr Perrone back to his hearse."

The taller of the muscular assistants led Erik back into the underground hall.

"What is in the other direction?" Erik jerked his thumb northward, away from the elevator of the crematory.

Hermann growled, "Another freight lift, under guard. Shoots up to the funeral parlor. You're standing underneath Albisriederstrasse." A distant tram thumped overhead, the muted vibrations disappearing.

Erik nodded as they turned left and hopped onto the crematorium elevator. At the street level, Erik trotted toward the carriage of the dead while Hermann returned below ground.

Erik slid to an abrupt stop, his shoes screeching over the gravel. A car approached, owlish twin lights knifing the black. Niemeier in his Mercedes!

Unable to leave the fenced enclosure without being seen, Erik spun about and whipped back into the red brick edifice. His thumb mashed on the elevator call-button. A commixture of Prussian and Italian intensified after three car-doors slammed shut with a triplet of thuds. Voices. Niemeier, Sierpinski, and a third man. Erik heard the sluggish grating of the elevator cease as it hit bottom and began a slow, return ascent. His frantic fist pressed into the button again.

Christ! Won't that infernal thing move up any faster? Icy fingers gripped his chest as footfalls and muffled tongues loomed closer. The phlegmatic doors of the elevator slid apart just as the three arrivals swung open the portal to the crematorium.

Erik leaped inside, hammering at the lever on the wall panel and then wiped cold perspiration from his forehead. The elevator grunted, lurching downward once more. No telephones visible. He wondered how could he contact Marlene and Joseph.

48

The Apartment, Monday, 8:00 P.M.

Marlene Sternschen paced back and forth in her flat at Freilagerstrasse. She and Joseph had seen the hearse drive up to the crematorium, but their infrared binoculars could not define the driver, his features hidden by a cap and tinted windows. Later, a car rolled through the graveyard gate on Albisriederstrasse.

"That Mercedes has Niemeier's license plate, but now it's hidden from our view by the crematory." Marlene's eyes riveted on the TV monitor. Feeling helpless, she resumed her tight journey about the room.

"Ease up, Marlene. There's little we can do now."

"I know, Joseph. I pretended to be Professor Roellein's secretary and called Niemeier's office. The clerk said that Doctor Landon drove to Cumaves with Niemeier, who later dropped him off at the Hotel Poly. But now, no word." She peered out the silver-toned window again.

"Strange, I admit. Especially when that Suzanne telephoned here. She could have known our phone number only if Erik had given it to her. And then informing us about this Sierpinski guy being associated with

Niemeier," scowled Joseph, his eyebrows knitting together.

"Do you think she told anyone else?"

"If she had, she would not have called us, I'm quite sure. And remember, Bjørn had been her husband. Just to be on the safe side, I have had that phone number disconnected and replaced. Tomorrow we'll have our people check out Sierpinski. We still have to hold tight until Wednesday, even if it means Erik's life. You must understand that, Marlene. There is too much...too many souls at stake now."

"I guess you're right, Joseph. I just wish we knew *something*." She clenched her fists and eyelids, attempting to picture where Erik might be.

"Terry Caldwell lands here tomorrow morning. Try to get some sleep while I keep surveillance for a while."

"Alright. I wonder what Cumaves has to do with all this?" Marlene stared out the window, her eyes glued to a tram rolling away, westward between the mortuary and the crematorium. She shivered, *Erik, darling, where are you?*

49

The freight elevator doors rattled and opened into the underground arcade below Albisriederstrasse. Erik hesitated under white bricked walls and a damp ceiling arching over reinforcing steel beams. Then he saw a bank of gray metal storage cabinets in the hall and squeezed between two, into their shadows. The icy silence crawled on, interrupted only by an overhead tram traveling westward. Then the lift returned with guards flanking the trio. The men continued conversing, now raising their voices in excitement, switching between German and Italian.

They brushed close by, Sierpinski's silver sleeve buttons scraping against the steel cabinets. Niemeier's forefinger pressed the electrical wall-stud powering the door to the operating chamber. Through the open portal Erik could make out most of the conversation, guttural voices clashing off one another. Standing in shadows, he peeked into the brightly lit room and listened.

"But Herr Doktor, the man must have gone past you. I left him off at the door of the crematory," cried a lackey they called Hermann, his voice tense, even brittle.

Niemeier shook with wrath, his face beat-red, a mass of knotted fury. "There is no one by the name of Perrone. How could you be so stupid!"

"But he passed the test. How would anyone but a colleague know about the radioactive tattoo?" questioned Pierre Montaut, trembling with rage, anger slipping into fear. "It was your idea, Herr Doktor, to assure absolute security."

"Someone knows now!" Niemeier's face, bristling, darkening with unappeased wrath, pushed within an inch of the Frenchman's. "And I intend to discover how the *SSV* has become compromised. Describe the intruder."

Pierre Montaut backed away. "Tall, black hair, strong build, hairy arms, wore a Trieste orderly's uniform, spoke German with a foreign accent."

"Lock! Doctor Lock!" screamed Niemeier. "From America. A spy. The hearse is still in the driveway. He did not pass us. He must still be nearby. Find him now and seize him!"

Hermann, dense eyebrows flickering out of control, punched numbers into a security panel and then pulled out a telephone. "Guards! Come immediately!"

Quietly, Erik slipped back behind the cabinets.

Joined by two arriving Thunderbird squads, Beretta AR-70 assault rifles slung over their shoulders, Niemeier and his henchmen stormed from the underground surgical chamber, splitting into small teams running toward the crematorium and the funeral home. As they trooped close by him, Erik held his breath until the muttering specters vanished, determination calming the anxiety of impending doom.

He stole from his hideaway. He could not stay there and could not leave without being seen. One of the elevators was returning. Looking about, Erik dashed toward the closed doors of the operating room, pressed the wall-stud, vaulted inside, and pushed another square lever to shut the massive sliding portal. He heard the unsettling vibrations of the elevator doors opening into the underground tunnel.

Erik rushed for the spiral stairway at the end of the operating room and dashed up into the crawl space. Wiggling his way along a steel beam, he then inched toward a corner where he could see below into the theater. Water conduits snaked through this aperture. The doors slid open again. The surgeon, the engineer, and the third man filed into the room.

"He cannot escape," hissed Niemeier, still fuming. "Others will continue the search. I've posted additional guards at both elevators. Now, we have work to do. Damn you, Frohmut, assist me with my surgical attire."

From above, Erik could see Niemeier change into his scrub suit as Frohmut, a middle-aged dwarf with a bald pate and long fringes of hair, scuttered about the room. Niemeier's servant was an elfin creature with small depressed eyes. He had a face fronting a prodigious head above a curved spine, the neck invisible. Soon he stood at fawning attention behind the doctor.

Niemeier, rage driving the surgeon, clamped the deceased Valentini's head into a surgical, three-point skull tong and then incised the scalp behind the hairline. Automatic drill-bits bore through the bloodless skull.

In the meantime Erik watched Sierpinski labor at the control panel, adjusting liquid helium and nitrogen cooling systems. The third man paced back and forth between Sierpinski and Niemeier. Erik now had a clear picture of the stranger. Five and a half foot in height. Obese. Middle-aged. Nearly bald. His left eyelid sagged, beads of sweat dotting the right side of his face.

From the description supplied by Helga to Jeffry, this is Jørgen Busche, Erik realized, recalling Jeffry's tape replayed by Stafford.

"Herr Doktor," growled Busch as he halted in front of the corpse, his eyes playing over Valentini's rubbery face.

"If your American is not apprehended, we must shut down our business in Zürich and transfer to another site. At any rate, your radioactive design, clever as it is, must be discarded. I shall notify our associates."

"*Verdammt!* What did Herr Dietz say about the delays at New York? Does he think U.S. Customs suspect our organization?" grunted Niemeier as he curetted out loose bone.

"We don't know, though there is intense pressure to locate the narcotic couriers. He is consulting with Masters.

"However, Dietz agrees that all units should proceed with Herr Sierpinski's brilliant suggestion. I already have notified our opium mills and mortuaries. If overseas customs officers attempt to uncover our shipments, you can be assured it shall be their final revelation. We have already shipped one such courier by vessel from Copenhagen to New York. And your surgical friend and his engineers in Hong Kong are preparing surprise packages for Taipei and San Francisco."

"Very good, Herr Busche. Today will not provide enough time to implant explosives. We shall just insert the heroin as usual. Tomorrow Sierpinski and I will prepare another captive we have in mind."

Busche squeezed his lips into an evil smile, nodding in agreement.

"My Polish friend," continued Doctor Niemeier with impatience. "Have you repaired the malfunctioning wire? Our argon mistress is becoming impatient."

"All is in order, Herr Doktor. You may proceed," confirmed Sierpinski, the shriveled, vulturine neck twisting toward the surgeon.

Erik was awestruck. The giant creature, a modern tapestry of metal and glass, lumbered into position as the mute and cretinous servant they called Frohmut, slavishly following the directives of Sierpinski, pressed a sequence of control buttons on the power supply panel. Niemeier aimed the huge laser gun. Overhead lights dimmed. A switch snapped, triggering a streak of shimmering white light targeting a burr hole. Niemeier paused until the rolling wheels of an overhead streetcar thrummed into the distance and vanished.

The three conspirators and the troll with a leonine head donned protective goggles, monstrous flies craving to devour a dead carcass. Niemeier commanded the release of energy—"*Los!*" and a blazing stream of blue-green pierced the air, slicing through the aperture in the skull.

Erik's eyes widened. Incandescent fumes shot upward as the electronic maggot vaporized the brain, eating its way through dead tissues. A thin suction tube in Niemeier's left hand spirited out liquefied nerves. With his right hand he maneuvered a small dental mirror into and beyond the hole. This instrument reflected the laser beam within the skull, through all reaches of the right brain. Then the left cerebrum suffered the same destruction.

"Excellent. Now, the milk from the poppy," ordered the gloating surgeon.

The obedient assistant shuffled to a cabinet and pulled out flexible strings of plastic containers. The thin, pliant packages encased the Marseille heroin which Niemeier inserted through the orifices. After packing the narcotic into the brain case of Louis Valentini, Niemeier sealed the openings with plastic and then glued the scalp edges together with acrylic adhesive. The doctor, lapsing into uncharacteristic tenderness while humming a waltz, washed the hair and combed the strands into place.

The shrill voice of the engineer startled Erik.

"Now, Louis," cackled Sierpinski, rising up in a messianic exhortation, taking center stage. His quiet, introverted demeanor spun into a evangelistic crescendo as shoulder blades hammered at the back of his shirt. "You are now a comrade-in-arms. In the name of Lenin, we shall destroy our imperialistic enemies!

"So Americans want the good life, do they? Weak and impotent, decadent and lazy, addicted to their child-like comforts. Yes, Louis, you will be a bearer of instant happiness. Let America suck on the breast of the poppy. *We shall rule the world. It is our manifest destiny!*" The human ostrich shrank back down and strutted toward the control panel.

Erik, stunned by what he just witnessed, tightened his grip on the steel beam, fighting to retain internal composure. He had to escape.

Hermann and Pierre Montaut, frustrated in their failure to locate the spy, reappeared in the surgical chamber.

"We cannot find this damn Perrone anywhere," cursed Montaut, mopping his perspiring face.

At that moment Erik jerked his head away from the opening in the ceiling. Fine dust from steel beams flittered down through the cleft and scattered into the air.

Sierpinski glanced upward. "Someone is in the crawl space," he shouted as the assistants drew firearms from shoulder harnesses.

"I would advise that you come down immediately, Perrone or Lock or whoever you are," bellowed Niemeier in English.

Desperate to escape, Erik searched for another exit, liberty denied. With reluctance he crawled back toward the shaft of light, to the stairway, and stepped down onto the tile.

"Escort him to the back room of the funeral home and bind him securely. It is late. We shall deal with him later.

"Yes, my friend," Niemeier barked as he shook his fist at Erik. "You will find death a pleasant release when we are through with you."

The armed lackeys grabbed Erik's limbs and shoved him into the underground hallway. They escorted him northward to the funeral home lift, ascending to the street level. The lumbering hoist-way doors rolled open into the rear of the mortuary.

Hermann, a giant of a man, wide eyes protruding as if pressurized gas were pushing forward from his missile-shaped skull, led Erik to the back room. An isolated chamber with mildewed wallpaper. And a single chair. Table. Cot. A tangle of pipes snaking along one wall. Musty air. Barren. Windowless.

With his AR-70, Hermann motioned Erik to sit on the thinly carpeted floor while Frohmut chained Erik's wrists to the metal radiator. The two subhuman spawns slammed and locked the oak door to purgatory, leaving Erik in his prison, an electronic jail surrounded by white noise and high-voltage insulation.

Erik listened to the sounds of footsteps fading, then the drone of an accelerating Mercedes. A small ventilator fan hummed overhead while dim light spread from a single, caged bulb.

Erik strained at his bonds. *Have to get word to Joseph and Marlene. Customs must be warned. Explosives in the skulls. And the reference to Lenin...was Harald on target again?*

The door creaked open, and Pierre Montaut returned with his two toadyish charges. Herman, the bullet-head, towering above the Frenchman. And Frohmut, the sooty gnome, straining to reach Montaut's shoulders. Demons from perdition, Erik concluded.

"Doctor Niemeier wishes that you sleep well." Montaut, his unlit tobacco stick teetering on the lip as he talked, leaned over Erik while the other two restrained his unwilling arm. A sharp point lanced his vein. The old man drove the piston of the syringe inward and withdrew the needle.

They departed, leaving behind the violent thump, thumping of Erik's heart. And the whirring of the fan.

50

Zürich, Tuesday, December 7, 1971, 10:00 A.M.

Terry Caldwell had landed in Zürich. He now sat in a straight-back chair while an overhead fan rotated slowly, attempting to drive warmer air down from the ceiling. He marked time, stewing in the chilly waiting room of Major Roland Reiter, head of the Zürich Division, Swiss National Police. Terry's fingers, unable to settle down, brushed his crew cut. Between glances at the wall clock the lanky BNDD agent studied detailed notes and then the tops of his cowboy boots. A siren cried in the distance.

"Major Reiter has just arrived," the secretary notified Terry. "He will see you now."

Terry followed her staccato steps to an immaculate office. Sunlight danced across a glass-covered credenza and reflected on a colorful portrait depicting a medieval harlequin. Behind a gray metal desk, finished with black acrylic, sat a tall, slim man in a blue, crisply-pressed uniform, carefully tailored to fit, his tie knotted precisely in place. Three inches of space separated his spine from a high-back chair.

He was pulling on a Dunhill, coils of slate-blue smoke hanging in the air, elbows perched on a green blotter as he waved Terry in. The police officer spoke excellent English textured with a sharp and precise Swiss-German accent, occasionally clucking his tongue against the roof of his mouth. He stood up.

"Good day, Herr...Mister Caldwell. Please take a seat. Your Director Stafford was quite insistent that I see you. I've set aside this hour. Cigarette?"

"No thank you, sir." A slight pause as Terry pressed his fingertips together, concentrating while the Major retook possession of his chair and leaned imperceptibly forward.

"My instructions, Major, are to report a remarkable, perhaps unbelievable, story of heroin, international intrigue, and massive transfers of moneyed capital in Europe. We have every reason to presume its authenticity. Only a handful of people are aware. Before you make any judgements, I beg you to hear me out."

"Do go ahead, Mr. Caldwell," the officer replied, his hands continually straightening and realigning the papers on his desk, as if marshaling imaginary soldiers on a battlefield, inch by resolute inch. "I am all impatience."

As Terry retailed the extraordinary circumstances, the Major's hands stopped traveling, his knuckles turning white, tense fingers interlacing and thumbs battling each other. The forefinger of law enforcement stabbed the intercom button after stubbing out a cigarette, twisting it violently in the ashtray.

"Have Captain Steimle report to me at once," Reiter ordered his receptionist, the whites of his eyes expanding with rising astonishment.

He shot another cigarette between compressed lips, but the Major appeared too stunned to fire it.

"Please continue, Herr Caldwell. If my friend, Stafford, had not called me first, I would have thought you insane, reeling off some crazy story."

"I understand your position, Major." Terry took a deep breath. "The organization we call Thunderbird has means to cache heroin inside skulls of the dead without it being obvious to our customs officers, even by routine x-ray examination. More recently, CAT scans disclosed the bizarre abnormalities to us, as I have explained. We had hoped that Doctor Landon would lead us to some answers, but he has disappeared."

"And you mean to tell me that many of the graves in Grünfeld are empty!" Reiter's voice struck a notch below a scream, the face flushed in anger. A thump on the desk and the harlequin tipped. "That our distinguished Herr Doktor Niemeier and his colleagues have actually shipped Swiss bodies to America! Swiss bodies? Impossible!"

The flat of the Major's hand smacked the desk again, a pen skittering on its surface. "I refuse to believe that. The paperwork, the logistics. How could they not be discovered?" Reiter's tongue now was snapping at a higher frequency against his palate.

"In the United States, a member of the narcotic cartel receives notice from Dietz in Europe that a new cadaver, a bearer of concentrated heroin, awaits transport to the USA. Someone under Thunderbird control in the U.S. State Department assigns the name and passport number of a recently dead and buried American to this deceased European. The syndicate operative flies to Europe with the falsified document. Or the item may be ferried in a State Department diplomatic pouch. In Zürich, the Society attaches a touched-up photo of the dead Swiss. The carcass, passing now as a deceased American visitor with passport, is returned 'home' for burial. Thus the powder, packaged inside the skull of the deceased Swiss, reaches our shores."

Terry surveyed the Major's stone-frozen face and resumed. "Without doubt, the Dietz organization has the seal for our Department of State and the appropriate imprinter to match that stenciled on the first photograph. Thunderbird obtains actual passport folders from State. Signatures are easily forged. As long as routine procedures are followed by Immigration and Customs, there are no problems. And with Dietz' connections…especially in our State Department…the red tape receives expeditious handling."

"This is…it's insane! What about the Swiss visa stamp on the false passport when he is supposed to have entered Switzerland?" argued Reiter, shaking his head in confusion as he snapped open his cigarette lighter.

"U.S. Immigration pays no attention to that. You know as well as I that the European countries often don't bother stamping the visa section on the passport if the traveler is just visiting. See, look at mine." Terry held up his passport folder. "I arrived this morning, and your Immigration Officer did not imprint it. Besides, I'm sure Dietz can provide an authentic looking Swiss immigration stamp if needed."

"*Lieber Gott!* What happens to your…our…the bodies in America?"

"Without doubt, the expired Europeans are cremated in ovens and scattered to the four winds, leaving their tomb empty in Grünfeld. Evidence would no longer exist…unless the body is a *real* American who dies in Europe and the family wishes a normal burial. This circumstance might appear more ideal to Dietz, I suppose. In fact, it was an American by the name of Campbell whose burial precipitated discovery of one of the Thunderbird principals."

"And at six tomorrow evening, you want us to enter the Braun Funeral Home, a venerable Swiss mortuary, and place everyone under arrest? My dear Herr Caldwell, we need a bit more evidence before such a rash undertaking."

The officer drew short, furious puffs on the cigarette while his eyes held Terry's in an unswerving gaze, the major's mind struggling to comprehend all facets of the bizarre intelligence.

"Later tonight, would the police be willing to breach the tomb of a Frederick Hoffmann at Grünfeld? It must be performed in the dark without arousing suspicion. If his grave is empty, perhaps you'll believe me," entreated Terry, his tone urgent, eyes focused. "We already have incontrovertible evidence that Hoffmann's body passed through New York Customs and needle biopsy confirmed heroin inside the skull."

"You are a persistent man, Caldwell." The police officer corkscrewed out of his seat and turned toward the opening door. "Ah…there you are Captain Steimle. You and I and this presumptuous American are going grave digging this evening. We will need shovels, picks, and flashlights. Tell your wife that you are working late. We must accomplish this in utmost secrecy."

Captain Steimle's mouth popped open at the bizarre order, speechless for a moment. "This must be a joke, Herr Major." His ramrod stance wavered.

"I am not jesting, and our audacious friend here had better not be either. Dress warmly. Snow is expected."

Grünfeld Cemetery, Tuesday, 10:00 P.M.

A fine veneer of wet leaves, mixed with carpets of pine needles and patches of snow, blanketed the soft contours of the resting ground. Barren trees, devoid of foliage, scratched the air with each burst of wind. Scattered rows of evergreens and low shrubbery dotted the field. Marlene Sternschen had located the grave marker of the Swiss, Frederick Hoffmann, now resting in America under the forged title of Sterling Mason.

Except for the distant, luminescent dots of metropolitan life, only probing flashlights interrupted the misty and palpable darkness, the cloak of night providing substance to collective suspense and skepticism. There were no signs of life at Braun. Marlene, Terry, and two police officers hefted their picks and shovels, proceeding to break up the frosted earth and frozen mud abutting the gravestone. Halfway to the casket, picks stopped in midair, a stranger's voice in the mist jolting the visitors.

"*Was ist los?*" What is going on? An elderly man dressed in caretaker's clothes materialized from the direction of the crematorium.

The Major, his hand on his holster, turned toward the approaching figure and snapped in Swiss-German, "Herr Major Reiter, here. *Polizei*. Authorized to exhume the body of one, Frederick Hoffmann."

"But that is absurd," charged Pierre Montaut, spreading his gloved hands. "I am keeper of this cemetery. This is an insult. The family will bring charges if you persist."

"Please stand fast until we finish," ordered the grim officer, lifting and snugging down his cap.

"Of course, Herr Major." He stepped back, flicking an ember of tobacco into the snow.

The low-pitched thud of picks striking a wooden coffin flew up from the burial pit. Dirt was cleared away and the top prepared for opening. Captain Steimle jumped into the crypt and removed the screws holding down the cover. The curious coterie looked on with a silent hush of nervous anticipation.

Reiter and Caldwell glanced at each other and then down at the coffin. Captain Steimle inhaled with a sudden gasp upon lifting death's doorway, flashlights spearing the black.

"Oh shit," hissed Terry. "Damnation!"

All eyes of the assembled gravediggers riveted on the decomposing body resting inside. A chagrined and contrite Caldwell, flinching at the sight, looked up with puzzled disappointment, refusing to believe what his eyes beheld. "Something is terribly wrong here," he muttered. Terry fisted his hands, still staring at the corpse dressed in a pressed railway uniform.

"Is there a problem, Herr Major?" growled the annoyed custodian still standing in shadows.

"Our apologies for disturbing the peace of this cemetery. We will fill in the grave," replied the abashed policeman, whipping his head about and glaring at Terry. His lips were tightly compressed, as if sutured together. "Well, Herr Caldwell?"

Terry opened his mouth to respond, then closing it, swallowing hard.

A sweet, nauseating reek hovered about the corpse. Something you could taste and feel. Marlene grimaced at the smell. Mortification of the flesh. "Strange! Why wasn't he embalmed?" she wondered aloud.

"May I take my leave now?" The caretaker stretched a wry smile across his sallow cheeks.

"Just a moment," interjected Marlene, her shaft of light refocusing on the marbled face of the dead. "You must not let that man escape."

"But we cannot hold him." The embarrassed Major shrugged his shoulders. "We've just proven Herr Caldwell to be dreadfully mistaken."

"That is not the body of a dead Swiss. This is Chester Phillips, our missing American CIA agent. And look. Several of his fingers have been sliced clean off. Quickly, grab that man!" Marlene spun about and torched her light at Montaut's face.

Pierre Montaut wheeled around and raced toward the crematory.

"Halt or I will fire!" commanded the Major.

The escaping figure whirled about, leveling his weapon at Reiter. The pistol flamed as a shot echoed in the night dampness. Scattering shock waves resounded, and a high-pitched whistle flew past Marlene's ear, the bullet creasing the Major's shoulder and striking an elm with a tight thud. Reiter leaped to the right while firing his sidearm, the missile cracking the air.

The human target grabbed his chest, twisted, and collapsed over an unmarked gravestone. They rushed to examine the victim, the Frenchman gasping as life slipped away, a milky sheen spreading over his eyes. Montaut's hand still held fast to his weapon while a crimson island spread from the breach in his shirt, crawling over a sea of white cotton.

"Take him to the city morgue," the Major charged the Captain, reality shattering his normally regimented infrastructure. "And my sincere apologies to you, Herr Caldwell."

"Herr Major, are you alright?" Marlene examined Reiter's shoulder.

"Yes. Just a scratch. And Herr Captain?"

"Yes, sir?"

"I want a tail placed on a Herr Doktor Niemeier and his friend from Cumaves. Tonight. Now come to my office for a briefing."

"Yes sir. I will be there," promised the bewildered officer.

"This is an unbelievable nightmare. Now, Miss Sternschen." The policeman turned to Marlene. "I wish to have you and your friend Joseph Smith explain how and why an infrared beam discharges from the top of one of our tram poles, bounces off the Braun windows, and strikes your apartment." Major Reiter pointed toward the funeral parlor. "All the details."

"How did you know?" queried Marlene, dumbfounded.

"Before entering the cemetery, I scanned the area with my heat-sensing binoculars. Your infrared beam is quite striking through these lenses, an unmistakable signature."

"Please come to the apartment. Agent Smith can relieve your concerns."

"Go ahead," said Terry. "The captain and I will retrieve the corpse and replace the lid on the coffin. I'll join you in a half-hour."

"And I shall arrange for the immediate removal of our assailant and this...Chester Phillips, you say? ...to the city morgue," asserted the Major. "We must fill in the gravesite so it appears undisturbed. The snow will cover our work. And Herr Caldwell, we must contact Director Stafford immediately."

A light drizzle slipped into flakes of wet snow.

51

Washington, Tuesday, December 7, 1971.

Thirty-four men and women, standing and sitting, had assembled in the conference hall at Justice. BNDD, FBI, and CIA. Their assignment—coordinate the destruction of Thunderbird. Electronic maps of cities and countries illuminated the walls, points of attack flashing in colors. Against an easel stood a graph reflecting the daily incidence of narcotic-related deaths. The curve was accelerating.

"Tomorrow afternoon we blitz the suspected Thunderbird operations in Washington and New York City." The Director's fist hammered the conference table top. "We will launch simultaneous hits at known narcotic nests in San Francisco, Taipei, and Hong Kong, as well as targeted European cities. In some cases, local governments are cooperating. In others, the CIA will have to handle it in their own way.

"Here in Washington..." Stafford pointed toward Agent Martin. "...Don will head the strike team. I have not heard from our Zürich operatives yet. A report should arrive from Caldwell any minute.

"Our enemy is vicious and cunning. One of the principals is the elusive Ludwig Dietz and his colleagues in Germany. Hopefully, we can confirm his role when the German police close him down. Try to abide by the local laws. In some cases, we cannot assist you if you exceed legal constraints. Use your judgment, but stop and decapitate this vampire. Each of you has your teams and assignments." He paused. "Any questions?"

"Sir, any word about Doctor Landon?" asked Don Martin.

"Sorry. Nothing yet. Our Zürich team is still seeking info. Okay, let's move…and good luck."

52

Zürich, Tuesday morning.

Still groggy, Erik's head and bones ached from lying on the floor. A day's stubble textured his face. He blinked his eyes as the jailed overhead lamp swam into focus.

Hermann returned with Frohmut shuffling in tow and released Erik's chains. The guards, smelling of cheap cologne mixed with sweat, hauled him, wrists now cuffed in front, down the hall to the toilet. Then to the elevator and underground operating room, a modern theater of horrors. His forearms, still fettered in chains, chafed from the iron bonds.

"Sit." Hermann, the taller henchman, shoved Erik down and lashed him to a metal chair.

The sliding door grated open. Niemeier and Sierpinski, conversing rapidly in German, entered the underground theater. Behind a screen Johann Niemeier, assisted by Frohmut, changed into a green scrub suit.

"Welcome to our 'debriefing center.' We do not wish to create bruises on your face, my friend. When we finish with you, your lifeless features must appear serene...especially to U.S. Customs. Today you shall witness what fate awaits in the morning. Should you cooperate and answer our questions, I will be humane and put you to sleep first. If not, then…

"Herr Sierpinski, prepare the explosive for our courier." The dungeon master screwed his frame toward Frohmut and Hermann, both literally bending from the violence of the surgeon's spirit. "Bring in the patient."

She looked familiar to Erik, and he felt like his bones were swimming in chilled blood.

The two stooges dragged in the terrified young woman, straining to break away, eyes wide, wet with fear. With sounds of ripping cloth, they stripped away her outer garments and roped her half-naked body to the operating table. On command, Hermann locked her head in his vise-like grip. She cried out as the former Nazi surgeon, without anesthesia, clamped the three pinions through her black hair and into her skull. His fist clicked the iron joints, locking her head in space. At first Erik did not recognize the newcomer without her glasses. Then his eyes snapped wide with shock.

"Suzanne," he blurted out. "You…how…?" Erik, recognizing the secretary from Cumaves, felt his heart stutter and then sink.

"I heard the tape of her conversation on the telephone yesterday," rasped Sierpinski, watery eyes darting about, undulating shoulder blades spiking the white laboratory jacket. He bore down on Erik. "From your presence and from what I overheard, you are working for some government—American I assume. And Fräulein Mullineaux is going to tell us all she knows."

"Of course," inserted a sanctimonious Niemeier, glancing at Erik, "if you wish to volunteer information, you would release her from the suffering of the condemned. Now let us aim the laser."

He focused the coaxial light beam on the victim's right index finger and then wound a string tourniquet about its base, her hand already yoked to an arm rest. Suzanne fought to disengage her limb as an electronic hum signaled photon charge buildup.

"Do you wish to talk, Fräulein Mullineaux?"

"Leave her alone, Niemeier. She doesn't know anything." Erik tried to hurl himself and the heavy chair at the man.

"*Los!*" Niemeier spit the biting command to fire.

A wire-thin beam of blue-green energy leaped through the air, striking Suzanne's straining finger. She screamed, her gaping mouth congealing in a rictus of pain as Niemeier swept the rapier of intense light, cleaving digit from joint, dropping the bloody flesh to the tile.

"You bastard, Niemeier! Your barbaric soul will rot in Hell," raged Erik, perspiration blanketing his forehead.

The corrupted surgeon barked his ultimatum. "Well, Fräulein. Perhaps you have reconsidered?"

"I know nothing of Bjørn's assignments. Please..."

The laser gun smote the defenseless woman, and another finger spun away. Shock waves rippled through her body, the flesh quivering with white-hot pain as defiance became more brittle.

"Stop it!" Erik cried. "I'll tell you what you want to know."

"No," gasped Suzanne, her breathing choppy, her words smudged by wrenching affliction. "Don't do it for me. I will be sacrificed anyway. Don't let it be in vain. Bjørn would have died for nothing."

"*Los!*"

A third finger tumbled to the floor. Fighting off the ghastly image, Erik squeezed his eyelids together.

"So... Then we must get down to business, Fräulein. Talk to me, and I'll administer morphine." The gloved fingers of the master race stroked her pale cheek.

No answer. The woman, impaled by the three points in her skull, had gone into shock, approaching the edge of death.

The predator, humming "The Merry Widow Waltz," proceeded to incise her scalp and drill two cranial apertures. He aimed the laser beam into the burr holes of the semiconscious woman, her brain melting, disintegrating into smoke and steam.

"For God's sake, Niemeier, have some compassion. You're a physician. You took the Hippocratic oath. Does that not mean anything?"

But Erik's entreaties only sharpened the blade of the doctor's ruthlessness. Stunned, Erik watched as Suzanne's eyes flickered open, seeing beyond the theater, peering over the final abyss.

"Bjørn...Bjørn, I love you." Her last, disembodied words trailed off into oblivion, replaced by the harsh static of electric charges. Her body arched backwards, limbs stiffening, Suzanne now a decerebrate animal teetering over the ledge and into a pale and lifeless form.

There will be a reckoning, Erik calculated, but he could not configure the form it would take.

The laser beam collapsed, and Sierpinski secured the weapon. The victim stopped breathing, her heart fighting for oxygen until its beat ceased forever. Sierpinski struck a switch and overhead vents swooshed away the odor of ozone.

Niemeier, failing to extract any telltale signals from Suzanne, packed the left side of her empty cranial vault with the Marseille heroin. Into the cavity on the right, he inserted Sierpinski's tubes of high explosive, a cordite derivative, attached to a miniature metal and plastic device powered by battery. The skull and scalp were sealed shut, and the crazed artist, still humming the waltz, tenderly combed Suzanne's lifeless tresses back into place. Hermann disconnected the skull clamp and placed the slain figure into a refrigerated vault within the chamber's south wall.

Niemeier peeled off his rubber gloves while assessing Erik's presence. "Tonight you must consider what you just witnessed. You shall be spared such pain and suffering tomorrow, if you talk. Take him away."

The two swaggering minions returned Erik to his cell in the mortuary and chained his wrists to the metal steam radiator. Frohmut carried in a sealed plastic bag filled with formaldehyde solution, three fingers floating inside. He threw the barbaric trophy on the floor in front of Erik.

"Herr Doktor sends his regards and wishes you to have something to think about tonight."

Frohmut drove another needle into Erik's arm. With his sense of time now in free-fall, the world began to spin. He tumbled into a suspended state, descending to the bottom of a bottomless ocean.

Wednesday, December 8.

The following morning, Erik awoke again with kettle drums hammering, bleariness fading as outlines of reality refocused. He sat up on the floor and attempted to force rational thoughts, shaking himself to throw off a mounting dread. He had to warn Marlene and Joseph about the explosives.

Only silence answered his shouts, and the early hours rolled by with agonizing slowness.

Early afternoon he heard clumping footsteps and the creaking of wooden flooring. The door flew open and the two dispassionate assistants, bottom feeders among the living, leaned over Erik.

"Herr Doktor Niemeier requires your presence in the operating room," snorted the dwarf, a cruel smile coiling his whiskered cheeks. He was picking shreds of tobacco off his lip.

"Tell the doctor I will talk. How about a comfortable chair in the front room?"

"Much too late for you now," needled Hermann. "But I will ask."

He left and returned with Niemeier.

"Ahah...so you have reconsidered. And as I expected, you prefer a bit more luxury. Don't even think about jumping through the plate glass window. Frohmut's bullets will hover only a trigger-pull from your heart."

"I understand," Erik responded, loathing the man in front of him. "What alternative do I have?"

Frohmut and Hermann marched Erik down a narrow hallway, past another guard with his assault rifle. Inside the front parlor Niemeier instructed him to sit in an armchair, its soft leather creeping around his body. His wrists remained shackled, his head still woozy.

"That Luger makes me nervous. Must your man point the barrel directly at me?"

"Niemeier turned toward the dwarf. "Lower your sidearm, Frohmut. This rash American has nowhere to escape."

"May I have some coffee?" Erik attempted to stall for time.

"*Nein*. I have a schedule to keep. Now, your real name? How did you know about the tattoo?" Niemeier removed his bifocals and rotated the stem in his left hand as Erik threaded the complex trail separating life and death, separating him from Marlene.

53

Zürich, The Apartment, Wednesday, 2:30 P.M.

Major Reiter, pacing about in Joseph's electronic war room, spoke with precision, measuring his words. "Our laboratory examined the missile from the old caretaker's gun. The late Harald Johnson and your CIA are absolved of any complicity in the death of Melita LaVecchia and her mother. They died by the hand of Pierre Montaut." He stopped, coughed, and lit another Dunhill.

"Armed units are moving into position for entry into the funeral home and crematorium at six tonight," continued the Major, his cigarette pointing out the window. "Three and a half hours from now.

"Our friend, Lugoso at Crédit Suisse, contacted colleagues at sister banks. He has verified that both Niemeier and Busche transacted huge sums of money over the past few years. Many of the bank drafts from Niemeier to Busche's account in Winterhur originated in Basel. We're tracing the paper trail to Basel."

"Who received the Niemeier and Busche drafts?" queried Marlene, her mind half on her intelligence job, half on Erik.

"Money passed on to Swiss bank accounts and to an offshore trust in the Bahamas. Our financial institutions won't reveal the owners unless we can prove illegal activities in Switzerland. We'll have that information in a few days."

"What about Sierpinski?" queried Joseph, resting on his knees as he recalibrated the null point on an oscilloscope.

"Originally Polish. This Jerzy Sierpinski is a curious man well known to West German Intelligence as an East German espionage agent and later a KGB operative for the Soviet State Security Committee. During the last world war, he fought the Nazi forces near Krakow. Even though he and a Kommandant Baumann at the Auschwitz concentration camp had campaigned on opposite sides, in later years they collaborated, growing wealthy together. Through the same Baumann in Mainz, Sierpinski met Dietz. This Dietz runs an international mortuary business, skilled at cutting red tape to transfer dead expatriots back to their homeland."

"But Dietz opposed communism. Our sources show that he was using his funereal activities to help smuggle people out of East Germany," interjected Marlene.

"True, except that, after the fall of Hitler's regime, Dietz, and Niemeier for that matter, neither endorsed nor disputed communism per se. They supported any ideology that put power and money in their pockets. There was more to it than that.

"Through Baumann, Serpinski, for reasons as yet to be clarified, was able to force Dietz to halt his transport of East German refugees and help Russia in their undercover work against the West. Perhaps the capture of the occupants of the Braun Funeral Home will shed some light. At any rate, this quiet and simple appearing engineer in Zürich may be the main link between Russia and your Thunderbird."

"How did you obtain the information so quickly?" asked Joseph. "Our own contacts have failed to come up with anything so substantial."

"Our Swiss operations devote massive electronic surveillance to track the rise and fall of currencies, including financial espionage hidden even from blinded governments and from manipulated CEOs. No regime or institution wants its clandestine fiscal activities jeopardized. With just a few phone calls to our banks, to Cumaves, and to the appropriate German and Polish officials, we ascertained our facts. And we have some counterespionage agents in the KGB on our payroll…as does your country."

"Then it would be mandatory to take this Dietz alive," emphasized Marlene.

"True. He works out of West Berlin, but I gather Director Stafford and West German Intelligence already have him under their microscope. It is this Herr Doktor Niemeier who interests me the most. We have discovered that some of the Swiss bank accounts protecting funds of Jewish families during World War II have disappeared, identical monies reappearing in various numbered accounts owned by Niemeier. He…"

"I see a small panel truck parking down the street." Joseph stood up and peered out the window.

"Belongs to us," explained Major Reiter, adjusting his cap. "More will be arriving. They'll park discreetly nearby. Captain Steimle is bringing us a radio to keep in contact with every police car. In the meantime…"

"Shh…listen. The infrared laser unit." Joseph turned up the loudspeaker as an automatic trip device triggered the tape. "It's coming from the mortuary."

"That voice—it's Erik! He's still alive," cried Marlene, jumping up from her chair. "…and Niemeier."

Deafening silence rolled through the room, only quiet electronic beeps and muffled whirrs slipping through the background. Marlene, her breathing nearly frozen, wiped away the moisture pooling in her eyes. Everyone leaned forward, tense, seconds slipping away on the ever-present digital clock as two brain surgeons battled with blades of wit.

"...name is Doctor Erik Landon. I arrived in Zürich to arrange for the return of my brother, Jeffry. You might know the name, except he called himself Brian Trent."

"Your brother? *Ja*, he was smart, but not smart enough for us," gloated Niemeier, checking his pocket watch.

"Why did you have to kill him? Why did you torture and slaughter Suzanne Mullineaux with that monstrous argon laser here in your underground operating room?" Erik asked, attempting to feed information to Marlene and Joseph.

"Ordered by the Kremlin. Your brother was interfering with my Helga. And that Suzanne knew too much."

"The Kremlin? The Soviet Union?"

"They pay us well to deliver heroin into your country. Our system is infallible. You shall be brought to your knees, begging for mercy." Niemeier stood over Erik and shook his balled-up fist.

"But why insert both explosives and heroin in the skull after vaporizing her brain with your laser?" Erik's brain ached with tension. *Christ, I hope they're listening to this.*

"Our people in New York will know how to remove the heroin without detonating the bomb. If anyone else touches the plastic cover or takes an x-ray photo, the head will explode and destroy a whole building," hissed Niemeier, his damp face now twisting into a burnt carmine. "Using a transponder, we shall arm the device after it has cleared European shores."

"An x-ray?"

"Indeed. Herr Sierpinski has developed a sensitive photo-detector. It requires merely a trace of radiation to send an electric charge into the detonator. Should your customs building go up in smoke, we'll know someone had discovered our courier system. Now, enough of this." His annoyance heightened, the voice now a half octave higher. "How did you come by that tattoo? How did you find out about us?"

"You treated a friend of a colleague once. Marty Campbell. We suspected foul play. That is how we got your name."

"Campbell? Yes, I recall the name. An American in an automobile accident. What was so unusual?"

"He was transferred from Winterthur all the way to Trieste, bypassing other hospitals. You were recommended by someone in Cumaves."

"Yes," smiled Niemeier, his jaw shifting. "My friend, Herr Sierpinski made the referral."

"And the other man?" Erik moved uncomfortably in the deep chair.

"You mean Herr Busche? Purportedly a Danish businessman. He heads an international ring skilled at providing espionage agents, money, sex, drugs, killers… whatever an unscrupulous government or corporate official desires. Russian funds are funneled into our organization through Sierpinski, and we pay Busche for services rendered. Busche also manages a funeral home like this one in Copenhagen for a man named Dietz. Quite an impressive place, don't you think?" crowed Niemeier, trapped by unrelenting pride.

"I marvel at the brilliance of someone who can carry this off," Erik agreed, again playing for more time. "And the source of your heroin?"

"Turkish opium. Processed by our new technique in Marseille. Quite pure."

"Who masterminds your division in America?"

"Someone at the very top in your State Department. Lance Masters. Busche had once arranged for your brother's friend, Helga, to compromise him on a hotel couch. It was a lustful affair he will never forget. He was first blackmailed and then offered large sums of money, which he could not turn down. Now he is one of us."

"This Helga. Why was she so important to you?"

Erik saw Niemeier flinch as the Nazi proclaimed, "In Auschwitz I made her what she was. The true alchemy. Not lead into gold, but Polish children into German Aryans...as surely as if I had spawned them myself. She...and others like her. Medical miracles. You are a colleague. Don't you understand? For the greater science!"

The apostle of self aggrandizement struggled to regain control of present intent, simmering in unintended silence. Then —

"Well now," growled Niemeier, "you have learned much. But of no value to a dead man. I suggest you tell me about your tattoo...in order to assure a painless death. How did you know it emitted radioactivity? Who is helping you? Whom did Suzanne Mullineaux telephone?" Erik observed Niemeier's annoyance moving to anger, a jowled countenance rising to violent shades of color.

Erik was determined that if he could not cheat death, he would make Niemeier work for his booty. "A friend of mine inscribed the tattoo."

"You astonish me, Doctor Landon — if that is your real name. I am losing my patience." He fingered his gold watch fob, stood up, and thumped Erik on his chest. "It is three-thirty and I must catch a plane tonight."

"Don't recall."

"Take him downstairs to the theater. We'll see how good your memory really is." He threw his massive body into the shaking of a threatening fist. Niemeier replaced his spectacles and spun toward Hermann, the surgeon's heavy brow darkening. "Where is Herr Montaut?"

"We do not know, Herr Doktor. We have not seen the old man since last night. This is very unlike him."

54

The Apartment.

"Major, would it be possible to advance the countdown?" implored Marlene.

"We are not fully prepared yet. A premature attack would jeopardize your missions here and elsewhere."

"He's right, Marlene," Joseph put his arm around her. "It's a precision operation with too many lives at stake."

Marlene sighed and sank back down in her chair, watching the luminescent green numbers of the digital clock flashing by, measuring, with a stealthy touch, the final moments of resolution. She abhorred her intelligence assignment now.

Joseph turned to Major Reiter and Terry Caldwell. "That third man must have been Jørgen Busche. He and this Sierpinski are somewhere else in that building. Our people in Copenhagen won't find him today. He sounds like a good catch too."

"I better contact Stafford and warn him about the explosive devices. Okay if I use your phone, Marlene?" asked Terry.

"Certainly." But her mind was on the man she loved. Marlene, her stomach seized with indecision, gazed out the apartment window toward the mortuary.

Terry walked into the kitchen and dialed long distance. He activated the scrambler.

"Hamlet here."

"Zürich speaking."

"What's up?"

"We know where Erik is."

The two henchmen, slaves to Niemeier's evil will, dragged Erik back down into the surgical dungeon. Chained to metal pipes, Erik glanced at the timepiece, its hands in irrevocable clockwise movement—4:45. Ticking. Ticking him away. Busche shuddered and excused himself. Helga's Copenhagen contact returned above ground, not wanting to digest this before dinner time.

Erik watched Sierpinski pace back and forth in front of the control panel, checking, tapping dials and computer readouts. Niemeier, garbed in surgical green, inspected the cranial drill. Frohmut, fine ropes of saliva swinging from smacking lips, hands shaking at the morbid thrill of witnessing the forthcoming execution, placed surgical instruments on the stainless steel Mayo tray, sharp echoes of metal to metal resounding. He pushed the stand close to the operating table. Hermann directed a surgical spotlight on the Mayo tray, the bright beam reflecting into Erik's eyes. The two then stepped back, whispering at an ominous timbre.

Niemeier rotated a handle on the OR table until its foot-end dropped down. The surgeon stepped back to analyze targeting and then elevated the head-end, the steel table now a surgical seat of torture.

"For this special guest, I have altered the routine. Strap our patient into the operating chair, facing the laser instrument. Bind his legs and chest but leave his arms free." Steam fogged Niemeier's spectacles. "I wish to watch our captive battle the laser aimed at his heart. Tell me, Landon. Do you still refuse to talk? I am giving you one last chance."

Niemeier wiped his glasses, his countenance now ox-hide dipped in fuchsia. Fiery, bulbous eyes glared as Hermann strapped Erik into position, Frohmut pushing and tapping his pistol against Erik's head.

Niemeier ripped off Erik's shirt and flicked on the narrow white beam to pre-set the aim of the argon laser. It targeted the center of Erik's chest, chinks of light bouncing from the tiny silver moon on his neck piece.

In the face of impending death, Erik fought to maintain composure as Sierpinski struck the triplet of switches kicking in the power supply. An intense humming signaled the charge build-up in electrical panels, photon energy accumulating in lethal quantities. The taste of brimstone in the air intensified. Niemeier peered over his bifocals at each man in the underground chamber and then prepared to order Erik's impalement. The devil incarnate and his two minions scuttled over by the control panel.

Sierpinski wheeled around and faced his instruments. He had seen enough slaughter yesterday.

"Goggles, everyone," charged the surgeon. "Herr Sierpinski, you should observe what your pet instrument can really do.

"Now...Landon, my friend. I shall count to five. When I cry out 'five,' Herr Sierpinski will release the death ray...and you can only imagine what will happen!" He pointed a wrathful, shaking finger at the drawer containing Suzanne's body.

Niemeier's other fist held up five splayed digits. "If you wish to talk, call out 'stop,' and we will hold the trigger."

Erik remained silent, a part of him battling an icy fear, another embracing contempt for death and danger. He kept thinking, *Marlene, where are you?* His heart raced, the mind reeling back in time, Suzanne a vivid memory.

The metallic taste of ozone in the air heightened. Niemeier shook both fists like a lunatic crazed with frenzied anger, his face churning deeper, into a livid puce.

Then Erik saw it—The tattoo on Niemeier's arm. The image leaped from gridlock into Erik's conscious scope—*the wings of the sphenoid.*

Niemeier barked, "Mark the laser at full power... One."

The flashing lights of the control panel intensified as Erik's mind, existing and long dormant neuronal circuits rapidly compressing, grappled to recall something from long ago, life now measured in milliseconds. He squeezed his eyelids closed, unshackled scanners running backwards in a labrynth, careening off walls, searching, groping for answers. A steeled mind over an imprisoned body—*wings of the sphenoid.*

"Two."

An eerie, warbling sound crescendoed in pitch and intensity as the deathly charge in the capacitors increased, violent sparks hissing, flashing, snapping. Erik's memory tape accelerated back in time, survival purely a matter of instinct, of concentration cracking through ancient synaptic barriers—*Can't breathe...Lauri Tucker...You're the surgeon...Stop the hemorrhage...Thunderbird...Birds of a feather...With the birds...*

"Three."

Erik felt his brain scaling fuzzy logic, speeding up pattern matching, while the serpentine coils surrounding the heart of the laser fluoresced a brilliant, almost supernatural and pale green color—*Green!* Daedalean images, retrieved from imprisonment, plunged forward into imperiled awareness—*Wings...Green...Wings...José's moth... Luna...Full moon...Silvery...Luna...Silvery!*

"Four."

Erik found himself fingering Marlene's silver moon. His heart slammed against tightened ribs as a living computer's deduction overcame deadly paralysis—*Silver... Metal...Reflections...The Mayo tray...A mirror!*

Just as Niemeier's eyes widened, his lips twisting into "five," Erik grabbed the shiny metal tray. Surgical instruments crashed to the floor, and he whipped the stainless steel armor before his chest. The tight lance of light knifed through the air, striking the center of the lunar shield.

The lethal beam ricocheted off the metallic mirror, the fusillade of reflected photons ripping into the ceiling. Gripped in a life-and-death struggle, Erik tilted the tray, guiding the reversed thrust of the fiery sword downward. The beam slashed into Sierpinski before anyone understood what was happening.

The engineer exhaled a truncated scream, grabbing his neck as bright red torrents spurted from the throat of communism. Blood draining rapidly, the man once known as Sierpinski, collapsed to the floor, writhing in his own expanding pool of blood, the ostrich neck jerking from side to side until all life had poured out onto the white tile.

"Shoot him!" screeched the hysterical Niemeier.

"Shh..."

In the next instant, Erik aimed the reflected death ray at the surgeon. The blue-green rapier sliced through Niemeier's shirt and skewered the doctor's chest, creating a gaping cleft, air rapidly sucked inward, the sharp, swooshing sound unmistakable.

Niemeier tore off his goggles, gasping and convulsing for oxygen, the lung collapsing before he could utter another word. Choking, he coughed up clots of blood and staggered towards Erik, the Nazi parasite clasping the bubbling wound with his hand. Another sweep with the beam and Niemeier's legs buckled under him, leaving him on the floor, gurgling sounds spilling from writhing lips.

In rapid succession, Erik fired at Frohmut, the kyphotic dwarf, now throwing off his own goggles and aiming the Luger. Erik slashed the laser across his face, and the blinded henchman spun to the floor, frontal lobes oozing through seared orbits, limbs convulsing until the Prince of Darkness reached up into Frohmut's evil heart.

"Hermann, drop your gun and unfasten my straps," Erik commanded the bullet-head, the man hypnotized—indeed, even enraptured—by the chaos. After what they had done to Suzanne and Harald, Erik craved to destroy them all.

The laser beam was dissolving the floor in front of the henchman, the thug quaking as tracers of light and sparks fired in all directions. Fearing a quick tilt of the shield, Hermann shuffled cautiously toward Erik. Niemeier's servant released the bindings while avoiding the path of the unnerving blue-green, a luminosity that could instantly deliver him into the netherworld.

"Place your hands behind your neck and move to the end of the room. Now!"

Erik slid off the operating table and left the Mayo tray against the raised backrest to reflect the deadly beam into the wall. He picked up Hermann's sidearm.

"Turn around."

After retrieving the manacles from the floor, Erik cuff-linked the Thunderbird lieutenant to a steel pipe. Erik had to get out soon. Busche and other guards were upstairs.

This hell-hole must be demolished. Erik rushed to the operating table and tilted the Mayo tray, rocketing the laser beam toward the steel cabinet shielding the explosives. Leaving the human debris, he turned and ran for the door, his pistol at the ready as Hermann struggled to free himself.

Apartment Twelve, 5:15 P.M.

With the transponder Major Reiter was giving orders to his police units. Suddenly the ground trembled. Terry dashed to the window.

"The street! The street is caving in between the crematorium and the funeral home!"

Terry saw a series of violent explosions with flashes of light. Shrieking metal and blasts of wind shook the apartment windows, glass fracturing as the earth quaked. The mortuary to the right of the thoroughfare crumbled, crashing toward the pavement. In slow-motion, the earth opened up a raw, gaping wound, the number three tram squealing to a halt within feet of disaster, blue-white flashes of electricity sparking from its overhead cable.

The foundations of the crematory to the left buckled, fire and smoke erupting, chunks of cleaved steel and bent girders ejecting from the walls.

"All units surround and move in. Arrest anyone trying to escape," shouted the Major. "Captain, call the fire department and rescue squads immediately."

Flames and detonations from both buildings leaped skyward, tearing the very firmament asunder. The pavement on Albisriederstrasse ruptured and sank deeper, dragging the two buildings in with it. Another explosion ensued, forcing the police to jump away, throats coughing and lungs wheezing from penetrating vapors of sulphur and ozone.

"Look," exclaimed Marlene. "Someone is running out of the funeral home." Joseph pulled her from the cracking window frame. She cried, "Erik? Yes, it's Erik…he's falling!"

Terry, Marlene, and Joseph, with the Major close behind, charged downstairs and raced across the street.

"Erik, can you hear me?" pleaded Marlene, coughing from the smoke. "Erik…"

She wiped the dust and blood from his half-conscious face. Erik's fist was gripping a small plastic bag.

"He's alive," yelled Terry as debris rained down. "Help me move him away before we're all injured."

Muffled sounds of a secondary, subterranean blast shook the earth. Then a singsong of sirens announced the arrival of an ambulance.

"Take him to Professor Roellein at the Central Hospital. Joseph, I must go with him." Marlene waved the emergency technicians over.

"Go ahead, Marlene. We'll comb the area for anyone else who might be alive," replied Joseph.

"Marlene, can you hear what he's saying?" asked Terry.

Marlene leaned her ear close to Erik mouth. "José," she repeated. "It sounds like 'José.'"

"I wonder what that means?"

The ambulance crew picked up one other injured man, still alive but lying half buried under bricks near the mortuary.

Through the back window of the ambulance, Marlene glimpsed a dark blue Volvo following them toward Central. Erik coughed up bits of blood and Marlene turned to assist. When she looked up, the Volvo was gone.

55

Zürich Central Hospital, Thursday, December 9, 1971.

"How is Doctor Landon?" Marlene anxiously looked at Professor Roellein. They stood near the nursing station while the Chief of Neurosurgery thumbed through the medical chart.

"Still unconscious, but improving. We did a CAT scan. He has some small superficial brain hemorrhages, but they will clear. I don't expect any permanent sequelae." Roellein snapped the file shut.

"Thank you so much. Might I see him now?"

"You may, but a brief visit. My colleague needs his rest."

Marlene approached the room. A policeman in blue stood at attention, guarding the door.

"*Guten Morgen*, Fräulein Sternschen."

"Good Morning, Officer. The professor says I may visit Doctor Landon for a short while."

"He seems restless," commented the guard, opening the door for her.

Marlene sat down next to the bed, her brown eyes following Erik's steady respirations. She grasped his left hand, though he was too insensible to realize it.

"I love you, Erik. Please get well. I need you so much," she murmured. "Heaven help us, I don't want to lose you." Marlene brushed away tears as she pressed his hand against her breast, Marlene's heart skipping a beat. She smiled, noting a slight blip in Erik's EKG at the same time.

She talked to him as if he were alert, distilling the actions of Major Reiter and Terry, almost like a form of therapy. Her closeness and warmth were comforting.

56

Office of the Swiss National Police.

*I*n Major Reiter's office Terry Caldwell leaned forward in his seat, holding a cup of hot tea to his lips. The Harlequin was perfectly aligned.

"Well, well, well, Herr Caldwell. We took the inventory of names from Fräulein Sternschen. Those listed as buried in Friedhof Grünfeld by Braun have been excavated. Over forty of the graves were empty. And there may be others." Major Reiter tapped a sheaf of papers with his pencil and then let the packet drop to the desk with a thud.

"Any chance of excavating under Albisriederstrasse?"

"Let us wait for Doctor Landon to wake up. He may be able to tell us what happened. Digging underneath that rubble would be difficult and a bit dicey if more explosives exist."

He lit up a cigarette and inhaled audibly. "Herr Caldwell, what would you like to do with our Jørgen Busche? We can shoot him back to Denmark or throw him in a Swiss jail and toss away the key. He is recovering from contusions. His doctors state that the man will be able to leave the hospital in three or four days. My government abhors the expense of maintaining security in a hospital."

Terry set his coffee cup on the black acrylic. "I would like to talk to Busche before you do anything. In the meantime, I'll check with Director Stafford."

"We have the register of accounts in our banks to which Niemeier and Busche had been making deposits. Your government will be very interested. Take this copy with you." The Major, permitting himself a condensed smile, handed over the file.

That evening Terry jumped on the tram back to his hotel. He telephoned Stafford in Washington, DC.

"Hamlet here."

"Zürich again. I've obtained a tally of off-shore bank accounts into which Thunderbird has deposited large sums of money. A John Tempest...Masters, no doubt...is included."

"Wow. Now we can initiate a grand jury investigation. Still, in spite of present evidence, it may be an exercise in futility to pin anything substantial on a man of his stature. By the way, Don Martin, ended the career of Ezra Thomas—permanent-like, so that thug won't be around to testify," responded Stafford. "The strike team trapped him in the raid, and Thomas wouldn't give up his firepower."

"Damnation."

"How is Erik today?"

"Still in a twilight zone, but improving."

"It's imperative that we find out what happened. The entire Dietz organization has crumbled. I suspect that the same types of operating rooms and laser units we found in Hong Kong, Mainz, Berlin, and Copenhagen were present in Zürich. Erik should be able to give us more details on how they were used."

"Last night you told me the Marseille processing organization had disappeared. Any idea what happened?" asked Terry.

"Too many political problems. No cooperation. By the time the CIA arrived to do their thing, the damn heroin operatives had been warned. Dissolved. Since we never nailed Dietz in Mainz or Berlin, we can assume Dietz had alerted them."

"Bet the West German government would like to get their hands on him," exclaimed Terry. "We should be able to convince Busche to testify to save his own neck. Helvetian jails can be very unpleasant. The Swiss do not take kindly to people abusing their banks or dealing in narcotics, and Busche did both."

"Call me when Erik is conscious."

"What are you doing about the bodies with explosives?"

"Customs will ship any corpse with a scalp incision out to sea. For deep-water burial. We're not taking any chances. I've warned Taipei, and they are doing the same," replied Stafford.

"Okay. Tomorrow I'll have a chat with Busch at Central Hospital."

57

Friday, December 10, 1971, 9:00 A.M.

Terry Caldwell walked into the hospital room of Jørgen Busche on the fifth floor. Two Swiss police guards remained posted outside the room.

"Feeling better today, Mr. Busche? I am Agent Caldwell of the United States Department of Justice."

"Much better. What is to happen to me now?" inquired the patient, looking up, his left eyelid lagging behind.

"That depends on you, Mr. Busche...or whatever your real name is. You entered this country under false documents and have flagrantly violated Swiss banking laws. You are an accessory to murder and attempted murder. And you're up to your neck in heroin traffic." Terry paused, assessing Busche's reaction. The man's face remained impassive, his eyes unfocused.

"In addition, you have compromised our Secretary of State in America. Swiss, West German, Danish, and United States governments all would like to get a piece of you. But especially the Swiss. I can guarantee they will put you away for life in a very lonely cell. I am offering you an alternative. If you agree to testify against Dietz in West Germany and against Masters in the U.S., the Helvetian government is willing to arrange for your extradition... By the way, I am taping this conversation."

"I guessed as much... You leave me very little choice, Mr. Caldwell. A hotshot lawyer in America can always get your prosecutors to cut a deal. I am told that my associates at Braun are all dead."

"No one could have survived the explosion, thanks to Doctor Landon. He did not take kindly to your having his brother killed." Terry gazed out the window, his hands, one with a notepad, clasped behind his back.

"Most unfortunate. One of the tragedies of war." Busche rolled his lips together. "His brother was a big help to our finding Helga Baumann. We monitored his reports to your office in Washington. Taped the calls and replayed them into our St. Petersburg...our Leningrad computer over long distance phone lines. Russia has most of your scramblers on file. It took only a couple of hours to come up with the conversation. We assumed our Miss Baumann was Ursa and your Mr. Landon played the role of Orion."

Busche pressed the bed lever to raise his head higher. "Might I have a cigarette?"

"Sorry, Busche. Not permitted." Terry briefly rocked back on his boot heels and then turned from the window. "Correct on the code names. But why did you have to kill Helga?"

"When she disappeared from Copenhagen and withdrew her account in Zürich, we believed that she had learned additional information from Bjørn Ljunggren before disposing of him. We could not risk her going to a western government and selling that intelligence. Our agents were instructed to drug her, not kill her, and bring her back to Zürich. But something went terribly wrong. I'm told her aunt buried her in St. Moritz."

"How did you employ Miss Baumann?" queried Terry as he jotted down more notes.

"One of her assignments was the seduction of Masters before he became Secretary. He was putty in her hands. She succeeded beyond our wildest dreams. Subsequently, we commissioned Helga to take out Mr. Piccollo, your former Secretary of State. The lady assassin from Copenhagen did an expert job, as you now know. Masters moved into Piccollo's office and became one of us rather than risk his position. The financial benefits were impossible for him to refuse. Now he runs the *SSV* in America."

"The *SSV*?" Terry recalled the mysterious initials with the tattoo.

"Yes, you tagged it Thunderbird, according to Masters. For us, *SSV* means 'Schlusssteinverein,' German for the 'Keystone Society.' This was the title of Dietz' organization shipping certain contraband. The icon, Niemeier's idea, was symbolic of the bat-shaped bone the neurosurgeon called the keystone of the skull."

"Was Heinz Baumann a member of this *Schlusssteinverein*, this Keystone Society?" Terry scratched his crew cut.

"No. He was responsible for bringing the four of us...Dietz, Sierpinski, Niemeier, and me...together. He knew about the Dietz international organization for transporting dead bodies, but remained unaware of our...uh...more profitable business. However, he had many friends in the German government, and Dietz paid Baumann well to lobby for his international mortuary interests, and unknowingly for the clandestine narcotic activity, all under the guise of a legitimate funereal service," replied Busche.

"Did Baumann ever realize what the Helga we knew had truly become?"

Busche thought for a moment and shuddered. "Yes, but I believe a part of him was in denial. In a rather convoluted way, he did love Helga as the daughter he could never have...as if caring for her later allowed his conscience to cope with the role he played at Birkenau.

"However, that other one...the brain surgeon. He was possessed with an inordinate, even a sadistic, interest in Helga. I don't know the reason. To this day, Helga has had no memory of Johann Niemeier. The man wrote voluminous notes on her progress, her mental state, and kept them locked up in a safe in Vienna, in a mental asylum once called Spiegelgrund. I believe it was renamed Baumgärtnerhöhe. It was he who had ordered her return to Zürich, to be canceled under controlled conditions following completion of her Copenhagen assignment. She fled before the scheduled termination."

"Controlled conditions?"

"Yes, he said her brain needed to be 'reprogrammed.' If that worked, Helga would no longer exist, even though she would not actually have to be killed. She would become some sort of mutant, an adult child, a medical case study that would make him famous. He made Dietz and me promise not to inform the former Kommandant of his extended plan."

"Where is Ludwig Dietz now? We can't locate him in Germany."

Jørgen Busche shook his head. "No idea. You might talk to his friend, Herr Baumann."

"I'll let you rest now. In the meantime, begin writing down a list of names and addresses of other *SSV* agents for us. Here, you may use my pen."

"Good day, Mr. Caldwell." Now eager to help expedite his transfer to America, the patient picked up Terry's ball-point and a tablet of paper.

"One other thing, Busche. Who was Anthony Salucci, the sailor found dead in Atlantic City four months ago?"

"Tony? I wanted him to assume my position someday, but he drank too heavily." Busche's face clouded over. "His death cut me to the quick, driving me towards revenge against the Americans."

"Revenge? Why so?"

"He was my son. I am not Danish. You are looking at General Mario Salucci, formerly of the Italian army. That is how I knew Kommandant Baumann. We battled the Allies together at Anzio."

58

Friday, the Zürich Central Hospital.

Erik opened his eyes and looked about. The room felt strange, and then a rush of claustrophobic terror flooded over him. He fought to refocus, images of viridescent circles and lines giving way to that of a human face. Marlene's face. Serenity returned as his love rushed over and sat down next to him on the bed, the darkness of coma losing its thickness and strength.

"Erik...Erik are you awake?" She squeezed his hands, joy welling up in her eyes.

He smiled and then lapsed into sleep until late in the afternoon. Later that night his sensorium cleared, and at ten o'clock, Erik asked for Marlene. The police guard notified Major Reiter, who arrived in forty minutes with Marlene, Terry, and Joseph.

Marlene informed Erik where he was, and Erik retailed the tragic events of Monday, Tuesday, and Wednesday.

"...and that's how they did it. Niemeier, Sierpinski, and several armed guards are buried under tons of earth. It would be difficult and hazardous to dig them out."

"I think we can leave them," said Major Reiter. "Cumaves has been very helpful in providing information about Jerzy Sierpinski. Also, their engineers have agreed to go to Mainz and check the laser unit there. I assume it is the same type as the one at Braun."

"Yes," reckoned Joseph Smith. "I am at a loss to understand how they were able to generate such raw power. Very likely they were working on something similar at Cumaves…or perhaps in Russia."

Marlene turned to the bedside. "Erik it's very late. You should rest now."

Erik suddenly sat up as a frantic nurse charged into the room, her palms clasped together. "The doctor needs you immediately, Major Reiter. It's about Herr Busche. It's terrible. Someone has killed him!"

"Corporal, stay close to Doctor Landon. He may be in danger." The officer turned to Marlene. "I suspect that Thunderbird has many clandestine operatives still lurking in the shadows of Europe."

On the fifth floor, nervous guards snapped to attention as the Major charged into the room. The carcass of Jørgen Busche, his purple face suspended in death, lay like a terrified giant beetle poisoned by venom, his left eye closed, the right half open. An arm hung over the mattress, Terry's pen on the floor.

"We aren't positive what caused his demise," exclaimed a consternated resident doctor. "You can smell the chloroform in the air. And check out his left arm."

"His tattoo…it's been cut away. What the hell is going on," blazed Terry, exasperated at the loss of so important a witness.

"Guards, was anyone allowed in here," demanded Major Reiter, livid with rage.

"Only the nurses and doctors as usual, Herr Major."

"Assemble everyone who has been here during the past hour."

One of the uniforms rushed out to round up the personnel.

"That's my pen on the tile," observed Terry. "And what is that mark on the sheet? Looks as if he was attempting to draw something."

Marlene analyzed the shaky ink lines trailing off over the edge of the bed. "Maybe a letter of the alphabet?"

"He must have tried to identify his killer. Anyone recognize the sketch?" Terry traced the lines with his forefinger, peering at it from Busche's perspective. "Almost like a cup or something?"

"We'll get a photograph and study it, Herr Caldwell." Major Reiter patrolled back and forth, hands tightly clasped behind his glistening blue tunic.

"Everyone is here, Herr Major," announced the perspiring sergeant. "Except for the floor maid and we're still searching for her."

Suddenly, a startling scream echoed down the hall, cleaving already tense conversation.

"Our Frau Müller—she's dead!" cried a frightened nurse, gasping in disbelief and holding a door open at a stairwell. "*Lieber Gott!* She's been strangled in the stairway. Look at the bruises around her neck. And the lady only in her undergarments."

Two of the policeman ran to the stairwell.

Reiter wheeled around to face his guards. "Who was the last person to come into the room?"

"The floor maid, Herr Major."

"Frau Müller, the usual cleaning lady?" He pointed toward the dead woman.

"No, Herr Major. The lady we saw reported that the regular maid was sick and she had come down from the sixth floor to help with the work."

"Idiots. You allowed a murderer in Herr Busche's room."

"But it was only a woman, Herr Major."

"Only a woman. And how do you know that, my brilliant corporal?" chastised the Major.

Reiter pivoted toward the rest of the stunned onlookers. "Tomorrow an autopsy will be performed. We also shall check for fingerprints, though it is unlikely we will find any.

"Herr Caldwell, the hour is late. Could you and your people assemble in my office tomorrow, Saturday afternoon at three? Perhaps we'll have some answers regarding the mysterious perpetrator."

"Yes, sir. We'll be there."

The police chief swiveled on his heels, muttering as he hastened toward the nursing station. "Insane…this is insane." He brandished a cigarette as he picked up the phone. "Yes, yes. Comb the entire hospital and grounds."

Marlene returned to Erik's room and filled Joseph and Erik in. They could hear the warble of police sirens approaching the medical center.

Later that Friday night, Terry phoned Washington from Erik's hotel room. Marlene and Joseph were sitting near the window. "Hamlet?"

"Speaking. How are things progressing?" asked Stafford.

"Here's Erik. I'll let him explain the situation concerning what is left of the Braun Mortuary."

Erik took the receiver and related the events covering his brush with death. Terry then followed with a description of Busche's untimely demise. He played the tape of his conversation with Busche.

"My God, Terry. You saw Busche earlier today. How did he appear then?"

"Seemed fine, boss. I talked to him about testifying and he was more than anxious to do so."

"Do you think Dietz got to him?"

"That's my number one guess."

"I have an idea how we can still use Busche to testify against Masters," stated Stafford. "I'll divulge the details later. In the meantime, arrange with the Major to have the body of Busche a.k.a. Salucci, shipped to Priestley & Dietz in Queens."

"But they're out of business now," replied Terry.

"Can't discuss it over the phone. When are you coming back?"

"I'm heading for Mainz to have a talk with Baumann. Then I'll come directly home."

"From your conversation with Busche it appears Baumann is on in years and knows little of the heroin activity."

"True. But he may lead us to Dietz."

"Call me as soon as you return. *Ciao*."

59

Zürich, Police Office, Saturday, 3:00 P.M.

While Erik's strength and balance improved with physical therapy at the hospital, his colleagues studied the lay of the land during a visit to Major Reiter.

Rigid, almost frozen in posture, Reiter perched on the edge of a chair behind his metallic desk. He faced Marlene and Terry, also seated. Then Joseph arrived, remaining standing, leaning against the wall. Blue smoke spun in slow motion over the policeman's head, layering above the picture of the harlequin.

"The autopsy was consistent with death from injection of a paralytic agent. No fingerprints." The Major waved the tiny ember of tobacco through the air.

"Major, Director Stafford would like to have the body of Jørgen Busche, or Mario Salucci, forwarded to New York City in care of the Priestley & Dietz Funeral Home. We'll assist with the details. He has a plan in mind to nail the *SSV* in America. Would the transfer be possible?" asked Terry.

"Busche is of no use to us here, and there is no one to claim his body. I must present this to our state government, but I am certain that we can arrange it."

The officer stood up. "One other thing. Fräulein Sternschen and Herr Smith have done an admirable job here. However, in large part it was done without the consent of the Swiss government. It would be prudent if both of you return to the United States as soon as possible, before I am put in the embarrassing position of having to place you under arrest. There are many Swiss already infuriated at the activities of foreign nationals on our soil."

"We understand, Major." Marlene glanced at Joseph. "We will leave on the first of the week for reassignment."

"There is something else. You may be interested to know that the West German police located Dietz." Reiter pressed spread his fingers together. "Motorists discovered him in a car not too far from the East German border. Murdered. My counterpart in West Berlin just telephoned me and is notifying your American Consulate. The cause of death awaits determination, but the local physicians claim it to be asphyxiation."

"You mean like Busche?" stammered Terry, aghast, another witness now gone.

"Your guess is as good as mine. But someone other than Dietz killed Busche."

"Why do you say that?" countered Marlene.

"Because Dietz had been dead for over twenty-four hours. The skin above his left elbow also had been sliced away."

"This doesn't make any sense." Terry slammed a fist into the palm of his hand. "I've got to talk to Baumann. I'm leaving for Mainz first thing in the morning."

"Careful," warned Marlene. "Something isn't right. Remember, Baumann once was the Nazi *SS* Kommandant at Auschwitz."

The next day, Sunday, Marlene helped Erik on with his sport jacket as Terry bounced into the hospital room, embracing both of them with a glance.

"How are you feeling today, Hoss?" Terry pumped Erik's hand and grinned at the two lovers.

"Super. All that rest and now I'm ready to go. What's this 'Hoss' bit?" Erik laughed.

"Just my kindly old Maryland eastern shore expression, Hoss. Not for the ladies, though," he winked. "I'm leaving in an hour for Mainz. I guess Marlene filled you in on what's happened."

"Yes, and I would like to go with you. This whole thing began in Mainz, and I'm very curious about the Baumanns. Especially after you told me what Reiter had discovered. Want some company, Terry?" Erik scratched his tattoo.

"Certainly, but there may be some risk. I don't know if you should."

"Nothing can be worse than last week. I really do want to go."

"Erik, why don't you come back to America with Joseph and me on Monday," pleaded Marlene. "You've done quite enough."

"Darling, the *SSV* started in Mainz. I expect it will end there. I have a personal curiosity about it after recognizing its symbol in Washington. Terry, if you can give me a lift to the Hotel Poly, I'll collect my things and we can be off."

"Okay. I'll meet you downstairs."

Terry left as Marlene grabbed Erik's hands.

"Honey, you don't need to go. I have a bad feeling about this."

"It's important to me, Marlene. Wait for me. I still want you to meet my mother in Minnesota."

"Hold me, Erik. It has to last me until I see you again."

"I love you, Marlene. I can't live without you."

He pressed his lips to hers and held her close, two rivers reunited.

"I get butterflies in my stomach when you do that, Erik. Now get going before I lose control again," she whispered, nibbling his earlobe.

They hustled down to the front entrance where Terry's car waited.

"Good-byes are difficult, but I mean the words, Erik."

"What are you saying, Marlene?"

"The word, good-bye. It means 'God be with you.'" The expression in her eyes—loving and tender, frightened.

She kissed Erik on the cheek and, after squeezing her hand, he stepped into the car.

"Hot damn! That's some girl." Terry sped away from the curb. "You're a lucky man."

"Is it that obvious?"

"Two people in love? Yes, sir."

Erik smiled as the car shot northward up Universitätstrasse.

Within the hour, Erik's mind was milling over the evil countenance of Busche in Niemeier's underground operating room. And now it was the deceased face of Mario Salucci, a missing *SSV* tattoo, and a strange drawing scrawled on the dead man's sheets. He wasn't sure why, but a shudder riffled through him.

Early evening was bearing down, hints of orange fringing the clouds in the western sky. Terry had driven the rented Audi to Basel where the two men shot across the border into Germany and barreled northward on the autobahn. The freeway paralleled the Rhine River on their left, separating France from Germany. They had already sped by the town of Freiburg and now closed in on the Heidelberg zone, the day clear and cold, the roads free of snow. Erik watched patches of white in the fields flash by as twilight descended, leaving blackness in its wake. Twin shimmers of moonlight glinted from steel train tracks on their right.

"Hey, Hoss, why don't we stay overnight at a hotel in Heidelberg?" suggested Terry, interrupting the monotonous drumming of rubber tires on asphalt. "It's late. We can check with the Baumanns first thing in the morning."

"Okay by me."

The shrill of a train's whistle suddenly stabbed the air from behind, the iron monster also rolling northward, dark rectangular boxes on wheels trailing, clickety-clack, clickety-clack, clickety-clack.

Erik's eyes followed, watching as the train dissolved into the sable night before them. The train to Mainz. Erik rummaged in his briefcase and pulled out the strange portrait.

"You look puzzled, Hoss. What are you staring at?"

"This photograph that Reiter made of Busche's drawing. I don't know which way to hold it."

"Well, I still think it looks like a cup with a long handle," reflected Terry.

Like a soup ladle, Erik mused. In studied silence he glanced out the window at a full moon, the disc shining like a silver-blue torch, a mosaic portrait etched into its lunar surface. Surrounding stars projected into families of constellations, and a small comet briefly rocketed through the firmament.

"Skoal." Erik toasted the falling star. *Skoal?* Suddenly his mind skidded, flipping open pages of that dictionary in Edina years ago—*Skoal...skull...cranial cup...dip...* He struck his forehead with the palm of his hand.

"Jesus, Terry. It's in the sky. The drawing...it *is* a cup, a dipper. Like in the stars, the floating bears of Greek mythology...the little dipper and the big dipper."

"I'm not big on astronomy, Erik. How does that help us?"

"Don't you see? The little dipper is called *Ursa Minor* and the big dipper, *Ursa Major*. Salucci knew you had code-named Helga as Ursa, the bear."

"But Helga is dead. Buried in St. Moritz."

"Was she? We were told that. What if her aunt only pretended to have her interred in the Engadin, a pact between Anna and Helga. Then Thunderbird, the CIA, and the Bureau of Narcotics would cease any effort to locate her."

"Hoss, if that's true, Helga would want the man she knew as Jørgen Busche dead — very dead. She would not only achieve her revenge but also block him from coming after her again. Permanently." Terry shook his head, wondering. "But why go after Ludwig Dietz, and how did she know where to find Busche?"

Erik's mind raced back in thought. "After her conversation with my brother, she knew that Dietz and Busche had been working together. Upon meeting up with Dietz again in Germany, she must have seen the tattoo on his arm. My guess is that Helga killed him near his Berlin office by administering the same drug she had used on Bjørn and, later, on Busche. Probably pancuronium.

"As far as her finding Busche is concerned, very likely she had discovered from Dietz that Busche was in Zürich. We weren't the only ones monitoring the mortuary. Once in Zürich, all she had to do was watch the events at Braun and then follow the ambulance."

"I don't know, Erik. If I were in her shoes, I would have gotten far, far away, assumed another name, and started over again."

"Sure, if you were mentally stable, perhaps. But from what you've told me of Jeffry's last conversation with her, she was both frightened and becoming a bit unglued...something that was rare for Helga."

The Heidelberg turnoff approached. Terry suddenly swerved away and back on to the main turnpike, rubber tread accelerating, squealing and skidding on the dark pavement.

"Damn. We better forget the good night's sleep and get to Mainz tonight." Terry stared ahead, twin beams drawing the Audi northward. "Dead people can't testify. When we get near Darmstadt, keep your eyes peeled for the autobahn to Mainz. This one goes on to Frankfurt."

"Okay. I hope the Baumanns provide some answers. Speaking of testimony from the dead, what does Stafford have in mind for Busche's body?" Erik quizzed.

"Got me. As soon as we're through here, we'll head for Washington and find out."

Erik's thoughts were still distracted by the two dippers in the heavens, the little one committed to the remote steppes of a black firmament, her mutant sister hurtling ungoverned back toward the distant points of fire.

Erik picked up the telephone in the speeding car and dialed numbers connecting across the border to the Swiss operator. "Zürich police, please... Yes, I'll hold."

"Hoss, what are you doing?"

"Hello. May I speak to Major Reiter? Yes, I know what time it is. It's urgent."

A minute passed. "Major Reiter here." Static frayed the transmission.

"Major, this is Doctor Erik Landon. Agent Caldwell and I are in a car en route to Mainz. We have reason to believe that the corpse buried in the grave under the Helga Baumann marker is not our Helga. Perhaps you should disinter the grave in St. Moritz. You might find some more answers there." Erik explained their reasons.

Reiter sighed, agreeing to carry out another bizarre request the next day. Erik's thoughts, now boiling over with an unfocused fear, turned to the ever more slippery present.

A half hour later he pointed to a road sign. "Here is our turn-off for Mainz. The Baumanns live near the university according to our directions. I visited some of my neurosurgical colleagues at the med center there last year."

60

Mainz.

Heinz and Ingrid Baumann were sitting quietly in the living room. The former Kommandant paced back and forth while his wife knitted a shawl. She rocked slowly, the ancient chair emitting hollow squeaks with each backward tilt.

"Ingrid, someone left the light on in the attic. Were you up there today?"

"No, dear. Not the past week." Her knitting needles clicked, a discordant backdrop to the rhythm of the chair. "Heinz, remember how I use to rock little Helga to sleep when the angels first delivered her to us?"

"*Sie ist tot!*" She is dead! he rasped, not wanting to mention the name that haunted him day and night. The wheezing of his lungs had worsened daily along with the twitching of the left side of his face. "We will not speak of her." But another name preyed on his conscience even more. A word he dared not mention.

"As you wish, my dear." Tears dimmed her vision.

Passing behind his wife, Herr Baumann halted in front of a bay window. He heard some dry leaves crackle.

As if underfoot. He pulled apart the drapes, and inhaled a choking scream. The head of a ghost, backlit by a driveway lamp, leaned into the frosted pane from the other side. Blond hair laced along her face in wet, salamandrian patterns. Dead-blue, unblinking globes peered at him. In her right hand she was holding up a black cap emblazoned with a Nazi eagle and its silver Death's Head, the *Totenkopfverbände* of the *SS*. In her left was a piece of tattooed skin. She mouthed the forbidden words, "My name is Halina."

An excruciating pain shot down the Kommandant's left arm, from his heart. He staggered backwards, falling to his knees, his left face in a spasm of terror. "Halina! My child..." His paralyzed lips could form no more sentences, a personal Hell preparing to serve up a banquet of remembrances and retribution. He was in a time warp, hurtling back toward Birkenau and 1943.

Ingrid, seeing her husband fall, jumped from her seat.

"Heinz, what is wrong? Shall I call our doctor?"

All he could do was clutch his chest with one hand and, with the other, point a shuddering finger toward the window. But the apparition was gone. The lights dimmed briefly.

Ingrid ran to the telephone. The line was dead. Then she caught the sound of heels walking down the hallway. On the other side of the door, a woman's heels. Drawing closer and closer.

61

Within the hour, Erik and Terry arrived in front of an old Gothic three-storied mansion, its peaked roof gripping the raven sky, a gray stone belly lying in wait, terraces at each story hovering, shielding darkened windows and glimpses of even darker souls. The dwelling, covered by moss-stained, blue slate roofing, lay protected by acres of manicured grass and fir trees surrounded by tangles of shrubbery. Far afield, a lone oak tree, split by lightening into two portions, strained to survive, one part gaunt and lifeless, the other with frozen tears of dried sap, slumbering in the winter.

The gate to a black, wrought-iron fence listed half closed, blocking their way. Erik gazed about, thinking on Marlene's warning as he stepped out to push the obstacle open.

They drove over a leaf-covered carriageway and braked to a halt between a dry fountain and the front portal. The auto now idled beneath an extended balcony supported by fluted pillars under a frieze of baby angels. Dead vines strangled the open trellis works flanking the porch, the flooring built of yellow-flecked black marble. A great, stone coat-of-arms embraced the chipped keystone of the doorway.

A stray cat, ribs showing, darted across the pavement and into a knot of bushes. Terry killed the motor.

"There are lights behind the shutters and someone is singing," Erik whispered, listening to the rise and fall of a lament. It sounded like that of a disembodied voice from a wee siren, and he wished he were anywhere but here.

"It sounds like a child." Terry fingered his pistol. "Let's go up."

"Meow," screeched the cat as she bolted across the drive and out under iron pickets, the high-pitched shriek causing two human hearts to backfire.

Terry, now perspiring, rapped the black wrought-iron door knocker. Erik thought it appeared like a twin to that on Aunt Anna's door—the beak and head of a raven.

No answer.

He lifted the raven's head again and let the beak fall, hammering a metal bolt.

"Terry, the girl is still singing. Maybe they didn't hear. Try again." Erik steeled himself against the unknown, forcing himself to resume steady breathing. His adrenals still had not fully recovered from his brush with death in the Zürich underground.

Terry knocked again, iron against iron. Still no answer. He turned the handle of burnished brass. It was not locked. The oak door, its hinges grating, swung open. They smelled the faint odor of smoke in a dimly lit alcove.

"Guten Abend. Ist jemand da?" Erik announced. Good evening. Is anyone there?

No response.

"Erik, there's some light at the end of the hallway. The music's from there. Odd. Stay behind me, Hoss."

Terry unholstered his automatic 9mm Smith & Wesson, the right thumb pushing off the safety, waiting for some form of beast to reveal its shape. As they crept forward, backs squeezed against a wall lit by recessed sconces, the stink of cauterized flesh violated their nostrils. They slipped around a brocaded settee, stole past a library, and edged toward the last portal, half closed.

Terry kicked the door open. And gasped. Smoke rolled out, escaping the terrifying chamber, grotesque shadows of the past stretching before them.

Erik stood speechless, his stomach knotting up at the macabre greeting. Propped up and sitting on the floor, backs against the wall, sat an elderly man and his wife half-dressed in bloodied clothes. The one dead body balancing the other. Garments on fire, searing the skin. Odors of embered hair and burnt flesh. Age-lined faces mangled beyond recognition. A bloodied medieval axe on the floor, spent after having inflicted havoc and a terrifying death. Furniture upturned in the living room, dishes and figurines lying broken on the floor, tendrils of blood and bits of flesh scattered everywhere.

Yet, something else appeared ghastly incongruous. A knife handle projected out of Herr Baumann's left orbit, the eye dangling by a single thread of muscle, under a black *SS* cap. The shirt and blouse had been ripped from the torsos of the old couple. The man's burnt chest stained ruby red. Not blood. Paint! And the old lady—rivulets of emerald green dripping from her breasts.

Turning through the haze of smoke, Erik and Terry witnessed a withered young woman with stringy blond hair, a creature hauled back out of the murky deep. She sat in a rocking chair on the far side of the spacious parlor, her back facing them. Dressed in the gray uniform of a hospital floor maid, she remained oblivious to the surrounding carnage.

"Helga? My God, is that you?" Erik softly asked.

Terry's forefinger tightened, gripping the trigger, yet holding fast, a supernatural power blocking detonation of the 9mm percussion cap.

Approaching her, Erik and Terry crossed the longitudinal expanse of the battleground, now a tapestry of bloody swirls and scorched patches on plush amber piling. In '43 it was a field of amber clay.

Suddenly, the screeching oscillations of the rocking chair ceased as Helga whipped around, lids retracted over glaring ophidian eyes confronting her intruders, her own face a vampire's mask with sunken globes. Her pupils dilated, targeting Terry's black cowboy boots.

And then it came—

The terrible shriek shook the very marrow of their bones. She screamed and screamed from her quaking gut until it was empty, screamed from the core of a convoluted brain hurtling toward meltdown, screamed from the recesses of a soul damned to eternal Hell. And when she was drained of all oxygen, her lungs heaved again at breath's end to emit one final cry.

Helga's vacant stone-blues, reflecting the hellish arena before her, pierced into the beyond, dismembering all of mankind. Then her lids snapped closed, as if sealing off the horrors of her past.

Erik saw Helga's left arm fastened around two floppy, cloth dolls—gifts from Jeffry, Raggedy Ann and Raggedy Andy, their heads pillowed on Helga's breasts, the three rocking back and forth. Helga resumed singing in a stuttering, child-like voice to the red and white striped effigies of calico—

"*Wie is es mmm...möglich dann,*
Dass ich dich la...lassen kann?"

A tremor crawled through Erik. "It's an old German folk song," he said. "It means, 'How is it possible that I could leave you?'"

Terry nodded.

Helga ceased the sad melody. She turned to Raggedy Ann and Andy. "*Mu...Mutti, Hali bleibt immer bei dir. Und Va...Vati, Halina schutzt dich. Du brennst nnn...nicht mehr.*"

"Hoss?" Terry approached the apparition, his hand still holding tight to his Smith & Wesson.

"She's talking to her parents. 'Mama, Hali will always stay with you. And Papa, Halina will protect you. You won't burn any more.' Halina must be her real name."

The specter, the stuttering spirit of the Helga Erik had met years ago, continued to babble, Hali's German now commingling with Polish. Finally, the German tongue faded out of existence, the four-year-old moppet speaking in Polish to a tiny, friend, a flower called Helga. With a strange detachment, her left hand kept brushing something which only Halina could see. The right arm, with its tiny golden cross of Jesus swinging from her wrist, remained crippled, the mystery unfathomable. A portrait of the world from which she had stepped years and years ago, an exhumation of a dead child.

Erik opened the windows to clear the air, letting in the shrill wail of a distant train whistle. Terry, shaking his head, picked up Helga's purse, discovering a syringe and several needles. An old photograph of a tattoo, two pieces of dried tattooed skin, a wallet, and three small snapshots occupied another compartment. On the back of Jeffry's picture—*Jeffry Landon, the only man I have ever loved! February 3, 1961.*

Terry handed one of the photos to Erik, who stared in silence at the portrait of his brother. He fought to choke back his feelings, struggling to stifle the quivering in his chin.

Then Terry passed over the other two faded pictures. Erik sat down and fastened his eyes on the sepia duplicates. In one, a little girl was standing with her parents before a railroad station in Krakow. In the other, Erik saw the same girl and a boy called Franz, according to the script on the back.

"Terry, I wonder if this is a picture of Helga...Halina when she was small? And maybe her brother, Franz? She must have been a very complicated person. Horribly tragic and beautiful at the same time. I wonder what drew her to my brother back then?"

Erik stood up and turned, his eye catching sight of an old record player, a Victrola. The music machine was on, the ancient record spinning like the black whirlpool of death, the needle scratching at the end of its play. Curiously listening for the tune, Erik replaced the needle onto its groove, back to the beginning—back to the points of light, the genesis, the birth of Helga Baumann, sculpted from the ashes of an innocent Polish child. The melody, a beautiful waltz and Hitler's favorite, twirled in three-step time as "The Merry Widow" painted its saturnalia of death in living sound.

62

New York City, Wednesday, December 15, 1971.

Days later, at Director Stafford's request, Erik boarded the Amtrak, rolling from Washington to New York City. He wanted time to think. About Marlene. About loose ends in his life.

Tim Stafford had received word the previous day that the casket bearing Mario Salucci, otherwise known as Jørgen Busche, had arrived at Kennedy Airport and awaited disposition from the cargo space of a Global Airways charter jet. Tim had called Lance Master's attorney, a Mr. Edward Ogden, and asked if the Secretary of State would be willing to travel to New York and help identify a body at Kennedy Airport. It had to do with providing guilt or innocence of Masters in the Thunderbird affair.

Ogden conferred with Masters. The lawyer insisted his client was innocent, but they would be happy to assist the investigation in any way possible. Stafford recommended they meet at ten on Wednesday morning at the Customs Office in Kennedy Airport.

Erik sensed that Tim had an ulterior motive, a grander scheme, believing fate and theater might reveal a chink in even the most carefully constructed veneer. With interest, Erik watched the players assemble. Marvin Cheverly and Theodore Burns, Customs. Timothy Stafford, BNDD Director. Terry Caldwell and Donald Martin, Bureau of Narcotics & Dangerous Drugs. Lance Masters, Secretary of State. Edward Ogden, Attorney.

After the last appeared, all, excepting Director Stafford, took their seats. Stafford initiated the meeting. Masters and Ogden had positioned themselves a distance from the agents and officers.

Tim Stafford faced the assemblage. "Mr. Masters, as a result of information obtained by the Justice Department, evidence has been brought forth, rightfully or not, that you may be involved with the procurement of illegal passports for the purpose of bringing heroin into the United States."

Masters feigned a gasp as Stafford held up a passport and, with a bit of drama, tapped his ballpoint against it. "It is my duty to warn you that anything you say can and will be used as evidence against you in a court of law."

Stafford paused, nodded toward the attorney, and then leveled his gaze squarely at Masters. "Your lawyer informs me that you have agreed to assist in our investigation by indicating whether or not you can identify a corpse, the remains just shipped from Europe by an organization code-named Thunderbird and consigned to the Priestley & Dietz Funeral Home in Queens."

"Dead body, huh?" Masters drew a deep breath through tight nostrils and pushed eyeglasses up on his damp nose. He popped a breath mint into his mouth.

"The refrigerated subject has been on the airplane for reasons of security. We have opened the coffin and confirmed there is a scalp incision behind the hairline. As we speak, the casket is being down-lifted to a gurney headed for the examination room." The Director cleared his throat. "And I must remind you that we are televising the proceedings."

"Yes, yes, quite so," interjected counsel, checking his wristwatch, a gentleman's Concord. "Let's move along. My client has agreed to leave his busy schedule and assist your office in any way he can. In doing so he does not admit to any absurd complicity with your so-called Thunderbird...uh...underworld alliance."

"Thank you, Mr. Ogden. Your patience is appreciated. I would like to ask the Secretary of State if he has ever known an assassin by the name of..." Stafford swerved his gaze back to Masters. "...Helga Baumann. She was working for the narcotic syndicate, and our sources have linked her name to that of Mr. Masters."

Erik took a second look at the Secretary. The years had treated Masters to thinning salt-and-pepper hair. He was dressed in an immaculate, solid navy-blue business suit. Smiling, he carried himself with an air of assurance, teetering over the edge of vain pomposity. Masters snapped his lighter, firing a cigar.

With tongue in cheek, Erik was going to ask about the promised payment for his services rendered to Dolores Piccollo at Masters' request, but then thought better of it. Ogden's brittle response redirected Erik's attention.

"You don't have to answer the question, Lance, if you don't wish to," snapped the attorney.

"Why, I never heard of the girl until I learned of your investigation." The Secretary spoke with his mellifluous, southern drawl. He waved his tobacco lighter in circles before pocketing it. "I understand the poor thing was killed in Switzerland."

"Quite the contrary, sir." Stafford cast a sharp eye at Masters, watching him rise to the bait. "She is very much alive and living in Mainz."

The Secretary of State siphoned an unintended puff from the Havana, choking as he squirmed in his chair.

With a handkerchief he dabbed moisture from the brush on his upper lip. Then, another breath mint.

"Well, Mr. Stafford, I'm certainly delighted to hear that. Very happy indeed. I'm sure she will verify that we have never met before." Master's initial grandiloquence began to lose its intensity.

"The room stands ready," Cheverly reported after cradling a telephone. "Shall we proceed? Please follow me."

Masters extinguished his cigar, jamming its smoky embers into a bronze ashtray.

The group filed into a large chamber. Additional BNDD agents, armed, hands clasped behind their backs, secured all exits. Erik stood aside to see the entire theater.

"Everyone wait here," signaled Cheverly. "We are bringing the item from the aircraft. It will be transported on that conveyer belt and through our fluoroscopic unit over there." He pointed, yanking his fishing pole to set the hook. "Then to the examination table. Any questions? None? Good, then...."

"Why can't we just mosey on over, open up the casket, and take a peek?" interrupted Masters, as if feeling the sting. "I have important meetings scheduled back in Washington."

Erik stifled a grin at the change in the Secretary's character.

"Standard procedure now, sir," Cheverly insisted. "We require a body check for contraband and any evidence of a breach in the skull."

"This is horseshit." Masters resumed his façade of bluster and indignation, unable to dislodge the barb. "Edward, I don't have to stand for this. Let's get the hell out of here."

"Lance, you agreed to come. Just play their game and be done with it," recommended Ogden, a bit puzzled.

The spit-polished shoes of Officer Burns cracked the linoleum, straight to the fluoroscopy unit.

"Slip on over here, Mr. Secretary," advised Burns, reeling in the line, his tone more like an order than a recommendation. "You can view the screen on the fluoroscope machine and ascertain what we see. Come now, it's quite safe, quite safe, indeed. All radiation is thoroughly contained."

Masters, swallowed hard and backed up a step, as if his own brain suddenly was on the rack. "Radiation! Never mind. I'll stay over here." His Alabama accent thickened, rational thought tripping.

"Okay. Fire him on through." Cheverly waved with his arm, snapping thumb and middle finger.

An electric dolly bumped through swinging doors opening before it and carried the coffin across the room. Four uniformed attendants heaved up the long crate and placed it on top of the conveyer. Rollers under the belt hummed, making clicking sounds as they accelerated.

The casket bearing Jørgen Busche, a.k.a. Mario Salucci, clacked along, traveling closer to the x-ray machine. Overhead lights played on beads of sweat trickling over Masters' brow. Just as the corpse disappeared into the fluoroscopy unit Masters shrieked, "Stop it! Stop it! Explosives in the head! We'll all be killed!"

He wheeled about and raced for the exit, but Terry and Donald grabbed his arms, immobilizing the Secretary.

"Not to worry, Mr. Masters, or should I say, Mr. Tempest?" Stafford tried to maintain a professional demeanor on his face, a victorious smile creeping toward his cheeks. "The casket won't bite you. The only way you could have known about the Thunderbird plan to place x-radiation sensitive explosives in the head is if you were a member of Niemeier's *SSV*."

"This is highly irregular, Stafford. And it hardly constitutes prior evidence of guilt," admonished the surprised Ogden.

The casket ferried on through and was lifted onto a low platform. Marvin Cheverly heaved up the lid in front of Masters.

"Jørgen Busche. But how?" sputtered Masters, too late to retract his words, the damning attestation now locked onto tape. "This is a trick. You must let me go. Ogden, do something!"

"Entrapment, gentleman. Pure entrapment. Lance, do not talk anymore," insisted his attorney.

The two men held on to the hysterical Secretary. Terry removed Masters' coat and rolled up the sleeve of the left arm. A fresh surgical scar appeared above the left elbow.

"What are you looking for? I had a mole removed." Masters strained to yank his arm away.

"This your mole?" Terry held up a piece of preserved skin with its tattoo and the initials *SSV*.

"How did you get that? I burned it in... You have no right..."

"This one came from Helga's purse, Masters. It matches the scar on Busche's arm. No, it is not yours, but your statements remain as corroborating evidence," warned Terry.

"Agent Martin, will you please take this gentleman into custody," instructed Stafford. "Mr. Lance Masters, you are under arrest for crimes perpetrated against the United States of America. I would advise you to follow the advice of your attorney."

The Director thrust the final harpoon into the great white shark. "We also need to discuss your relationship to an Ezra Thomas...sir."

Another mortar round landed, the face of the Secretary blanching.

"You have to go with them now, Mr. Secretary." Ogden glared at Stafford. "Don't worry, Lance. I'll have you out in an hour."

"Terry?" Tim beckoned to his agent.

"Sir?"

"Please arrange to have Salucci buried next to his son. We have no further use for him."

As they walked back down the hall, Terry reported to Erik, "I got word from Major Reiter, Hoss. You're correct. The body buried in St. Moritz was a blond woman shot several times in her face. Unrecognizable. Dressed in Helga's clothes. She had lived in some Italian village. Strange, though."

"How so?"

"Buried under the sod over her grave was a rather unusual neck-piece. Titanium braided with silver. Two wooden crucifixes attached. Helga's fingerprints on the crosses. Traces of blood in the wire mesh."

Erik nodded, thinking of the necklace at the home of Helga's aunt. Something still lay amiss. He had to seek answers in Switzerland.

63

St. Moritz.

"So nice to see you again, Doctor Landon. Please have a seat." Frau Anna Baumann nodded toward the colorful Afghan-covered chair in her home. She gave Erik a worried look.

Erik settled down, and Aunt Anna, black beads and a gold cross of the rosary about her neck, faced him from her love seat. They had an invisible bond. Jeffry and Helga.

"Since returning to America, I found myself compelled to revisit St. Moritz and search out the answer to something nagging at me. I hesitate to ask, but..." Erik glanced at the statuette of the Madonna.

"About my niece, Helga. Why did I deceive you about her death, her burial in St. Moritz. Isn't that it?" Her voice, her eyes reflected the anguish and weariness of a woman grappling with a past pressing down, her shoulders slumping with the weight of history.

"My God, Frau Baumann, after what I witnessed in Mainz..." Erik closed his eyes, the scene refusing to go away. "If there is anything you can tell me."

Anna fell into silence while fixing her gaze on a wedding ring. Agony clouded her features, fine crowfoot lines clutching deeper at the corners of her eyelids. She spoke, very slowly at first.

"Doctor Landon, what I'm about to reveal must not leave this room. There are personal reasons for that request." She hesitated, and Erik nodded his assent.

"My brother, Heinz, was a Nazi, a terribly evil man. During the Second World War, I refused to join the Party. Even so, I was sightless to what truly was happening, blinded by years of the inculcation of hatred towards the 'Christ-killers,' *der Jude*, the Jew…or so we Germans were taught from infancy."

"But Jesus was crucified by the Romans." Erik was puzzled.

"We had a living scapegoat on whom to blame all of our ills. 'Eliminate the Jew,' preached Hitler, 'and the cancer is eradicated.' There were no Romans to destroy…except, perhaps, by staring into a mirror.

"*Ja…Ja*, I understood that Heinz was Kommandant in the army, in the *SS*, but that was all I knew…or perhaps all I wanted to know. Yet, even I, God forgive me, embraced the concept of genocide, as long as I did not have to witness, to harbor any conscious knowledge of the tortures, the killings… The point? Please bear with me."

Her voice wavered, and Erik realized that Anna's once-youthful brain, carved by the teachings of The Third Reich, was struggling to withstand the painful lash of a deeper morality. While fingering her beads, she ventured toward the Madonna and touched the sculptured hands of healing. Tears trailed down aged cheeks as she returned to her seat and resumed talking.

"After Helga disappeared from Scuol with my help, I took the train to Mainz and informed my brother and his wife, Ingrid, that Helga was truly dead, foully murdered in the Engadin. The next day he brought me into his study, not wanting Ingrid to hear the truth about her daughter, Helga. He said he had to relieve himself from a miserable burden before his own time came. God save us, this is what he divulged.

"Only four people knew what had occurred at an evil place known as Birkenau. Kommandant Heinz Baumann and a Herr Doktor Niemeier were present in the year 1943 during the horrific psychological experiment on a Polish family, a four-year-old girl and her mother and father. A man by the name of Jerzy Sierpinski from Poland and an Italian, Mario Salucci, later knew some of the morbid details. All four now are dead, from what you have told me. And now I also know the unspeakable story. In a way, I'm glad you are here, doctor. I must tell someone or I'll go insane." Anna bowed her head, droplets falling through fingers, the tips clutched almost convulsively to her face.

"*Gott in Himmel*… I realize now that my niece was not the only child to travel through Niemeier's inferno at the Spiegelgrund psychiatric asylum in Vienna. Heinz told me there were many others, many such children from various Nazi camps…and many of his subjects still exist. Adopted. Living in Europe, South America, and even in your own country. Other small patients, the so-called 'unfit,' underwent 'euthanasia' and autopsy, their brains preserved in jars for medical review. To prove some theory of Aryan superiority, thus satisfying Niemeier's personal 'Gestalt psychology.' Gestapo psychology would have been more correct."

Anna hesitated while dabbing her eyes with a lady's handkerchief. She then retailed the barbaric events leading to the electrocution of Halina's parents, the termination of Halina Vozniewski, and the inception—the parthenogenesis of Helga Baumann. Anna hesitated while Erik attempted to assimilate the full meaning of her words—the tabletop toys of green and red.

"There is more, Doctor Landon. Herr Doktor Niemeier, in his zeal to identify all of the factors affecting his medical research, had sought out more information on Halina's past. Before the end of the war, he had located documents on the child, papers in the archives inside Poland...in Krakow. He was shocked to discover that Halina had been *adopted* at birth by the Vozniewski's, that her original family name was not what he had thought."

"Why did that agitate him so much, Frau Baumann?" Erik was on the edge of his chair, disbelieving what he had heard.

She looked up. "You see, my good doctor, the last name of her natural parents, close friends of the Vozniewski's from Poland, was Kapozi. Her real name was Hali Kapozi. She was born to German Jews. In Dresden. The Kapozis sought to hide Hali and her brother, Franz, in the Catholic family, Vosniewski."

Anna Baumann fastened her gaze on Erik. "Can you imagine? Heinz and the Herr Doktor thought they had engineered an obedient Aryan out of a Christian. And now God had thrown their nefarious scheme for the master race into checkmate."

Erik fought to understand the enormity of Anna's revelation. The apocalyptic deeds—and the deeper meaning of the conflagration he witnessed at Mainz. Red and green—the American colors of Christmas. Ambivalent roots. Jew? Christian? Nazi?

"As the years passed by, my brother, Heinz, struggled with very conflicting feelings toward his adopted Jewess. Only he and Niemeier knew the truth of her origin. Ingrid and I loved Helga for what she was, a beautiful, wonderful child. But the surgeon—his experimental animal now tainted by the blood of Kapozi in her veins—waited patiently for the day when the research would end, though the final protocol was to be altered. He wasn't about to allow the Almighty or anyone else to interfere with his corrupted plan.

"In those days we God-fearing Germans believed that a Jew was the minion of the Devil, an antichrist residing in a *Fremdkörper*, an alien body, a being to be eliminated if it refused to be purged or even if it recanted. The blood of such a person could not be permitted to flow in the vessels of a true Aryan. Such purity of Prussian blood was the elixir for the German master race.

"Accordingly, the Herr Doktor's mind set about to formulate a sickening and devious plot not only to reprogram Helga's brain but also to perform an exchange blood transfusion on Hali in his operating theater. In Zürich.

"*Mein Bruder*...my brother, fighting to escape Niemeier's expanding orbit, refused to have anything further to do with the surgeon's plans. Heinz was becoming more and more apprehensive of the real creatures he and Niemeier had constructed. And, God knows, I have no idea how many now walk the earth. But the Herr Doktor wielded more power than anyone could imagine."

Erik shifted uncomfortably. He could not discuss the role of the Thunderbird Society.

Anna shook her head. "Nothing was going to prevent the Nazi surgeon from completing his research. So Heinz begged me to help Helga disappear and assume a new name. He knew his daughter would come to me after she left Copenhagen. Then Helga called me from Scuol, and you know the rest. Even Heinz believed she was truly dead.

"Doctor Landon, it wasn't Helga that crucified my brother and Ingrid that night in Mainz. It was little Halina...Hali Kapozi, a tortured Jew inside Helga's skin. I would not be able to conceive of a living creature so completely desolate and forlorn as my Helga, our little Hali, must be now."

"Oh, Jesus... Uh, pardon me Frau Baumann." Erik folded his hands, white knuckles pressing against his chin, elbows on his knees. "Does...did Helga ever know she was born of Jewish parents?"

"No, Heinz never told her. But, of course, he couldn't without revealing Hali." Anna paused. "Oh, I see. Your brother, Jeffry, being Christian, I suppose..."

"Helga's religious beliefs would have had no effect on Jeffry's feelings for the woman he loved so deeply..."

"There is yet more, Doctor Landon."

"More?"

"*Ja.*" She gathered her thoughts, clapping her eyes on Erik's. "Herr Doktor Niemeier, during his investigations in Krakow, discovered that the Kapozi family in Dresden were extremely wealthy. Multimillionaires. Just before the great war, Hali's natural father, Mattaus Kapozi, had transferred their assets from their home in eastern Germany to Swiss banks in Zürich. The Kapozi's and the Vozniewski's are all dead now. Except for Hali...though she is reported to have had the brother, Franz Kapozi. The doctors sent him to Vienna. Treated for idiocy at the Spiegelgrund Asylum. He was never seen again.

"Apparently, my brother and Niemeier tried to get their hands on the money, but without success. The funds still gather interest in Switzerland."

"That means..."

"Unless the brother should surface, Helga...Hali is the only Kapozi survivor. Proof of her rightful inheritance may be impossible to locate. Of course I would be willing to testify should the opportunity arise. Doctor, she may be one of the wealthiest women on this planet."

"Whew. Yet a state she would gladly relinquish to be free, I should wonder." Erik closed his eyes, seeing two calico dolls held tightly by an unwilling prisoner, a weeping thespian portraying a four-year-old blonde, her lips begging answers to *"Wie ist es möglich dann?"* How is it possible?

64

Stockholm, Sunday, June 4, 1972.

A cool breeze rustled the new leaves on nearby trees. Pristine sunlight danced over the blue rolling waves of the Baltic Sea. Marlene and Erik stood before three burial sites, the third one freshly excavated to the left of Christian. On the right lay Christian's father, Bjørn Ljunggren. Erik felt that Harald was standing there with them. The grave digger finished, wiped his forehead with a bandanna, and stepped aside. Pastor Svensen pulled a well-thumbed Bible from the coat pocket and repeated the words of David from the Twenty-third Psalm—

> …Yea, though I walk through
> the valley of the shadow of death,
> I will fear no evil: for thou art
> with me; thy rod and thy staff they
> comfort me…

Erik lifted a sealed plastic bag from his coat pocket. It seemed somehow heavier now in his hand as he laid it inside the shallow grave. He blanketed the three fingers of Suzanne with sandy soil.

After the minister and his assistant departed, Marlene and Erik collapsed into each other's arms and sat down on the hillside overlooking the Baltic Sea. As Erik looked beyond the white phosphorescence of cresting waves, he heaved a great sigh, thinly buried grief breaking through, washing down his face.

He finally unburdened his soul, confessing what had happened to Suzanne and how he had refused to talk to ease her pain. Marlene, steady as a rock, listened, not so much with her ears, but with some deeper, more sensitive organ of hearing. She said little, the telling cathartic. She took his hand in her firm grip and held him close, the warmth annealing, mending the broken threads of Erik's life.

"That's all bygone now, my love. Let's go home." Marlene kissed his cheek. They walked arm-in-arm down the grassy knoll and toward the waiting white Mercedes.

65

Washington, Monday, June 12, 1972.

Sitting in his office, Timothy Stafford was discussing another case with Terry Caldwell, the new Section Head. Martha Farnsworth walked in with a leather case in her grasp.

"For you, Mr. Stafford. The parcel came from a Mr. Lugoso of the Swiss Credit Bank."

"Thanks Martha. Call Doctor Landon and see if he can join us at two this afternoon. I suspect it contains some of his brother's personal effects."

Erik arrived on time to meet with Terry and the Director. Stafford pulled five items from the package and placed them on his desk. Jeffry's diary. A photograph of a tattoo. One passport. A postcard dated Christmas 1960. And a letter. The missive read,

> Dear Mr. Stafford!
> I am herewith returning the articles which your Mr. Brian Trent/Jeffry Landon left in our care.

As per your request, the funds in the Landon account have been put in escrow to be used for the welfare of Antonietta, the only surviving daughter of Martino and Melita LaVecchia.

Our legal department is looking into the matter of ownership of the Mattaus Kapozi accounts funded before the Second World War. So far, we have uncovered ledgers totaling over eight-hundred million Swiss francs.

It is always a pleasure to serve you.

With kind regards,
A.T. Lugoso

The three men walked away from the meeting at BNDD, rather silent as they headed toward the elevator leading to the underground parking lot. Erik carried the package from Lugoso under his arm.

"Well, I guess you can close this file, boss. Thunderbird is out of existence and that assignment is finished." Terry pressed in his key-card to call the express elevator.

They entered the lift and initiated descent.

"Just about, Terry. The narcotic traffic is down...for now. But we've cut off only one head of a serpent with many. Already trouble is brewing again in Colombia."

Erik watched the lights blinking as the elevator shot by each level, sharp pings announcing the floor. The door opened on to parking level D.

"I'll drop you at your office, Erik. I feel bad about your brother. Must be Jeffry that's buried under the mountain slide in Scuol." Stafford held the door as they exited.

"Yeh," added Terry. "What a shock, the hair and dental studies revealing that the mutilated body in Zürich was Giovanni Molinari. Erik, your brother will remain a loose end in the 'Bird file'."

Epilogue

Mainz.

The tall blond woman, chained to a bottomless depression, hobbled beside the male attendant. She was dressed in a flowered hospital gown. At the far end of the long hallway points of light flickered. On the door — *Labor für Schocktherapie.*

The patient, her stomach churning, had not spoken since entering the asylum. Suddenly she turned to the man in white and stammered in Polish, "I...I knew a Hel...Helga once. She was very pr...pretty. Bu...but they took her away. Helga was mmy friend."

The door opened and Hali shuddered. Standing before her was a man, his eyes exploded by edge-thickened glasses.

Washington, D.C.

The last patient of the day departed Erik's office. He turned to gaze at the two photos on his credenza. The one of Halina and her adopting parents before a Krakow train station. The other, Hali and Franz.

The intercom buzzed.

"Yes?"

"Doctor Landon, an overseas call on line two. He says he knows you."

"Thank you, Jennifer. I'll take it."

Erik lifted the receiver. "Doctor Landon here."

"Good evening, Doctor. At least it's evening in Zürich."

Startled into a smile, Erik recognized the sharp voice. Major Roland Reiter. "Hello, Major. It's been a long time. What can I do for you?"

"First, I wish to give belated congratulations on your marriage. I heard from Professor Roellein that you and that lovely lady tied the knot."

"Thank you, sir. Marlene and I have an infant son. We named him Jeffry, after both my father and my brother. What's new in Europe?"

"The West German Immigration Office just called. Thought you would like to know. Their computer recognized a man passing through from Switzerland into Germany. The name on the passport was Brian Trent."

The thunderbolt ricocheted off the Atlantic satellite.

"Jeffry!" Erik jumped out of his seat, nearly leaving his heart behind.

"The name was listed in their files, but the authorities had no reason to detain him."

"Dear God…where was he headed?"

"Your brother was on the train to Mainz. And his hair…the border guard said he had a *Pferdeschwanz*. In English you call it a ponytail, I believe."

About the Author

John L. Fox, M.D., Professor of Neurosurgery, has written numerous articles for the professional literature, including two highly acclaimed surgical books published by Springer-Verlag. Now the author has turned to a psychological thriller, *The Thunderbird Covenant*, a novel drawing on the author's medical and research experience as well as travels to foreign lands.

After three years at Trinity College in Hartford, Connecticut, Doctor Fox entered the George Washington University School of Medicine in Washington, DC, graduating summa cum laude. He completed his surgical training at UCLA Medical Center in Los Angeles and at GWU in Washington. At government and private institutions, some requiring top secret clearance, the author led investigations into the explosive effects of pulsed laser radiation aimed at the head. He has practiced medicine in the USA and taught neurological surgery in several countries, including Denmark, Japan, Sweden, Taiwan, and Saudi Arabia.

The Thunderbird Covenant, a story of international intrigue, surgical drama, and a woman called Helga, evolved after the author's return home from a year of microsurgical studies in Zürich, Switzerland. Dr. Fox is currently teaching and working on his next novel.